D0481613

THE EXPLOSION CHRONICLES

YAN LIANKE

THE EXPLOSION CHRONICLES

Translated from the Chinese by
Carlos Rojas

Grove Press
New York

First published as *Zhalie zhi* by Shanghai 99 in 2013

Printed in the United States of America
Published simultaneously in Canada

ISBN: 978-0-8021-2582-8
eISBN: 978-0-8021-9001-7

First Grove Atlantic hardcover edition: October 2016

The Library of Congress has cataloged the Grove Atlantic edition as follows:

Yan, Lianke, 1958- author. | Rojas, Carlos, 1970- translator.
    The explosion chronicles : a novel / Yan Lianke ; translated by Carlos Rojas.
Other titles: Zhalie zhi. English
Description: New York : Grove Press, 2016. | Orginally published in Chinese as Zha lie zhi (Taibei Shi : Mai tian chu ban, 2013).
Identifiers: LCCN 2016023950 (print) | LCCN 2016032248 (ebook) |
    ISBN 9780802125828 (hardback) | ISBN 9780802190017 (eBook)
Subjects: LCSH: Upper class families—Fiction. | Cities and towns—Growth—Fiction. | Competition—Fiction. | Power (Social sciences)—Fiction. | China—Fiction. | BISAC: FICTION / Literary.
Classification: LCC PL2925.L54 Z413 2016 (print) | LCC PL2925.L54 (ebook) | DDC 895.13/52—dc23

Grove Press
an imprint of Grove Atlantic
154 West 14th Street
New York, NY 10011

Distributed by Publishers Group West

groveatlantic.com

17 18 19 20   10 9 8 7 6 5 4 3 2 1

Translator's Note

*" . . . So, they withdrew and wrote their various accounts to
vent their frustrations, intent on handing down empty words
to make themselves known."*
                              Sima Qian, "The Letter to Ren An"

As every Chinese schoolchild knows, Sima Qian's first-century BCE
historical classic *Records of the Historian* was—as the Ming dynasty
literary critic Jin Shengtan memorably put it a millennium and a
half later—the product of a "bellyful of stored-up resentment." Jin
Shengtan's characterization can be traced back to Sima Qian's own
lamentation, in a letter he wrote near the end of his life, that many
rich and powerful figures end up disappearing from the historical record—after which he proceeded to list several famous works
authored by figures who, he argued, had found themselves stymied
in their quest for worldly success, and consequently withdrew from

political life and turned to writing in order to "vent their frustration" (*fafen*).* For Sima Qian, writing functions as a sublimated expression of the author's personal frustrations in response to setbacks in the real world—offering the author the possibility of realizing through his writing the fame and influence he was unable to achieve in real life.

As Sima Qian made clear in this same letter, his discussion of the visceral resentment that may drive literary production had clear autobiographical resonances. He complains bitterly about how, in 99 BCE, he had been accused of offending Emperor Wu of the Han, as a result of which he was sentenced to be castrated. Given that castration was regarded as a fate worse than death, it would have been expected for someone of Sima Qian's stature to then promptly take his own life—but he instead resolved to live so that he might fulfill the promise he had made on his father's deathbed twelve years earlier, to complete the monumental historical project his father had begun just a few years earlier. Sima Qian labored for decades over this massive and extraordinarily influential historical chronicle that traces China's socio-political history from the legendary Yellow Emperor up to what was then the present-day. Like the earlier literary figures to whom Sima Qian tacitly compared himself, he managed to leave an indelible historical mark after his death despite having suffered devastating dishonor and humiliation while still alive.

Sima Qian's monumental text would go on to not only be an invaluable source of information on early China, but also to provide

* For a discussion of the "stored-up resentment" quote, see David Rolston, ed., *How to Read the Chinese Novel* (Princeton: Princeton University Press, 1990), 131. For a discussion of the "vent their frustrations" quote, see Stephen Durrant, et al., *The Letter to Ren An & Sima Qian's Legacy* (Seattle: University of Washington Press, 2016), 28ff. A partial translation of Sima Qian's historical text itself, meanwhile, can be found in Burton Watson, trans. and ed., *Records of the Historian* (New York: Columbia University Press, 1993), in 3 vols.

a structural and literary model for the cycle of dynastic histories that followed. There are twenty-four official dynastic histories in all, beginning with *Records of the Historian* and concluding with the Qing dynasty's *History of the Ming*. Each of these subsequent dynastic histories was formally commissioned by the imperial court of a new dynasty, and uses a similar approach to chronicle the history of the preceding dynasty. In addition to these official histories, *Records of the Historian* also provided a model for another historical genre known as "local gazetteers." Numbering in the tens of thousands, these local gazetteers were regional histories compiled by officials and local gentry. Both the dynastic histories and the local gazetteers typically consisted of a combination of narratives, biographies, anecdotes, and other historical materials, and Yan Lianke uses these two interrelated historiographic genres as a loose narrative model for his novel *The Explosion Chronicles*. In particular, Yan's novel uses a similar compositional structure that brings together individual biographies, clan genealogies, and descriptions of pivotal events in order to trace a broad swath of a community's history.

In *The Explosion Chronicles,* Yan Lianke relates the history of the community of Explosion, located in the same Balou Mountain region of Henan province in which Yan has set many of his other fictional works. The novel surveys more than a thousand years of Explosion's history, but devotes by far the most detailed attention to the post-1949 era, and particularly to the post-Mao period. Two years after Mao Zedong's death in 1976, his successor Deng Xiaoping launched the Reform and Opening Up Movement, which generated a long period of economic expansion, and in Yan's novel the community of Explosion capitalizes on this opportunity as it metastasizes from a modest village into a town, a county, a city, and finally a provincial-level megalopolis. *The Explosion Chronicles* tracks the community's explosive growth by focusing on the complicated relationship between individuals belonging to three of the community's major clans, using a set of intersecting biographical narratives to detail the history of the community as a whole. At the same time, even as the novel chronicles the history of Explosion, it simultaneously uses the community to offer an ironic commentary on China's own hyperbolic growth, as the novel uses Explosion as a metonym for the Chinese nation as a whole.

As the narrative of *The Explosion Chronicles* traces Explosion's development, it employs a variety of different measuring systems. For instance, the novel initially refers to the months of the year using the traditional Chinese lunar calendar, but by the end of the novel it is clearly using the Western calendar. (In Chinese, this shift is subtle, since under both systems months are referred to simply as "second month," "third month," and so forth, though there is always a one- or two-month gap between, say, the second month of the lunar calendar and the second month in the Western calendar). Similarly, for units of length, weight, and so forth, the narrative often uses a combination of metric and traditional Chinese units. In the translation, I have preserved the metric units, but have translated some of the traditional Chinese units into English ones, for units in which there is a close equivalent. For instance, a Chinese *chi* is roughly equal to a foot, and a Chinese *cun* is roughly equal to an inch. On the other hand, for Chinese units that lack a close equivalent in the English system (such as a *mu*, which is equivalent to about 0.16 acres, or a *jin*, which is equivalent to 1.3 pounds), I have simply retained the Chinese unit.

Many of the specific elements in *The Explosion Chronicles* are clearly fantastical. For instance, one character collects shards of moonlight in order to dry out the smudged ink of an old almanac that contains the fates of the other characters. At the same time, however, some putatively fictional elements actually have real-life correlates, such as a reference to a torrential downpour that is described as being the largest Beijing had seen in more than six centuries, and which was directly inspired by record-breaking rainfall that inundated the capital in July of 2012, just as Yan was completing the novel. As a result, the novel's use of hyperbolic mimicry has not only a defamiliarizing effect, in that it invites readers to view familiar practices in a new way, but also an uncannily familiarizing one, in that it invites readers to consider the relationship between the novel's fictional content and the "real world."

This interplay between reality and fiction, meanwhile, is further developed in the paratextual material positioned at the margins of the novel itself. The main text of *The Explosion Chronicles* is framed by a metatextual preface and postface written by (a fictional) Yan Lianke, who is introduced as the author and editor of the chronicles themselves. Modeled loosely on the real-life author, this fictional figure is presented as a prominent novelist who lives in Beijing, where he is a professor at Renmin University. Since this fictional Yan Lianke is originally from Explosion, local municipal leaders have recruited him to write and edit a historical chronicle of their community. He accepts this assignment, but insists that he be given complete autonomy to compose the work as he sees fit, explaining that he does not wish to merely model it on traditional Chinese historical chronicles, but rather to treat it as a creative literary endeavor in its own right. The municipal leaders agree, though the result is perhaps not what they expected.

Moreover, the entire work (including the main text, as well as the preface and postface) is itself embedded within yet another paratextual frame consisting of a pair of notes that offer additional reflections on the novel and its literary context. First, the book opens with a translator's note by the work's English-language translator, which situates the novel within a tradition of Chinese dynastic histories and local gazetteers, while also commenting on the structure and contents of the text itself. At the end of the book, an author's note by (the real-life) Yan Lianke positions the novel in relation to a literary practice that Yan calls mythorealism, which he defines as the use of a nonrealistic narrative style to explore contemporary China's underlying reality. In this note, Yan describes how his recent novels are motivated by a sense of righteous indignation in response to the horrifying realities of contemporary China (such as the hundreds of dead pigs that suddenly appeared floating down China's Huangpu River during the Lunar New Year holiday in early 2013, just as Yan was carrying out the final revisions of the novel), and he implies that the *The Explosion Chronicles* itself may be viewed as a product, like Sima Qian's *Records of the Historian*, of a process of venting frustration—frustration of not only with the situation in which China currently finds itself, but also with the authors' limited ability to intercede with that same reality.

At the same time, however, the novel suggests that the process of writing about this history and contemporary reality may be productive in its own right. From the text of the old almanac that can only be read after its pages have been dried out by shards of moonlight, to the fictional text of the Chronicles themselves, Yan's novel suggests that through a careful study of the past and present, it may be possible to gain insight into the future, establish a new legacy, and create a new historical record. Or, as Sima Qian describes his own project, "I have cast a broad net across the old accounts that have been lost or neglected. Examining these in light of past events, I have gathered together all the evidence for cosmic and dynastic cycles, having studied the underlying causes of success and failure, and of rise and decline. . . . I have tried to probe the boundaries of heaven and man and comprehend the changes of past and present, thereby perfecting a tradition for my family."**

—Carlos Rojas

** Stephen Durrant, et al., *The Letter to Ren An & Sima Qian's Legacy*, 28–29.

THE EXPLOSION CHRONICLES

CHAPTER 1

Prefatory Material

1. AUTHOR'S PREFACE

Esteemed readers, permit me to use this Note to clarify a few points. If these thoughts are not to your liking, feel free to curse me but please don't criticize our other comrades on the Chronicle Committee.

1) I agreed to put aside the novel on which I was working to accept the role of author and editor of *The Explosion Chronicles*. Apart from the fact that I grew up in Explosion, another motivation (or tacit motivation) for this decision was the enormous financial compensation that Explosion City offered me—a sum so large it left me speechless. I hope readers will forgive me, but I really needed the money, just as a man with too much testosterone needs a woman. The mayor sent his secretary to Beijing to visit me. "Mr. Yan, the mayor says you should tell us how much you want, and as long as you don't claim all of the city's banks, we are willing to agree to anything." I was overwhelmed by this offer, and was captivated by the promise of riches. Please don't

ask me how much I ended up earning for writing and editing this. All I can say is that after completing *The Explosion Chronicles*, I'll never again need to worry about money—whether it be to purchase a house or a luxury car, or even for reputation and social status.

I therefore agreed to serve as the author and editor of *The Explosion Chronicles*. I spent quite a bit of time and effort on this project, not only for the sake of my readers and for Explosion City, but also to earn the vast sum of money specified in the contract.

2) Before I began work on *The Explosion Chronicles*, Mayor Kong Mingliang and the entire editorial committee agreed to my three requests: (A) That I would use only materials and facts I could trust, and reserved the right to decline any examples or requests people might bring me. (B) Given that I am a novelist and a novelist's primary significance lies in a process of defamiliarization, I wanted to write these chronicles in my own fashion, and not simply copy the format and narrative conventions of traditional Chinese historical chronicles. (C) I asked that the editorial committee assign me a cute and clever secretary, ideally a recent humanities major.

3) Regardless of how Explosion City decides to print and publish these chronicles, the city and I, as the primary author, will jointly hold the copyright, but if Explosion decides to stop printing the text, I will retain exclusive rights over any subsequent reprintings.

4) The authorial and financial rights for all translations (including translation into traditional characters for Hong Kong and Taiwan editions of the work), adaptations for film or other media, Internet serialization, and other adaptions will be retained by me, Yan Lianke, as the primary author, and Explosion City and the members of the editorial board will relinquish further rights.

And so on, and so forth.

Dear readers, I have recorded all of this, though ordinarily it should not have been made public, just as a gentleman should not air his dirty laundry. Go ahead and read it, and curse me. Any of you can stand on that arch of chastity and curse me for being a prostitute, a whore, and a novelist completely lacking integrity. You may curse me to death and drown me in an ocean of spittle—but before you bury me, I have but one request, like a criminal sentenced to death who wishes to make a final statement:

Read these chronicles! Even if you read only a few pages, it will be as if you deposited a flower on my grave!

2. THE *EXPLOSION CHRONICLES* EDITORIAL BOARD

Honorary director: Kong Mingliang, mayor of Explosion City

Acting director, author, and editor: Yan Lianke, author and professor at People's University, Beijing

Associate director: Kong Mingguang, professor at the Municipal Teachers College, and former chair of the editorial board of the *The Explosion County Chronicles*

Members of the editorial board (listed by the stroke order of their surname):

Kong Mingyao: A famous industrialist from Explosion City

Chen Yi: Professor at the Municipal Teachers College

Li Jinjin: Cadre in the Municipal Culture Bureau and folklore expert

He Zhaojin: High school language teacher

Su Dianshi: Lecturer at the Municipal Education Academy

Ouyang Zhi: Female, worker

Yang Xicheng: Worker

Zhao Ming: Video artist for the municipal literary federation

Graphics: Luo Zhaolin

Copyeditor: Jin Jingmao

Treasurers: Liang Guodong, Dang Xueping

3. CHRONOLOGY OF THE COMPILATION PROCESS

1) August 2007, the municipal government decided to compile *The Explosion Chronicles*, for which it agreed to consult *The Explosion City Local Gazetteers*.

2) September 2007, the editorial board of *The Explosion Chronicles* was constituted and headed by Kong Mingguang, a professor at the Municipal Teachers College.

3) October 2007, the editorial board held its first meeting and began the formal editing process, using existing local gazetteers as its foundation.

4) March 2008, the process of collecting documents was basically complete.

5) March 2009, the first draft was written and printed, and then distributed to all of the county departments for review and comment.

6) December 2009, *The Explosion Chronicles* was sent to the printers.

7) February 2010, printing was completed.

8) October 2010, in order to help *The Explosion Chronicles* circulate more widely, the municipal government decided to hire a famous local author to undertake a thorough rewrite, to make it an outstanding literary achievement. The objective was to document Explosion's transformation from a village into a town, from a town into a city, and from a city into a provincial-level megalopolis, while also celebrating Explosion's heroes, personalities, and citizens.

9) October 10, 2010, the renowned author Yan Lianke returned to his hometown, formally took over as head of the *The Explosion Chronicles* editorial board, and immediately got to work.

10) Late November 2010, after completing extensive research,

interviews, and reflection, Yan Lianke offered his suggestions on how *The Explosion Chronicles* might be revised, and requested that the text be entirely rewritten from an individual's point of view. In the end, this suggestion was approved by the mayor.

11) February 2011, Yan Lianke drafted a new narrative frame for the work.

12) October 2011, he began the formal process of rewriting and editing *The Explosion Chronicles*.

13) March 2012, while Yan Lianke was serving as a foreign writer in residence at Hong Kong Baptist University, he finished the majority of *The Explosion Chronicles*.

14) August 2012, the first draft of *The Explosion Chronicles* was completed.

15) September 2012, the manuscript of *The Explosion Chronicles* was distributed to the Explosion municipal government and to all levels of society, to read and evaluate. The work incited an uproar and received a steady string of critiques and denunciations, such that it became a legendary metropolitan chronicle that was privately circulated throughout Explosion.

16) 2013, *The Explosion Chronicles* was released in Chinese simultaneously by publishers in Mainland China, Taiwan, and Hong Kong, but virtually all of the cadres, administrators, intellectuals, and common people of Explosion refused to recognize this fantastic and absurd text, which incited an unprecedented antihistorical movement. As a result, Yan Lianke was prohibited from ever returning to Explosion, where he had grown up.

CHAPTER 2
Geographic
Transformation (1)

1. NATURAL VILLAGE

Song dynasty

During the Northern Song, the former capital, Luoyang, was located 350 kilometers from the new capital, Bianliang (present-day Kaifeng); and 70 kilometers west of Luoyang was Gaoyi county, where beneath the peaks of Funiu Mountain the earth's crust was still molten. The volcano erupted and the smoke did not disperse for several months. At the time, people did not know anything about the earth's crust or tectonic plates, and so they simply said that the land itself was rupturing and exploding. The people living in the vicinity of the volcano ran for their lives when the ground fractured. Some of them fled to the Balou mountain range more than a hundred *li* away, where they settled down and began farming. This community came to be known as Explosion Village, in commemoration of the mass migration that had been precipitated by the earth's fracturing and explosion.

Yuan dynasty

When Explosion Village was first founded, it had about a hundred residents. Because the village had the Yi River in front and the Balou mountain range in back, and because its fields were wide and flat, farmers would often gather there to barter and to buy and sell goods. As a result, the village gradually became a small marketplace.

Ming dynasty

The village's population grew to over five hundred, with most of the residents surnamed either Kong or Zhu. Many of them claimed to be descendants of Confucius, though there are no genealogical records to corroborate this claim. The village had a custom whereby on market day—which was held on the first, eleventh, and twenty-first of each month—everyone would congregate to buy and sell goods.

Qing dynasty

During the Qing, the formerly prosperous society began to decline, and there were revolts throughout central China. After the Li Zicheng peasant uprising, farmers living in Explosion and surrounding areas were subjected to theft and looting. When the farmers went to tend their crops and livestock, they were robbed. Moreover, at the time there had been a drought lasting several years, as a result of which the wheat sprouts produced no grain and plants produced no flowers. The residents of Explosion couldn't survive and fled west to Shaanxi, Gansu, and Xinjiang provinces. Explosion Village was left virtually deserted and was effectively destroyed.

The Republican period

As people came and went, Explosion became repopulated, and the village once again began to thrive. According to Gaoyi county gazetteers, by this point Explosion had several hundred residents, and given that there were several nearby waterways and transportation was convenient, the town became a market center in the region, with an industrious and upright atmosphere. In the middle of the Republican period, after large coal reserves were discovered in neighboring counties, a railway line was extended to the region, and a train station was constructed only twenty *li* away. Explosion soon lost its former tranquillity and developed quickly, as the natural village was integrated into the modern social village system.

2. SOCIAL VILLAGE (1)

After the founding of new China in 1949, the history of Explosion Village replicated in miniature the pain and prosperity undergone by the nation itself. The village experienced attacks on local tyrants during China's rural revolution, as well as the shock and ecstasy of the land redistribution movement. There was one incident in which the wife and two concubines of local landlord Zhu were reassigned to three farmworkers. One of these farmworkers was surnamed Kong—he was the grandfather of Explosion's future mayor, Kong Mingliang—and after receiving the landlord's second concubine, he took her to bed on the first night. He didn't dare touch her fairylike body, and instead merely knelt down next to the bed and repeatedly kowtowed to her until the sun rose in the east. Once the concubine saw that he was in fact simple and honest, she pulled him onto the bed, removed his clothes, and told him to lie on top of her. That was the night Kong Dongde, the father of Explosion's future mayor Kong Mingliang, was conceived, and so began the prosperous Kong lineage that is the subject of this spectacular *Explosion Chronicles*. Post-Liberation, the land that had previously been assigned to individual peasants was reassigned to local collectives. As a result, Mayor Kong's grandfather sat at the front of his field and cried his eyes out. He cried continuously for three days and three nights, and attracted the attention of the heads of virtually every other local household. They went to the front of their fields and wept over having lost their land. His wife, landlord Zhu's second concubine, however, merely stroked her hair and laughed. She laughed for a long time without speaking, and this was the origin of Explosion's "crying convention" (a more detailed explanation of which will follow below). Later, during China's Three and Five Overturnings campaign,* residents of Explosion Village chopped down trees to make hoe handles and wooden stools, and for this they were sentenced to imprisonment, beatings, and labor reform. This was a startling development. During this period, Kong Dongde accidentally destroyed some farming tools belonging to the collective, and he was sent to prison on charges of having broken the law by harming socialism's tools. This became the Kong family's deepest trauma, but it was also what spurred the author of this history to take up his pen and begin writing.

In 1958, China implemented a process of collectivization, and Explosion Village was designated a production brigade under the People's Commune. This further reinforced the glory and trauma the village shared with the People's Republic.

---

* In 1951 and 1952, China's development extended throughout the country. As socialism was implemented from the city to the countryside, the nation initiated an "anticorruption, antiwaste, and antibureaucratism" campaign, followed by an "antibribery, antitheft of state property, antitax evasion, anticheating on government contracts, and antistealing of state economic information" campaign.

When the Cultural Revolution broke out in 1966, the Kong and Zhu clans were designated as Explosion's two major factions. Meanwhile, the village's third major clan, the Chengs, observed these developments from afar but continued to lead a peaceful existence. In Explosion, conflicts between different clans developed into a more general class struggle, and during the years of revolution and fighting, some people died, others were imprisoned, while others lived off the land. Because Kong Mingliang's father Kong Dongde spent so much time hunched over working in the fields, bird droppings would often fall on his back, and on one occasion these droppings became soaked in sweat and spread out to form what looked like a map of China on his white shirt. Given that he wouldn't wash his shirt for weeks at a time, this bird-dropping map stayed there for days, until someone finally noticed it and reported it to the village chief. Zhu Qingfang then determined that this was a very serious matter, and reported it to both the commune and the county seat. As a result, Kong Dongde was imprisoned again and sentenced to labor reform. When he was finally released and quietly returned to the village, Explosion was undergoing a new historical cycle.

It was with this that the history detailed in *The Explosion Chronicles* enjoyed a new point of departure.

3. SOCIAL VILLAGE (2)

In early winter, when the air was cold and the ground was frozen, everyone stayed shacked up at home and the trees outside were barren. Sparrows circled under the eaves of the houses, and the entire village was enveloped in peace and tranquillity.

Kong Dongde was released from prison and returned home to the village. He returned surreptitiously, and no one even realized he was back. He spent the next month locked away in his house.

By this point he was sixty-two years old and had been in prison for the preceding twelve years. No one knew what he had endured, or what he had done there. He had knocked on the door of his house in the middle of the night, startling the household and bringing his wife and sons to tears. After this, the family fell silent and, apart from asking him what he wanted to eat or drink, no one said a single word.

He had originally been sentenced to death, and everyone in the village assumed he had already died. In the end, however, he returned alive. By this point his hair was gray and he was as thin as a reed. He sat so still that, had it not been for the slight movement of his eyes, he would have been indistinguishable from a corpse. Indeed, when he lay down, he no longer resembled a living person.

But after half a month of deathly silence, signs of life once again returned to his face. He called his sons over to his bed and made a series of astonishing pronouncements:

"The world has changed. In the future, production brigades will not be called production brigades, they will be called villages.

". . . The land will be distributed back to the peasants, who will again be able to make a living.

". . . In Explosion, the Zhu and Cheng families have met their end, and now it is time for our Kong family to take over."

He had married at the age of twenty, and at the age of thirty he started having sons. Now, his four sons gazed at him like a litter of pups that were already grown and ready to go off on their own. Kong Mingguang was the eldest, followed by Kong Mingliang, Kong Mingyao, and Kong Minghui. They stood in a row in front of the bed, beneath which was a brazier of scholar-tree embers, the sweet fragrance of which filled the room and enveloped their faces in a yellow glow. When the gecko on the wall heard Kong Dongde's soft voice, it turned to gaze at this man who appeared far older than his sixty-two years. The gecko's clear, tiny round eyes were a combination of pitch black and pure white. Above Kong Dongde's head, the gecko wagged its tail like a dog greeting its master, while the gray spider on the eastern wall also heard Kong Dongde's voice, and when it turned in his direction, it lifted its head and exposed its belly.

"You should all leave," Kong Dongde said, pointing to the door. His face, which had not smiled for over two weeks, appeared as though it were plated in gold. "You should all leave, and each of you should proceed in one of the four directions of the compass. You should continue forward without looking back, and when you find something you should pick it up—and whatever it is, it will determine your future life-course."

His sons didn't say a word, since they assumed their father had gone mad.

However, Kong Dongde repeated these instructions three times, almost as though he were begging them. Finally, Second Brother Kong Mingliang gave his elder brother Mingguang a meaningful look, then led their two younger brothers, Mingyao and Minghui, away from the brazier, the stools, their parents, the gecko, and the spider, as they all hesitantly made their way out the door.

Afterward, everything changed, and the world would never be the same. Following this juncture, the historical chronicles of Explosion entered a new phase.

When Kong Dongde's sons left, their mother, who had been sitting on the edge of the bed staring at her husband, asked, "Are you ill?"

He replied, "I want a bottle of wine."

She said, "You seem different."

"Our family will produce an emperor," he said. "But I don't know which of our four sons it will be."

His wife prepared to fetch him some wine and to make several small dishes to accompany it. During the time since Kong Dongde had returned, he hadn't even touched her, as though he no longer had any interest in sex. But at that moment, as his sixty-year-old wife was about to leave, he grabbed her from behind and pulled her into bed, so that the bed once again became the site of those nearly forgotten sounds of screams and of clothes ripping.

It was the middle of the night, and the moonlight poured down like water.

The sparrows under the eaves of every house were tucked into their nests, and periodically they would emit a series of chirps and tweets. There was an exaggerated feeling of calm, and the shops that lined the village streets were like tombstones in a cemetery. After Kong Dongde's four sons left home, they quickly arrived at the main intersection in front of the village. Mingliang said, "Let's divide up, and each of us can proceed in a different direction. As soon as anyone finds something, he should return here."

They parted ways and proceeded north, south, east, and west, respectively.

The eldest son went east, the second went west, the third went south, and the fourth went north, like four chicks leaving the nest in the middle of the night. The village was located at the base of a mountain, and the main road ran from east to west, while there was a smaller alley running from north to south. The intersection was located to the east of the village, and therefore the eldest, third, and fourth sons quickly left it behind, while the second son, Kong Ming-liang, had to first go back through the village itself. In the depths of night, apart from moonlight, air, and the sound of dogs barking, he initially didn't encounter anything.

But just as he was losing hope, he heard the sound of gates opening.

The gates in question were located in the village's only tile-roof gatehouse, which had wide double-paneled willow gates that had just been painted red. The gates creaked open; they were also red and emitted a pungent smell of fresh paint. This was the home of the former village chief, Zhu Qingfang. After the gates opened, the mayor's daughter Zhu Ying walked out. She had taken only a few steps when she saw Kong Mingliang—who was a few years older— striding toward her.

They both stopped in surprise.

After a second, they had an exchange that would resonate for the rest of their lives.

Mingliang said, "Fuck, I've encountered a demoness."

"I didn't expect I would run into you," Zhu Ying remarked with shock. "Where are you going, in the middle of the night?"

"I was coming here." In the moonlight, Kong Mingliang gave Zhu Ying a fierce look, then added, "I was planning to climb the wall to your house, to strangle your father and rape you. But now, I'm no longer in the mood." He turned around and strode down the village road, heading back east toward the intersection where he would meet with his elder brother, who had gone east, and his two younger brothers, who had gone south and north. He walked quickly, but his steps seemed full of sorrow, as if there were something explosive hidden in his veins. Yet in those same veins that seemed as though they were about to explode, there was also something unutterably joyful. He wanted to shout and wake all of the sleeping villagers, but as he was about to do so he heard Zhu Ying call out from behind him,

"Kong Mingliang, it was truly my misfortune to run into you today.

". . . Now that I've run into you, I have no choice but to marry you.

". . . I must marry you, and embrace your Kong family for the rest of my life."

As Zhu Ying's shout bolted like lightning, Kong Mingliang turned in the direction of her voice and saw that the Cheng family's daughter Cheng Qing was walking out of a small alleyway, carrying a red lantern. Her neighbor Yang Baoqing walked out of another alleyway, using a lighter to illuminate her path, while a villager named Second Dog also walked out, shining a flashlight on the ground.

Suddenly, the village was illuminated on all sides, as the sound of footsteps accelerated like a torrent of water. Everyone walked forward under the light of his or her lamp, as though searching for something. By this point quite a few people had congregated at the intersection and were discussing how something significant seemed to have occurred at the national level—something as momentous as the death of an emperor. Otherwise, how could the officials have ordered that the communes, which had been in place for several decades, be converted back into countryside, that the production brigades be renamed villages, that the production teams be renamed villager groups, or that the land that had been reclaimed by the state now be reassigned to individual peasants? The officials even encouraged people to start their own businesses. Previously, if you went into private business, you would be arrested and paraded in the streets, but now everyone was encouraged to do precisely that.

There was a dynastic shift and an attendant process of geographic transformation, as place-names were all changed. The entire world was turned upside down, with black becoming white and white becoming black.

Because of this dynastic shift that overturned heaven and earth, the people of Explosion reported that while they were sleeping that night, they dreamed the same dream: that there was a skeletal man in his sixties or seventies who had just been released from prison and came over their beds to shake their shoulders and tug at their hands, urging them to quickly go out into the streets. He urged them to go straight ahead without looking back, and whatever they encountered first would determine their fate. Some people didn't believe him, and when they woke up they simply rolled over and continued sleeping, but then they proceeded to dream the same dream. This process was repeated over and over, and each time it was that skeletal man who had been released from prison urging them to go out into the streets and proceed straight ahead. If they found a coin or a feather, this meant they would earn a lot of money, and if they encountered a woman's item that had fallen to the ground, it meant they would have a good marriage or an endless string of affairs. The villagers struggled to wake up; then they put on their shoes, grabbed a lamp, and went outside. There, they all discussed their dream and related what strange things they had seen or encountered on their way over. One person excitedly held up a coin or a bill and said that he had found money immediately after stepping outside, while someone else held up a red rope or a girl's plastic hair clip and asked what it prophesied.

There was also that girl named Cheng Qing, who was not much more than ten, and who had also dreamed the same dream. She had grabbed a lantern and proceeded outside, where she found a white finger-shaped condom in the middle of the street. She didn't know what this was or what it foretold, so she rushed over to the crowd and asked if anyone knew what it could be. The more experienced men all laughed and said this was something that men and women use when they go to bed together. Cheng Qing became excited and curious, and wanted to ask why men and women need to use this, but at that moment her mother reached through the crowd and slapped her face, then dragged her away.

The crowd exploded with laughter.

Kong Mingliang did not join this crowd full of light and laughter. He didn't know what his encounter with his enemy's daughter

Zhu Ying—who was the first person he encountered as he proceeded west—prophesied. What Zhu Ying had shouted to him remained engraved on his heart, but he couldn't quite figure out what it meant—as though he had walked up to a door and had a bunch of keys but didn't know which was the correct one. He stood hesitantly at the westward side of the intersection, feeling as though something hard was digging into the sole of his foot. He wanted to pick it up but at the same time suspected it was merely a pebble. As he was standing there unwilling to bend down, that object bore into the sole of his foot like a drill. Eventually, he leaned over to get it but then held it tightly in his fist and couldn't bring himself to look. Instead, he gazed at the crowd gathered in the intersection.

In the crowd all sorts of lights and lamps jostled together, like two sheets of iron rubbing against each other. At that point, Mingliang saw his elder brother Mingguang returning, accompanied by their two younger brothers, Mingyao and Minghui. The three brothers were smiling brightly, as though each had found his heart's desire.

At that point, Kong Mingliang took advantage of the light of the lamps and opened his right hand, which was clenched tightly into a fist. His palm was covered in sweat, which had soaked the object he was holding. It turned out to be a square seal wrapped in a sheet of white paper. Its owner had apparently lost it before having had a chance to inscribe anything, and now that Mingliang had found it, it became his destiny.

CHAPTER 3

Year One
of the Revolution

1. A RECORD OF TEN-THOUSAND-YUAN HOUSEHOLDS

Everything happened suddenly, like a torrent gushing out of a dream. People began farming their own parcels of land, picking fruits and vegetables in their own fields, and after they had eaten their fill they would take the remainder to sell at the market.

In this way, the market, which had been discontinued for many years, once again regained its vitality.

Because the riverbank in front of Explosion Village was wide open, it was used as a marketplace. On the first day of each lunar month, the riverbank would be lined with people selling chickens, ducks, and pork, as well as lumber, local specialties, and new clothes and shoes from the city. The most important thing was that the government issued a statement saying that it wanted to establish and cultivate a group of "ten-thousand-yuan households."* In other words, it wanted to let a minority "get rich first."

Everyone went crazy. Pig farmers, goatherds, cow and horse breeders, weavers, furniture sellers, and house builders—all aspired to be among the small minority who would get rich first, and to be the first to get a no-interest loan from the government, which would allow them to brag and let them live a dream life.

That spring, Third Brother Kong Mingyao ended up joining the army. On the night when the villagers were following their dream paths, Mingyao had proceeded south. When he left the village he saw an army truck pulling a cannon, and therefore he knew he was fated to join the army and leave Explosion. In fact, during the next recruitment that spring, the army was no longer concerned with recruits' family or political history, and as long as recruits talked about protecting the nation and physically there was nothing wrong with them, they were welcome to apply.

So, Mingyao joined the army.

Eldest Brother Kong Mingguang went on to become an elementary school teacher. He himself had completed only middle school and didn't know many Chinese characters, but the most notable thing he saw when he left the intersection that night was a piece of chalk sitting in the moonlight. He didn't think that a piece of chalk could be his fate, so he continued walking east until he reached a mountain range. Apart from the chalk he had picked up in the moonlight, however, he didn't find anything else on the road, and therefore his fate was that piece of chalk. This was also an excellent omen. By this point he was twenty-eight years old,

---

* The phrase *ten-thousand-yuan households* refers to those households that, in the early 1980s, were the first to attain a net worth of ten thousand yuan.

but because his father was in prison he was considered the relative of a criminal and consequently had not yet succeeded in finding a spouse. Afterward, however, he became the village intellectual and in no time found a local girl who liked him. They quickly married and established a family, and went on to enjoy a calm and pleasant life.

Soon, it was time to think about Second Brother Kong Mingliang's wedding.

Their father said, "You should get married."

"Will marriage help put ten thousand yuan in my bank account?" Mingliang asked his father with a mocking look, then walked out the door. He didn't farm, sell goods, or weave fabric. Instead, every day he just left the house after each meal and returned when it was time to eat again. Whenever his parents asked him to do anything, he would grin and snort, then disappear from the house and the village.

In turns out that Kong Mingliang was very ambitious. While everyone else was farming and engaging in small trade, he left the village every day as though nothing were happening and went to a nearby gully to retrieve a couple of baskets and some hemp sacks. Then he would proceed to the railroad tracks at the base of the mountains several *li* away, where he would wait for a train bringing coal and coke from Shanxi. When the train arrived, he would reach up and pull down coal and coke from the railroad car. The sky was blue and wide open, and the crops in the mountains had all awoken, blanketing the mountainside in green. Mingliang sat alone on the hillside, watching the train as it came up the mountain. The train was emitting thick smoke, as though it were a smoldering pile of wet firewood or an enormous stove laboriously climbing the mountain. When the train finally slowed to walking speed, Kong Mingliang would emerge from the field on the side of the road, lift the long-handled hoe he had prepared, and proceed to pull down some coal and coke from the top of the passing railcar, like picking feathers from passing geese. He was able to get about a basket or half a sack of Shanxi coke from every car. As soon as he had enough coal and coke to fill his cart, he would take it all to the county seat and sell it for two or three hundred yuan. By summer, the grass along the train tracks was completely black from coal dust, but Kong Mingliang had become the first person in Explosion to save up ten thousand yuan, thereby making himself a nationally acclaimed model ten-thousand-yuan household.

He went to the county seat and held a three-day conference on how to get rich.

The day he returned to the village, he was accompanied by the town mayor. The mayor's name was Hu Dajun, and he arranged for the residents of Explosion to gather in the village's main intersection, which functioned as the village square. There were more than six hundred residents in all, including four villager groups. Everyone—including men and women, young and old—was called upon to assemble in the open area in the square. After the people filled that open area, the mayor pinned a bowl-size red blossom to Kong Mingliang's chest, then held up a door-size copy of his bankbook, so that everyone could see the name *Kong Mingliang*— printed in characters as a big as a man's head—followed by a 1 and four 0s: 10,000.

The villagers were speechless.

They were as silent as a mountain.

At a time when even the most industrious households had not managed to save a thousand yuan, Kong Mingliang had somehow saved ten thousand. As the rays of the setting sun shone over from the westward mountains, the villagers all stared at that enormous bankbook, and at Kong Mingliang's sunlit face. They saw the look of excitement in his eyes, while the corners of his mouth were twisted into a smirk. When the mayor asked Kong Mingliang to come forward and discuss how he had earned his wealth, Mingliang gazed at the villagers and said simply,

"There is really nothing to say. Just one word: Diligence!"

The mayor proceeded to reflect on the word, saying that *diligence* was the spirit of humanity's wealth and the warehouse of its silver and gold—and as long as individuals had a diligent pair of hands, then even if they were blind or crippled, they could still gallop along the road to wealth. As the sparrows were preparing to return to their nests, and as the chickens, pigs, dogs, and cats were preparing to return home and go to sleep, the mayor gazed out over the heads of the assembled villagers and found the old village chief Zhu Qingfang, who was crouched at the back of the crowd.

"Can you earn ten thousand yuan in a year?"

Zhu Qingfang bowed his head.

The town mayor asked, "Are you determined for your village to have not one but *ten* ten-thousand-yuan households by the end of the year?"

Zhu Qingfang glanced up at the mayor's face, then bowed his head even lower, to the point that it was virtually tucked between his legs. The mayor turned to Kong Mingliang standing next to him and asked, "Brother, how many ten-thousand-yuan households can you have the village produce by the end of the year?" After taking a step forward, Kong Mingliang looked at the mayor, then out at the crowd of villagers. He pounded his chest three times with his fist, hopped onto a boulder that people sat on while eating, and announced to the villagers that if he were village chief, he would ensure that at least half of the village's 126 households, which is to say 63 households, would become ten-thousand-yuan households—and if he failed, he would go to the field, walk around it three times, then distribute his own savings to the other villagers and leave Explosion, never to return.

The villagers all went crazy. They wanted to jump for joy, and their applause sounded like the tide rushing in. The chickens that had already returned home had no idea what was going on, so they came out and began clucking excitedly around the courtyard. The sparrows and pigeons that had been tucked under the eaves of the houses alighted on the courtyard walls and the rooftops, to watch this unprecedented performance that was unfolding in the square. The mayor announced that he was relieving the old village chief Zhu Qingfang of his responsibilities and was instead appointing Kong Mingliang to serve as Explosion's new village chief for the first year of the revolution. Because it was already late in the day, the major added a few more words after his announcement and then rushed back to the town center about twenty *li* away.

After the mayor left, the new village chief did three things. First, he repeated his governing objectives and guaranteed that everyone in the village would get rich, and that by the end of the year half of the village's households would be ten-thousand-yuan households, by the following year all of them would be ten-thousand-yuan households, and by the third year they all would be able to bid farewell to their thatched-roof houses and move into new tile-roof houses. Second, he asked each family to stay and watch his father Kong Dongde spit in the face of his enemy, Zhu Qingfang. Third, he said he would give ten yuan to anyone else who spat at Zhu Qingfang, twenty yuan to anyone who spat at him twice, and a hundred yuan to anyone who spat at him ten times.

Zhu Qingfang sat stiffly under the final rays of the setting sun, his face pale and his eyes dull. He removed the village commit-tee's official seal from his pocket and handed it to the new village chief, Kong Mingliang. Then he pushed the stool on which he was sitting over to his daughter Zhu Ying and, without saying a word, he lowered his gaze and squatted there and waited for the torrent of saliva.

Standing next to him, his daughter Zhu Ying cried out, "Father!"

Without looking up, Zhu Qingfang shouted back, "Let him spit! Let him spit!"

As he was shouting, Zhu Qingfang closed his eyes, and the villagers watched as Kong Dongde—who had barely left the house since returning home after being released from prison—walked up to Zhu Qingfang and stopped in front of him, with a smirk. With a loud *ptui*, he spat at Zhu Qingfang's forehead.

Kong Mingliang pulled a wad of ten-yuan bills from his pocket and, hopping onto a boulder, announced, "I will give one bill to whoever spits once, and two bills to whoever spits twice!" He then riffled through the bills, waiting for someone to accept his offer.

No one moved. The setting sun covered the village in pink light, like a sheet of silk lying on the water's surface.

"Will anyone spit? I'll give twenty yuan to anyone who does."

The young man known as Second Dog asked Kong Mingliang with a smile, "Will you really give twenty yuan for one spit?"

Kong Mingliang hopped down from the boulder and handed Second Dog twenty yuan. The man accepted the money and proceeded to spit in Zhu Qingfang's face. Kong Mingliang gave him another twenty yuan, and he spat again. Second Dog kept spitting, and Mingliang kept giving him money. Upon seeing this, the other villagers happily went up to Zhu Qingfang and spat at him as well. The sound of spitting filled the evening air like a thunderstorm, and in the blink of an eye Zhu Qingfang's head, face, and body were completely covered in spittle. This continued until everyone's throat was dry and no one could spit another drop, but even then Zhu Qingfang continued squatting there without moving.

He looked like a statue made out of spittle.

2. STELE OF THE REVOLUTION

Zhu Qingfang was drowned in spit.

When his family were changing him into his funeral clothes, they had to wash his body five times just to get rid of all the spittle. The responsibility for taking care of this fell to his only daughter, Zhu Ying. She scrubbed his body, washed his face, changed his clothes, built his coffin, and found someone to dig his grave and bury his corpse.

That night, when the villagers were spitting at her father, Zhu Ying had heard him say, "Don't mind me, let them spit away!" So she stood motionless as the villagers spat at her father's head and face. She silently counted how many times each of them spat and remembered which of them spat hundreds and even thousands of times. It was not until everyone had finally dispersed, and her father had toppled over like a chopped-down tree, that Zhu Ying went over and pulled his body out of the pool of spittle and carried it home. When she arrived at the entranceway to their courtyard, and as she was about to carry the corpse across the threshold, she noticed that the youngest of the Kong family sons, Kong Minghui, was helping her carry the body. Someone turned on the entrance light, and Zhu Ying saw that Minghui's face appeared pure and ashamed, as soft and delicate as a piece of paper that had been scrubbed with water. "It's you! I don't need any help!" With this cold remark, she pushed Minghui's hand away, then struggled to carry her father's body across the threshold on her own. Minghui was left standing outside under the lamplight and continued standing there until the door to Zhu Ying's house was closed.

Zhu Ying buried her father in the same location where he had drowned in a pool of spit—in the center of the village square. This was a public area where the villagers often ate, so naturally there shouldn't be a funeral mound there. Everyone discussed this development and reported to the new village chief, Kong Mingliang. When Mingliang came to intervene, however, Zhu Ying said,

"Mr. Kong, you forget that on the night when you came out to follow your dream west, the first person you encountered was me!"

Mingliang stood there and remembered that Zhu Ying had called out to him that night. She now told him in a mocking yet painful tone, "After I bury my father I'm going to leave the village, and I won't return until you have knelt down before me."

Kong Mingliang stopped trying to prevent her from burying her father in the middle of the village and explained to the other villagers that the reason he didn't want to stop her was that her father was a former village official. So they buried Zhu Qingfang on the third day after his death. The people who attended the burial were the same ones who had drowned him in their spittle, and the person who had spat the most was also the same person who worked up the biggest sweat digging his grave. Second Dog had spat at him 106 times, but when it came to digging the grave, laying out the body, lifting and lowering the coffin, and then refilling the grave again, there wasn't any task to which he didn't contribute diligently. Furthermore, after Zhu Qingfang was buried, he stood in front of the grave and said,

"I have now repaid my debt."

It was also Second Dog who used a cart to haul over the tombstone—a meter wide, two meters high, and half a foot thick—from a site several dozen li away. Before they completed the burial process, the Zhu family, in accordance with the family's conventions and traditions, draped both a clan flag and a national flag over the corpse, and recited an emotional eulogy (people would later learn that the eulogy had actually been written by the Kong family's Kong Mingguang). After they buried the corpse and removed the red flag covering the gravestone, everyone saw that it had the following inscription:

TOMB OF THE MOST LOYAL OLD COMMUNIST, ZHU QINGFANG.

With this, someone who had been a party member since the founding of the nation penned a coda to that era and disappeared from the village forever. His daughter would go on to become a leading figure in the village, town, and city—though it was unclear whether her fate would be more tragic or glorious than that of her father. The day Zhu Ying decided to leave the village was the seventh day after her father's death. She bowed in front of the grave, burned some funeral money, then left the village without looking back. She departed with a solemn expression and a hard gaze, but as she passed the entrance to the Kong household she paused and, with a-tooth-for-a-tooth logic, she spat in their doorway. Then she left the village, climbed the mountain ridge, and disappeared. Her parting silhouette was hard and firm, as though she were a tombstone heading out into the mountains.

3. EMOTIONAL ELEGY

In turned out that Explosion Village's grand plan to have all of the villagers move into tile-roof houses within two years was actually rather conservative. In reality, this process took only six months. Kong Mingliang led the entire village to the mountain ridge to unload goods from the trains, and as a result cash came pouring in like rain. From summer till winter, from the rainy season till the snowy season, the villagers worked day in and day out, rain or shine, so that there would always be someone waiting on the ridge overlooking the train tracks. They had already mastered the schedules of the trains running through the Balou Mountains. For instance, they knew that the trains running from north to south would generally be hauling coal, coke, and lumber, while those running from south to north would haul goods such as electrical cables, cement, and construction materials, as well as oranges, bananas, mangoes, and other fresh fruits that are rarely seen in the north. After half a year, Explosion's villagers became as disciplined as a military brigade, adhering to a strict schedule dictating when they should come on and off work. They even developed their own terminology and system of distributing profits.

Village Chief Kong Mingliang didn't permit anyone to utter the word *steal*. Instead, everyone would refer euphemistically to "unloading." When greeting someone returning from the mountains, the villagers would ask, "How many goods did you unload today?" "What did you unload?" They would ask those who were leaving the village for the mountain ridge, "Are you going to work?" "Is it your turn to go to the office?" Everyone found this rather amusing. When Kong Mingliang distributed salaries at the end of every month, he began deducting one or two hundred yuan from the salary of anyone who uttered the words *stealing* or *theft*, and these words immediately disappeared from the village vocabulary. Later, no one would believe that the villagers had gone every day to steal from passing trains. In a gully located about two *li* from the train tracks they built a warehouse, which they filled with apples, oranges, electrical cables, coke, toothpaste, cigarettes, soap, and all sorts of clothing and shoes from the south, as well as a vast array of odd products and commodities that were being transported to be sold in the city. Kong Mingliang issued the villagers their monthly salary together with their performance bonuses. Initially, a household could earn several hundred yuan a month, which then became several thousand, and even tens of thousands. When spring arrived, the villagers saw that in the third lunar month on the day when the scholar trees lining the street would normally bloom white, their blossoms were instead all gray, as their former whiteness had become the color of north China's yellow earth. The paulownia trees' pink bell-shaped flowers, meanwhile, all became snowy white—as white as snow at a funeral. Everyone was surprised, and people came out of their houses to look at those flowers that had changed colors. At that point, Second Dog returned from the mountain ridge, shouting that someone had fallen and died on the tracks. The villagers immediately ran up to the ridge and stopped paying attention to the scholar-tree blossoms that had turned gray and the paulownia blossoms that had turned white.

The Kong family was having dinner. By this time they were living quite comfortably. They had hired a servant to wash their clothes and cook for them, because they didn't want their mother—whose hair had already turned gray—to work near the stove or go to the river to fetch water. At dinner they had more than enough dishes for seven or eight people, and were eating in their courtyard with the gate closed—treating themselves as though it were New Year's. When Second Dog suddenly rushed in, he stopped in the middle of the courtyard and then said something that was both brash and yet very ordinary:

"Chief Kong, there's been another one!"

Kong Mingliang quickly threw down his chopsticks and asked, "Who?"

"Zhu Qingfang's nephew, Zhu Damin. He is Zhu Ying's uncle." As Second Dog was saying this, he went over to the table, picked up an enormous white bun and took a couple of bites, then took Kong Mingliang's half-finished bowl of soup and guzzled it down. He added, "That fool. After climbing onto the train, he noticed a car that was full of wool suits and designer clothing. He shouted to me, 'This is it! I've found some valuable goods!' and then began tossing down one box of clothes after another. But by the time he had thrown the ninth box, the train had reached the top of the ridge and was beginning to pick up speed as it headed down again. I was running behind the train yelling at him to hurry and jump off, but he said that he had just noticed a box of red ties, and felt that if they were going to sell Western suits they should pair them with red ties. When he had unloaded that final box and was about to jump off, the train was already flying down the mountain. He fell onto the tracks and his blood spurted out like a geyser." Upon saying this, Second Dog stood under the paulownia tree in the Kong courtyard, as the snow-white blossoms fell into the soup bowl he was holding.

Everyone in the Kong family stared at Second Dog, who had brought these tidings of death. A smile crossed the father's face as he got up from the table and walked into the house. Eldest Brother Ming-guang had a calm expression, as though he hadn't heard anything, and he proceeded to take a fat but not greasy piece of pork from his soup bowl and, reaching past his mother, placed it in his wife Cai Qinfang's rice bowl. Only Minghui, who was sitting farthest from Second Dog, dropped his chopsticks in surprise as his face turned pale and a layer of sweat appeared on his forehead.

"What should we do?" Second Dog asked.

Mingliang replied, "Let's treat him as a martyr." He reflected for a moment, then said to Second Dog, "Go buy a top-rate coffin and the biggest and thickest tombstone you can find." As he said this, he picked up an army coat that was hanging on a nearby tree branch and draped it over his shoulders. Then he tore open a steamed bun, placed several pieces of lean meat inside, and headed outside. When he arrived at the home of the deceased, the parents were wailing in grief. They repeatedly draped over the body the clothing that had been unloaded from passing trains—wanting to call their son back into the world of the living. Everyone surrounded the elderly couple and tried to restrain them, saying that although it was true that their son had indeed died, he was actually a martyr. But the couple wouldn't listen, and they kept trying to rush up to the casket while wailing with grief. At this point, Chief Kong arrived, wearing his army coat as though it were a thick suit of armor.

The crowd opened a path for him.

Zhu Damin's parents abruptly stopped wailing. They glared at Mingliang with pure hatred, as if they wanted to tear him apart and devour him.

Kong Mingliang calmly made his way through the crowd and lifted the jacket that was covering the face of the deceased. The man's face looked as though he had been badly beaten. Mingliang turned pale and his lips trembled, but he quickly recovered and, in a brusque but calm voice, told the elderly couple,

"Damin is a martyr. He died for the sake of the prosperity of the entire village."

The elderly couple stared at Kong Mingliang's mouth.

"We'll give him a grand burial. We'll bury him in the center of the village square, right next to his uncle—who is also my uncle—Zhu Qingfang. From now on, I want the entire village to emulate him."

The elderly couple looked as though they couldn't fathom what Kong Mingliang was saying, but the fury in their eyes abated.

"Next month, the village will come together to replace all of its thatched-roof houses with new tile roofs." Kong Mingliang presented this simply and clearly to the confused elderly couple, saying, "When your daughter-in-law brings her son back from her parents' home, tell her that I said . . . for the villagers to build a new house for your family. You won't have to pay a cent, and the new house will be funded entirely by the village. The village will also cover all of your grandson's expenses until he turns eighteen. But you mustn't let your daughter-in-law remarry until your grandson is of age. Do you understand? And if, at that point, she is still determined to remarry, you mustn't let her take your grandson with her. OK?"

The elderly couple's sorrow was gradually transformed into delight, and smiles appeared on their faces like the sun coming out. As Kong Mingliang was about to leave the corpse, the couple suddenly knelt down and repeatedly kowtowed, telling him how great he was and how they had never seen such a good village chief. Kong Mingliang turned and said a few comforting words. He urged them not to worry, assuring them that those who died while unloading goods on behalf of the village would be considered martyrs, and their parents would live even more comfortably than their children. He then told the crowd that anyone who needed to go eat should leave, and anyone who was supposed to go up to the mountain ridge to unload goods should leave as well. As for the others who were responsible for burying the corpse, they should remember to collect the clothing off the deceased, wash away the blood, and take the clothing to the warehouse so that it could be sold to the city.

Then, they offered the deceased, Zhu Damin, a most solemn burial.

On the ninth day of the third lunar month, the villagers were permitted to take a day off. Apart from one person who remained in the mountains to keep an eye on the warehouse, everyone else stayed home—including the villagers assigned to unload goods from the train hauling imported cigarettes (each carton worth several thousand yuan). The entire village attended the funeral, as though they were attending a wedding ceremony and banquet. The Zhu family used the biggest, deepest, and most expensive coffin they could find, and the smoothest and most transparent marble slab for the tombstone, on which they engraved in bowl-size characters: TOMB OF THE MARTYR

ZHU DAMIN, WHO WAS A MODEL FOR THE PURSUIT OF PROSPERITY. Then they set off fireworks. Everyone in the village who was younger than the deceased put on mourning apparel and began wailing, while everyone who was older dressed in black and carried a small paper blossom. The coffin was draped in a national flag, and the area in front of the grave was covered in wreaths and elegiac couplets. Even Mingliang's elder brother Mingguang wrote an elegy, which Mingliang read aloud to the entire village:

> *Comrade Zhu Damin was born in 1956, and as an infant he lived through the Great Leap Forward and the famine of the Three Years of Natural Disaster. Later, he lived through the Cultural Revolution, during which he never had enough food to eat or clothes to wear. When presented with the opportunities offered by the Reform and Opening Up period, he worked diligently and was willing to endure hardship as he exerted himself on behalf of the village's enrichment plan. In the end, he died in the line of duty when he was only twenty-eight years old. He was regarded as a national hero, and as a paragon for how to get rich. . . .*

The elegy went on and on in this vein.

Kong Mingliang read the elegy solemnly and sonorously. Although he spoke with a heavy Balou accent, and more specifically with an Explosion accent, the residents of Balou nevertheless were very moved by his words. As they were burying Zhu Damin's coffin, tears started streaming down their faces, but afterward they began grinning enviously. They continued until the sun was high in the sky, whereupon it turned out that the silver blossoms on the old elm tree next to the grave had all changed to the color of black jade. With this, they collected their tools, gazed at the sky, and remembered that at noon there would be a train hauling mushrooms, enoki, and hericium from northern China to dinner tables in the south. At the thought of how a case of wild hericium could sell for several thousand yuan, or how sometimes they could even find a case or two of gastrodia tuber or wild ginseng, they quickly dropped their grave-digging tools and rushed to the mountain ridge.

With this, the village quieted down again, since only children and the elderly were left behind.

In the village square, first there appeared the grave of Zhu Qingfang, who drowned in spit, followed by graves of those who died unloading goods from trains and fighting over unfairly distributed items. Wild grass appeared on all of those graves, and on Zhu Qingfang's grave there even appeared several wildflowers. Before long, there were sixteen graves in the square, located on both sides of the road, so that the people of Explosion would always have to walk right through them.

4. OBSERVATIONAL DELEGATION

Within two years—a mere seven hundred days—Explosion was completely transformed.

In the blink of an eye, the village's old thatched-roof houses disappeared and were replaced with tile-roof ones. Some of these new houses were built with imitation old-style bricks while others had new artificial red tiles, and the village as a whole smelled of sulfur from all of the new bricks and tiles. The main road running from east to west was repaved with cement and lined with electrical poles, just like a city street.

One day, when the sun was several rod-lengths high in the sky, the county mayor led a delegation consisting of more than a hundred village chiefs and town mayors from throughout the county, and they all enthusiastically drove into Explosion to observe its transformation.

They saw that in front of every house there were flowers, and in back there were pigpens, goat pens, cattle and horse stables, and other corrals and breeding rooms—built with brand-new tiles and filled with live-stock that had been rented or borrowed from neighboring villages. The villagers had purchased truckload after truckload of fresh vegetables from the city and placed them in front of the village, then performed a play about going into the city to sell vegetables. At the same time, a few people serving as local "vegetable kings" had spent the first half of the year in the fields next to the mountainside road—erecting a series of large plastic tents and preparing a piece of land for farming, and then planting mid-season and green-season spinach, celery, pumpkin, and bitter squash, to which people in the city had recently taken a liking.

The delegates parked their sedans at the entrance to the village, and the first thing they would do was walk to the village square and solemnly leave a wreath for the martyrs who had given their lives on behalf of Explosion's quest for prosperity. Only then would they pro-ceed, under the direction of the village chief, Kong Mingliang, to visit each house and observe the new tile roofs and television sets, washing machines, refrigerators, and brand-new bicycles and motorcycles, not to mention tractors capable of bringing in prosperity. At that time, Kong Mingliang was the youngest village chief in the entire county and the youngest prosperity leader in the entire province. Later, when people recalled the arrival of the observational delegation, they felt a surge of pride and smiled like autumn chrysanthemum blossoms.

Mingliang first led everyone to the graves in the middle of the square and kowtowed three times, then explained that everyone who had died for the sake of the village's quest for prosperity was buried here so that whenever the villagers, their children, and their grandchildren passed through, they would remember the efforts and sacrifices their ancestors made so that they themselves could have better food, clothing, and houses: "Those who drink water should not forget who brought the water from the well; and when you drink the water, remember its source." He recited two couplets for the benefit of the county mayor and the delegation of cadres from the city, then led the delegation to one house after another, each of which had been carefully prepared beforehand, and he recounted what hardships each family had endured. Just before the delegation was about to depart, its members visited Chief Kong's house, and it was only then that the town mayors and village chiefs were truly moved. It was only then that they understood how extraordinarily difficult things had been for Kong Mingliang.

It had never occurred to anyone in the delegation that while all the villagers were living in new tile-roofed houses, Chief Kong's family would still be in a thatched-roof house built before Liberation. The house had three main rooms and four straw-covered side rooms facing the courtyard. For ages, the house had been located at the eastern edge of the village, giving off a malty scent of fresh thatching.

The observers stood astonished in front of the mayor's house.

The county mayor also stood there, tears streaming down his cheeks.

A sigh filled Chief Kong's house like water filling a lake. There was no television, refrigerator, or washing machine in his house, and it had none of the couches that had begun appearing in the village or the wicker chairs that were popular in the city. Instead, there was only a row of ancestral tables and portraits of Mao Zedong and Deng Xiaoping, flanked by a pair of red couplets written in gold dust, which read:

> *The first to worry about the future of the people*
> *And the last to enjoy the happiness that future may bring.*

Such a simple saying, and such a simple person. The county mayor didn't say anything, and instead merely wiped away his tears

and drank a bowl of poached eggs the wife of the village chief prepared for him. Then, he led the hundreds of town mayors, village
chiefs, and other cadres back to the village, where he watched as the
other town mayors and village chiefs all got into their sedans and
made their way down the Balou mountainside. It was only then that
the county mayor summoned Kong Mingliang over to his car. He
stared at Mingliang for a moment, then said something that would
make Mingliang's career take off:

"How old are you?"

Kong Mingliang replied, "I just turned twenty-six this year."

"Can you lead all of the surrounding villages into prosperity?
If you can, I will immediately promote you from village chief to
town mayor."

CHAPTER 4
Revolutionary Biographies

1. KONG MINGLIANG

Kong Mingliang resolved to lead some neighboring villages along the road to prosperity. The local town and county mayors had agreed that they would help the two villages closest to Explosion to get rich first, and as soon as the annual salaries of those village residents reached a designated level and they were all able to live in tile-roof houses, like the residents of Explosion, Mingliang would be promoted to deputy town mayor, and eventually he would become the town mayor. The villages of Liu Gully and Zhang Peak were therefore administratively classified as belonging to Explosion. Explosion Village had originally been but a single natural village with six hundred residents, but with this reclassification it now included three natural villages, fourteen village teams, and a total of 1,956 residents. The village board decided to erect a two-story building on an empty plot along the bank of the river near Explosion, surrounded by a redbrick wall with an iron gate bearing a heavy sign reading,

THE COMMUNIST PARTY VILLAGE BOARD OF EXPLOSION, with each character as large as a watermelon.

The village board had already issued each household in those two villages several thousand yuan with no strings attached, thereby permitting the villagers who wanted to raise pigs to do so, and those who wanted to farm to do so. The board also took the young people from the two villages and then led them to another set of train tracks on a mountain about twenty *li* away, to unload goods. The board taught them how they could use an iron hook to grab the coal and coke off the top of the train car as the train was going up the mountain, and if the train car didn't have a roof and the goods were simply sitting in plain view, they could hook a box, a basket, or a sack of goods. The board also had the young people from Explosion take on disciples, to teach them how to climb onto trains and, after they had unloaded their goods, carefully jump down again.

The most important thing was to make sure that everyone in the two other villages followed the same rules as the residents of Explosion, and signed an oath of secrecy about their practice of climbing onto trains and unloading goods. Once this was accomplished, everyone quickly became rich. Those two villages previously led a bare-bones existence, but in the blink of an eye their lives became opulent. Some households became ten-thousand-yuan households and began building new tile-roof houses.

The residents of Explosion felt as though a severe winter had just passed and spring had finally arrived. When they woke up one night, they found that all the trees in the courtyards, along the village streets, and in the fields outside the village had burst into bloom and were sprouting new growth. The entire world was peach red and lily white. It was said that, because Explosion had been designated a model village, the current town mayor, Hu Dajun, was therefore transferred to the county seat to be the new deputy county mayor.

Moreover, since the current county mayor had overseen the first ten-thousand-yuan household in the entire province, and furthermore all of the other villagers had moved into new tile-roof houses within two years, a photograph of a tile-roof house standing on that poor loess soil and accompanied by an inscription was therefore passed around by the leaders in Beijing, who even took the photograph home with them at night to show to their wives and children. A leader was so excited by the photograph that one evening he ate three extra golden buns and drank an extra half bowl of rice congee. After this, the county mayor was sent to Beijing to report on the glories of the Reform and Opening Up campaign.

In sum, this one event ended up having far-reaching implications. It was as though a window had been opened, which in turn illuminated the entire world. But it was precisely at this point—in autumn of that year—that the speed of the nation's trains suddenly increased. The residents of Explosion didn't know how this change had occurred, but suddenly all of the trains—be they passenger trains or cargo trains—no longer huffed and puffed as they struggled up the mountain ridge, and instead they had considerable speed and energy, like an old man who has become young again and walks as though he has been given wings. Now, the trains climbed the mountain as though they were on flat ground, but it was only after five villagers fell to their deaths while unloading goods that everyone finally noticed that the average speed of the trains passing through that region had increased dramatically, to the point that it was no longer possible to climb aboard to unload goods.

What was worse, Zhu Qingfang's daughter Zhu Ying returned to the village just before autumn. When she had left two years earlier, she was wearing simple clothing that she, as was customary in Balou, had sewn herself; but now she was decked out in imported clothing that cost thousands of yuan. Her shirt, pants, scarf, and shoes were all printed with English words that no one in Explosion could understand. Most remarkable was the unbuttoned gray duffle coat she wore everywhere, which had a bright red foreign logo stitched along the outside of the left sleeve. She swaggered through the village, giving everyone she saw cartons of cigarettes and boxes of chocolates she had brought back from the city.

In so doing, she was issuing Explosion a challenge and a promise.

She was issuing Kong Mingliang a taunt and a confirmation.

What Kong Mingliang found completely incomprehensible was that without having gone through Explosion's village board, and without using the board's certificate or seal, Zhu Ying had somehow received from the county a certificate for a homestead, and that autumn she proceeded to build, on the edge of the village board's land, a three-story house that was an entire story taller than the board's own buildings. The board's buildings were made from bare bricks, while the outer walls of Zhu Ying's house had a layer of white ceramic tiles. The windows of the village board's buildings were made of plain glass, while Zhu Ying's windows were tinted red. The day that Zhu Ying's house was completed, five villagers trying to unload goods from a train fell to their deaths within five minutes, and after those five martyrs were buried, Zhu Ying suddenly appeared in the doorway as Kong Mingliang was sitting alone in his village board office, staring blankly into space. Zhu Ying was smiling brightly and was leaning against the door, her wool duffle coat sitting high on one shoulder and low on another, like a department store mannequin whose clothes have not been arranged properly. At that moment, the sun was setting in the west and the entire village was quiet.

Kong Mingliang's office was as large as a conference room, with an enormous desk and a leather swivel chair, and on the desk were a telephone and an envelope containing some document, which he had deliberately placed there in order to display his authority. Behind a sofa were a palm tree and an ingot tree that the mayor had bought in the county seat market, while the floor was made from floral-patterned bricks and had water marks left behind by the mop. In Zhu Ying's eyes, however, all of this appeared very rustic and lacking in authority. She stood in the doorway with her back to the setting sun, staring intently at Kong Mingliang, who looked at her in astonishment. She laughed softly and asked,

"Are you anxious? Don't you know how to earn more money?"

This was the first time since her return to the village that she had come to see him, and the first time he had spoken to her so close up. He therefore simply looked up at her and stared. She walked into his office and stood in front of his desk, and in a soft but painful voice she said,

"The trains are faster now, and if you keep trying to steal from them, countless people will die. You could end up transforming the entire village square into a cemetery.

". . . If, within the space of a year, you are unable to make Liu Gully and Zhang Peak as wealthy as Explosion, you shouldn't even think of becoming town mayor, the current town mayor shouldn't think of becoming county mayor, and the county mayor shouldn't think of relocating to the city to become city mayor.

". . . I, however, have a way to make those villages rich. I can make them so rich that by next year every family will be living in a tile-roofed house."

The setting sun shone in through the windows, and those two rooms were filled with a red glow, as though a flame were jumping around before his eyes. Mingliang heard Zhu Ying's Balou-accented speech, which carried a hint of urban inflection. He looked at Zhu Ying's face and noticed that she was prettier than she had been when she left. At that time, she had been as pretty as a village flower, but now she was as beautiful as a bonsai plant or a carefully groomed balcony flower. Between her eyebrows, which somehow had become very long and thin, there was a seductive hint of evil.

"How will you make them rich?" he asked her.

"First you'll have to marry me," she laughed. "I'm twenty-three, and you're twenty-seven. So it's time for both of us to get married. Outside, I could easily marry someone far better than you, but you were the first person I saw that night the people all followed their dreams, so I have no choice."

Mingliang stared at her for a long time, then suddenly laughed and asked:

"Do you think I don't know what you were doing while you were away? . . . You were working as a prostitute, as a whore! Do you think I don't know?"

Zhu Ying shuddered, and she said, "If you don't agree to marry me now, then next time you'll have to kneel down and beg me, but even if you do, I still won't marry you." Upon saying this, she turned around and stalked out. Her footsteps were as light and poetic as they had been when she walked in, and her maroon high heels clicked along the floral-patterned yellow brick floor. For an entire year, until she left again, that sound of her high heels would periodically echo in Kong Mingliang's head when he was thinking of something else, or even just staring blankly into space.

2. CHENG QING

Cheng Qing, who by this time was almost seventeen, was working as a secretary for the village board. Her responsibilities included wiping down the tables, mopping the floor, notifying people when it was time for meetings, and pouring water for the village chief.

As Zhu Ying walked out of the village board courtyard, Cheng Qing stared at her red leather shoes and resolved that she would also buy a pair and click her heels like Zhu Ying as she walked into and out of the village board building. But just as Zhu Ying was leaving, Cheng Qing noticed that the village chief's face had turned orange, as though he was dehydrated from having sweated too much. She hurriedly grabbed a thermos of boiled water and went to pour him a glass, but when she entered the room she saw that his face was now as green as a spring bud. His eyes, however, appeared to be shrouded by an acute sense of loss. By this point the village chief had already turned away from the window and was gazing at Cheng Qing's face, as though looking at a girl he had never seen before.

Cheng Qing went up to pour him a glass of water.

He grabbed her hand and asked in a trembling voice,

"Are you seventeen yet?"

"Not yet."

Cheng Qing took a step back, pulling her hand from the village chief's grasp, then dashed out of his office. As she entered the courtyard, she heard him yelling after her, "Do you think you're as capable as Zhu Ying? . . . Go look at your brother's grave—I can arrange it so that not even weeds will grow there!"

Cheng Qing stared blankly in the courtyard, and after Mingliang's voice faded she left the premises. To the south of the village board building there was a small forest, and from there she took a path that looped around behind the building. As she was heading home she saw a house, recently built by a family surnamed Yang, which was as large and beautiful as a temple. She saw a family surnamed Zhu, who wanted their son to go to become an electrician, and his mother would go to the village chief's house every day to bribe him with spinach, celery, hens, and eggs—to the point that she ended up giving him virtually everything they owned. When

Cheng Qing saw the Zhu family's mother, the mother also saw Cheng Qing and smiled. Cheng Qing smiled back, but when she arrived at the graveyard she stopped smiling and remembered what the village chief had said. Her brother, having been one of the first martyrs to die while unloading goods from the trains, was buried in the southwest corner of the village square. It was because of her brother's death that she had been hired to work as a secretary for the village board. The villagers and the village chief felt they should look after her, given that she was after all the sister of a martyr. Every day when she went to work, she had to pass by this square, and where there had previously been only one grave—that of Zhu Ying's father, the former village chief—now there were several dozen. She had long since grown accustomed to this scene, so that walking through these graves was like walking through her own house, and she usually couldn't be troubled to look around. But on this day, as she walked through the graveyard she was startled to notice that apart from several new graves with wreaths and bare soil, all of the older ones—which were really not that old, since the oldest of them was only three years old—had already become overrun with weeds and wildflowers, as though they had been painted in an assortment of different colors. White and red flowers, together with dark, dark yellow chrysanthemums, were blooming happily over the graves, singing and dancing, and even the bees and butterflies were hopping around, shouting and laughing. However, Cheng Qing also noticed that over her brother's grave there were no bees and butterflies, and instead the grave was as bare as a slab of stone on a barren wasteland. She stood staring into space and then began walking toward her brother's grave. As she approached, she saw that on the graves around her brother's, the plants—including wild chrysanthemum and mountain asparagus, together with some white jasmine blossoms that the villagers had planted—were all green and blooming, and the air was filled with a strong scent of osmanthus blossoms. Spring was over and summer had arrived, and even though jasmine blossoms elsewhere had already withered, over these graves they were still blooming brightly and seemed to have no intention of admitting defeat.

This is what Cheng Qing saw, that on all the other graves grass was growing vigorously, and it was only her brother's that was completely bare, without any grass or flowers. Not even bees or butterflies were willing to land there.

After a while, Cheng Qing left her brother's grave. She followed the path she had taken and returned to the office of the village chief, Kong Mingliang. When she saw that Mingliang was getting his coat and was about to leave, she rushed up to him and blurted out,

"I'm already seventeen. I'm an adult!"

Mingliang noticed that her forehead was drenched in sweat. He reached over to wipe the sweat from her brow and saw that her entire body was trembling like the surface of a drum. Without waiting for him to say anything, she closed the door and began disrobing right in front of him. In her hurry, she accidentally ripped off a black button from her collar and it fell to the floor, rolling under the sofa like a ball. At this point, sunlight that was still casually strolling in through the window began making running sounds as it clattered around the room, lighting up some parts while leaving others in darkness. In the end, a patch of light from Cheng Qing's face shone down on her chest, and under this light Mingliang noticed a pair of objects that had not yet fully taken form, like buns that were not yet fully baked. He reached out to stroke those bun-like objects, then pulled her clothing up to cover them up.

"You aren't yet seventeen. . . . Wait, because the town mayor has asked me to make a quick trip into town." With this, Kong Mingliang quickly headed to the door. When he opened it, as sunlight streamed in and illuminated his body, he turned to look at Cheng Qing and said, "Go see your brother's grave. It is now covered with flowers."

Then Mingliang left.

Cheng Qing stood in front of the village chief's desk until the footsteps in the courtyard had faded away and dusk had fallen. Then she put all of her clothes back on and headed toward the village—to her home. When she arrived at the village square, she saw that the withered grass over her brother's grave had burst into bloom and had attracted a swarm of bees, butterflies, and chattering orioles.

3. HU DAJUN

I.

Town Mayor Hu Dajun drove to Explosion in the sedan Zhu Ying had purchased with the money she had earned from prostituting herself and had donated to his town.

It was winter, and the yellow sun was directly overhead, like a flaming orb shining down on the mountain ridge. Mayor Hu took the deputy mayor and several other officials in the new sedan, and together they drove through the mountains. As they gazed out the window at the scenery, their faces were shrouded in a bright red glow, and it seemed as though the color would flake right off if you were to touch it. Mayor Hu looked extremely pleased, and the entire way over he kept chortling quietly to himself. The former county mayor was going to the city to become the new city mayor and had agreed to recommend that Mayor Hu replace him as county mayor—because out of the entire county, only Hu had managed to come up with a village like Explosion that was able to become a model of prosperity. Furthermore, Zhu Ying had exerted considerable effort on behalf of this model village, and now Mayor Hu wanted to return to Explosion to host another enrichment conference and to erect a commendatory monument in Zhu Ying's honor.

II.

A year earlier, after the speed of the trains increased, the residents of Explosion could no longer go to the railroad tracks to unload goods, and as a result the town's growth had ground to a halt. Town Mayor Hu and Village Chief Kong Mingliang became so anxious that they couldn't eat or sleep, and in the end the mayor clenched his teeth and stamped his feet and ordered several large trucks to wait in the road just outside Explosion. At the same time, Mayor Hu and Chief Kong held a mobilization meeting in the village, where they announced that representatives from the city had come to Explosion to hire workers, and that all able-bodied men and women in the village between the ages of eighteen and forty—as long as they were able to walk or crawl and were willing to go into the city to work, and earn between three and five thousand yuan a month—could immediately pack their suitcases and their bedding and board the trucks at the base of the mountain.

All of the village's young people went to investigate.

After everyone departed, the village was left as empty as a wheat field after the harvest.

Those trucks full of villagers from Explosion and the neighboring villages of Liu Gully and Zhang Peak were sent by the mayor and the village chief to a city several hundred *li* away, where the villagers were deposited on a corner next to the train station. The trucks then parked in a quiet area, and the town mayor and the village chief both got out and proceeded to give every villager a blank letter of introduction with official stamps from both the town and the corresponding village. They said, "You are welcome to fill these out as you wish, and whatever kind of work you want, you are welcome to go find it." The village men went to work in construction, while the women went to work in restaurants as waitresses and dishwashers. Regardless of whether they were working for Zhu Ying as female or male prostitutes, or were using their tongues to polish people's shoes or lick their asses, they were not under any circumstances permitted to return home to the village. The town levied a fine of three thousand yuan on anyone who returned to the village after staying in the city for less than six months, a fine of four thousand yuan on those who stayed for less than three months, and a fine of five thousand yuan on those who stayed less than one. Anyone who dared buy a ticket back to the village would be not only fined, but also treated like someone who had more children than permitted under the One-Child Policy.

Following the announcement, the mayor and Kong Mingliang boarded a truck and rode back to the village. Afterward, the residents of Explosion were like drops of water that fall into the ocean and disappear. Occasionally, there would be an incident, which usually involved the villagers orchestrating a theft and then being arrested. Given that there were too many detainees to fit in the jail, the police would drive them back to their hometown, whereupon Mayor Hu would have to take the policeman out to dinner and fete him with alcohol; as he was leaving, he would give him some local specialties.

The policeman said, "Fuck! Your village really does specialize in producing thieves!"

Mayor Hu slapped the face of each thief.

The policeman said, "If we arrest them again we'll have to enforce the punishment."

Mayor Hu put the gifts in the police car.

After the car drove away, only the mayor and several dozen thieves were left behind. Mayor Hu looked over and asked them,

"What did you steal?"

"Manhole covers and steel pipes."

"What else?"

"Television sets from the city dwellers."

The mayor walked right up to the eldest of the thieves and said, "You should learn from Explosion and not waste your time with petty theft. How much do manhole covers and steel pipes sell for, anyway? And television sets get cheaper every day, to the point that they're now as cheap as carrots and cabbage. Is it really worth your time to steal this sort of thing?" He continued, "Get lost! All of you, go back to the city, to the provincial capital, to Guangzhou, Shanghai, and Beijing. I won't punish you for stealing, but within two years you must build several small factories in the village. And if you don't succeed, and instead are arrested again, I'll parade you and your families through the streets." After those youngsters from Liu Gully and Zhang Peak were reprimanded by the mayor and given the new blank letters of introduction, they didn't even return home to see their parents and instead proceeded directly to take another bus back into the city, and from the city they took the bus to the provincial capital or to other cities.

Following a few more of these incidents, the city police stopped sending the villagers they detained, and instead would simply call up the mayor and ask him to come into the city to collect them—saying that if he didn't, not only would the city not let the detainees go, it would even publicize the details of the arrests in the newspapers and on television. Whenever the situation grew tense, Mayor Hu had no choice but to go to the police station in the provincial capital or Jiudu City. As soon as he entered, he saw more than a dozen young women from Liu Gully or Zhang Peak squatting in a row along the wall. Each of them was naked except for a bra and a pair of colorful panties, revealing her nubile body.

While the mayor was looking the girls over, one of the police officers walked over and spat on the ground in front of him.

"Are you Mayor Hu?"

The mayor said, "I'm sorry we've given you so much trouble."

The police officer cursed him, saying, "Does your town fucking specialize in producing prostitutes?"

The mayor replied, "When I return, I'll make sure each of these girls walks through the streets with an old shoe hanging from her neck. We'll see if they ever dare go out in public again, and furthermore who the fuck would be willing to marry them?"

He led the women away, telling them to get dressed and follow him out of the police station, like students following their teacher out of school. They first crossed one street, then another. When the mayor turned around, he saw that they were all still following him. He stared at them and said, "What are you following me for? If you follow me, will you get food to eat or money to spend? All of you should follow the example of Zhu Ying, who has returned from Guangzhou and opened a store in the provincial seat."

The young women stared at him in astonishment, then looked at one another. They proceeded to walk away, like a row of flowers planted along the city streets. Only after they bade the mayor farewell did he reprimand them as though he were their father, calling out,

"You should each become your own boss, like Zhu Ying. You should hire some young women from other towns and counties to work as prostitutes for you. Then you should go straighten out the policeman who spat at me, so that his wife and children abandon him and his family falls apart. You should then become that policeman's wife, and make sure he doesn't enjoy a day of happiness for the rest of his life.

". . . You should all leave. Get lost! If you aren't able to replace your thatched-roof house with a tile-roof house within half a year—or able to then replace your tile-roof house with a small building—you will have truly earned the right to be called a whore. You will have lost face on behalf of your ancestors back in Explosion and Balou and will be too depraved to return home and stand before your parents and grandparents."

From a distance, the young women heard the mayor's remarks. They gazed at his face that was as plain as dirt, then turned and walked away. They went into the city, their tender flowers blooming as if they were about to bear their plentiful corporeal fruit.

III.

Liu Gully and Zhang Peak followed Explosion's lead and became extremely wealthy. The villages acquired not only electricity but also roads and running water, as well as a flour factory, a wire factory, a nail factory, a brick factory, and a lime kiln that was still under construction, and all the villagers instantly became rich. It turned out that the ordinary workers who had been charged with building chicken coops and brick kitchens in Jiudu all became foremen in the blink of an eye. Similarly, all of the young women who had worked in hair salons and waited on men at night went to learn from Zhu Ying. First they worked as her disciples, then they were masters, and finally, with Zhu Ying's help, they went to other cities to establish their own businesses. The most talented among them succeeded in becoming owners of their own hair salons, and passed on their former clients to other young women. This is how things progressed, as the residents of Explosion surged into the cities as though chasing chickens and ducks, and within a year the villages had begun to acquire some urban characteristics. The streets of Liu Gully and Zhang Peak, for instance, were both soon lined with tile-roof houses and other buildings, just like Explosion. Each house had a tall gate with stone lions in front and several stone steps inside.

Why didn't they simply erect a stele in Zhu Ying's honor at the entrance to the village? Without Zhu Ying, would those girls have been able to make their villages rich? Zhu Ying did not merely help bring wealth to the families of the young women of Liu Gully and Zhang Peak, she even donated a new sedan to each village.

A directive was sent out to all local village chiefs, instructing them to come to Explosion to attend a meeting. Kong Mingliang had gone to the provincial seat to curry favor, so Mayor Hu himself mobilized the residents of Explosion to clean their houses, sweep their courtyards, and tidy up the streets and alleys. They hosted over a hundred visitors from other villages and towns, who followed Mayor Hu around. The visitors first went to see Liu Gully's factories and kilns, and then they went to see Zhang Peak's poultry and livestock. They asked questions as they walked and were able to visit any household they wanted and query the residents on anything they wished.

Eventually, Mayor Hu led everyone to Zhu Ying's home, which was next door to the Explosion village board building. Everyone saw that the Zhu family home resembled a new-style temple. It was located on one *mu* of land, and it was a three-story building oriented from east to west. The Zhu family had lived there for only half a year before completely renovating it. The blackish-gray bricks had been artificially distressed, and the windows were made from steel designed to look like carved wood, and inlaid with copper and brass. As for the courtyard wall, because it was made of iron it came to function as the wall around the city park. Although it was winter, grass and bushes grew along the wall, as holly bushes and winter grass added greenery. Everyone stood at the base of the building, exclaiming in delight, and then rushed away to see everything else before the sun set. The visitors reluctantly left Zhu Ying's house and proceeded back to the village to erect a marble stele in her honor.

There was a large open field in front of Explosion, right where the main road entered the village. It was there that the town mayor erected the stele in Zhu Ying's honor. The stele was made of marble and was an inch thick, eight inches wide, one foot two inches high, and it was carved with bowl-size Chinese characters.

The base of the stele had already been placed in a pit.

Around the base, the villagers added not only dirt but also a ring of concrete. There was a fresh smell of cement in the air. When the sun was directly overhead, the town's cadres either stood in the sun or sat on their cotton shoes, staring intently at the mayor's face and watching his mouth open and close as he spoke. He said,

"Tell me, who here is Zhu Ying's equal? Does anyone know? When Zhu Ying first arrived in Guangzhou, she was merely an assistant in a hair salon, but now she has opened an amusement park in the provincial capital, which is large enough to accommodate nine hundred men and women bathing at the same time. Every day she earns enough money to buy several sedans or even build a small house!

"How can we not erect a stele for her?" the mayor asked. "Not only did she help her family build a new house, she also helped the families of a hundred other young women construct new tile-roofed houses and other buildings." He added, "She not only helped the families of these young women construct new tile-roofed houses and buildings, she also helped provide Liu Gully and Zhang Peak with electricity, running water, and a paved road. Where did all this money come from? It was donated by Zhu Ying and the other women! It was all donated from the money earned by these hundred-odd young women working for Zhu Ying.

"There is also something else." The mayor paused, gazing down at the cadres, then he cleared his throat and said, "Zhu Ying said that next spring she is going to repave the cement road leading from the town to the village. She is going to convert the dirt road into a national-standard paved road. Do you know how much it will cost to repave this road?"

The mayor shouted, "It will cost millions!"

He added, "As mayor, I have no way of rewarding Zhu Ying other than to erect this stele in her honor."

Accordingly, an enormous stone stele as big as a wall was erected, and everyone in attendance saw the basket-size characters inscribed on its front:

TO GET RICH, LEARN FROM EXPLOSION

TAKE ZHU YING AS A MODEL

His listeners began applauding the erection of the stele, applauding so hard that their palms were soon covered in blood.

4. KONG DONGDE AND HIS SONS

I.

As everyone was appealing for spring to return, the paulownia tree sprouted its pink blossoms and the apricot tree sprouted its jade-white blossoms. When spring finally did in fact arrive, Kong Dongde saw that all of the graves in the village square were covered in winter jasmine—but while at this time of year they normally would be bursting into green and sprouting flowers, these particular plants were neither green nor flowering. The willows along the river and next to the well were also no longer producing new growth. There was no lingering winter chill, and each day was warmer than the last, as people removed their padded clothing. Once you passed the Qingming holiday and began approaching the fifth solar term, spring should have started to arrive. But this year, even though it was already the beginning of the third lunar month, the spring greenery was still not willing to emerge.

One morning, Kong Dongde thought about the spring, then took a couple of mynah birds he had raised and hung their cage from the willow tree next to Zhu Qingfang's grave in the middle of the village square. Then, like city residents who go to the parks in the morning to do their daily exercises, he proceeded to exercise in the open area in the square in front of the graves. He didn't really want to exercise, but it was just that the preceding few years had convinced him that life was good, and he had now entered a period of calm and refinement. During the first half of Kong Dongde's life Zhu Qingfang had always forced him to crouch in submission; now Kong Dongde was smiling happily while Zhu Qingfang was buried six feet under.

So, every day after getting up, Kong Dongde would take those two mynah birds and hang their cage in front of Zhu Qingfang's grave, and then he would exercise right there in the square, happily greeting everyone who passed by. The days were gradually becoming warmer, and after exercising he would soon be covered in sweat. He would remove his jacket, but rather than hang it from a nearby tree, he would instead make a point of walking past several graves to hang it on the same tree on which he had already hung the cage with the pair of mynah birds. He would then walk back over the same graves, would stomp several times on Zhu Qingfang's grave mound, and only then would he return to his exercises.

During that period, the air was brisk and there was a humid breeze. Every morning, Kong Dongde would walk back and forth over Zhu Qingfang's grave. There was a path leading up to the grave, and the earth of the mound itself was packed down very hard. The new soil that had been deposited during the Qingming grave-sweeping holiday had already been stomped into the ground, to the point that the grave mound appeared quite low. One day, Kong Dongde decided that the MOST LOYAL OLD COMMUNIST inscription on Zhu Qing-fang's tombstone was displeasing, and therefore proceeded to plaster it with mud. Another day, he decided that the entire gravestone was displeasing, so he asked some villagers to knock it down—but before they had a chance to finish, he told them to stop.

"Let's just leave it like this. For better or worse, he did live and walk this earth, so let's leave his gravestone as it is." From that point on, the gravestone stood at a precarious angle, as though it were about to topple over. Kong Dongde felt that the grave and tombstone were somehow more acceptable this way, as though Zhu Qingfang was forever bowing down before him. It was as though Zhu Qingfang's grave was abandoned. Every morning Kong Dongde would get up and go down to the village square to do these things—thinking about the good fortune his family had enjoyed. Kong Dongde's eldest son was now a teacher and was now the assistant principal at an elementary school; his second son was the village chief and the emperor of the village; his third son was in the army, and, although not a general, he was nevertheless a security officer for his regiment, and sooner or later he would surely be promoted to cadre; and his fourth son was enrolled in high school in the city, receiving excellent grades, and would soon take the college admissions exams.

With luck, he would be able to pass the exams easily.

Kong Dongde had absolutely nothing to complain about. Had Zhu Qingfang's daughter not gone into the city to earn money to buy a house, and had the town mayor (who was also someone who should have met with misfortune) not erected an enormous stele in front of the village, there would not have been a single thing in this life that would have given Kong Dongde any displeasure.

Several months earlier, Mayor Hu Dajun had erected this enormous stele for Zhu Ying, the first line of which read, TO GET RICH, LEARN FROM EXPLOSION, while the second read, TAKE ZHU YING AS A MODEL. However, Zhu Ying was herself a resident of Explosion and therefore should be under the direction of the village chief—which is to say,

Kong Dongde's son, Kong Mingliang. But this made Kong Dongde feel as though there were a needle pricking his throat. He naturally couldn't simply go knock down the stele the mayor had erected, and furthermore Mayor Hu could very well end up being promoted to county mayor. So Kong Dongde had no recourse but to blur out the inscription on the tombstone that had been erected in the name of the father of that whore, Zhu Ying. Moreover, he had to settle for blurring out the inscription on the nearly overturned tombstone of that whore's father, because he naturally couldn't blur out the inscription on the enormous stele the mayor had erected.

In the end, Kong Dongde felt that everything was again as it should be, and it was as though that bone in his throat had been removed.

He exercised in front of that grave, humming a tune while swinging his arms and legs around. He did this every day, coming every morning to announce his feeling of victory and delight to the person in the grave. On this particular morning, however, as he was exercising in the square, he suddenly noticed that the winter jasmine had not yet begun flowering, even though it was already the end of the third lunar month; and while there were a handful of willows that had begun to bud, those buds had already dried up and the hint of green had retreated to the very center of the branch.

Kong Dongde felt rather unnerved by this.

He remembered that when Mingliang returned from his meeting in the provincial seat the previous day, he had mentioned that both the county and the town wanted to initiate a reform movement. They wanted to use Explosion as a model and have the villagers hold an election for village chief. At the thought that Zhu Ying might be elected, however, Kong Dongde's heart skipped a beat and his arm froze in midair. He turned to look at Zhu Qingfang's grave, then listened as the two mynah birds squawked, "I'm better than you!

I'm better than you!" He nodded and exchanged a few words with villagers who passed by, accepting everyone's greetings and well-wishes. Then he completed his exercises and walked over toward Zhu Qingfang's grave.

After waiting until no one was around, he proceeded to urinate on the grave, peeing all over the area where Zhu Qingfang's face would have been. Then he put on his clothes, picked up the two "I'm better then you!" mynah birds, and returned home.

II.

There was indeed an election.

On the ballot provided by the town there were two names: Kong Mingliang and that whore, Zhu Ying!

Kong Mingliang had bags under his eyes. He rushed to the town and the county seat, and bought a lot of wine and expensive cigarettes to give away. It turned out, however, that there was no way to change things. There would be an election, and one of the candidates would in fact be that person who had opened the Worldly Pleasures brothel in the city and the provincial seat. As a result, Kong Mingliang and Zhu Ying would inevitably collide on this narrow path to the village chiefdom, and only one of them would succeed. From the break of dawn until the sun was high in the sky, Kong Mingliang struggled to predict who in the three villages would vote for him and who would vote for Zhu Ying. He understood that every family in Explosion was like a watertight bucket and family members would definitely vote for whomever they said they would. He ripped two empty pages from his brother Minghui's school notebook, and on one sheet he wrote *Village Chief* followed by his own name, and on the other sheet he wrote *Whore* followed by Zhu Ying's name. He calculated from Explosion Village to Liu Gully, and then from Liu Gully to Zhang Peak, and after he tabulated his totals he concluded that most of the residents of Explosion would vote for him, though most of the residents of Liu Gully and Zhang Peak would vote for Zhu Ying. He was the one who had enabled Explosion to grow wealthy, while she was the one who had enabled those other two villages to achieve prosperity. By Mingliang's calculations, there were 105 households and a total of 525 individuals who would vote for him, while there were 165 households and a total of 825 individuals who would vote for Zhu Ying.

So, it appeared that he would lose.

Kong Mingliang threw away those two sheets of paper and walked out into the courtyard. He stood there for a moment, but when he looked back he saw that those two sheets of paper were fluttering in the air like white funeral paper. Then, those two sheets became rain clouds, floating for a while before drifting away. He turned his face toward the sun overhead and, frowning, repeatedly wet his lips with his tongue. As Mingliang was worrying about the election, his father emerged from his bedroom, and when he arrived at the doorway he saw the birdcage hanging outside. He came over and stood in front of his son, and asked,

"Do you realize you won't be elected village chief?"

Kong Mingliang looked at this father without saying a word.

Kong Dongde handed his son two sheets of paper covered in writing. Mingliang took the sheets and saw with surprise that they were also labeled *Village Chief Kong Mingliang* and *Whore Zhu Ying*, respectively. On the sheet labeled *Village Chief*, there were the names of some of the households in each village, and below, written in red: "Total: 105 households, or 535 individuals." On the sheet labeled *Whore*, there was an even longer list of names of households, below which, in red: "Total: 165 households, or 825 individuals."

This was identical to Kong Mingliang's own calculations.

Kong Mingliang stared in shock at those two sheets of paper, until finally his father asked, "Given that you won't be elected village chief, do you know what you need to do to be elected?" It was only at that point that Mingliang snapped out of his daze. He simultaneously nodded and shook his head. In a fog, he seemed to hear the words "Come with me," then saw his father turn around and head back to his bedroom. His hunched shoulders resembled a pair of balls rolling forward. Mingliang followed in his father's footsteps, into his father's room.

III.

In accordance with their father's arrangements, the Kong family sprang into action. They rode a tractor into the county seat to purchase malted milk, crackers, cigarettes, and wine, and when they returned they distributed cigarettes and wine to all of the heads of household who smoked and drank, and gave health supplements to some of the elders. Mingliang himself also went out, accompanied by his elder brother Kong Mingguang and his fourth brother Kong Minghui. Together, the three of them visited the families of those villagers who had lost their lives unloading goods from the trains. In the families' homes, they placed the gifts on the table, exchanged some pleasantries, and then Mingliang said very bluntly,

"When it comes time to vote for village chief, I hope your family will vote for me.

"At the end of the day, we are all Kongs, and it is ultimately better for a Kong to serve as village chief than for an outsider.

"The plot of land on which your home rests is somewhat smaller than everyone else's. Once I'm elected, the first thing I'll do will be to grant you a larger plot."

The brothers went to visit another family, and similarly offered them gifts and exchanged a few pleasantries, then asked, "Are your parents still bedridden? Why don't we send them to the hospital!" Irrespective of what the illness happened to be, they carefully propped up the invalid and assigned someone to take him to the hospital for an exam, while also providing the family with money to cover the medical expenses.

After visiting all of the households in Explosion, the Kong family split up to visit the families in Liu Gully and Zhang Peak. In order to convince everyone to vote for Mingliang, Kong Dongde and three of his sons rode to battle. Kong Dongde unloaded the tractor-full of gifts on the mountain ridge road. He told his eldest son, Mingguang, to go pay a visit to all of the families with school-age children and told Mingliang to visit the families whose daughters had followed Zhu Ying into the city. Meanwhile, Kong Dongde himself went to visit those families with sick elders, and he told Minghui to stay on the mountain ridge to keep an eye on the remaining gifts and wait for them to return.

Kong Mingliang went to visit a family whose daughter had followed Zhu Ying into the city. As soon as he entered the courtyard, he saw the newly constructed residence and exclaimed, "Great house! Great house!" He proceeded inside and looked around both upstairs and downstairs, then suggested to the family where they could install a water faucet and put in a couch. Finally, he sat down in the living room and sipped tea from a large teacup the home's owner brought him. Smiling, Mingliang made small talk, and once his hosts were in good spirits, he went in for the kill, saying,

"Do you know what your daughter is doing in the provincial seat?"

Neither of the parents responded.

Kong Mingliang said sternly, "She is working as a whore! For her to have to work as a prostitute is worse than our going to the train tracks behind the mountain to unload goods. Please vote for me for village chief. Once I'm elected, the first thing I'll do is bring your daughter back from the city and help her find a good job—a job that will be easy, respectable, and well-paying. Then I'll help her find a husband from a good family, so that she'll live out her days in comfort!"

The parents were both embarrassed and deeply moved. The look of anguish on their faces gradually softened and they agreed to vote for Kong Mingliang, explaining that although their family had become wealthier and they were able to live in a new house, their feeling of resentment toward the daughter of the Zhu family could never be erased. Upon leaving this family's home, Kong Mingliang offered the couple some additional suggestions and promises, then went back up to the ridge to fetch gifts for the next family. Because the next family was more cultured and dignified, Kong Mingliang didn't go in for the kill as he had done with the first family, and instead looked over the house and the yard, and repeatedly complimented his hosts. Finally, he sat down to chat and told them that they mustn't believe others who claimed that their daughter was in the city following Zhu Ying's example and engaging in dissolute activities. He said he had recently been in the city and had seen their daughter, and that she was working in a factory and had relied on her skills and labor to earn enough money for her parents to build a new house. The parents maintained a dignified expression and said that they never believed their daughter could engage in those sorts of activities either, given that she had, after all, received a good upbringing.

"But it is true that Zhu Ying has engaged in these sorts of dissolute activities," Mingliang asserted. "It is definitely the case that Zhu Ying is a whore, though for some reason the higher-ups still permit her to be a candidate for village chief."

"No one will vote for her," the family said emphatically. "We, at any rate, wouldn't vote for her even if our lives depended on it."

In this way, this family was accounted for, and it was certain that the members would vote for Mingliang. He therefore left them and approached the gate of another new home, grasped the owner's hand, and pleaded for her help, then headed back to the mountain ridge. In the truck, the Kongs originally had one gift for each family, and there were still some gifts left. It was another two or three days until the election and, taking advantage of the fact that Zhu Ying had not yet returned, Mingliang rushed to distribute the remaining gifts. He ended up visiting every family that had originally been planning to vote for Zhu Ying, and in this way Explosion would become the Kong family's, and Kong Mingliang would be able to realize his life's dream.

IV.

On a mountain path between Liu Gully and Zhang Peak, Kong Minghui waited as his father and brothers repeatedly returned to the tractor to fetch more gifts—as though waiting for the sun to rise and set. He felt that the colorful gifts in the trunk of the tractor, which were still in their original bags, resembled a flock of sparrows locked in a cage. He wanted to set these sparrows free so they could fly home and so that he, too, could return home to finish his homework. He actually wasn't interested in passing the college entrance exams, but when he did well on his homework and his teacher held up his assignment and praised him to the rest of the class, he felt as though this were a form of bribery. Although he would usually bow his head in embarrassment, afterward his classmates would gaze at him enviously. Their envy made him feel reassured, and even joyful. He was still young and had not yet begun worrying about practical matters like establishing a family, and a career. He didn't yet have a trace of facial hair, and his classmates who had already hit puberty all said that he looked like a girl, as white and pure as a girl's untouched breasts.

He was this sort of a child, a typical middle-school student.

When Kong Minghui returned home on the weekend to get some more grain money, he found his father and elder brothers busy

64

preparing for the election. His eldest brother, who was twelve years older, was a teacher. Minghui felt he could talk most easily with his eldest brother, since they were both in a school. But when Minghui asked, "Does Second Brother really need to be village chief?," Mingguang merely stared at him in surprise and asked in return, "If Second Brother doesn't keep his position as village chief, how will Explosion end up belonging to the Kong family?"

Kong Minghui didn't understand what relation there was between Second Brother's becoming village chief and Minghui's own studies or Eldest Brother's teaching, but he nevertheless recognized that this was what their father most desired and what Second Brother was most excited about. Minghui therefore agreed to accompany his father and brothers and take a carful of gifts to a mountain path between Liu Gully and Zhang Peak. He looked at those two villages separated by a ridge and saw that virtually every house was a brand-new building with a tile roof. By this point, spring had arrived but green growth had not yet begun to appear along this mountain ridge, and those new buildings resembled splotches of paint on a blank canvas. Minghui simply couldn't understand how those villages had grown wealthy so fast, and that now everyone had money and was strolling around in the latest fashions.

Indeed, everyone in Explosion was so interested in earning more money that no one seemed willing to slow down, and instead the villagers ran around frantically all day long. Everything was done in a mad rush, and only the mountain range and the sky itself remained peaceful and unchanging. Kong Minghui rested quietly in the mountains, either sitting by the side of the road watching the beetles and sparrows in the fields, or climbing into the driver's seat of the tractor and gazing at the instrument panel, the clutch, and the hand brake. He continued fiddling with those instruments until he saw his father and brothers returning from Liu Gully and Zhang

Peak with broad smiles on their faces. Only then did he notice that the trunk was now completely empty and all of the gifts had been given away. He then hopped down from the cab.

It appeared he had fallen asleep there.

Seeing the delighted expressions on his family's faces, Minghui exclaimed happily, "Are you done? If so, we can go and get a good meal." It was unusual for them to be in such high spirits, and they were confident their family would retain control over Explosion—to the point that if Mingliang didn't give the word, the wind wouldn't blow and the grass wouldn't sway. So, they went to a restaurant called Xiangcui Pavilion, which was located in front of the village board headquarters. There were other villagers at the restaurant, including many young people, and the room was filled with the white aroma of alcohol and the bright red scent of fresh meat. When the other villagers saw Mingliang, they remarked angrily that they would burn down the house of anyone who dared vote for Zhu Ying. Mingliang then glared at them and asked, "How dare you? Don't you know what democracy is?" The villagers didn't utter a word, and instead they just stared at him. Kong Dongde then called his sons over to eat, whereupon they all gratefully sat down. They let Minghui order the food, saying that since he was doing well in his studies he could order whatever he wanted. Minghui ordered many dishes and said they could pack up what they didn't finish and take it home. Kong Mingliang, meanwhile, looked over the menu, then went to the counter and examined the restaurant's collection of wine and beverages. The restaurant owner was the wife of one of the villagers who had fallen to his death unloading goods from the train, which is why she had been granted permission to open a restaurant directly across from the village board headquarters. Business at the restaurant was good—as though it had wedding banquets every day—and the profits rolled in. The owner had been devastated by her husband's death, and Mingliang had arranged for her to open this restaurant. When Mingliang and his family came to eat, the owner acted as though the emperor himself had arrived—and seeing Mingliang at the counter looking over the restaurant's wines, she came over and said,

"Chief Kong, you can have whatever you want. And if we don't have it here, I'll go somewhere else to buy it for you."

Mingliang said, "Have you ever considered expanding the restaurant?"

The woman laughed, and replied, "This is already more than enough to feed my own family."

Mingliang appeared displeased and said, "If it has never occurred to you, then no matter. However, someday you may want to expand this restaurant into a banquet hall, and then make the banquet hall a major hotel for the entire metropolitan area, with rooms, restaurants, a swimming pool, elevators, security guards, and a shopping mall, and even an amusement park and a theater—just like the hotels you see on TV."

The women stared at him, speechless.

Mingliang was again displeased and asked, "What are you staring at? Don't you recognize me?"

The woman quickly smiled and nodded, saying, "Brother, how could I not recognize you? My children even address you as Uncle."

Mingliang then asked, "Did you hear what I just said?"

The woman quickly replied, "I did, I did . . . you said that someday I should expand the restaurant into a major hotel."

Pleased, Mingliang was silent, then went to the cabinet and selected ten bottles of alcohol. He returned to the woman and asked, "How many dishes did my brother just order?"

"Twelve," she replied. "Four cold ones and eight hot ones."

"Then bring us twenty-four dishes," Mingliang said. "Let's have your cook show us what he's got."

The restaurant owner was startled but quickly recovered her composure and hurried to the kitchen. By this point it was almost dusk, and the setting sun appeared pale red. When Mingliang turned around, a sheet of red sunlight was streaming in through the door, making his face glitter like an auspicious cloud—like the gold plating on a statue of a deity in the village temple. When the diners looked at him, they all stood up in surprise, unable to believe that this village chief was in fact the same Kong Mingliang that they knew, or that the Kong Mingliang they knew was now this village chief. Even Mingliang's elder brother, Mingguang, and his fourth brother, Minghui, almost didn't recognize him, and instead they just stood there speechless.

Only Mingliang's father, Kong Dongde, continued sitting, looking at his son as though nothing were out of the ordinary. His delighted expression seemed pasted onto his face, the way red couplets are traditionally posted on door frames for New Year's.

Kong Mingliang carried over the bottles of high-percentage alcohol and slammed them down on the table. He said in a low voice, "Explosion is currently still a village, and in front of the village there is only this one market street. But next year or the year after that, I intend to make Explosion a town. I will also remove the administrative town board from Cypress Town, so that Cypress Town will then fall under our jurisdiction and the new town board will be located here, where we are now eating. Within three or five years, Explosion will be no longer a town but rather a city. Then, the county seat will be relocated here as well, since we will be as developed as the city. Most of our streets, however, lack traffic lights, so the buses and cars will continually run into each other, and the police will be kept busy from morning to night."

Everyone gazed at Kong Mingliang, eager to find a clue in his expression. But Mingliang, who was of average height and stocky build, maintained a very serious and solemn expression, as strict as a mountain range blocking an underground river. No one could predict what he was going to say next, so they each simply watched him, as he stood there like someone who had stepped out of their dream and was standing in front of their bed. Mingguang, looking as though he wanted to check on something, walked over and grasped his brother Mingliang's hand, but Mingliang, as though feeling he were the object of suspicion and ridicule, immediately pushed his brother's hand away. Kong Minghui, meanwhile, stood up with a start and took half a step back. He covered his mouth with his hand, as though afraid he might say something that his brothers could take the wrong way.

Their father, Kong Dongde, suddenly began weeping and, his shoulders shuddering, he exclaimed that he would be willing to spend another decade in prison if it meant he could have a son like Mingliang. Everything then changed, to the point that Kong Mingguang and Kong Minghui had no idea what was happening and simply stood there blankly in front of the window of the restaurant as the red rays of sunlight continued to stream in—making it appear as if they were blushing with embarrassment, like clay statues in the sunlight. There were some youths from the village who also stood in shock, like clay statues that had just been struck by lightning. They stood there expressionless and immobile.

Kong Mingliang, however, remained as lively as before, since he understood what was going on. He looked with disdain at his brothers and glanced mockingly at the other villagers. Then he walked over and patted his father on the shoulder and said,

"Dad, take it easy . . . you will be able to see everything."

His father stopped weeping, and Mingliang gazed at those village youths, explaining that they should endeavor to learn some things out in the world, and after the village was transformed into a town, a county seat, and a capital city, they would all become senior figures in the industry and would be appointed section, bureau, and division chiefs. The last thing they wanted was to reach that point and find that they had no skills—that they couldn't speak, make appointments, approve documents, or even schedule meetings. He concluded, "When the time comes, don't blame me if I'm not generous and don't give you responsibility for any big business or important administrative duties!" As he said this, he expected to hear complaints, but instead as he was speaking the restaurant owner brought over some dishes. The stir-fried vegetables were steaming hot and the steam enveloped her face. Mingliang shouted through the steam,

"Twenty-four dishes are not enough. We need at least thirty-six, or even seventy-two. You should prepare at least ten banquet tables' worth of food. . . . I intend to invite the head of every household in Explosion to come dine with me; I intend to invite everyone in the entire village to come dine with me. . . . I want everyone to know that within a few short years, Explosion will become a town, then a county, and finally a wealthy and prosperous metropolis!"

V.

By the time the men of the Kong household finished their meal and headed home, the moon was already high in the sky. The streetlamps and the moon combined to light up the scene as brightly as though it were daytime. The street was filled with the smell of sulfur from newly built tile-roofed houses; there was also a midnight quiet. The father and sons took home the leftover food, and on the road Mingliang asked Mingguang,

"Did you get a receipt?"

Mingguang replied, "Yes, and I even had them add an extra thousand yuan to the total."

"You could have added more, and I would have signed for the reimbursement." When they got home, Mingliang and the others saw with surprise that of all the gifts they had given away that afternoon, nearly half had been returned to them in the middle of the night and left piled up next to their front door. The gifts had not been returned directly to the Kongs, and instead they had been deposited anonymously on their doorstep. In the moonlight, the gifts looked like a pile of pumpkins and other vegetables. The father stared at that stack of returned gifts without moving. Mingliang and his brothers also stood looking at the gifts. Under the moonlight, they could hear the light passing through the doorway. Suddenly, the entire family began cursing, "God . . ." Minghui leaned over to pick up a bag but then put it back down again and said, "In that case, our family can enjoy everything that was returned." Mingliang stared at him coldly, then kicked the pile of gifts and smelled the rich cookies and pastries. The first thought that came into his mind was, "Do you fucking want to die? How dare you return our gifts?!" Then he remembered that Third Brother, when he was in the army, had been issued a gun, and it occurred to him that if only he could borrow it for a day, everything could be sorted out. When he looked over at his father, Kong Dongde said something that was completely consonant with what he himself was thinking:

"Why don't you send a telegram to Third Brother, and see if he can bring his gun back for half a day?"

Mingguang and his brother Minghui stared at their father in confusion, but Mingliang saw he had a look of evil excitement that even the dim moonlight couldn't conceal.

5. KONG MINGYAO

Kong Mingyao returned from the army.

He was now much taller and stronger than before, and was as powerful as a galloping horse. When he entered the village, a yellow travel bag in hand, he walked down the street with an excited expression. He nodded to everyone he saw, and handed out cigarettes and candy. He gave cigarettes to the men and candy to the women—as was customary in Balou for people who had left the village and then returned in glory. The quality of the cigarettes and the candy was taken as evidence of one's relative success or failure while away. When Mingyao returned, the cigarettes he distributed were the most expensive ones available at the time, and it was said that only national leaders could afford to buy them. These were the cigarettes that Mingyao distributed to the villagers. As for the candy he distributed to the women and children, the villagers didn't feel this was necessarily the best or sweetest candy available, and in fact they found it rather bitter. However, the writing on the tinfoil wrappings of the round, rectangular, and triangular candy was definitely not in Chinese, and instead was in some foreign script. From this, everyone realized that the chocolate must be a foreign delicacy, and therefore Kong Mingyao's return became even more legendary. When he walked over from the village street, the spring sun had flowers bloom for him and enveloped him in tints of tender green and fresh red. The scholar tree to the north of the village was covered in flowers in his honor, including red roses and white peonies. The air was filled with a fresh aroma, as the flowers glittered brightly in the sunlight.

It had been several years since Mingyao last returned, and now he was wearing a blue uniform and black leather shoes. As he strode along the main street, he spoke to everyone he knew. After he passed by, some villagers thought how excellent it would be if their daughters could marry him!

Kong Mingyao returned to the Kong family home, to the south of the village square.

With this, all that was left was rumor and speculation, together with the sound of footsteps running to and from the Kong household.

By afternoon, however, everyone's feverish speculations had begun to fade. The villagers saw Mingyao reemerge from his home, followed by countless other members of the Kong clan—including men and women, young and old. None of them retained their earlier look of excitement, and instead they each had a barely concealed expression of murderous rage. The men followed immediately behind Mingyao, while the women and children came after them.

When Kong Mingyao emerged from the Kong home, he was no longer wearing the same blue uniform he had worn when he first returned to the village. Instead, he was wearing the military fatigues he had worn while in the army, together with a red leather munitions belt. In his hand, he was carrying a jet-black pistol—the likes of which the villagers had not seen for decades. The villagers did not know what Mingyao and his family had discussed while he was inside, but when he emerged the air in the village was tense with anticipation. Like his face, the atmosphere was also somewhat cloudy. The two badges on his collar were bloodred and reminded people of a decapitated head. Neither his father nor either of his brothers dared walk behind him. Meanwhile, Minghui was studying in the city and had no idea that Mingyao had returned to the village.

When Mingyao emerged from the house, he proceeded directly to the village square, where he looked at all of the people gathered there and said with a smile, "I hear that the village is going to vote on a new village chief. Democracy is good. Whomever you want to elect, that is your right, which no one can take away from you." He took out his pistol, looked at it, wiped it with his handkerchief, and casually aimed it toward the sky. Then he said to himself with a smile, "I hear that Liu Gully and Zhang Peak have become so wealthy that they have replaced all of their houses with new ones. Shall we go take a look?"

The people of Explosion all cheered, "Let's go to Liu Gully! Let's go to Liu Gully!" The crowd grew larger and larger, forming a black mass that pushed and shoved the young soldier Kong Mingyao, while at the same time opening a path for him, as they left the village and surged toward Liu Gully a couple of *li* away.

At this point the sun was directly overhead, and the mountains were warm and indolent. By the time the tide of several hundred residents of Explosion had surged to the entrance of Liu Gully, the news of their arrival had already preceded them. Therefore, the people of Liu Gully had closed their windows and locked their doors, as though fearing a bloodbath. But in the end they discovered that the situation was not as they had feared, which is to say that Kong Mingyao had simply returned home from the army to visit his family, and he gave away cigarettes and candy. Then he opened his door, and everyone saw he was wearing his military fatigues and was holding a pistol. By this point he had already walked out of his family's house, and people surrounded him as he stood in the doorway of a new three-story house. He then aimed his gun into the sky, and with a *Hu!* he opened fire. After waiting for all of the birds in the trees to fly away, he blew the muzzle, wiped down the gun with his handkerchief, then tucked it under his belt and proclaimed, "Democracy is good. You should vote for whomever you wish!" Then he proceeded from Liu Gully to Zhang Peak.

After Mingyao left, and as the sound of his gunshot reverberated through the air, all of Liu Gully's green leaves suddenly wilted and the spring flowers died. The villagers were left speechless.

Zhang Peak was actually right next to Liu Gully, with a dirt path connecting them and a river separating them. The Kong family didn't have any relatives in Zhang Peak, so Kong Mingyao didn't need to visit their houses to socialize and distribute gifts. Instead, he just said he had a small matter to attend to there, and he also wanted to see how Zhang Peak had changed and how its new buildings were sprouting up like mushrooms. He took a group that quickly grew from one hundred to two hundred, and then again to three hundred, and together they proceeded from Liu Gully to Zhang Peak. When they reached the middle of the village street, as everyone was crowding around, Kong Mingyao stood on a millstone that had been left in the village and looked at those new houses and other buildings. He asked to whom each house belonged, and what the owner had done to be able to build it. He asked in particular about a house with a roof made of glazed tiles, saying it was pretty good and was just like the villas he had seen while he was away. Then, he took out his pistol and aimed it at a gray tile pigeon on the roof of the house, then closed his left eye and placed his index finger on the trigger. There was a *Bam!* and the tile pigeon was shattered. The tree leaves all fell to the ground and the grass dried up. Then the villagers heard Mingyao shouting in the street, saying, "Democracy is good. You should vote for whomever you wish." At that point, it began half-raining and half-snowing in Zhang Peak, and everything quickly froze over.

After Mingyao left, Liu Gully and Zhang Peak both suffered a devastating drought and a hard freeze. The trees wilted and the sprouts died, and the villagers were not able to harvest even a few *jin* of grain. In Explosion, which was separated from them by only a single mountain ridge, however, the weather was fantastic that spring and the villagers had more grain than they could eat.

CHAPTER 5

Political Power (1)

1. THE ELECTION

I.

Democracy mixed with a thunderstorm, leaving Explosion completely soaked.

Zhu Ying returned from the provincial seat the day before the election. By this point the rain had stopped, the sun had come out, and the air was fresh. A sedan brought Zhu Ying to the entrance of the village, where she saw the enormous stele the town mayor had erected in her honor. Then she strolled into the village.

When Zhu Ying entered the village it was ten in the morning. The muddy road had been washed clean by the rain, and hovering over the street there was a cold mist, which made the stones and bricks along the road look like grayish-white chunks of ice. Because of the election, the peddlers didn't go into the town or county seat to sell their goods, and neither did the peasants go into the fields. Instead, everyone gathered in the village streets, under the sun, waiting for an unprecedented exercise in democracy to unfold in Explosion.

One of the candidates—the young Zhu Ying—returned from the provincial seat with a bang. Her return this time was completely different from the last. Before, she had returned to help refurbish the new house that her family had just built, but which they felt was already out of date. That time, she had been dressed unlike the other villagers. She had worn lipstick and mascara, and had plucked and penciled in her brows. Her hair had been dyed red, so that the villagers, and even the village sparrows, couldn't take their eyes off her. She had looked as though she wasn't from Explosion at all but rather was an enchantress from the city. This time, however, she was returning for the elections and looked like all of the other villagers. Her hair was black again, and she was wearing low-heeled shoes. She had a short wool skirt and a red sweater, and resembled not so much a city dweller but rather a villager who had struck it rich. The first person she encountered when she entered the village was a boy. She held the boy to her chest and slipped a hundred-yuan note into his clothes. She told him that she had been busy working and had not had time to buy him a gift, and he should use this money to buy himself something tasty to eat. She then ran into a teenage girl. She took the girl's hand and slipped her two hundred-yuan notes, saying that she hadn't had a chance to buy her a dress, but when the girl went into the city she should buy whatever caught her eye.

In this way, Zhu Ying walked through the streets distributing money in amounts ranging from one hundred to several hundred yuan. Her behavior resembled that of Kong Mingyao, though the weaponry she was carrying was somewhat different. Cash was her weapon—fistfuls of hundred-yuan bills, which she distributed to the villagers. She proceeded from one end of the village to the other, giving away who knows how much money along the way. Eventually, she reached her father's grave in the village square, and immediately knelt down and began kowtowing. She burned real bills as though they were fake funeral money and mumbled to herself. Then she proceeded back up the street distributing money, before disappearing into an alley. In the end, all of the villagers were left wondering what had just happened in Explosion, what was happening now, and what would happen in the future.

In a moment of quiet after Zhu Ying disappeared, one of the several hundred villagers who had gathered in the square cried out, "Zhu Ying has returned . . . Zhu Ying has returned, and has given money to everyone in Explosion!" With that, everyone began surging toward the Zhu family's new house. It was on that day that the people of Explosion first glimpsed the possibility of a twenty-four-hour bank from which they could withdraw money whenever they wished. They discovered that although Zhu Ying wasn't wearing new clothes when she returned to the village, in her house there was a cape made from an assortment of red, yellow, and blue bills. Moreover, that money was not simply printed on the fabric; rather, the cape was made from real hundred-yuan bills that had been pasted on. This had been done so skillfully that they looked like part of the fabric itself. In Zhu Ying's living room hung her other clothing, including sweaters, undershirts, underwear, coats, socks, and shoes—all with real hundred-yuan bills pasted on them. Two decades later, when Explosion would be transformed from a county seat into a city, the most valuable possession of the newly established Explosion Development museum would be Zhu Ying's money clothes.

It was because Zhu Ying had been busy having this new clothing made that she was delayed in returning to Explosion.

Eventually, the living room of the Zhu family's three-story house would be transformed into a gallery. Men and women, young and old, including those people who previously had been on good terms with the Kong family and who regarded themselves as the enemies of the Zhus, all took the opportunity to visit the Zhu home to see the various articles of clothing—which featured cut-up hundred-yuan bills arranged into images of flowers and trees, bees and butterflies—suspended on clothes hangers and displayed along the wall of her living room, or else they were being passed around from hand to hand. Unlike the Kong family, who brought a tractor-full of gifts and distributed them to everyone in an attempt to buy votes, Zhu Ying didn't go to anyone's house; instead she simply waited for everyone to come to her. On that day, the road in front of her family's house, together with the mountain ridge behind the village, was full of people talking about Zhu Ying and her money clothes, as well as the election for village chief.

People whispered to her, "It would be best if you were village chief."

Zhu Ying waved them away and said, "You should vote for Mingliang. I've declared my candidacy only because the town and county mayors required that I return."

Everyone complained, "You're as rich as a stallion; how can you leave us to live like fat sparrows?"

"Then who would look after my business in the city and the provincial seat?" Zhu Ying asked, unwilling to sacrifice something valuable for something inferior.

Everyone was quite disappointed, but then became even more determined to elect her. Zhu Ying proceeded upstairs and downstairs, to the living room and the courtyard, pouring tea for the villagers and chatting with them. For those households that were still rather poor, she offered three or five hundred yuan to help them out. Those young women who, like her, had gone out into the cities to work—including those from Liu Gully, Zhang Peak, and other villages in the Balou mountain range—all came to Zhu Ying's home for her to take care of them. They said, "Sister Zhu Ying, you absolutely must not become the new village chief, because if you do, what will happen to us? Would not every factory, every store, as well as the region's largest and best amusement park—would they not have to close down within days?" Later, after the first group of observers left the Zhu household, another group entered and said the same thing. At midday, the Zhu family prepared a lot of home-cooked food, and Zhu Ying invited everyone who had come to see her money clothing to come in and eat. This continued from the afternoon into the evening, and only then did Zhu Ying take her money clothing and carefully fold it. It was then that she turned around and saw Kong Mingliang standing in the doorway, smiling coldly. He resembled a stone statue as he stood there, with the light from the setting sun shining on his face. The pomegranate trees planted in the courtyard sprouted apple blossoms, and there was a peach tree that sprouted not only pomegranate blossoms but also crab apple blossoms and camellias. Some flower blossoms fell on the bricks and tile floor, like a poem in which people were like miswritten words. Kong Mingliang looked around and, with a mocking expression, asked,

"You've returned?"

Zhu Ying also laughed, and replied, "These money clothes were not put on display for you."

Mingliang's smile evaporated. "Money is more powerful than munitions."

Zhu Ying said, "If you aren't going to come inside and sit down, then you should just leave."

It was hard to tell whether they were quarreling or merely chatting. When they parted, Mingliang headed toward the entrance to the courtyard and Zhu Ying accompanied him—both to walk him out and also in order to close the outer gate and lock out the entire day's tumult. Just as Zhu Ying was about to close the gate, however, he turned around and said,

"You whore, do you still want to marry me?"

After a shocked pause, Zhu Ying said quietly, "I may be a whore, but tomorrow I'll be the new village chief. You can then come kneel down and beg me."

"Do you really think the villagers are going to pick you?"

"They aren't going to vote for me, they're going to vote for money. Right now, I've got a lot of money."

Kong Mingliang didn't say anything. His heart was pounding and he bowed his head; then he suddenly rushed back into the court-yard. Zhu Ying tried to keep him out, but he continued to force his way in. They struggled, until finally Mingliang succeeded in push-ing Zhu Ying aside. By this point dusk had fallen, but the courtyard seemed to be full of the scent of spring combined with the warmth of summer. The air was full of birds chirping, as a flock of sparrows alighted on the pomegranate tree and the peach tree in the courtyard. The two of them stared at each other coldly for a long time.

"You should leave," Zhu Ying said. "If you continue standing here, soon you'll have to beg me. "

Kong Mingliang stared at her intently. "You should withdraw from the election—and leave the position of village chief for me!"

Zhu Ying laughed. "Are you begging me?"

After a pause, Mingliang laughed as well. "If you don't withdraw, then after I'm elected I'll have you killed!"

Zhu Ying, still laughing, asked, "When you were sleepwalking that night, apart from running into me, what else did you find?"

Mingliang didn't reply, and instead he just stood there until eventually he turned and headed back out. He walked toward the village board building. The entire day, he had been in the village board building, watching the gate to Zhu Ying's home, but now, as he was preparing to head back there, he heard Zhu Ying shout behind him, "You once again missed your chance to ask for my hand in marriage. . . . You have now twice missed your chance, and you will regret it to the point that you will want to bash your brains out against the wall."

After that, he heard the sound of Zhu Ying slamming her gate.

II.

That night, footsteps echoed through Explosion like hailstones. Some people went to the Kong household, others went to the Zhu household, and still others went back and forth between the two. These would be village chief elections with national consequences and would be the topic of a major report that the county mayor would give to the provincial city, before he was promoted to city mayor. The residents of Explosion didn't know how many reports the county mayor had filed and how many preparations he had made, all so that he could take this election as a gift up to the city and offer it to the entire province.

So they prepared to elect their new village chief.

At ten in the morning on the day of the election, the residents of Liu Gully and Zhang Peak, both of which were under Explosion's jurisdiction, were summoned to the riverbank in front of the village. There, they used an assortment of house doors to construct a stage, and on the stage they placed a table. The table was covered by a new, red tablecloth, and the stage was draped with a large banner, on which was written EXPLOSION VILLAGE'S FIRST DEMOCRATIC ELECTIONS. In this way, the proceedings were granted a degree of solemnity. There were reporters and police cars, as well as more than a dozen spectators from the county and the town. The officials placed a ballot box in the center of the stage and then issued each villager (or citizen) over the age of eighteen a ballot printed with the names Zhu Ying and

Kong Mingliang, and asked the voters to make a check mark after the name of their preferred candidate. Then, each villager would go up onstage and insert the ballot through the slot in the ballot box. The result would be democracy, and their responsibilities would be over. After this, they would only need to wait for the ballots to be counted and tabulated, and then it would be announced how many votes each candidate received.

The candidate with the most votes would thereby be elected village chief.

There was nothing particularly extraordinary about any of it. Explosion had already experienced this sort of thing many times before. The only difference was that previously the voters had been electing battalion chiefs, but now the battalion had been replaced by the village and everyone was now electing a village chief. Previously, they would simply drop a pea into the bowl of the candidate they wanted to elect, but now they had to use an anonymous ballot box. In the past, the villagers organized the elections themselves, but now it was the police and the town and county mayors who had come to organize and observe the elections.

The county and town mayors arrived in the village at the crack of dawn. In order to avoid the appearance of impropriety, they didn't go to the house of either of the candidates for breakfast, and instead they brought their own soy milk and fried dough sticks, and ate in their cars. After breakfast, the villagers (citizens) started heading toward the meeting site. They arrived one group after another, each carrying a small stool as though they were going to the theater. By ten o'clock, thousands of people had gathered along the riverbank, where a loudspeaker announced that the election was about to begin. The former county mayor served as election mobilizer and said a variety of things about the earth-shattering nature of democracy and elections. The town mayor then announced the general rules of the

Yan Lianke

election, and also what was improper and illegal. Next, the candidates gave their speeches. Kong Mingliang stood onstage and read aloud the text that his brother Mingguang had written for him a couple of weeks earlier, though it wasn't clear whether the audience was listening or not. There was a droning sound, as though there were thousands of flies buzzing around the meeting site; the entire area came to resemble a cesspool in the middle of summer—becoming a performance stage for the flies. Mingliang glanced down at the audience in surprise and saw that in front of him there was a mother holding her child while he relieved himself. The mother was using that stiff, yellow ballot as toilet paper, and Mingliang couldn't resist going down and slapping her. While the county mayor was speaking, the audience had been completely silent, but once the town mayor began speaking, the audience had started mumbling, though it was impossible to make out what they were saying.

By the time the sound reached Kong Mingliang, it was a dull roar.

He had taken out a sheet of draft paper and looked at the county and town mayors. He saw that the county mayor was being interviewed by a reporter, so Mingliang had gone up to the town mayor and whispered, "You must tell the police to come maintain order!" To his surprise, the mayor had whispered back, "Read it now. Otherwise you'll miss your chance." Then Mingliang had cleared his throat and had begun reading his speech out loud. His dream, he explained, was for the drawers of every family to remain full of cash year-round. Within a few years he wanted Explosion to become a town, and a few years afterward he hoped it would become a city. After reading his speech, amid the sound of fighting from the ground, he slipped away like a cloud and returned to his seat next to the town mayor, and just as he was about to complain, the mayor did so first, saying,

"Your speech was too long."

He glared back in consternation.

Looking at Mayor Hu's face, Mingliang noticed that his eyes never once left Zhu Ying, who was sitting beside him. He wanted to curse the mayor, calling him a pig and a whoremonger. Suddenly, however, Mingliang felt the ground beneath his feet begin to tremble, to the point that he couldn't even keep his balance. He discovered that Zhu Ying's attractiveness and appeal were all concentrated in the area around her eyes. Her red sweater, straight-legged pants, low-heeled leather shoes, and flesh-colored socks, together with the scarf she kept either wrapped around her neck or draped over her chest and shoulders, were very tasteful and attractive. Although these were from the city, and although she had acquired her fashion sense there, that seductive expression and that glow around her eyes, which produced a laser beam that could stop men in their tracks—these were something that even city women didn't possess. The town mayor stared at that milky-white and bright red area between her eyebrows, as though looking at a virgin's bare genitals. At that moment, Mingliang had a sensation that almost knocked him off his feet. A shudder ran down through his heels. He abruptly sat down and heard someone announce that it was Zhu Ying's turn to go onstage and read her nomination speech. He saw her walk past the town mayor like a breeze. She gazed at the mayor and he looked back at her. For an instant their eyes met, whereupon she walked to the front of the stage, as though floating through the air.

At that point, Kong Mingliang's only thought was, *This is it—I lie in defeat between the gazes of this whore and the mayor*. In order to forestall the defeat that had not yet come to pass, he forced himself to calm down and see whether or not the audience would be louder during Zhu Ying's speech than it had been during his. Even now, his palms were still sweaty from hearing the audience's roar as he was trying to read his speech. He stared at Zhu Ying as he waited for her to begin, as though waiting for a thunderstorm to arrive. However, she simply stood there without opening her mouth. There was a long pause, and then another, until finally Zhu Ying used silence to quiet the audience. After waiting until everyone's gaze was fixed on her to begin speaking, she suddenly pulled a thick wad of bills out of her pocket and tossed them down to the audience. Those bills fluttered through the air like so many flowers or snowflakes, and before the audience had a chance to recover, Zhu Ying made a promise:

"If I'm elected village chief . . . I will make sure that every family has more money than it can spend—so much that it will be able to toss money out the door, like this. . . ."

And that was it.

Her entire speech—from her initial act of tossing the money into the air until her final word—lasted less than twenty seconds. As she was waiting for the audience to rush forward to retrieve the money, she returned to her seat. Before Kong Mingliang was able to recover his senses, everyone onstage and in the audience erupted into thunderous applause, which seemed to last for a full day and night. Eventually, the loudspeaker announced that it was time for all citizens, under the direction of their village organization chief, to come up onstage to cast their ballots.

This election was like a theatrical performance. Everything Kong Mingliang had done dissipated like smoke under the gaze of the county mayor, the town mayor, and the police. Mingliang got up from his seat in the middle of the stage and sat down in a corner, then watched as Zhu Ying, the town mayor, and the county mayor chatted and laughed as they proceeded to a table beneath a tree in back of the stage. Zhu Ying was acting as though she had already been elected and was accompanying them as though accompanying familiar guests.

A whore and her pimps! Mingliang cursed them to himself, as a feeling of lonely hatred rose up from his heart. He truly wanted to knock over the ballot boxes and the table. Eventually, however, he saw his father and eldest brother, as well as his fourth brother, who had returned from his high school in the county seat for the express purpose of voting for him, and Mingliang decided that things were not yet over and that the villagers would not necessarily elect Zhu Ying.

She was, after all, a whore.

And who didn't know what kind of business she had engaged in while in the city?

It was decided that during the period between when the ballots were cast and when they were counted, the local leaders and the candidates would leave the ballot box area and wait at the tea table behind the stage. It turned out, however, that Kong Mingliang was not willing to leave, and he didn't want to wait with the others. As Zhu Ying led the men away as if she were an enormous golden butterfly, Mingliang thought he should hate her with the sort of disgust one feels when one sees a swarm of flies circling around a pile of dung. But for some reason, even as Mingliang was calling Zhu Ying a whore, he couldn't find it in his heart to hate her. He simply couldn't forget that entrancing expression in her brows. He therefore smoked a cigarette—having taken up smoking when he began preparing for the election—and watched from a distance as everyone came up onstage in an orderly fashion to vote, including the people . . . villagers . . . citizens. He saw a magpie that looked as though it was about to alight on a tree next to him, but just as it was about to land, it flew away. In the end, it landed on a tree next to Zhu Ying, then sang happily for a while before flying away again. The county and town mayors pointed at the magpie and spoke with Zhu Ying for a long time, as the sound of their laughter came over in waves, piercing Kong Mingliang's heart. He wondered whether they had slept together or had visited Zhu Ying's brothel. Did they have the girls at the brothel bathe them, wash their backs, massage their feet, and then sleep with them? Kong Mingliang was certain they had. He thought that only this could explain why they were so friendly toward her and cold toward him. Otherwise, how could they all be over there chatting and laughing without thinking of inviting him (the other candidate) to join them?

After voting, many people headed back toward the village. The sun was high in the sky and it was already lunchtime, so the citizens needed to return home to prepare meals. Watching as the villagers departed, Kong Mingliang stood under the tree, as a patchwork of light fell on his face and body. He felt alternately hot and cold. The question of whether Zhu Ying had slept with the county and town mayors kept pricking his mind, making it impossible for him to settle down. In theory this should not have been any of his business, since after all Zhu Yu was neither his wife nor his girlfriend, but at that moment it occurred to him that if Zhu Ying and the mayors had indeed slept together, it would mean that the election for village chief would be forfeit. And if the election were forfeited, then the building he had been constructing in his dreams would collapse. His life would come to an end, like bubbles by the riverside that suddenly get popped. Life would lose all meaning and would no longer give him any pleasure. He didn't know if he could continue living. He had come back to Explosion in order to transform it from a village into a town, and then from a town into a city. When he was stealing goods from passing trains, there were several times he had almost fallen to his death. Explosion had become rich because of him. By this point, everyone else in the village lived in a new tile-roofed house, and only the Kong family still lived in their original thatched-roof house.

Even if everything he had done had merely been a performance, he had nevertheless done it all for the sake of Explosion and in order to become village chief. But now, that slut . . . just because she was attractive and dissolute—combined with the fact that after the trains sped up, he could no longer take the villagers to unload goods—thought she could waltz in with her cash-covered clothing and contest him for the position of village chief.

Fuck! Kicking the tree trunk, Kong Mingliang saw that as the last citizens—villagers—were leaving the riverbank and heading back to their homes, Zhu Ying was also leading the county and town mayors back to the village.

They were going to have lunch.

At that point, Kong Mingliang also walked toward the village, alone.

III.

Before going home, Kong Mingliang first went to the village board.

The village board building was completely deserted, and apart from himself and his secretary, Cheng Qing, the only thing present was that particular kind of sunlight that you see only in the fourth lunar month, together with a flock of sparrows that had returned for the spring. Mingliang sat in his large, empty office, where the exceptionally high ceiling made the couch and the plants feel unusually small. Cheng Qing was wearing a red sweater, straight-legged pants, and low-heeled leather shoes and appeared incredibly pure and beautiful, but Kong Mingliang felt that her face was not quite as seductive as Zhu Ying's. He didn't return home for lunch, but Cheng Qing brought him from somewhere a bowl of noodles, which he ate at his desk. As he was about to begin eating, he suddenly stared at Cheng Qing and asked,

"If I were to ask you to marry me, would you be pleased?"

Cheng Qing replied, "The county and town mayors each had a meal in every house in the village; they said that this was a good way for them to get to know the common people."

Mingliang asked again, "Tell me the truth, do you think that the county mayor and the town mayor have slept with Zhu Ying?"

"The vote counters went to the stage on the riverbank," she said. "After lunch, the votes will all be counted, and when the villagers return to the assembly area they will announce which candidate—you or Zhu Ying—received the most votes."

Kong Mingliang suddenly froze, with the bowl of noodles held up to his mouth. Without saying a word, he stared out into the empty, silent room. Cheng Qing was standing in front of him, her face registering an expression of concern and disappointment over his having lost the election. She looked at him as though she had done something wrong. "Run over to the riverbank to assess the situation, then report back to me." After Mingliang placed his bowl on the table, he gave Cheng Qing this order, and she nodded and hurried off.

The first time Cheng Qing returned from the riverbank, she said, "Chief Kong, you and Zhu Ying are virtually tied, but you are leading by a few votes."

The second time she returned, she said, "Zhu Ying's count is increasing, and now she is leading by fifty votes."

The third time she returned, she said, "Half of the ballots have now been counted, and you have 201 votes, while she has 409."

The fourth time Cheng Qing returned, she was soaked in sweat. Her face was pale and her hair was matted on her forehead. She stood in front of Kong Mingliang and was about to speak, but he waved her away, indicating that she should remain quiet. There was a silence as he chewed his lip, almost making it bleed. Then he sent Cheng Qing next door to bring Zhu Ying to the village board. In inviting her over, it was as though he were making a monumental decision, after which he seemed exhausted. He sat back, his body so limp it seemed as though he were about to slide out of his chair. But after Cheng Qing left, she immediately reappeared and reported, "Zhu

Ying says for you to go to her house. She says that if you want to ask her something, you should do so in person." Kong Mingliang sat there in a daze. After a long pause, he finally sighed and slowly got up. He rubbed Cheng Qing's head, releasing an intoxicating scent of hair and shampoo, then kissed her forehead and walked limply toward the door. He turned around and gazed nostalgically at his three-room office, like an emperor who is being forced out of the imperial palace but cannot bear to leave. An aura of loss enveloped his face, and the room itself.

He left the village board building, each step bringing him anguish.

"What about me?" Cheng Qing asked, as she followed him into the courtyard. "After Zhu Ying becomes village chief, will she still want me to be her secretary?"

Kong Mingliang paused and considered for a moment, then he said softly, "How can I not serve as village chief? What do you mean, you crow's mouth? How could I possibly not be reelected as village chief?" Then he turned away and headed toward Zhu Ying's house. Their buildings were several dozen steps from each other, but he proceeded extremely slowly. At times, he was tempted to stop and turn around, but in the end he didn't and instead permitted the history of Explosion to continue moving forward.

The sunlight poured down on his head like a gush of water, and sweat from his head ran down his neck. Cheng Qing followed behind, watching him carefully. She suddenly regretted that, several times when he had grabbed at her in the village board building, she had slipped away, unwilling to give herself to him. But, seeing him about to step down from his position as village chief, and seeing him hobbling along like a seventy- or eighty-year-old man, she rejoiced that she had not done so. Yet on the other hand, she also felt she should have given herself to him, since after all it would not have been a big deal, given that it would have merely been a physical encounter. If she were to give herself to him now that he was about to step down, she wouldn't in fact be giving herself to the village chief. She stood there and reflected, until he turned into that court-yard, but Cheng Qing still couldn't decide whether she should give herself to him or not.

The light in the Zhu family courtyard was hot and bright, leaving everyone covered in sticky sweat. Kong Mingliang would have preferred to first wash his face with cold water and cool himself off before going to see Zhu Ying. After stepping through the gate, he looked around the courtyard and saw that, under the wall, Zhu Ying was washing her dishes with water from a faucet that had been placed there to irrigate the plants. "Why don't you wash your dishes in the kitchen?" he asked. When Zhu Ying didn't turn around, he suspected that maybe he had just thought this question to himself and hadn't actually uttered it out loud. So he mustered the courage to ask in a louder voice, "Why don't you wash your dishes in the kitchen?"

Zhu Ying still didn't turn around, acting as though she hadn't heard a thing.

In reality, of course, Zhu Ying knew perfectly well that he was standing there. When the gate opened, she knew he had arrived. But she ignored him, acting as if she were completely unaware that someone had come in. It was only after he had asked three times in a row that she finally finished washing her dishes and turned around and looked at him, as though looking at a mule that had gotten run over. She saw that he appeared pale and that his brow was covered in beads of sweat. The loudspeaker by the riverbank began blaring, announcing that the citizens of Explosion Village should finish eating and hurry back to the assembly site, because the vote-counting had almost concluded, and the officials would soon announce the first democratically elected village chief since the founding of the People's

Republic of China. The sound from the loudspeaker was loud and coarse, and the voice stuttered, with every syllable spat out like a string of pebbles. After the announcement, Mingliang and Zhu Ying both took a moment to recover. They stood in the courtyard looking at each other for a long time, but in the end it was Zhu Ying who could no longer restrain her mockery, and as she pursed her lips traces of a smirk remained visible around the corners of her mouth.

"Have you come to ask me to withdraw?" she asked, still facing the interior of the courtyard.

He asked, "Why didn't you dine with the town and county mayors?"

"I didn't have time. I've decided to be the village chief."

"Tell me the truth—Zhu Ying, did you sleep with the county and town mayors?"

"The kitchen faucet is broken." She put the newly washed electric rice cooker and dishes in the kitchen. "You've already missed your chance."

"I know you received more votes," Kong Mingliang said, following behind. "I just want to know what your relationship is with the county and town mayors."

"The loudspeaker is urging everyone to convene," Zhu Ying said. "You and I should also return to the assembly site."

He then stood in front of her and said, "Give me the position of village chief, and I'll do anything you ask."

She looked at him, and said, "What can you do for me?"

"You just need to tell me one thing." His lips were trembling slightly. "Did you or did you not sleep with the county and the town mayors?"

She asked again, "What can you do for me?"

"I'll marry you."

"Will you kneel down and swear?"

Yan Lianke

He looked at her.

"Kneel down and swear!"

He finally knelt down and said, "If you let me be village chief, I'll marry you immediately. After the marriage, I'll take responsibility for everything outside the household and you can take responsibility for everything inside, and in this way all of Explosion will be ours. In the village, you'll be able to do whatever you want." When he finished speaking, he looked up at her. He felt that the tile floor of her house was as hard as iron, as though he were kneeling on a bed of nails. Outside, the loudspeaker continued to blare, calling out his and Zhu Ying's names and urging them to quickly report to the assembly site. At forty-five minutes past the hour there would be an announcement of who had been elected the new village chief. Mingliang ignored the loudspeaker and continued to kneel there, gazing at Zhu Ying's tantalizingly attractive appearance with a pleading expression. Zhu Ying, however, listened carefully to the loudspeakers, then looked down at him. Slowly pulling him to his feet, she said, "I knew that this day would come sooner or later. . . . Let's go, or we'll be late for the announcement."

CHAPTER 6

Traditional Customs

1. WEEPING AT THE TOMB

I.

After the announcement that Kong Mingliang had been elected village chief, it occurred to him that it had been more than a year since the villagers last went to weep at their families' grave sites in the mountain ridge cemetery. This custom of weeping at the family grave site had been almost forgotten. It wasn't even necessary to really cry; rather, one would just go and kneel to one's ancestors. Kong Mingliang, however, suddenly wanted to go to the grave site and weep. Initially, Zhu Ying had received 820 votes, while he had received only 410—which is to say, he received precisely half the number of votes that she did. Moreover, those who voted for Zhu Ying were all young people, most of them under forty, while those who voted for him were all older people in their fifties and sixties who wanted to spit in disgust whenever they heard about prostitution. Among the village's young people, there was not one who wasn't entranced by Zhu Ying's money, which flowed like water. Nearly everyone had daughters who claimed their money came from working in the south, but virtually all of them had in fact followed Zhu Ying and were earning their money doing sex work. This is something every family tacitly recognized but wasn't willing to acknowledge out loud. As new houses sprouted everywhere like mushrooms, the village became increasingly wealthy, and even though the villagers were not willing to say nice things about Zhu Ying, they thought well of her. As a result, she received twice as many votes as Kong Mingliang.

The announcer, however, stated that Kong Mingliang had been elected village chief, with 820 votes, while Zhu Ying received only 410. Upon hearing this, the audience first reacted with a stunned silence but then broke into wild applause. Amid the applause, the county and town mayors came to congratulate Kong Mingliang on his election. Music began playing over the loudspeakers, and there were fireworks outside the assembly hall. Kong Mingliang walked to the front of the stage and took a bow, thanking everyone who had elected him and promising that within two or three years Explosion would become as prosperous as a major metropolis. Zhu Ying also congratulated him and shook his hand the way that city people do. While doing so, however, she whispered, "In a few days, we'll get married!" He shook her hand as though accepting her congratulations and felt that her hand was light and soft, without a single callus. It felt as though he were shaking hands with a wad of cotton. Responding to that hand's warmth and softness, he nodded in agreement.

At that moment, he suddenly remembered that for two years the village had not maintained its practice of weeping at the grave site. So, after Mingliang had taken the county and town mayors out to lunch and had let the reporters from the city take some photographs, the mayors both said that they needed to go take care of some business and Mingliang escorted them to their cars. He watched as they drove out of the Balou Mountains, and the citizens who had gathered in the assembly site returned to their homes. The sun exhaustedly made its way west, as the entire world transitioned from tumult to quiet. As stillness unfolded, the riverbank was empty apart from a handful of people dismantling the stage. The broken stools had been simply tossed aside, and discarded shoes and ballots were scattered all over the ground. Kong Mingliang stood in the road seeing off the mayors, until their cars faded from sight, like horses galloping into the sunset. Only then did Zhu Ying turn around and repeat very solemnly, "I want to get married right away."

Mingling replied with a wan smile, "It appears that you and the mayors really didn't have any kind of relationship."

"Don't you want to get married?" Zhu Ying asked. "Marriage is good."

"What I want is to go to my ancestors' grave and weep in their memory," Mingliang said. "I haven't wept for them in a long time, and I have to tell them what has happened in the village."

Some people called out something from onstage, and they both headed toward the stage. Mingliang went first, and Zhu Ying followed behind. When Zhu Ying caught up to him she grabbed his arm like a city girl, at which point Mingliang felt so dizzy he almost collapsed. Her arm, however, held him up, like a rope, while also making it impossible for him to walk away.

Even more than before, he wanted to go to his ancestors' grave site and weep.

II.

The Kong family grave site was located several *li* outside the village. It was oriented from south to north, so that the sun shone down on the graves all day long. The cemetery contained more than ten generations of ancestors, including dozens of graves. Each one had a willow or a cypress growing over it, making the scene look as if a forest had suddenly sprouted in the middle of the mountains.

As the sun was setting in the west, there was a tiny sound of something moving. The field of wheat had turned green. Everything appeared very peaceful, but there was a sense of emptiness. For some reason, after Kong Mingliang was reappointed village chief, he wanted to cry. He proceeded alone to visit his family's grave site, and before he even got there his face was covered in tears. When he arrived, a breeze blew over from the graves and caressed his face, and only then did he begin to wail like a small child. He collapsed in front of the grave of one of his ancestors, as though he had suffered an unfathomable indignity. Because the grain in front of the graves had already begun to transition from its winter state and to sprout new spring growth, each stalk straightened its back, then turned to watch him cry. No one could understand why he was crying like this. Even Mingliang himself didn't know; he simply cried and cried. Some wild hares that had just come out of hibernation were watching him, and several crows landed on the grave. His hoarse sobbing was like a river of mud, covering the entire mountain ridge in yellow sludge. His shoulders shuddered as his tears poured out from between his fingers as he held his hands up to his face. As he wailed, however, he resembled a child performing in front of its parents. He continued until he didn't feel like crying anymore. By this point the sun had almost set in the west, and he heard a voice in his head say, *Stop crying!* Therefore, he stopped. He wiped away his tears and the snot on his hands, and felt that the crying spell had left him refreshed, as though there were a bright light shining in his heart. He wanted to use that light to see something, and after resolving to do something, he got up, but then saw his brothers Mingguang and Minghui half-squatting and half-kneeling behind him. There were tears behind Mingguang's eyes, though in the end he did not cry them out. Minghui, meanwhile, did not appear particularly sorrowful but rather was very quiet. When the sun finally set, the last rays of light shone down onto Minghui's face. He appeared simple and pure, as though he were artificial—as though he were a jade statue with a square face, broad shoulders, and thick red lips. He was quite tall, but had it not been for his clothing and short hair, he might have been mistaken for a girl.

Mingliang stared silently at Minghui.

Mingguang, however, wiped away his tears, then smiled as he walked forward. He said, "Today, you received twice as many votes as Zhu Ying."

Shifting his gaze from his fourth brother to his eldest brother, Mingliang suddenly blurted out,

"Zhu Ying and I are going to get married."

Kong Mingguang stared at Kong Mingliang in surprise, as though he no longer recognized his own brother.

"Has our father agreed?"

"*I* have agreed."

There was another pause, whereupon Minghui, as though trying to break the silence, announced happily, "Today we received a letter from Third Brother that he has received a commendation in the army, and he'll be promoted."

Mingliang was pleasantly surprised. With a smile, he stared at Minghui for a while, then brushed off the dirt on his knees and his butt and began walking toward the grave. His two brothers followed behind. There was a long silence, as though a curtain had been draped over their heads. By this point the sunlight had completely disappeared, and the mountain path became dark and quiet, and their footsteps resonated as though they were drumsticks tapping on the earth's crust. But in the blink of an eye, the moon emerged from behind a cloud. You could see that in Explosion there were many villagers who had come out of their houses, and they were all going to weep at their families' graves. They didn't really want to weep, but rather they were merely following tradition. Every year, on one day in the month following the Qingming grave-sweeping festival, all families would return to their ancestors' graves to weep and to tell their ancestors what was on their minds. In this way, their hearts could be at ease for the rest of the year. It was also said that on this day when the village chief went to his ancestors' graves to weep and tell them what was on his mind, he also visited the graves of the ancestors of the other villagers as well. There were the sounds of countless footsteps, and there were many lights and voices emerging out of the stillness. He heard a family crying beside a grave and mumbling something. Lights appeared wherever there were graves—appearing in all directions, along the hillside and in the ravine. There was the sound of crying everywhere, as though each family had suffered a boundless injustice.

The three brothers proceeded through that cascade of tears back to the village.

They initially assumed that since the villagers had gone to weep at the grave sites, the village itself would therefore be empty and quiet; but when they arrived in the village square they discovered that there were some villagers who had not gone to the graves in the mountain but rather had come to these new graves in the square—to weep and burn incense and paper money, filling the village streets with dense clouds of smoke. As the brothers approached, they saw that one of the mourners was Zhu Ying. She was kneeling at her father's grave and was burning three incense sticks, and she had laid out three bowls of offerings. In a loud, clear voice, she announced to her father,

"I'm about to get married. You can rest in peace. In the future, Explosion will continue to belong to our Zhu family.

". . . I'm about to get married. In the future, Explosion will continue to belong to our Zhu family!"

The Kong brothers immediately stopped to listen to what she was saying, as though watching her perform a scene in a play. Next, Cheng Qing came out. She and her mother were carrying a basket full of funeral money and sacrificial offerings. They were also each carrying a flashlight, whose beam shone back and forth under the moonlight, like a big round piece of yellow silk fabric being dragged along the ground. As Cheng Qing and her mother passed in front of the Kong brothers, the mother stopped and exchanged some warm words with them, then stroked Minghui's face and asked how could he have grown up so quickly? However, Cheng Qing, who as the village board secretary would have been expected to say something upon seeing the newly elected village chief, merely nodded her head. Since the announcement that Mingliang had been elected village chief, she had not appeared in his presence. Even now, she did not address him as Brother Mingliang—as village custom would have dictated—and neither did she address him more formally as Chief Kong. Instead, she tried to avoid his gaze as she walked toward her ancestors' graves to weep.

Mingliang stared at her in surprise. She proceeded a few paces, then turned around, and their gazes met under the moonlight. Only then did she ask somewhat awkwardly,

"Will I still serve as the village board secretary?"

"Of course," he said, coming up to her. "Why wouldn't you?"

"Are you definitely going to marry Sister Zhu Ying?" She looked over toward Zhu Ying and saw that Zhu Ying was looking over at her.

"We'll get married right away," Mingliang said. "Isn't that a good thing?"

"Of course it's a good thing . . . I just want to go weep at my ancestors' graves." As Cheng Qing was speaking, her eyes filled with tears, and she urged her mother to hurry. The two of them disappeared into the moonlight, like a couple of yellow leaves on an autumn day. At that moment, Zhu Ying walked over from her father's grave, held Minghui's hand, then gazed at Mingguang and addressed him familiarly as Eldest Brother, as though she and Mingliang were already married and she were already a member of the Kong family.

2. WEDDING INVITATION

When Mingliang's father Kong Dongde heard that Mingliang and Zhu Ying were going to get married, he immediately dropped the birdcage he was holding. The cage door opened and the container of birdseed spilled out. A pair of parrots, which had been pets their entire lives, squawked in surprise and flew away.

The parrots were never seen again.

Kong Dongde had been sitting under the house awning and using a piece of bamboo to clean up the bird droppings in the cage, as Mingliang stood next to him and told him about the marriage.

"Zhu Ying and I are now engaged."

His father had frozen, and after a long pause he slowly turned and asked,

"Doesn't Cheng Qing treat you well?"

"I promised Zhu Ying we would immediately get married."

It was at that point that Kong Dongde had dropped the birdcage.

The swallows that had flown back for the spring were busy building nests under the awnings, and their cries seeped into the cracks of the silence between father and son. The old elm tree in the courtyard was full of pear blossoms, and a strong smell of Chinese toon wafted over. Watching his parrots fly away, Kong Dongde knew that they were going far away and would never return. He was heartbroken and regretted his reaction. He looked at his son, who had appeared unusually somber ever since being elected village chief, and said,

"Did Zhu Ying give you the position of village chief?"

Mingliang replied, "We are ready to get the marriage certificate."

"She will be the death of me," his father said. "It is on account of her dead father that she wants to marry into our Kong family."

"Send her a wedding invitation," Mingliang said. "Can't several hundred votes for village chief be exchanged for a wedding invitation?"

Everyone knows you can't have a wedding without a wedding invitation, which should be printed on red paper and should say something propitious like "Together for a hundred years" or "Auspicious marriage." Several hundred yuan should be placed in a red envelope, to serve as engagement money. A banquet should be arranged, at which the groom's father or mother should hand the bride the wedding invitation, thereby signaling that the groom's family approves of the marriage. After this formal engagement, the couple can then get married.

One morning in the fourth lunar month, Zhu Ying came over to the Kong family home to receive her wedding invitation. The sky was clear, and it was market day along the river in front of the village. All of the villagers had gone to the market to buy and sell their goods and were busy doing their own things. Zhu Ying was also in a hurry to return to the county seat to get on with her business, so she picked this date to meet with her fiancé's mother and decide on a day for the wedding. After going to the city to make a reservation at Pleasure World, she would return for the wedding and then spend the remainder of her days helping Mingliang with Explosion's business. It was also on this day that Zhu Ying, wearing the money-covered dress she had brought with her from the city, went to the Kong family home bearing countless wedding gifts.

"What if my father doesn't agree to the marriage?" Mingliang asked.

"As soon as he sees me, he'll definitely agree," Zhu Ying replied confidently. "In this world, there isn't anything I can't do." Then she turned and asked Mingliang, "Is there anything *you* can't do?"

"No, there isn't anything I can't do," Mingliang replied.

They rushed to the Kong family home to fetch the wedding invitation. As they passed through the village streets, side by side, they saw a middle-aged man taking some vegetables to market and stopped to talk to him. Zhu Ying asked how old the man's daughter was and suggested that he let his daughter go into the city with her—saying that in a single day in the city his daughter could earn as much as he himself could earn in an entire year from selling vegetables. The man looked at her, whereupon Mingliang glanced at the new tile-roofed house the man had built, and added, "Let her go—if you have some more money, then when the village becomes a town you'll be able to open a grocery store selling fresh vegetables. And after Explosion becomes a city, your daughter will have seen the world and could return to serve as a manager and open a department store or something. After she becomes a boss, you won't even need to button your own clothes, since there will always be people to help you get dressed and put on your shoes." Then they proceeded down the street and saw a child with a book bag on his way to school. Zhu Ying patted the child's head, and Mingliang asked her,

"Shall we have a child next year?"

"Sure," Zhu Ying replied. "Next year, when the village becomes a town, my child will be born into the town's new prosperity."

"Study hard," Mingliang said with a smile as he patted that child's head. "Work hard, and after you finish school you can become an engineer in Explosion City's Bureau for Urban Planning."

The two of them proceeded along. The conjugal affection they had felt for each other in Zhu Ying's home—a feeling of love that surged up to their heads—hadn't yet subsided. Love, like fire, was burning them up, making them feel that the entire world was full of promise. When they reached a street corner, Kong Mingliang said that in the future he wanted to build a one-star hotel on this street corner, for the people who would come to Explosion on business trips. Zhu Ying smiled at him mockingly and replied that he was being shortsighted. She said that if they were going to build a hotel, they should build a five-star one. That way, they wouldn't risk opening it and feeling that it was already out of date.

"We should build a ten-star hotel!" Mingliang kissed her and said, "That way, when people from all around the fucking world come to this hotel, they'll be left speechless."

Zhu Ying smiled even more mockingly and said, "Five stars is as high as it goes!"

"Do you not believe that I can build a ten-star hotel with walls that are made entirely of gems?" Mingliang asked seriously. "Do you think that there is anything in this world that I can't do? If you don't believe in me, then why did you agree to marry me?"

This question left Zhu Ying speechless—and immediately reminded her of their urgent post-wedding plans. She did not say anything about believing in him but merely told him that he must have someone immediately write an announcement about Explosion being redesignated as a town and send it to the town government. One copy of the announcement should be sent directly to the county seat, and another should be taken to the city, to be placed on the mayor's desk. In this way, they returned to reality, and to the things at hand that urgently needed to be done. They continued chatting until they arrived at the door of the Kong family home. All of the houses in the village now had tile-covered roofs, and only the Kong family was still living in their original thatched-roof house. The old building abutting the courtyard wall was made of mud and crushed tiles, and under the wind and rain it was on the verge of collapse. There was a strong smell of dirt and dust around the gate. Zhu Ying walked up to the gate and looked at it and at the old house inside the courtyard.

"We should build a new house. . . . Wait until I am town mayor!"

"Reporters from the newspapers and the television stations are no longer interested in your affairs." She replied coldly, "I don't want to get married and live in this old house." At this point, Mingliang's mother walked out of the house. When she saw Zhu Ying, she stared in shock at her dress, then broke into a smile and accepted the clothing and gifts Zhu Ying was carrying. Smiling brightly, she led her son and Zhu Ying into the house.

In the morning air, there was the green scent of spring combined with the smell of wheat from the fields outside the village. Mingliang's mother went into the kitchen to help Mingguang's wife with the cooking, while Mingliang's father and eldest brother sat in the living room. There were already five or six dishes on the dining table in the middle of the room, including chicken, beef, and fish. The aroma seeped out from under the dishes' lids and filled the room. Several village cats had come over, attracted by the aroma, and were wandering around the table legs and Zhu Ying's pants legs, their mewling sounding like music. A flock of magpies and orioles flew over and were circling the courtyard, then they flew inside and even circled around Zhu Ying's head. When they began to tire, they alighted on the tree in the courtyard to rest. Zhu Ying's body was covered in perfume, which smelled like fragrant osmanthus blossoms. A couple of canaries landed on her shoulders, and were followed by a flock of sparrows that also flew up to her in search of that aroma. As a result, the entire house was filled with the sound of birds chirping and the smell of dirt. Only after Kong Dongde shouted at them did those birds begin to settle down.

No matter where Zhu Ying went, the canaries always landed on her shoulder, pecking at the coins printed on her clothes. She had to keep waving her arm to shoo them away, but it was not until she picked up a bowl of bitter melon that they finally scattered. Then, Kong Dongde led everyone into one of the interior rooms, where the family all sat around the table. There were more than a dozen dishes, all artfully arranged. The wineglasses and chopsticks were waiting impatiently in front of them. The father sat at the head of the table and his daughter-in-law Cai Qinfang sat with Zhu Ying. Cai Qinfang leaned over and smelled Zhu Ying's clothes and said that it was no wonder the sparrows and butterflies were circling around. She also told Mingliang that he had a good eye, and that in finding Zhu Ying he had ensured that he would be able to spend the rest of his life in a honeypot.

Mingliang smiled, but after looking over at his father he immediately wiped the smile from his face.

Mingliang's elder brother Mingguang didn't say a word. Instead, with an expression of disappointment, he gazed first at Zhu Ying and then at his wife, Cai Qinfang.

The warmth in the room was unevenly distributed and alternated between warm and cold. Zhu Ying had considerable experience and had hosted guests from all over of the world, including rich and poor, high officials and lowly fishmongers—but everyone knew that today she had come to the Kong household to receive the wedding invitation, and that she would be subjected to a sort of vengeance banquet. Zhu Ying, however, was neither anxious nor angry. Before sitting down she brought out the wedding gifts and distributed them to everyone. Zhu Ying gave her future mother-in-law a pair of flannel shoes like the ones people wear in the city, and gave Elder Brother a Western suit he could wear when he went to teach. She gave her sister-in-law a half-wool dress and two bottles of perfume and face cream covered in foreign writing—assuring Qinfang that this perfume and face cream were better than what she was currently using, and if she used them for a few days she would look a lot younger. Her sister-in-law's hand trembled as she happily accepted these gifts. Then, Zhu Ying took out the jeans she had brought for Fourth Brother but set them aside, saying that the family should give them to him as soon as he returned from the city.

In the end, she would present a gift to her future father-in-law, Kong Dongde. When she gave him the gift, Kong Dongde naturally would take out the wedding invitation he had prepared and give it to his prospective daughter-in-law. After this ceremonial gift exchange, Zhu Ying would open the wedding invitation and read aloud the auspicious words written on it (while someone else would take the money in the envelope and count it out aloud in front of everyone). Finally, there would be a celebration, and the wedding invitation would conclude with a banquet.

Under the family's expectant gaze, Zhu Ying pulled out a letter from the bottom of her bag of gifts. As everyone watched her with a smile, she returned to the table, opened the letter, and produced blueprints for two new mansions—one for a Chinese-style courtyard compound and the other for the kind of expensive villa you might find in the city. She asked her future father-in-law to pick one of them, saying that the following month she would begin construction on whichever one he preferred. She exclaimed that it was humiliating for her father-in-law to have to live in such a dilapidated adobe house, and that he should instead live in a large Western-style mansion. She would install heat and air-conditioning in the new house, so that it wouldn't be cold in the winter or hot in the summer, and this way she hoped to grant her father-in-law everything that he previously lacked.

"Father, please pick one of the houses, and I'll have it built for you this year," Zhu Ying said loudly, then handed the blueprints to him.

Everyone's gaze was riveted on Kong Dongde. He was in his sixties, with a thin but sturdy frame, and although his hair was beginning to turn gray, his face was increasingly bright. He looked at the blueprints Zhu Ying handed him, with a vigilant and depressed expression, as tears began to flow from his eyes as though trickling out from behind a dammed-up river. He looked at the blueprints but didn't take them. Then he looked at his two sons and their wives sitting around the table, and saw that everyone was watching him expectantly. When Mingliang caught his eye, he subtly gave his father a look indicating which blueprint he should pick. Kong Dongde turned away from the table and took the two blueprints Zhu Ying was holding. With a smile, he said, "Please let me think about it before deciding." Then he stared at the blueprints and saw that the one for the courtyard compound included a living room with a row of furniture, and next to the wall there was a kitchen cabinet that looked just like a rectangular coffin. He said, "This looks like a large pantry but also resembles a coffin." The pleased look vanished from his face. He quickly turned to the blueprint for the villa and saw that in the living room there was one item that resembled a piece of furniture but was nevertheless clearly a coffin. Kong Dongde looked at Zhu Ying in astonishment and saw that she was not looking in that direction but rather was saying something to her sister-in-law. He immediately realized what was going on—she had hidden a coffin in each of the blueprints she gave him. He slowly accepted the blueprints, with a hard look on his face. Then he cleared his throat to get everyone's attention and he pulled a red envelope the size of a regular letter out of his pocket. On the envelope were written the words "Good Fortune for a Hundred Years." He stared at these words for a moment and read them aloud. Then, as everyone was watching, he walked toward Zhu Ying.

Everyone smiled and applauded as he read those words aloud again. Zhu Ying's look of concern vanished and was replaced with a peaceful expression. But when Zhu Ying received the red envelope and was about to open it in front of the family, Kong Dongde suddenly picked up his chopsticks and said, "Let's eat first—there isn't very much money, so you can open the envelope after you return home." He smiled again. Zhu Ying smiled as well and put the red envelope in her pocket.

They all enjoyed the engagement banquet and, as they helped one another to more food, the family's happiness spread to the entire table and gathered inside the house. The eldest son, Kong Mingguang, kept looking over at his new sister-in-law Zhu Ying's face, then back at his own wife's, and would crack a stupid joke to cover up his actions. Zhu Ying noticed what he was doing but feigned ignorance, and instead periodically peeked at Mingliang's face, and then at her father-in-law, Kong Dongde. She detected something in their expressions and noticed that as Kong Mingliang ate his food, his gaze remained fixed on the pocket in which she had placed the red envelope. As everyone else was still eating, she suddenly excused herself, saying that she was going to the kitchen to get some more soup.

In the kitchen, she opened the red envelope Kong Dongde had given her. Inside, she found that there was no money but rather only a white sheet of paper that read: "You whore, what are you trying to do to the Kong family?"

She stared at these words for a long time, until she was finally able to master the cloud of emotions that covered her face. Once she recovered her composure, she refolded the sheet of paper and put it back in the envelope, then ladled out a bowl of egg-drop soup. When she walked out of the kitchen, she ran into Kong Mingliang, who was heading into the kitchen. He knew she had gone inside to open the red envelope. Whenever a woman marries in Explosion, she is always eager to know how much money will be in her red envelope. So, when Zhu Ying took such a long time to emerge from the kitchen, Mingliang decided to look for her.

"How much was there?" Mingliang asked. "As long as you have me, you'll have everything you need. Don't worry about how much my father gives you."

Zhu Ying smiled and said, "It's a bankbook, which I'll never be able to spend down for as long as I live."

When the two of them went back into the room, Zhu Ying and her father-in-law exchanged a meaningful glance, then each of them immediately turned away. At that point, Zhu Ying began acting as though she were one of the Kong family's daughters-in-law and proceeded to pour a bowl of soup for everyone at the table, then placed it in front of each person. When she came to give Kong Dongde his bowl, she took the red envelope out of her pocket, waved it around, then laughed loudly. "I just looked at this. It's a bankbook, which I'll never be able to spend down as long as I live." Kong Mingguang's wife turned pale. When she entered the Kong household, she received not a bankbook but rather just an envelope containing two hundred yuan. As Dongde's wife was trying to grab that red envelope to see for herself, she accidentally knocked over a bowl of soup. The bowl broke into three pieces, and the egg-drop soup spilled all over the floor.

Everyone stared in shock, and only Zhu Ying reacted to the broken bowl with a bright smile on her face, as though it were a red curtain onstage.

3. LIVING ROOM

The Kong household quickly replaced their thatched-roof house with a tile-roofed one.

The day of the wedding, the entire village went crazy.

The village chief and Zhu Ying, who was the village's richest resident, were going to get married. At the time of the election for village chief, the two families were clearly still enemies, but now they were joining into a single family. Some people said that the town mayor had served as a matchmaker. Whatever the case may be, this wedding was a momentous event for Explosion. Both the town and the county mayors came to attend, and they each brought astonishing gifts. There wasn't anyone in Explosion, including the residents of Liu Gully and Zhang Peak, who didn't send a wedding gift. In the entrance to the village there were two tables for depositing gifts, and next to the enormous stele that had been erected in Zhu Ying's honor there were two accountants recording the name of everyone bringing a gift, and the type of gift or amount of money—and the accountants wrote so much that their wrists became swollen. So many people gave bedding and blankets that the gifts wouldn't even fit in the Kong family's two granaries. Every girl who had gone out with Zhu Ying to engage in romantic work in the city rushed back and gave her so many rings and necklaces that she needed a large bamboo basket to hold them. Throughout the whole day, these seductive women wandered through the streets and alleys of Explosion. Their perfume drove the men of Explosion mad with desire and attracted all of the sparrows in the world to fly overhead. To prepare the banquet for everyone who had come to offer gifts, the Kong household built countless stoves along the village streets. Everywhere that they could set up tables, they combined the Balou region's traditional square tables with round tables they had borrowed from hotels in the township seat several dozen *li* away. The banquet began on the morning of the sixth day of the month and continued uninterrupted for three full days. The cooks used two large barrels of MSG just to prepare the vegetables. The wine and cigarettes were brought over in a large truck from the county seat, and after the owners of those stores sold out their entire stock of cigarettes and wine, they squatted in front of their shops and regretted they didn't have more goods in stock. Finally, at dusk on the third day, everyone began to drunkenly head home, as a modicum of peace and quiet was finally restored to the streets of Explosion.

After three days of festivities, the horses and oxen that had been frightened away by the tumult slowly made their way back to the village.

The startled chickens, ducks, and geese also returned from wherever they had gone. They could be seen walking up and down the streets, as the chickens started laying goose eggs and the geese started laying duck eggs.

Dusk arrived in the village, and brought the peace and quiet the village had previously enjoyed. The men who planned to eavesdrop outside the bridal chamber had already hidden in the courtyard or leaned their ladders against the Kong family courtyard wall. In Balou, it was considered a veritable disaster for a wedding not to have any onlookers roughhouse the newlyweds and eavesdrop on the bridal chamber: that would be taken as evidence of the family's isolation and reclusion. Only if the eavesdroppers were able to listen from dusk till dawn was the event thereby considered auspicious. Everyone therefore began making preparations early, with some people hiding under the chopping board in the Kong family kitchen, others hiding at the base of the courtyard wall, and others climbing a tree and hiding amid the leaves. There were the young men who had helped Mingliang unload goods from passing trains, and the young women who had gone with Zhu Ying to the south or to the country seat—all of them were now happily chatting as they walked into and out of the bridal chamber. They kept pushing Mingliang on top of Zhu Ying, and pushing Zhu Ying into Mingliang's arms, and then would burst out laughing. In this way, they turned the Kong family's enormous courtyard upside down.

After Mingliang and Zhu Ying had kowtowed first to the heavens and earth, and next to the Kong father and mother, Mingliang's father, Kong Dongde, disappeared from the festivities and wasn't seen again by the crowds of visitors.

Kong Mingliang's elder brother, Mingguang, and his wife, Cai Qinfang, had spent all day on the wedding, and that evening when they retired to their own bedroom the visitors who had come to eavesdrop on the bridal chamber also heard them making a tumult. Then the visitors heard someone's face being slapped, and the bedroom became as silent as a grave.

Fourth Brother Minghui had taken a leave of absence from his school in the city and returned to the village for the wedding. He was assigned to serve as the page boy who would fetch Zhu Ying from the Zhu household and bring her to the Kong household. Since both families lived in the same village, their houses were less than half a *li* from each other, but when the magnificent caravan had set out from the Zhu home it circled around the whole village and through the township, loudly playing drums and setting off fireworks. As a result, although the caravan had set out at nine in the morning, it did not make its way back until eleven. In the luxurious caravan sedan, Minghui had been sitting on Zhu Ying's left and a twelve-year-old flower girl had been sitting on her right. The girl was dressed up in Western attire, and during the entire ride she sucked on a candy and leaned her head on Zhu Ying's shoulder. The only thing she had said to Zhu Ying was that when she grew up she wanted to go out into the world as Zhu Ying had done, and then return home to marry the village chief or town mayor. Minghui and Zhu Ying had said a lot to each other. She asked him about his studies in the city, and what he wanted to study in college. She also asked,

"After college, do you plan to return to Explosion?

". . . What kind of job and wife do you plan to find?"

Finally, she told him very solemnly, "I'm your sister-in-law, so listen carefully to what I have to say. After college, you mustn't return to Explosion. After I marry your second brother, Explosion sooner or later will be destroyed by us." Minghui didn't understand what she was saying, and when he turned to look at her he saw that her eyes were filled with tears as big as the diamond on her ring, but the crooked smile on her face made the blood freeze in his veins. He stared at her in bewilderment, until she finally laughed, wiped away her tears, and gave his cheek a sisterly pat.

This is how the day had proceeded.

That night, no one knew where Minghui—who most needed to participate in the bridal room tumult—had gone.

After the room in the Kong home directly across from Mingguang's was renovated, it was designated as Mingliang's and Zhu Ying's bridal suite. The entire room and courtyard were filled with red *double happiness* characters, the courtyard and streets were filled with red couplets, the street and the village were filled with fireworks, while the entire world was filled with the smell of burning paper. As the tumult gradually faded in the moonlight, it was replaced by a humid stillness. In the bridal chambers, there was not a sound to be heard. Some people placed their ears against the wall, while others climbed down from a nearby tree and tiptoed up to the bridal chambers and placed their ears under the window. When they still couldn't hear anything, they looked in surprise at the window to the darkened room and used their tongues to poke tiny holes in the paper window shade. One person squatted so that another could stand on his shoulders. The latter closed his left eye and peered through the hole in the window shade with his right eye, but apart from some red furniture and a table with a candle that was about to burn out, there was only the bed made up with a combination of tumult and quiet.

The person on top climbed down to let the person on the bottom climb up, but apart from the red tumult on the bed and the quiet in the room, there was nothing else to be seen or heard. At this point, however, there was a movement in the matrimonial bed. Someone who had hidden under the bed in order to watch and eavesdrop on the bridal room had fallen asleep, and after waking up he slowly crawled out, looking disappointedly at the enormous bed. Apart from the bride and groom, who were both sound asleep, everything was completely peaceful. The interloper tiptoed out of the bedroom, and everyone asked him what was wrong. Had the bride and groom whispered something to each other? The interloper didn't say anything, and instead cut through the crowd. Only after he reached the Kong household's outer gate did he finally turn around and say to those who had followed him:

"After an entire day of excitement, the bride and groom went to sleep without even taking their clothes off."

The second night, it was the same story.

The third night, as all of the children and young people were in the depths of their disappointment at not having been able to satisfy their voyeuristic fantasies, they had no idea what astonishing and earth-shattering things were unfolding in the bridal chamber.

Love exploded with earth-splitting force.

Following the house-toppling excitement, Kong Mingliang and Zhu Ying had fallen asleep, and when Mingliang woke up he hugged Zhu Ying and exclaimed,

"My god, my god! I've found a nymph!"

Zhu Ying laughed and said, "In the future, you should listen to this nymph!"

Then, they engaged in a second round. When they were done, Mingliang rubbed the sleep from his eyes and got out of bed. He knew that Zhu Ying had sucked the strength from his legs, and if he didn't lean against the walls he would probably collapse. The sky was overcast, and the sunlight was being captured by the clouds. When he opened the doors to the bedroom, Kong Mingliang looked out and saw that the courtyard was virtually full of the young people who had previously gone with him to unload goods from passing trains. They all had mysterious expressions of envy and excitement, but in their eyes there was a look of puzzlement. There were also a couple of fifteen- or sixteen-year-olds who had kept their ears pressed against the bedroom door until Mingliang came out.

Kong Mingliang kicked those two youngsters in the butt.

The two youngsters hopped like a pair of springs and said with chagrin, "Chief Kong, you and your wife were so animated in the bridal chamber last night that even our own beds were bouncing."

Everyone crowded around the village chief and asked what was the best part of being married to Zhu Ying? What had they done differently? Kong Mingliang spun around and, with his arms folded across his chest, he kept repeating over and over again, "Incredible! Just incredible!"

Everyone else spun around with him and kept asking,

"What was incredible?"

"It was like a volcano."

"Could someone have burned up?"

"Someone who was weak could have been burned alive."

The young men of Explosion resolved that they wanted to imitate Kong Mingliang, and would get engaged and married to those young women who had gone out to seek romantic work in the city. The young men were heedless of the disdain of their elders, as long as they could earn money from the outside world. As long as their fiancées desired money and a family, the young men could pretend that their past never occurred. They surrounded Kong Mingliang and asked what he would do next. After all, he couldn't keep spending money that someone else had earned. Kong Mingliang then announced to those youngsters that if Explosion Village really wanted to get rich and be redesignated as a town and then a city, it wouldn't be able to rely on the money the young women earned in the city doing romantic work, but rather it would have to open factories, and the factories would need to be as crazily prosperous as the young women in their bridal chambers.

"I've experienced all sorts of hardships," Mingliang shouted. "During the Reform and Opening Up period, you could earn whatever you wanted. If you had money, you could be a grandfather or grandmother, but if you didn't, you would be a grandchild or a lowly rat. If you had money, the town and county mayors would listen to you, but if you didn't, the town and county mayors would treat you like a grandchild or a great-grandchild." As he was shouting this, he observed that the villagers crowded around in ever-greater numbers, and after they filled his family's courtyard, he stood on one of the newlyweds' chairs and shouted even more loudly, "All of you elected me to serve as your village chief, casting 820 votes for me, while casting only 410 for Zhu Ying. Because of my vote count, which was precisely double hers, her dreams of becoming village chief were shattered. She admitted defeat, and in order to marry me she went to the village board and knelt down, crying like a child. She cried so hard, as though she were made of tears, that I agreed to marry her. She then agreed that, after the marriage, she would bring in her outside business and install it in the streets of Explosion. This included foot-washing parlors, hair salons, and amusement parks—she would create an entire amusement avenue here in Balou. In this way, she would attract those rich people to pour into Explosion to spend their money. They would come to Explosion with their pockets full of gold and silver, and then return home with their pockets empty. Within two or three years Explosion will become a town, and a few years later it will become a city. If girls and women love Explosion so much, and are willing to sacrifice their bodies, their reputations, and even their lives for the sake of Explosion's prosperity, then what about the men?" As Mingliang was shouting this, he looked out at the crowded courtyard and saw that it contained not only strong young men from the village but also old people, children, women, and girls—all of whom were surging into his courtyard as though he were holding an assembly. Kong Mingliang let them take one of the newlyweds' tables from his house and place it outside the main gate, as though he were holding an oath-taking meeting in the village streets. He stood in front of the table decorated with red matrimonial *double happiness* characters and gazed out at the dark crowd of villagers. He even sent people to fetch those families who had not come. The sun appeared from behind the clouds, as the village streets became warm and bright, and the villagers in attendance became drenched in sweat. They looked at the groom standing on the red table, as though watching a young Buddha dancing in midair. They listened as he shouted, his voice thundering through their veins.

"If our girls and women are already like this, how can our men live in the houses built with the money the women earned, eat the food bought with the money the women earned, and not do anything? We'll create factories and companies, and as long as you can earn money and become rich, you should be willing to do anything—even kowtow to people or lick the dust from their shoes. As long as you can earn money, then apart from murder and arson there is nothing you shouldn't be willing to do. There is nothing that should appear undoable. After Explosion is transformed from a village into a town, the vast majority of you will become factory bosses and company managers. You'll become national cadres in the town government— you'll become standing committee members, deputy town mayors, secretaries, and bosses. Every household will have a large truck and a car to use, and even a bicycle for when they go buy vegetables at the market. You'll drink milk in the morning, and at night you'll have chicken tonic soup. You'll have nannies to take your children to and from nursery school. This is what I, Chief Kong, promise you, and this is the direction in which I will lead you over the next few years! If Explosion does not become a town that is as active and thriving as a county seat, then don't vote for me in the next round of elections!

"You can pull me down from my position as village chief and spit on me, to the point that I drown in your saliva and phlegm, just as my father-in-law Zhu Qingfang did!"

By this point Mingliang was hoarse from shouting, and sounded as though some grass had gotten stuck in his throat. He lowered his head and coughed, and as he was doing so the crowd erupted in applause, which continued until after the sun had set. The applause lasted for eight and a half hours, and many villagers clapped so hard their hands bled, to the point that they used up all of the village clinic's astringent and cotton gauze.

CHAPTER 7

Political Power (2)

1. TRANSFORMING THE VILLAGE INTO A TOWN

In the end, the directive to convert the village into a town wasn't approved.

The directive was sent to the county seat the same way a relative would deliver eggs and pastries, and who knows how much money was spent preparing for this figurative banquet. Zhu Ying even sent several of the village's most beautiful girls to the county seat to serve as nannies for the political leaders. She sent seven or eight girls in all, but the directive to have the village redesignated as a town remained stuck in a cul-de-sac. Every girl she sent into town ended up being wasted, like cow droppings left in the middle of a field.

Mingliang began to have a sense of despair.

Going from disappointment to despair was like going from one end of the village to another, and had it not been for Zhu Ying's perseverance and determination, Mingliang would have been tempted to simply kick Mayor Hu Dajun in the shins, saying, "You got to be promoted from town mayor to county mayor, while Explosion only wanted to be redesignated from a village to a town. All you need to do is call a meeting with the county officials, sign the order, then send it down—but you are simply not willing to do so."

Kong Mingliang was exhausted and exasperated. By this point, he no longer held out any hope that Explosion would be promoted to a town—but just as he was succumbing to despair, they received news that the directive was about to be approved, because significant molybdenum deposits had been discovered in the Balou Mountains. It was said that the fuses of all of the world's lightbulbs were made of molybdenum, and consequently without molybdenum the entire world would go dark. While previously the train station in the mountains had only a couple of passenger trains stop there each day, and for only a couple of minutes each time, now the station was being expanded to serve as a transport hub, in order to ship out the region's molybdenum. Explosion was already on the path to prosperity, but as the residents waited for the village to be redesignated as a town, they became increasingly anxious, frustrated, and exhausted.

That winter, it snowed heavily in the village and in the mountains. In this cold, snowy weather, Mingliang sat in the village board building, his eyelids growing heavy. The previous night he and Zhu Ying had again engaged in nuptial activities, and that mouth of the volcano had virtually burned him alive. When they finished, he exclaimed, "You are a demon incarnate," and she replied, "I'll have to hire a maid to wait on you." He said, "I'll need to hire an engineer, to redesign the village roads," and she replied, "When it snows, visitors rarely come to Explosion, and business becomes as frigid as the weather." Then they fell asleep in each other's arms. Even after Mingliang woke up and went to the village board, the exhaustion from his nighttime exertions had not been wiped from his eyes.

As in the past, he dozed at his desk and slept for a while. But this time when he opened his eyes, he saw that there were two documents sitting on the corner of his desk. One was titled "Official Reply to the Directive to Permit Explosion's Redesignation from a Village to a Town," and the second was titled "Announcement of Comrade Kong Mingliang's Designation as the Inaugural Mayor of Explosion, Once Explosion Village Has Been Redesignated from a Village to a Town." Each of the documents was relatively short, but their impact was like that of a dozen trains running into him head-on.

Kong Mingliang felt somewhat light-headed. His vision blurred, and he became as dizzy as if he had just slept with Zhu Ying. Beads of sweat—from a combination of fear and excitement—began dripping from his forehead.

> *In order to permit the Balou mountain district in the northern part of the county to enter into the national reform and development program, we will let businesses based in Explosion—including private industries, private enterprises, and tourist industries, as well as the new molybdenum mines—to each develop systematically based on their own conditions and needs, therefore permitting Explosion to become a development zone in this southwestern region of the province. It is reported that the city board and city government have agreed to establish a new Explosion town. The town government will be located in what is currently Explosion Village. At the same time, the twenty natural villages in the western part of Cypress Town, together with the nine natural villages surrounding Explosion, will all fall under the administrative supervision of the new Explosion Town. The new town will have 460,000 square kilometers of land, and a population of 112,000. The map of the new Explosion Town will be printed and distributed as soon as the county finishes revising it.*

The announcement contained only these dozen or so lines. There was also a short appointment letter, which read, "In accordance with the decision by the county board and the county government, Comrade Kong Mingliang is hereby appointed the first mayor of the newly established Explosion Town." These two documents, both printed in red on white paper, were inscribed with the names of the county board and the county government. They also both had large red stamps from the county board and the county government, together with the signatures and seals of the county party secretary and the county mayor. These two pages, together with the words printed on them, made Kong Mingliang shake with excitement. Reacting as though he were charged with electricity, he trembled for a moment and read them, then trembled and read them again. By the time he read them for the ninth time, he noticed with surprise that the dried-up fern on his desk had suddenly come back to life. The fern had previously withered as a result of the cold, since every time he tried to water it the water would merely freeze at the bottom of the pot. But now, after he had given it up for dead, Mingliang saw that in the blink of an eye the plant's tiny leaves had begun to turn green. He had no idea what was happening. He tried waving the two documents above the fern, whereupon the plant's dried-up leaves fell off and tiny new buds emerged. As if to demonstrate something, he then faced the fern and read the documents out loud, and before his eyes the fern produced a cloud of green vapor.

He walked toward a stunted evergreen bonsai sitting on his desk and stroked it with the two documents, whereupon the plant's branches began producing tiny white flowers, making the village chief's three-room office resemble a greenhouse. In order to further confirm the phenomenon, Mingliang placed the two documents in the branches of a cycas tree in front of the couch. The tree, which was as tall as a person and had a trunk as wide as a bowl, had for over three years been more dead than alive, but at that moment the faint sound of summer corn sprouting could be heard from its branches, as though someone were grinding his teeth in his sleep. Mingliang took back the document declaring Explosion a town, leaving only the letter appointing him town mayor hanging from the branches of the cycas tree, as those dried branches gradually turned green like a willow in early spring.

When he placed both pages on the tree roots that emerged from the pot, the cycas burst into bloom.

He then held the documents up to a cockroach that was climbing on the couch, and the cockroach reacted as though it had just ingested poison and immediately fell down. The insect lay on the ground with its legs in the air and its belly turning white, but even in death it continued staring at the two documents in Mingliang's hand.

With an awkward smile, Kong Mingliang felt a rush of excitement. At this point, his secretary, Cheng Qing, walked in and poured him a cup of freshly brewed green tea. As she was about to leave, Mingliang remarked with feigned nonchalance,

"Explosion Village has become Explosion Town."

Cheng Qing stopped in her tracks.

"I am now the town mayor."

Cheng Qing's face flushed with excitement.

"Are you happy?" she asked, and Mingliang replied with a smile, "I'm delighted."

"You're the new town mayor?" Cheng Qing asked with a smile. "Are you really the new town mayor?"

She looked over at Kong Mingliang's youthful and passionate face and saw him nod. Unsure what she should do to congratulate him, she hesitated, standing there like a rag doll. Mingliang waved the appointment letter in front of her, and she seemed to wake up and smiled as she took off her jacket and began unbuttoning her sweater. Mingliang waved the appointment letter in front of her a few more times, and she laughed, removing the rest of her clothing. Completely naked, she lay down on the sofa, as the light from her body illuminated the entire room as though it were under the sun.

The new town mayor stared in astonishment.

Cheng Qing had never before been willing to disrobe for him, but now she silently removed all of her clothes and lay down in front of him. Mingliang stared at her as though at a cluster of white flowers floating in water. He wasn't sure whether she was doing this for him or for that appointment letter. He wanted to caress her body with the letter, to see whether it would turn out to be a mere fantasy. But in the end, he couldn't restrain himself and, faced with her naked body, he started to tremble uncontrollably. The appointment letter fell from his hand and fluttered to the ground. Meanwhile, she also started trembling as she lay naked waiting for him, filling the room with the sound of her body rubbing against the couch. It was the middle of winter, but the room was very warm and they both began to sweat. "Come here!" she commanded him with a trembling voice. "The village has been redesignated as a town, and you are the new mayor. I should give myself to you."

He tiptoed toward her. He removed his outer coat and his padded jacket as though they were a pile of straw and cotton, and threw them to the floor. Just as he was about to caress her, her body seemed to give him an electrical shock, causing his fingers to recoil. But this shock passed almost immediately and, given that he was already married, he immediately knew what to do.

And, without any hesitation, he proceeded to do it.

Her body was as tender as if it were filled with water, and was completely different from Zhu Ying's. Unfortunately, at that moment he failed to live up to expectations, and although the conditions were perfect, the performance was as brief as a one-act play in which the coda begins as soon as the curtains open. It was as if everything concluded before he even knew what was happening. He felt somewhat depressed to think that he was already the town mayor—and no longer merely the village chief—and yet it had still been so quick. He got up and put on his clothes, and as he was debating whether or not to see a Chinese medicine doctor for his condition, he noticed that Cheng Qing was curled up on the red leather couch, her face pale like a pile of leaves after an autumn frost. Her forehead was covered in sweat and strands of wet hair. Her pants and socks fell off the couch as though they felt aggrieved.

"What's wrong?" he asked her.

"It hurts." Cheng Qing hugged her knees and then, with a smile, offered an unexpectedly poetic line: "Mayor Kong, you have deflowered me."

As Kong Mingliang was in the process of putting his pants back on, he directed his gaze toward the area between Cheng Qing's legs and immediately froze. The area was all red, and there was the smell of spring. Kong Mingliang didn't say a word but suddenly felt feverish from head to toe, and his member once again grew engorged. He climbed onto Cheng Qing, and they did it again on the couch. The first time he had been very rushed, as though he were anxious to escape through a crack in a door. This time, however, he was not rushed, and instead he used the skills that Zhu Ying had taught him. He acted as though he were opening the door to his own house and returning to his own home, where he could fetch whatever he wanted. Finally, exhausted, he rolled off her—and it was only then that he could confirm he was, in fact, the new town mayor. There was a difference between being town mayor and being village chief, and there was also a difference between the member of a town mayor and that of a village chief. Satisfied, he watched her, as a radiance extended across his face. He asked once more,

"What's wrong?"

"You've deflowered me again," she replied with a smile, her face resembling a golden sunflower.

"Do you want me, as town mayor, to do anything for you?"

"I'd like you to rent me a house in the town square; I'd like to open a store there."

He had assumed she would be more ambitious and would ask to be appointed deputy town mayor, party committee member, factory director, or manager of one of the town's industries, but instead she simply wanted one of those buildings in the town square. This made him feel disappointed but also comforted. In the end he agreed to give her the building rent-free and let her run whatever business there she wanted. He treated this as his gift to her, upon his being appointed town mayor.

"Really?" She gazed at him with a look of surprise.

"I am the town mayor, and what I say goes," he declared. Then he picked up the appointment letter and read it to her again, and they both burst out laughing. Still laughing, they walked out of the office and saw that the sky was once more filled with snow. Amid these snowflakes that were as large as goose feathers, the two paulownia trees in the courtyard of the village board building, which had been bare, suddenly burst into bloom, with large, red, bell-shaped blossoms. Staring at the snowy sky and the paulownia trees full of red blossoms, Cheng Qing cried out in delight,

"God, the paulownia trees are blooming in the middle of winter! Just a moment ago, both trees were completely bare."

Mingliang said, "Now that the village has been redesignated as a town, this courtyard of the village board building will become a grand courtyard of the town board."

2. FAMILY GOVERNMENT

Mingliang returned home at midday, and his family's delight exploded over their faces, the house, and the courtyard. The snow did not reach the top of people's feet, and when they walked their footsteps sounded as though they were treading on fried fruit chips.

Initially, Kong Dongde and Zhu Ying had not been willing to speak to each other, and Kong Dongde had refused to acknowledge Zhu Ying as his daughter-in-law. One day when no one else was home, Zhu Ying had bowed to him and called him Father. Kong Dongde stepped backward in surprise and continued retreating until his back was against the wall. She then went up to him and bowed again, saying, "If you don't acknowledge me as your daughter-in-law, I will kneel before you, and will continue kneeling until I die!"

He therefore had no choice but to acknowledge her.

As a gesture of filial piety, Zhu Ying had hired him a maid. The maid was neat and tidy, and even though she was in her forties, she still retained her youthful beauty. Her hair was still jet-black, and she had barely any wrinkles. The only problem was that she had put on some weight. When she was younger she had been so slight that she appeared to float when she walked. She lived in a building in the corner of the courtyard, and every day she would silently cook the family's meals, wash their clothes, and sweep the courtyard—thereby permitting Kong Dongde to live as though he were a rich landowner. She quietly worked for the Kong household until the day Mingliang was appointed town mayor, but that afternoon—after the maid had prepared a tableful of dishes, and as the family was celebrating Mingliang's new appointment—there was a sudden change.

Just as the food had been brought out and the entire family had sat down at the table, Mingliang strode in. His parents and Zhu Ying, as well as his eldest brother, Mingguang, and his fourth brother, Minghui, who had failed to pass the college entrance exams—all turned around and looked through the door, where they saw Mingliang shaking the snow off his clothing. He laughed and announced in a loud voice, "From now on, Explosion Town will belong to our family. Whatever you want, just tell me." He sat in an empty seat and, staring intently at his father, said, "The town has established a nursing home. Would you like to be appointed the director?" When his father merely laughed and looked at him, Mingliang then turned to his mother and said, "In the future, when you have a toothache, you won't need to go to the hospital in Cypress Town. After we establish our town's clinic, the doctor will be able to make house calls and see you at home."

Mingliang turned to Mingguang and asked solemnly,

"Do you want to be a cadre? Do you want to be appointed to the town board, to serve as deputy town mayor, and to be in charge of education?" Initially, his brother was surprised, but then he reflected for a moment and replied very seriously, "All I want is to be transferred from primary school to a high school. I want the other teachers to listen to my lessons, and if they say I'm knowledgeable and my classes are the best, then I'll be satisfied." Mingliang was rather scornful of Mingguang's lack of ambition. Finally, he turned to Minghui and asked him what he wanted to do, saying that he could have any job he wanted. Mingliang saw that Minghui no longer appeared depressed as a result of having failed his university entrance exams, and instead was smiling like a sunflower at dawn. This reminded Mingliang of the amorous activities he and Cheng Qing had engaged in that morning in the village board office—he remembered how, afterward, Cheng Qing's face had resembled a sunflower, and it occurred to him that Cheng Qing and Minghui would make a good couple. But the thought of Minghui with Cheng Qing made him feel as though a bowl of boiling water had been poured onto his heart. His entire body began to tremble, and he quickly turned to his wife, Zhu Ying, and asked, "What do you want to do? Do you want to be the director of the town's Women's Federation and oversee all of the women's jobs in the entire town?"

Zhu Ying replied, "I don't want to do anything. I just want to be a housewife and take care of our parents. With that, everything would be perfect." She initially said this merely as a social nicety, but after she uttered these words the entire Kong household stared at her in astonishment, as though they had finally seen through her—as though she were completely naked. In that instant, the room became so quiet that you could even hear the sound of the snow falling outside. As they stared at one another in embarrassment, not knowing what to do next, the maid walked in with a plate of stewed chicken and placed it on the table. Her face lit up and she looked at Mingliang, then said in a warm voice, "Chief Kong . . . no, you are now the town mayor . . . Mayor Kong, may I ask you a favor? Can you have me transferred, to serve as a cadre for the Women's Federation? If your wife Zhu Ying doesn't want to be a town cadre, then I'd like to serve as a cadre for the Women's Federation. Let me oversee the jobs of all of the town's women."

She added, "I've already served as a maid in your home for half a year and have not received a single cent, so I deserve this compensation."

She also added, "Mayor Kong, I don't count as a member of your family, but since I wait on your family's elders, I should at least count as half a member. So, please make me a national cadre."

That evening, Zhu Ying packed the maid's bags and spat in the maid's face, then slapped her. The maid left the Kong household, and no one had any idea where she went.

3. TOWN APPEARANCE

The village's redesignation as a town had enormous historical significance, and before the unveiling ceremony the people had to make countless preparations. All of the houses and shops on both sides of the street had to take down their original signs and replace them with new ones. For instance, if a sign read ZHANG FAMILY LOCK-SMITH, it would have to be changed to read EXPLOSION TOWN LOCK CITY, and if a sign read WANG FAMILY SEWING, it would be changed to read EXPLOSION TOWN SEWING WORLD. Similarly, someone who had been selling roasted chicken from a street cart labeled ROAST CHICKEN would now be required by the business and tax administration to rename the cart EXPLOSION TOWN CULINARY MANSION. By the same logic, a shop selling flatbread would be called EXPLOSION TOWN'S FLATBREAD KING, and a small noodle shop would have to change its sign to EXPLOSION'S CLASSICAL CUISINE or EXPLOSION TOWN'S CULINARY CAPITAL. The store names needed to be stylish and forceful, to reflect the majesty and grandeur of Explosion's redesignation from a village to a town.

The busiest stores were those that specialized in printing signs. Several of these moved to Explosion from the county seat and then worked day and night printing all sort of different signs.

The snow stopped falling.

The sun came out and was blindingly bright. Along the river in front of Explosion, the streets that had suddenly become prosperous were lined with trees full of green leaves and colorful flowers. It was winter, but given that the village was being changed to a town, the climate had no choice but to change as well. The cold receded and was replaced by warmth, everything came to life, and a spring fragrance circulated. The cement roads that had been constructed two years earlier were washed clean by the melted snow, filling the air with an appealing moist odor that made people feel as though the world had changed. A few days later, the county mayor brought several groups to Explosion to announce the official inauguration of Explosion Town, and naturally they wanted to visit Explosion's streets, its factories, and the various small businesses that were scattered around the town's periphery. Mayor Kong had been busy preparing for the arrival of the county mayor, Hu Dajun. After everything was established, he took a group of town cadres preselected by the county and led them from one end of the town to the other, to observe the appearance of the streets and to see the progress of each family's preparations. They saw the new buildings that had been erected, the walls of which had been given a fresh coat of red paint. The street resembled a blazing fire, as the scent of fresh paint mingled with the snowy sunlight, yielding a scene that was as beautiful as a sheet of silk. Every store had a new sign, either printed in red on a white background or printed in yellow on a green background, and in front of each door there was a couplet printed in red, together with at least four flowerpots. The shops that didn't have fresh flowers had bought plastic ones from the city, and the street resembled a flower street.

Mingliang led the group. Everyone crowded around, and when people saw him they shouted, "Mayor Kong, Mayor Kong!" He smiled and said, "It hasn't yet been announced." Someone replied, "But it will be soon!" Mingliang was delighted by this, like someone dying of thirst who suddenly receives a cold drink. He saw a house that wasn't decorated with either fresh or plastic flowers, but an old lady was inside using scissors to cut out eight red paper blossoms, each of them larger than a basket. Mingliang remarked to those accompanying him, "This is one of the village's famous martyrs. She doesn't have any children. However, as of next month the town will issue her an extra five hundred yuan a month, so that she will have enough money that she won't even be able to spend it all."

They reached a store run by a family named He, which specialized in cooked pork entrails, and as everyone was debating between the names Explosion Cooked Meat and Explosion's He Family Meat Stand, Mingliang told the shop owners, "You should use the name Delicacy of the Century." They then wrote OLD DELICACY OF THE CENTURY RESTAURANT on their sign.

The group reached the southernmost end of the street, where there was a Healthy Amusement Park and a Satisfaction World featuring hair salons, pedicure shops, and a variety of other restaurants and shops that Zhu Ying had transferred from the county seat. The Amusement Park and Satisfaction World signs had been replaced with new ones printed with beautiful, artistic characters, and the girls standing in the doorways were all dressed modestly and neatly, and appeared quite happy. The group walked by, then crossed the street and visited a small shop. The shop specialized in designing and printing different sorts of documents, such as high school diplomas, certificates for government agencies, IDs for military cadres, and police badges for city police. The shop had steel and wooden stamps, as well as a variety of ID cards and an assortment of blank receipt booklets for people to use when getting reimbursed. After the certificates were designed and printed, they were shipped to be sold in the city, where they enjoyed robust sales; the shop received one order after another. In front of the shop there was a large sign that read RED STAR PRINTING COMPANY, and inside there were numerous imported printing presses and piles upon piles of revolutionary books and student notebooks. Everything was in accordance with specifications. A smell of ink surged out of the shop like the scent of summer wheat in the mountains. They led the group on a tour, then walked out satisfied. As they were about to leave, they accidentally stepped on several seals lying in the grass, and when they leaned over to take a look, they saw that these were the big round seals belonging to the county and municipal governments.

Mingliang called for the director of the printing factory.

The factory director had previously helped Mingliang unload goods from the trains, so when he came out he addressed Mingliang familiarly as Brother Mingliang. Mingliang showed him the two seals, then hit him over the head with them. He kicked the factory director in the stomach and stalked out, his face pale with fury.

The factory director squatted on the ground in agony, as though his intestines had been ruptured. Only after Mingliang and his group disappeared down the street did the factory director finally get up and go look for another job.

CHAPTER 8

Integrated Economy

1. INDUSTRY AND INDUSTRIAL WORKERS

The new town's industries included wire factories, cable factories, cement factories, and printing shops, as well as prefab factories making cement products for use in construction. Family industries included shoe factories that used recycled car tires to make rubber soles, and factories that used recycled plastic to make buckets, bowls, and washbasins. There were also textile plants and agricultural processing plants. One agricultural processing plant was located in a compound next to the river, and mountain products such as walnuts, mushrooms, and tree fungus all went in smelling of dirt, only to emerge as highly refined swallow nest soup. At a rubber factory, rubber shoe soles collected from the city went in, and what emerged were water buckets, washbasins, and tooth-brushing cups for people in both the city and the countryside. Someone's colorful plastic cup might be made from the rubber soles of that same person's shoes or sandals, while someone else's tooth-brushing cup might be made from former toilet plungers.

There was also a newspaper story processing plant, and the factory director was Yang Baoqing, who on the dream-walking night had picked up an old conch shell. He loved to read, and on top of that enjoyed the benefits of being in a favorable position. At a time when the entire nation's journal and periodical industry was flourishing, Yang bought subscriptions to countless newspapers and magazines, and directed his children to take scissors, glue, and colored pens, and every day cut out stories of events happening in the south, then change the reference to time and location, repaste them, and send them to newspapers in the north. They would also take stories from the north, turn them around, and send them to newspapers in the south. Alternatively, they would copy an article from a journal, add their own names to the byline, and send it to another editorial office. Those manuscripts were all published quickly, and the royalty checks came flooding in, with sacks upon sacks of checks arriving in the mail every day. The family's strategy was to take stories from the south and send them north, and take ones from the north and send them south; to transform stories from Shanghai into stories from the heartland and send them to Xi'an and Lanzhou, and to take stories from Xinjiang and transform them into coastal stories and send them to Shanghai. Their acceptance rate was 98 percent, and they became a famous news processing plant in the new Explosion Town.

In the end, everyone in Explosion stopped farming, though no one was left idle. The various industries and factories made this new town bustle like a pot of boiling water. Every day, the sky was filled with black smoke from the factories' smokestacks, producing a burning stench that you could smell in the air and taste in the water. But everyone in Explosion quickly grew accustomed to this odor, so much so that when it was washed away by a rainstorm, the fresh air would leave everyone with a cold. As a result, the hospitals became extremely busy, having more sick patients than the schools had students. With this sudden increase in patients, the town needed its own pharmaceutical factories and medical packaging plants, and with this increase in packaging plants there also developed an increased need for tax collection and sanitation services. With the rise in tax collection, the town was even busier than before, and virtually every day there was a ribbon-cutting ceremony celebrating the opening of a new industry. Later, when Kong Mingliang recalled the initial period of Explosion's growth and development, he told me:

"Those were good times, when you could open a new newspaper story processing plant with nothing more than some glue and a pair of scissors. I'm afraid that China will never see times like those again."

2. AGRICULTURAL INDUSTRY AND AGRICULTURAL WORKERS

Once, the sound of shouting and crying could be heard coming from the top of the mountain ridge. It continued for three full months, until finally someone went to the town government to report it. At that point, the town government's new compound was still under construction and several new buildings had just appeared. The construction site was in complete chaos, the cement mixers and paving machines shook the earth, and if you didn't shout at the top of your lungs, no one would be able to hear you. One of the town residents appeared in front of Mayor Kong and began noisily issuing directions, but Mingliang simply stared at him and asked,

"What did you say?"

The other person then shouted in his ear,

"The peasants have gone mad! The peasants in the mountains are all crying like crazy."

"What are they crying about?"

"They are crying over the land!"

Mingliang reflected for a moment, then followed the man to the mountain ridge behind the town. When they were halfway up the mountain, they turned and the mayor noticed with surprise that buildings had suddenly sprouted up everywhere, and the streets were bustling with activity that was quite different from the kind of rustic excitement the town had enjoyed when it was a mere village. Streetlamps now lined the streets like chopsticks, and each house's chimney spat out thick smoke like clouds on an overcast day. Everywhere, the ground had been opened up and resealed, like a patient randomly cut up by a surgeon, and things were vibrant but also covered in scars.

"But Explosion is developing so quickly!" Mingliang sighed.

"They are crying because they don't have any land to farm," the other man replied with a laugh.

"How many of the town's families are living in villas?"

"They have been crying continuously for three days and three nights, and look as if they're about to collapse."

They hurried up the mountain. The road they followed was the same one Mingliang had taken every day back when they were unloading goods from the train. As he walked, Mingliang had a sense of warmth and couldn't help glancing over to the other side of the road. The landscape flowed past like water, and he saw that there was an electrical line and cable factory on the hill. The workers were drinking beer in the entranceway to the factory and in the streets, eating peanuts and pork, and throwing wrappings all over the ground. Mingliang asked a passerby why they were drinking beer when they should be at work, and the man replied that the factory had just received a large order from a certain city in which all of the electrical lines and cables came from this factory in Explosion. These electrical lines were embedded within the city walls and the electrical cables were buried underground, but within a few years they would both start to disintegrate, as the insulating rubber became degraded and the cables leaked electricity. Consequently, they would produce short circuits and electrical fires, often resulting in casualties. People from other places might use wires and cables from this factory, but after they suffered a fire they would invariably go somewhere else for their supplies. This particular city, however, once had a fire that killed over a hundred people, but even now it still bought wires and cables from only this factory in Explosion.

"But why is that?" Mingliang asked.

"Because the city gets enormous kickbacks," the other man responded with a smile.

Mingliang then asked the other man to go notify the factory that he would give an extra 10 percent in kickbacks to all who came to make purchases after suffering a fire—if they ordered ten million yuan's worth of goods, he would give them an extra million yuan. "I'm not at all concerned that those fuckers might not come to buy our electrical lines and power cables!" Mingliang cursed. Then he told the passerby to relay this message to the factory, while he proceeded alone to the top of the ridge. The factories and workshops lining both sides of the road swept by him like village houses. The leaves of the trees were covered in dust, and an enormous assortment of plastic bags were caught by the branches, so that whenever the wind blew the bags would inflate and make a crackling sound. The mayor looked up at these plastic bags that filled the sky and began to wonder when Explosion could be redesignated as a county. When would the county seat, in recognition of Explosion's prosperity, be relocated from its current location forty kilometers away?

Some workers approached and waved to him. "Come have some beer!"

Mingliang shouted back, "We can drink together after Explosion becomes a county!"

By the time he reached the top of the mountain ridge, the sun had reached its zenith. On the mountain ridge were a wild chicken and a wild hare looking around, but when they saw the mayor they immediately ran away. Hu Dajun had erected a massive stele for Zhu Ying in what had been the village square, but given that the town was increasingly prosperous and visitors from out of town all wanted to be down by the river, the stele appeared solitary and lonely. Even Zhu Ying herself rarely visited. It was as if this event had never even occurred in her life. The inscription on the stele was so covered in dust that it was virtually invisible. The elders from Explosion Village—meaning all of the old peasants over sixty—wept beside the stele and said, "We don't have any land, nor do we have anywhere to plant our crops." They had recently entered their sixties, but appeared as young and strong as the sun at high noon. However, the town's rising prosperity had sent them into a retirement home, and didn't permit them to use their hoes and shovels to interact with the soil. They couldn't get used to this life of not interacting with the soil, so they came to weep at this empty field, which was previously a plot of farmland.

Zhu Ying's stele was like a storm wall. Previously, in the land around the stele there had been wheat in winter and corn in the autumn. Every spring, the wheat sprouts grew black, and when they ripened in the summer a fragrant odor would enter the village and circulate to the dining table of every home. But now, no one planted anything. The weeds were as tall as a person, and the wild birds and hares were going in and out, as though this were their heavenly park. Old people gathered there, weeping and wailing, shouting and hollering. On large sheets of white paper they scrawled phrases like RETURN US OUR LAND! WE WANT TO LIVE AND DIE WITH OUR CROPS! and so forth. Some of these slogans were posted on the stele itself, while others were posted as freestanding signs in the middle of the field. The elders shouted and wept, and when they tired of shouting and weeping they ate the food they had brought with them, and then began shouting and weeping again.

The demonstration was like an uprising. People gathered for three days and three nights, and while there were initially only a handful of people, they soon grew to several dozen, and by the third day there were more than a hundred. Even peasants from Liu Gully, Zhang Peak, and other nearby villages—who had had their land confiscated for mining and road building—all came here to protest. They didn't realize that their behavior constituted a form of revolution, and instead merely saw themselves as resisting development and post-industrialization. Their simplicity helped create this protest peasant movement, even as it also helped destroy the great peasant movement. By the third day, a dark mass of more than two hundred people had gathered, as those banners with slogans such as WE SWEAR TO THE DEATH THAT WE'LL REMAIN WITH OUR LAND fluttered over the mountainside like flocks of white homing pigeons tumbling down the hill. Mayor Kong stood before the crowd of sixty-year-olds and shouted emotionally,

"Go home. Aren't you concerned that you will hurt yourselves from weeping so much?"

Everyone stopped talking and gazed at him silently.

"Go home and ask your sons and daughters—and other young people—whether they want to farm the land or make Explosion a city."

No one said a word, and instead everyone just watched him silently.

"If you don't leave, I'll summon your children to come fetch you!"

No one said a word, and everyone just watched him silently.

The silence was like black ink on the faces of those elderly peasants. They had deep wrinkles, which made them appear sedate and powerful. Virtually every one of the peasants had gone gray, and when they stood in the middle of the field, they resembled random pieces of straw. No one responded to Mingliang, and no one wanted to leave the field and return to the newly constructed houses and retirement homes. They knew that Mingliang wouldn't dare force them to return home and also wouldn't dare summon the town's police to drive them away. They had watched him grow up, and even now—when he encountered them individually—he would address them as Uncle and Grandpa. They continued standing there, until suddenly a yellow leaf blew over and passed in front of the mayor, as though it were a message that had been sent out from Mingliang's brain. At this moment, Mingliang was standing on the base of his wife Zhu Ying's stele. He gazed down imperiously at those elders who were asking for their land back, then shouted in his most forceful voice,

"Uncles and Aunts, Grandpas and Grandmas, please listen to me and return home. I will agree to one thing . . ." Looking down at that sea of expectant faces gazing up at him, the mayor looked as though he had just encountered a drought-stricken piece of land. He said, "In a few years, the nation, on account of a shortage of land, will implement a policy of mandatory cremations, whereby corpses will be placed in furnaces and burned to ashes. At that point, none of you will be permitted to be buried, and instead your weeping sons and daughters will push you into a large furnace, where your flesh and bones will be reduced to ashes." Mingliang paused and looked again at that sea of dry and hard faces, which all appeared pale with fear, like ashes from freshly cremated corpses. With expressions of terror, everyone turned to everyone else as though searching for something. "How about this . . ." The mayor stood even taller than before and shouted even louder, "Everyone disperse and return home, now! I promise that after the mandatory cremation policy goes into effect in a couple of years or so, those who go home now will not need to be cremated and instead can be buried, as they would have been in the past. You can all be buried in a coffin with a funeral shroud and have a traditional burial. That way, after you die, you will never have to leave the land and will instead remain with the land for eternity. On the other hand, those of you who refuse to listen to me, and continue insisting that your land be returned—you will be cremated when you die, and your ashes will be stored in a cinerary urn measuring only a few inches in diameter. The urn will be placed on a cement ledge, and you will never be reunited with the land. Whether it be before birth or after death, in this life or the next, either way you have only these two options. So you should consider carefully and decide which one you want."

With this, Mingliang climbed down from the stele platform.

As everyone looked at each other, one of the elders holding a sign that read RETURN OUR LAND! got up and went home, and then everyone else followed him, leaving that empty field and heading back into town. In this way, a significant peasant rebellion developed, like a corpse being cremated.

3. SPECIALIZED INDUSTRIES

I.

Explosion's flourishing was a result not only of industrial expansion and the corresponding loss of its rural economy, but also of a more specialized development that produced the scaffolding behind its integrated economy.

Although the northern portion of Explosion's main street was virtually silent during day except for an occasional dog bark, by evening it was brightly illuminated with colorful lights, so much so that everything was a blur and no one knew where to go next. There were salons, pedicure shops, massage parlors, and amusement sites. Their names were all hazy, but each had a distinctive flavor. For instance, there was a *Mini Hair Salon*, *Dead Drunk Flower Garden*, *Come Again*, *Always Return*, and so forth. These names were ones that Zhu Ying had copied down while in the south and in the provincial seat, and had brought back with her.

Since the street already had these sorts of names and buildings, it occurred to someone to install a bathing room with wood-burning stoves and saunas with electric stoves, where it was said that you could irrigate plants over the fire and everything you would need to take a steam bath would be arrayed in front of you. Everyone therefore went to visit. First it was the men and elders from Explosion who lined up to get in, and once inside they would get undressed and bathe. Then they would enter the sauna and begin boiling water, producing clouds of steam. They would inhale the white clouds of hot steam, and within ten minutes or so their bodies would be covered in sweat, and the dirt and grime would flake off their bodies like plaster off a wall. Their exhaustion from a long day at work would disappear in a cloud of steam, and when they reemerged from the sauna they would be floating like celestial beings. The first building along that street to install this sort of sauna was Zhu Ying's Otherwordly Delights, and the first person to try it was Kong Mingliang, who at the time was still serving as village chief. When he came out, he was completely naked and said to the men waiting in line outside,

"It feels like you've just entered a woman's you-know-what."

People entered the sauna in small groups, and each group remained inside for about ten minutes at a time. Meanwhile, those waiting outside formed a line that stretched down the street and halfway up the mountain ridge. People wanting to use the sauna had to wait in line from dawn until after dusk. Some people even had to pack travel rations and spend up to three days on the road in order to reach Explosion and be able to use its sauna. Later, there were additional electric saunas and a coal-burning one, so that women could also take turns using them. In addition to the saunas themselves, there were also other services such as massages, pedicures, and sexual services. After people had enjoyed themselves, they would want to drink, have tea, and play mahjong. In this way the most prosperous figures in the world quickly entered Explosion.

It wasn't clear whether the mountain ridge began to have mines and miners because Explosion developed this sort of service industry, or whether Explosion developed this sort of service industry precisely because there were mines and miners in the nearby mountain ridge. In the end, however, everything happened virtually overnight. There was a foreigner with a big nose and big eyes who drove from the mines into Explosion. He parked his sedan and swaggered down the street, stopping to buy a plate of dumplings. Because he had too much money, he paid with a hundred-yuan bill for a plate of dumplings that cost only five yuan. When the owner of the dumpling restaurant gave the foreigner his change, the foreigner left the entire ninety-five yuan as a tip. The shop owner stared in astonishment, unable to believe that the world's foreigners had this custom whereby if you smile at them when they are paying for food, they will give you even more money.

Explosion's residents believed every foreigner must own a bank.

Everyone watched until the foreigner entered the sauna, and only then did people spread the news that a foreigner had arrived in Explosion, describing how he spent money as though he owned a bank. A large crowd arrived, including virtually the entire population of Explosion, and they all gathered in front of Otherwordly Delights. They chatted and laughed as they waited for the foreigner to come out—waiting to see his large nose, blue eyes, blond hair, and hairy arms. But as they were waiting, they gradually stopped talking and laughing, as a stifling feeling began to permeate Explosion. It dawned on them that they didn't know whether the foreigner was American or European, or what he had gone into the sauna to do. A sauna bath—including the time necessary to get undressed and get dressed again—shouldn't require more than about half an hour, but this foreigner had already been inside for over an hour. After two hours he still hadn't emerged, nor after three hours. When he arrived, the sun had been high in the sky and the streets were filled with an autumn warmth like a sauna that had just opened its doors, but everyone waited for the foreigner for so long that the sun had begun to set in the west and he had not emerged.

The doors to the shop had glass windows in wooden frames, and on the glass appeared the words WELCOME CUSTOMERS, PLEASE MAKE YOURSELVES AT HOME. But behind the glass, a curtain had been pulled shut, preventing people outside from seeing what was happening inside. As a result, the villagers could only speculate about what was going on. By this point, the foreigner had been inside for more than three hours. This was the first Westerner to come to Explosion for business, and there was no telling what kind of practices he had brought with him and was flaunting in front of the villagers. They held their breath as they waited for him to emerge, but they didn't know why they were waiting or what they would say to him once he reappeared.

Time became like dammed-up water, pooling between the waiting crowd of people and the newly constructed town streets. It was not until the bright midday sun had been replaced by the red rays of the setting sun that those glass doors finally opened. The villagers' throats tightened and their hearts trembled as they saw the foreigner saunter out. He was wearing a pin-striped gray suit and a red tie, and his face was as red as pig liver. His hair had been washed and blow-dried, every strand neatly combed from left to right. As the sun set over his hair, the sunlight slid down from his head to the ground or onto the wall. In the crook of his left arm was a young woman wearing a miniskirt and showing off her thin legs and pert breasts. As the two of them walked out, everyone waiting in the doorway stared in amazement, but after the onlookers realized that the woman was not from Explosion, they began throwing clods of dirt, eggs, apples, and baked sweet potatoes at Zhu Ying and the foreigner, shouting, "Whore!" "Slut!" "Swine!" "Shameless!"

The woman quickly retreated back inside.

The foreigner stared at the onlookers in surprise and babbled something to them about rights and law that they couldn't understand. Finally, a dust-covered shoe struck him in the face, and only then did he have no choice but to step away from the door. At this point, Zhu Ying stormed out of the building and stood in front of the foreigner, shielding him from the curses and projectiles that were being hurled in his direction. Then she said something that made everyone fall silent:

"Do you know what Reform and Opening Up is?"

She added, "Is it possible that you don't want to grow prosperous?"

She added, "Don't forget that it was with the money sent back by your own families' daughters and sisters that you were able to build your new tile-roofed houses!"

Everyone was silent.

In the silence, Zhu Ying personally escorted the foreigner across the street and accompanied him all the way to his sedan, which was parked outside the village.

II.

Prosperity is something that needs to be supported every day. Everyone gradually came to accept the activities along that street and to regard them as commonplace. The first thing Kong Mingliang did as town mayor was to pass a law of protection on behalf of the entertainment industry, certifying that not only were these customers engaged in legal activity, but furthermore their activity was supporting the Reform and Opening Up campaign. In this way, their patronage was placed aboveboard with considerable fanfare, and business took off. People surged toward that entertainment street that would come to be known as Otherworldly Delights, just as they would surge into the market on holidays. They treated this as nothing unusual, particularly given that not only were the girls working there not from Explosion, but they were not even from that county or city. Instead, they were from Sichuan, Guizhou, and Hunan, together with some tall and forthright girls from the northeast. As for Explosion's own girls, in the interest of preserving their reputation and future marriage prospects, either they went south to earn this sort of money, or else they returned to help Zhu Ying with her businesses—becoming Otherworldly Delights' supervisors and directors.

There were also some who tried to open their own romance businesses, but because of the cost of preparations, services, and salaries, they were ultimately unable to compete with Zhu Ying's. Some of these new businesses ended up closing, while others gamely attempted to carry on. The following year, meanwhile, Cheng Qing opened a romantic establishment called Peach Blossom Spring in an intersection to the north of Otherworldly Delights. She used a building that had previously been a restaurant, which she renovated and rebuilt with a new storefront. The shop provided the same sauna, bath, and massage services as the others, but unlike them her business flourished, as workers from surrounding factories and from the silver and molybdenum mines in the mountains came surging in, day and night.

Zhu Ying watched this new establishment warily, and one day took the opportunity to go see Cheng Qing. On that particular day,

Cheng Qing was in her office discussing something with a foreign client, and when Zhu Ying arrived she discovered that the foreigner was none other than the same man who had visited her shop when it first opened, and who had been beaten by the villagers. She smiled at him and said, "So, you've come here? In the future, I'll give you a fifty percent discount, and if you're not satisfied you'll get a full refund." The foreigner looked at her happily, as though he couldn't believe what he was hearing. Zhu Ying then added earnestly, "You should go now. Today, you can pick as many girls as you want—you can take two, four, or even eight at a time, and I'll charge you for only one." The foreigner laughed with delight, added some awkward and stilted words of gratitude, then left Cheng Qing's office. It was only then that Zhu Ying had a chance to examine Cheng Qing's office, which was located directly across from the check-in counter, and through the door or window you could see every customer who arrived as well as the girls she employed. Zhu Ying saw several girls pass by in front of the door. Their faces were almost perfectly round, their bodies were slightly plump, and they all had very ample breasts. They looked as if they were under eighteen, and they appeared to be as pure and unaffected as freshly picked melons or fruits.

"Oh, they're all fresh firewood girls. No wonder your business is so good!"

After teasing the girls, Zhu Ying examined the office's decor and saw that it was nothing out of the ordinary. There was a woven couch cover, some random desks, and some hardwood chairs. The large bureau next to the desks was brand-new, but the door was full of white cracks. Zhu Ying looked down on Cheng Qing's business, particularly when she remembered the source of Cheng Qing's success. "Are your girls all virgins?" When she asked this, she noticed the two bouquets sitting on Cheng Qing's window ledge. The bouquets surprised her and made her feel inferior. The plants were autumn chrysanthemums, which typically bloomed at that time of year, but on their stems there were peony blossoms, which usually bloom only in spring. The peony was bright red and as large as a person's face and a mixture of peony fragrance and chrysanthemum scent emanated from that windowsill and wafted into the room. Cheng Qing sat next to those flowers, her face reflecting a sense of energy and beauty characteristic of this business where you would succeed if you were younger than your competitors. Zhu Ying stood in front of her, with a desk between them. When Zhu Ying had entered, Cheng Qing had not stood up to greet her and neither had she invited Zhu Ying to sit down or offered her any tea. Even after escorting the foreigner out, Cheng Qing still didn't utter a word to Zhu Ying.

Cheng Qing's confidence was as hard as a bone, and her calm expression was like a pool of water that not even the wind could touch.

"You've stolen my business," Zhu Ying said. "It would have been OK if you had come into town to earn a salary, but you shouldn't have opened this establishment."

Cheng Qing replied with a smile, "The mayor himself asked me to open this business."

"I'll have him reassign you to a job in town. With a single word, I can have you reassigned."

"Do you think?" Cheng Qing smiled again and replied, "He has slept with me. He wouldn't do what you tell him."

Zhu Ying felt her legs grow limp, and she almost toppled over. But she made a considerable effort to support herself and didn't let Cheng Qing observe the sound of her heart lurching. Zhu Ying didn't want Cheng Qing to witness that her words had almost leveled her, so she made an effort to adopt a mocking expression like Cheng Qing's.

"Did you sleep with him?" Zhu Ying said. "Then my husband was cheated."

"We slept together many times," Cheng Qing replied. "He says that I'm better than you. He even asked me if I wanted him to divorce you so he could marry me."

Zhu Ying didn't say anything. She shifted her gaze from Cheng Qing's face back to the flowers. She noticed that there were some black chrysanthemum leaves supporting the large peony blossoms. Several of the peony blossoms had pink petals, but the petals in the center of the flower were delicate pink and white, like a young girl's innermost kernel. Zhu Ying looked at that cross between a chrysanthemum and a peony, and noticed that in another pot next to it a large garlic plant had sprouted little red fruits like wolfberries. There was a small cherry tree in a pot beneath the window, together with a pepper plant covered in red thorns. Then Zhu Ying stared at Cheng Qing, who had been sitting there without moving, and noticed that she had a satisfied smile, making her appear like one of those flowers.

"If he wants you, he can simply move in with you."

"There's no need."

Zhu Ying looked away and said, "Over at Otherworldly Delights, everything is like this. The oddest thing is that the dogtail growing on the wall around my courtyard is blooming with chrysanthemum blossoms, and even the wormwood is as fragrant as osmanthus blossoms. If you have time, you're welcome to come over to take a look."

"Really?"

"Do you want to come right now? I'll go with you."

"I'm afraid the mayor might arrive at any moment. He likes to drop by periodically."

And so it concluded. As Zhu Ying walked out of Peach Blossom Spring and passed through a courtyard full of cars, tractors, and bicycles bringing customers to the brothel, she felt that the sunlight appeared black, and the buildings and walls looked as though they were floating on water. The sound of pedestrians and street hawkers was like an uprooted tree hurtling toward her. She felt faint, as her brain finally began to process what Cheng Qing had just told her.

III.

Kong Mingliang felt that the best things in the world were power, women, beds, and pillows. When Zhu Ying returned exhausted from seeing Cheng Qing, she immediately fell asleep, wanting to bury her head in the pillow and call for her father. The night enveloped Mingliang like a pool of water, and in this autumn evening, which was neither warm nor cold, he felt as though he had returned to an enormous womb, as his exhaustion slowly melted away. His typical day involved attending meetings and ribbon-cutting ceremonies, eating and reading documents, and going down to the site where the new town hall was being built. If he didn't go down to the construction site one day, the construction workers and foremen would steal all of the cement and rebar beams. The truck drivers would even haul away an entire truckload of bricks and sell them. The amount of nails that drivers delivered to the construction site paled in comparison with the amount that they stashed under their beds. Mingliang took the town police down to the house of Second Dog—who was working as a guard at the construction site warehouse—and they discovered that his house was like a warehouse in its own right, with ropes, sacks, lumber, and steel pipes, together with piles of hammers and nails. Kong Mingliang summoned Second Dog and slapped his face.

Second Dog held his cheek and cried abjectly, "But Mingliang, I'm your brother!"

Kong Mingliang slapped him again.

Second Dog cried, "Even though you are now the mayor, I'm still your brother! Don't forget that I was the first one to spit at Zhu Qingfang, on your behalf."

Kong Mingliang launched a kick at him, until finally Second Dog stopped insisting on that brotherly form of address and instead just stared at him fearfully. Second Dog clearly saw that the person standing in front of him was Kong Mingliang, whom he had originally helped elect as village chief, but now this person's bearing and disposition were different. Second Dog wasn't sure what had changed, but somehow the person in front of him was no longer Kong Mingliang. It was not until Mingliang signaled with his eyes to the two policemen accompanying him—who in turn put a pair of jangling handcuffs on Second Dog's wrists—that Second Dog finally realized that Kong Mingliang was no longer village chief but rather town mayor.

Second Dog abruptly knelt down and began kowtowing to Kong Mingliang, saying, "Mayor Kong, please let me go. I promise I'll never steal again!

". . . Mayor Kong, please let me go. I promise I'll never steal again!"

Kong Mingliang then gave another signal, and the police released him.

In the course of a single day, Kong Mingliang visited several households in Explosion, ranging from that of the chief of the construction team to those of the construction team workers charged with tasks such as moving bricks. All of the workers were from Explosion, and each of them had stolen tiles, cement, rebars, and lumber from the construction site. When Mingliang entered these houses, the owners would immediately greet him as Mayor Kong and wouldn't even bother to hide the goods they had stolen. Mingliang would then slap them, and that would be the end of that. Kong Mingliang asked one of them, "Will you steal again?" The man replied, "No, I won't." He then asked, "Why not?" The man replied, "We have already grown wealthy, and now we must follow the rules so that we don't damage the reputation of Explosion and of the mayor." It turned out that this thief was wise. Kong Mingliang walked out, satisfied, and proceeded to another house. There, he encountered someone who was not as wise. This other man addressed him not as mayor but rather as Brother and Nephew. Kong Mingliang felt his heart lurch, but he didn't say a word and instead merely stared intently. The police proceeded to put the thief in handcuffs, then kicked him until he was kneeling on the floor. The thief was at his wit's end and begged the mayor, saying, "Mingliang . . . we're both from Explosion. Don't forget that you should address me as Uncle!" The policemen's fists rained down on the man like thunder, and as they was beating the thief they asked, "Are you still going to steal? The mayor is frank and forthright, but what he hates most are thieves. Do you know that?" Finally, the man came to his senses and stopped addressing Kong Mingliang as either Mingliang or Nephew, and instead addressed him as Mayor Kong. He promised he would never steal again and would never again disgrace the town.

There was another man who didn't understand what was going on, and as he was being slapped he merely stared in astonishment and asked,

"How dare you hit me? I'm the mayor's uncle."

They slapped him again.

He said, "Mingliang, how can you stand there and watch them hit me? Don't forget that my entire family voted for you when you were elected village chief."

The mayor didn't respond and instead merely looked at the courtyard, which was full of items that the man's family had stolen from the town. The mayor had a pale, disdainful expression, and as the police who had accompanied him understood its meaning, they turned to the man's family and asked, "Did you participate in the thefts? All of you, kneel down. . . . Damn it, if you don't kneel down now, you'll have to spend the next six to twelve months in jail." The entire family hurriedly went out to the courtyard and knelt down. They stopped addressing the mayor by name and stopped calling themselves his uncle or aunt. They stopped discussing how they had voted for him when he was elected village chief. Instead, they simply said, "Mayor, mayor, you are very magnanimous. We'll stop stealing and will never again bring dishonor to you and Explosion." Eventually, the mayor gave a signal and the police let the family go, and soon a series of cars and trucks arrived to haul away the goods the family had stolen.

The mayor gave so many signals with his eyes that day that his eyelids developed a callus, and he became so exhausted that he almost fell asleep before dinner. He began feeling drowsy even as he was walking down the street, to the point that he almost walked right into an electrical pole along the side of the road. In this manner, however, the wealth gradually accumulated, and the pile of confiscated goods became as big as a mountain. Outside the town, in a field next to the river, they built an enormous warehouse, and what didn't fit in the warehouse they left on the roadside. It was in this way that a modern town was constructed. Where one day there had been just a messy array of scaffolding, now there was a tall building. Workers were cleaning up trash from in front of the building. Where in the morning they had been breaking earth to build a road, by evening they were pouring asphalt, and by the next day there were cars driving up and down the new oil-scented road.

In this halting fashion, the town was erected. Using as models the town's five-hundred-*mu* committee building and the two streets leading out of the town, Explosion's economy, development, and modernity all expanded like a balloon ascending into the sky. The mayor was exhausted and wanted to get a good night's sleep. It had been a month or so since he had slept in his own bed, and once he had a chance to go home he proceeded to sleep for three days straight—a full seventy-two hours. Apart from waking up twice for a sip of water, or three other times to go to the bathroom, he slept soundly for more than seventy hours. When he did finally wake up, it was past midnight and the milky-white moonlight was shining in through the window, while a cool feeling of autumn circulated through the room. The red *double happiness* characters on the bed from the wedding had already faded, and there was a cobweb in the corner above, on which the tiny spiders were crawling around. He heard the soft footsteps of the spiders walking along the web, then turned over, rubbed his eyes, and saw that his wife, Zhu Ying, was sitting on the bed, staring at him as though she didn't recognize him. She had a strange glint in her eyes.

He asked, "You haven't gone to sleep yet?"

She replied, "You've already woken up?"

He asked, "How long have you been there watching me? From the look in your eyes, it seems like you want to kill me."

She replied, "There is no woman in the entire world who loves you as much as I do."

"I've reclaimed all of the things the people of Explosion stole," he told her with a smile. "Now, everyone addresses me as Mayor Kong, and no one dares address me as Uncle, Nephew, or simply neighbor."

Smiling back at him, Zhu Ying poured him a glass of water. She told him that while he was sleeping, he kept talking, saying that he wanted to become county or even city mayor. Upon hearing this, he stared in surprise, then laughed. He looked at the clock hanging on the wall, then out the window at the moonlight, and finally he took off his clothes and crawled under the covers. As Zhu Ying was waiting for him to finish drinking his water, she took off her clothes and curled up beside him. Finally, when their hands and lips were exhausted and he could no longer shout how much he loved her body, she turned on the light and sat up and asked solemnly,

"Don't you like me anymore?"

"I'm tired."

"If you don't like me, you can go find someone else, such as Cheng Qing and her Peach Blossom Spring. It must be exhausting being mayor."

He stared at her in shock.

"You should sample other people," she told him with a smile. "You can't just be town mayor. You should speak as though your voice were the law. You should be like the emperor, and have six courtyards full of wives and concubines, together with thousands of palace maids. You can't only be town mayor." She asked, "Who ever heard of an emperor who didn't have six courtyards full of wives and concubines, thousands of palace maids, and the ability to send people to their death at will?"

Kong Mingliang stared at her intently as though he were reading a book.

"The town should have more brothels and entertainment districts. It's not enough for it to have only two successful brothels like Peach Blossom Spring. Instead, it should have six, seven, or eight—to the point that the entire town becomes a red-light district. We should have all the girls in the world come to Explosion. Once they come, rich businessmen will follow, and in the process they will invest in Explosion. And then there are foreigners—foreigners are particularly fond of visiting Chinese red-light districts, and once they come they will build factories and set up companies. Once the streets are lined with cafés, dance halls, and bars, and are full of foreigners and rich people walking around with their girls—at that point Explosion will be recognized as one of China's famous towns and cities. As the town and future city mayor, you will be recognized as the emperor of the entire Balou mountain range."

Zhu Ying described her plans for her husband as though she were sketching an image with the tip of her tongue. As she was speaking, she brushed aside her hair, revealing that her face was flushed like a spring day full of pink blossoms. Furthermore, as she was speaking, her body kept writhing back and forth on the bed, her breasts moving through the air like a pair of wild rabbits hopping through a field. Kong Mingliang stared at those wild rabbits with a gleam in his eye, but this gleam vanished as he knelt down naked before her and said,

"You're still willing to help me, even though I've let you down?"

"You're my husband. If I don't help you, who am I going to help?"

After she said this, they both started to laugh. Naked, they hugged each other, laughing and crying, as their tears poured onto each other's shoulders, completely soaking each other's bodies as well as the bedsheets and the bed itself. Everything became as wet as though it had just been pulled out of a well.

CHAPTER 9

Nature

1. SPARROWS

I.

Kong Mingguang decided he wanted to divorce his wife, and the reason involved none other than the new maid Zhu Ying hired for his family. Her name was Little Cui, and she was in her twenties. She was as delicate as water and her breath was so sweet it smelled as though it had been dipped in honey. She was one of the girls Zhu Ying had brought back from the city to work in Otherworldly Delights. However, no one realized that she worked there, and when people asked where her family lived she replied simply that they were in the mountains. When people asked her how old she was, she told them to guess. When people asked if her parents were still in good health, she burst into tears and said that her parents had already passed away. When she said that she had to work as a maid because her parents were dead, people took pity on her and she would smile like an orphan who is being treated with kindness.

She always had a smile on her face, like a colorful cloud. She had a sweet voice and spoke in a whisper. She talked and worked very quietly, and it was almost as if she wasn't even there. The moment you said you were thirsty, she would immediately bring you a glass of water, and the moment you began to feel sweaty, she would immediately bring you a change of clothes.

She was like a celestial being.

Zhu Ying had assigned Little Cui to work at the Kong household only a few days after Kong Mingliang was promoted to town mayor and the middle-aged maid left. Previously, no one in the family had noticed the middle-aged maid with Kong Dongde, and consequently no one suspected her of having any unseemly relations with him. The maid remained in the Kong household for half a year, washing clothes, cooking, and serving tea. She would bring tea when they wanted tea and would bring wine when they wanted wine. When they needed her to retire to her room, she would discreetly do so. Only a few days after she left, Zhu Ying noticed that at mealtimes her father-in-law would push his bowl aside and complain that his wife had put too much salt in the food and that his daughter-in-law Qinfang had not washed his clothes well. When he went to bed, he would complain of a toothache or say that he was running a fever. He would call a doctor and buy medicine, but he wasn't really doing this to treat the illness; rather, he was simply acting out.

One day, when Zhu Ying was home alone with her father-in-law, he had beseeched her,

"Please, arrange for the maid to return."

Zhu Ying knew that the time was ripe for her to proceed with her plan. She therefore brought Little Cui from Otherworldly Delights and told her to wear the sort of homespun clothes usually worn by people from the mountains. Little Cui scrubbed her face so there wasn't a trace of makeup left. She stood in front of the Kong home and greeted the family elders, then rolled up her sleeves and began sweeping the floor and scrubbing the tables, from time to time kneeling on the ground to look for things Kong Dongde had dropped. In general, she acted as though she had just returned to her own home and behaved as though she were waiting on her own parents, without any sense of restraint or separation. Kong Dongde wanted Zhu Ying to bring back the middle-aged maid she had originally hired for him, but Zhu Ying declined. She said the other maid had already gone home and wouldn't return for any price, and therefore Zhu Ying had no alternative but to bring in a younger one. She said that perhaps Little Cui didn't cook as well as the other maid, and perhaps she didn't wash clothes as quickly, but she was nevertheless diligent and respectful.

So, Little Cui stayed on in the Kong household.

Three months later, Kong Mingguang decided to divorce his wife and marry Little Cui. He made this announcement one afternoon after lunch, as the sluggish sun's rays flowed muddily through the Kong family courtyard and the sparrows in the trees sang like pigeons. The steps of people walking by outside were as soft as leaves fluttering down. Following Explosion's explosive expansion, there were people in the village who built houses facing the road along the river. After they finished these new houses, they used them for business or rented them as street-front stores. As soon as new buildings and tile-roofed houses appeared on the hillside, everyone immediately moved away and everything suddenly grew quiet, and even the sound of footsteps faded away. Mingliang was often busy working in the town government complex and didn't have time to return home. He ate and slept in his office—and it almost seemed as though he were prepared to die there. Minghui, who hadn't passed his university entrance exams, had gotten a job in town, and specifically was in charge of overseeing the town's birthrate and its new households. He said that signing the daily reports on Explosion's population growth was so exhausting that his wrist was constantly in pain. Therefore, he would return home only for meals and would leave as soon as he was finished. The eldest brother, Mingguang, meanwhile, was often at home, claiming that classes at his school had been canceled owing to some emergency or that the entire school had closed for several days. As a result, on this muddy-sunlit day Kong Dongde was sitting in his chair and, as Little Cui was idly giving him a shoulder massage, Mingguang happened to walk out of his room. He had a book in his hand and a box of chalk in the crook of his arm. He was headed back to school to teach a class, but he first went to the courtyard to look around. Little Cui said, "Teacher Kong, are you going to class?" He nodded first to her and then to his father, and then proceeded to leave as usual. After he left, the sparrows flew away as they usually did, and the magpies perched on the roof of the house and sang as they usually did. Everything was as usual, and nothing seemed to be out of the ordinary. But only a few minutes later, Mingguang returned. His face was pale with fury, and he slammed the outer gate shut, stood in the middle of the courtyard, his back as straight as a board, and stared at his father and Little Cui, whose alarmed faces were turning red and white.

"Father . . . there is something I want to tell you," he blurted out.

Kong Dongde stared back at his son.

"I want to get divorced," he announced to his father, "and then I want to marry Little Cui. I can't wait to marry her!"

Kong Dongde turned pale. He sat up in his chair and turned to look at Little Cui, who had stopped her massage and was standing there with her hands suspended in midair. Her face was like a cloud that had suddenly been struck by a gust of cold air. Her mouth was half open and her eyes were wide, as though she had no knowledge of what was happening and had no idea what to do. At this point, Kong Dongde heard the sparrows in the courtyard start cooing like doves, and heard the magpies in the trees and on the roof start squawking like crows. He didn't know what kind of relationship his eldest son had with Little Cui, nor did he know why his son's wife, who had gone to visit her parents for a few days, still had not returned after more than two weeks. He asked Mingguang,

"When will Qinfang return from her mother's house?"

Mingguang replied, "If she returns, I'll kill her!"

Kong Dongde's pale face was covered in sweat. He looked at his son's contorted expression and, in a trembling voice, said, "You're committing a sin, do you know that?"

"I'll kill whoever tries to interfere with my marriage to Little Cui!" Mingguang shouted, as though he really was capable of killing someone at the drop of a hat. With bloodshot eyes, he glared at his father, then added, "After Little Cui and I get married, we'll move out of this house. We'll live alone. Even if you don't give me a cent when we leave the household, I still want to live alone with Little Cui. I want to spend the rest of my life with her!"

Then he left.

His footsteps echoed loudly as he stormed out and slammed the gate behind him. The sparrows on the wall and the magpies in the trees also flew away, as the sparrows cooed like doves and the magpies squawked like crows. After watching Mingguang leave, Kong Dongde spun around and grabbed Little Cui's arm and asked,

"Is this true? Is this true? Is this really true?"

II.

A few days later, Mingguang's wife, Qinfang, came back from her mother's house.

After she returned, she and Mingguang locked themselves in their room and began arguing, and there was a thunderous sound of things being smashed. The sky was overcast, and that morning it was full of dark storm clouds that galloped across it like horses. Mingguang's wife hurled the washbasin into the courtyard, threw their water bottle to the ground, then struck her husband's face until it bled. She used his chalk to draw countless turtles and tortoises on the walls, to symbolize adultery, then used kindling to burn all of her husband's textbooks and his students' assignments. In the light of the fire, she glared at her husband and asked,

"Are you an adulterous turtle?"

"Let's be civilized about this."

"Are you a cheating tortoise?"

"Be civilized!"

His wife grabbed an electric water kettle and threw it at her husband's head, and Kong Mingguang ran out into the yard. At this point, he noticed his father was standing in the middle of the courtyard facing their house. He peered into his father's eyes, then spat at his feet and said, "I know it was you who summoned Qinfang from her mother's house. . . . You should be careful!" With this, he ran outside, closing the double gates behind him—wedging them closed so that his wife wouldn't be able to follow him. His wife, hair disheveled, still ran out to the entranceway, where she furiously shook the gates. Then, like a madwoman, she rushed back into the courtyard and stared at her father-in-law, who was still standing there. She cursed, "Your son is a pig, a dog, a tortoise!"

Her father-in-law said, "You must not divorce him!"

She cursed, "He is even lower than a pig, a dog, or a tortoise."

Her father-in-law said, "You must hold on to him and not divorce him. If you need anything at all, I can provide it."

Like Mingguang, Qinfang spat on the ground in front of her father-in-law, then went inside to get her clothes, in order to return again to her mother's house. She planned to leave the Kong household forever. The floor of her room was covered with things, and she kicked them all out of the way. She even leaned down to pick up a teacup and hurled it against the wall. Then she proceeded into the inner room, took a travel bag out of the cabinet, and began packing her clothes. When she was only half finished, someone's shadow passed in front of the house, and she turned to see her father-in-law enter the room. He stood in front of her, with a beseeching look on his face.

"If you leave, you'll just be following your beastly desires."

She listened.

"You shouldn't leave. You shouldn't divorce him."

She listened.

"Do you know that sooner or later Explosion will become a county seat, and even a major metropolis? Do you know that your brother Mingliang sooner or later will become county mayor, and even city mayor? If you remain in the Kong household, you will become the county's or the city's first lady. But once you get divorced and return to your mother's house, you will no longer be a resident of Explosion. After that, you will no longer be regarded as an urban resident, and instead you will remain a peasant and a mountain resident for the rest of your life."

Her hands, with which she was packing her bags, slowed down. The bed in front of her was as messy as an overturned flowerpot. It remained overcast outside, and the air was full of a mugginess that precedes a rainfall. Under the light of the lamp, the air resembled a piece of illuminated silk. She stood in front of the bed for a while, then looked at her father-in-law's pale, yet still somewhat rosy face.

She looked at his hair, which was graying but still thick. She looked at his hands with their dark liver spots and throbbing veins, and bit her tongue as she waited for her father-in-law to finish.

He said, "If you don't leave the Kong household, I'll make sure you're treated very well."

He said, "If you treat Mingguang well and give the Kong household a son, he will surely have a change of heart, and you'll have an exalted position within the Kong family."

He said, "After you become the county's or city's first lady, you will be treated like an emperor's wife. I can't even imagine what kind of life you will be able to lead then."

Kong Dongde's wife walked in. She had been waiting right outside ever since her son and daughter-in-law started fighting. She had been standing anxiously in the entranceway, like an invalid unable to walk, but now she quietly came in and, without saying a word, she began picking up everything that was scattered on the ground. She used a dustpan to sweep up the broken glass and porcelain, and dumped it all at the base of the courtyard wall. Then she returned and, as she was cleaning the debris, her daughter-in-law Qinfang walked over from beside the bed, brushed past Kong Dongde, and said, "I'll do as you say." She then proceeded to help her mother-in-law tidy the room.

III.

After borrowing a house outside the village from Second Dog, Mingguang and Little Cui moved out of the Kong household and proceeded to lead a peaceful domestic life. Kong Dongde went to look for Kong Mingliang, and asked why he was focusing only on his responsibilities as town mayor and ignoring the needs of his own family, while his cuckolding brother had his head buried in his pants. So Mingliang went to see his elder brother Mingguang and found him in the street in front of the middle school—by this point Mingguang had already been reassigned from primary school to middle school. The two brothers engaged in some idle small talk, then each went to attend to his business.

Mingguang's school was located on a flat area on the mountainside. Mingliang slowly walked over, seeing several rows of new buildings and a surrounding wall, together with scaffolding for some new construction. There were also a lot of lively students, who ran to wherever they needed to go. That was Explosion's middle school. The two brothers stood at a corner of the wall surrounding the grounds. The sun shone down on them, casting a mottled patchwork of dark yellow and light black shadows on their faces and bodies.

"I never expected you would end up being such a good-for-nothing." Mingliang looked at his eldest brother, and said in a soft voice, "There are so many girls at Otherworldly Delights, but instead you have an affair with your maid."

Mingguang blushed and replied in an equally soft voice, "When I'm with Little Cui, I understand what true love is."

Mingliang pursed his lips and said, "If you break up with Little Cui, then first thing tomorrow I will dismiss the school principal and announce that you will replace him."

Mingguang smiled and said, "I don't want to be principal, because now I know what love is."

Mingliang said, "Fuck love. Love is a pile of shit. You should stay with Qinfang, and after you have finished your term as school principal you can serve as deputy town mayor or county mayor."

Mingguang said, "Love is like a chrysanthemum blossom blooming on a peony stem. No one but the peony and chrysanthemum can understand it."

"One day, the middle school will become a college, and if you don't maintain your reputation, will you be able to serve as college president?"

"I couldn't care less whether it is a high school or a college," Mingguang said. "Now I know what love is. You're my brother, so you should help me secure a divorce from your sister-in-law. She is an obstacle standing in the way of love."

The two brothers then separated. A car from the town was going to take the mayor to the county seat for a meeting. When Mingliang got into the car, he shouted back to Mingguang, "Brother, please think this over carefully!"

Mingguang replied, "I've found love—and now realize that up till now my life has been pointless!"

Mingguang and Little Cui moved in together, to enjoy a spring-like love life. Their new house had previously belonged to Second Dog, and came with furniture, beds, and pots and pans. After Second Dog stepped down as the warehouse guard, he resumed his former career as a thief and, in addition to stealing from trains, he also stole from the forests and workshops, or from neighboring villages. In this way, he, like everyone else, became increasingly wealthy, and along the town's main street he built several houses that he could either live in or rent out, meaning that his own former house was left empty. After Mingguang and Little Cui moved in, the house suddenly became very animated, but Second Dog told Mingguang three things:

First, he said, "You are the mayor's elder brother. You can live here as long as you like."

Second, he said, "Will you ever become an official? If you do, I'll simply give you the house."

Third, he said, "There is one thing you have to agree to, which is that you convince the mayor to call me Brother, as he used to."

Mingguang and his wife therefore moved in and proceeded to sweep, clean, and wipe everything down. They also posted red *double happiness* characters on the walls, like newlyweds. In the large courtyard, several apple and pear trees were slowly growing. On the apple tree there were pear blossoms, and in summer the pear tree was full of red apples. When the outer gate was closed, they felt as though they were in a fruit orchard. In the middle was the apple tree with its pink and white flowers, while walnut-size green pears hung from its branches. Mingguang cooked food and took it over to Little Cui. The dining table was under the fruit trees and was surrounded by the fragrant smell of flowers and fruits. Previously, it had always been Little Cui who would cook for the Kong household, but now love changed the color of the sky and Mingguang cooked for her. Little Cui was pampered like a princess. When it was time for Mingguang to go to school, he would wait until the last moment before leaving, and in the afternoon he would return home before school was even over. When he returned, he would bring either vegetables or grain or rice. Little Cui didn't go anywhere, and at most, after Mingguang left for work, she would walk to Otherworldly Delights to see her sisters and exchange a few words with Zhu Ying, but then she would immediately return home. When she returned, she would bring either some meat or a fresh fish, as though she had gone out grocery shopping for Mingguang.

Once, Mingguang was returning from school with a bag of fresh vegetables and Little Cui was returning from the market with two *jin* of beef. They ran into each other in what had formerly been the Explosion village square. They both saw the graves there, and laughed. Mingguang said, "The weather is quite good. I hear that the town has discovered another sizable copper deposit."

Little Cui said, "Really? I hear that over in the mountains, they have discovered a deposit of gold ore. In the future, when the people of Explosion buy fish and meat, they will simply pay for it in gold."

They laughed, gazed at each other for a while, then kissed in the middle of the square. Seeing that the street was completely empty and as peaceful as though it were the middle of the night, and that everyone was at work either in town, in the factories, or in the mines, they placed their bags of vegetables and meat on one of the tombstones and proceeded to engage in a raucous bout of sex. After they were finished, they got up, put their clothes back on, and brushed off the dust, then noticed that a dog was standing there watching them in surprise. They threw several rocks at the dog and returned to their house in back of the village. They held hands as they walked, and their fingertips tingled with love, like a dog running up and down the street unable to find its way home. When they got to Second Dog's house, they shut the gate and looked at the bees and butterflies flying around the fruit trees. Little Cui said to Mingguang, "I'm going to cook some food. I'm the maid, and you're the bookworm."

He replied, "Books are dog shit. You are the empress and the dictionary of all of the world's intellectuals." He then took the vegetables, beef, and washbasin from her and proceeded to wash the vegetables while watching her remove her shirt. By this point she had already taken off the rest of her clothes and hung them on a branch of the fruit tree. Her red dress and purple underwear fluttered in the wind like a couple of flags. Her thin yellow sweater resembled a wild chrysanthemum blossom. Every time he completed a certain task, she would remove a different article of clothing and either hang it from a tree branch or drape it over a chair. By the time she removed all of her clothing, he had already cleaned and cut up the meat and vegetables. One of them stood inside the kitchen, while the other stood outside, as the early summer humidity washed through the courtyard like a sauna. The redbrick courtyard wall surrounded her like a wall of fire, and the sound of machinery could be heard coming from the distant factories, while at the base of the mountain the roads running along both banks of the river were loud and grating. They proceeded to embrace each other passionately, as though there

were nothing left in the world but sex. Mingguang smelled her body's
sweet fragrance and once again saw her naked body in the sunlight
produce a glow like a soft thorn. Her body's aura resembled sunlight
shining through a cloud. She had a peach-like smile, like a shining
lamp immersed in water.

She asked, "Am I beautiful?"

He said, "I want to get divorced."

She smiled and said, "I want to marry you, and I wouldn't care
even if you were unimaginably poor or ugly."

He replied, "I can earn a lot of money. I can have every student
in the school pay significantly more tuition every semester, and all of
that tuition will then belong to us. We'll have so much money that
you won't even be able to spend it all. We'll have so much money,
you won't even be able to hide it all."

She suddenly turned serious and said,

"Hurry up and get divorced. I can't keep waiting anymore."

"I'll get divorced later this year."

"I can't wait that long."

"I'll get divorced later this month."

"I can't wait that long."

"I'll get divorced later today."

"I can't wait that long!"

"I'll get divorced as soon as we finish eating."

She considered for a moment, then nodded. Her hair bun had
come undone, and her black hair now covered her shoulders. Then
she brushed past him as she went into the kitchen to cook the food.
As she walked back and forth naked in the kitchen, cooking him
lunch, she resembled a glimmer of sunlight. When they encountered
each other, he touched her breasts with his fingertips, but she pulled
his hand away and said, "Go get divorced. I can't keep waiting."
She glanced at him, then continued cooking. In all, she prepared

eight dishes and two bowls of soup. She carried these dishes into the courtyard, where she placed them on a reed mat. The sun was shining brightly, so that the mat glowed in the sunlight. Completely naked, she lay down on the mat, her tender skin resembling white jade and her body like an agate statue. Then she carefully picked up each of the dishes on the mat and placed them on her chest, on her breasts, on her belly, and on her thighs—so that he could sit next to her and eat off her own body the banquet she had prepared for him. She also poured him a glass of wine, and handed him both the glass and his chopsticks. Then she repeated,

"Go get divorced. I can't keep waiting."

His right hand, holding his chopsticks, trembled slightly. He wanted to use his left hand to stroke her jade-like body, which was covered with white and blue dishes, but discovered that his entire right arm was shaking. He saw her jet-black hair hanging down from her apple-red face to the snow-white reed mat. He saw her black, round eyes right under the tree's shadow. He saw her nipples peeking out from between several of the dishes. He also saw her porcelain-like skin and her navel, which resembled an eye staring back at him. He licked his lips, swallowed his saliva, then looked up. He looked at the sun overhead and at the sunlit courtyard, and then in a voice as dry as fire he asked, "Do I have to go get divorced right now?"

"I'll serve you a naked banquet every day."

Without saying a word, he placed his chopsticks on a plate of grilled fish that was sitting on her belly and immediately headed home to get divorced. He walked quickly and resolutely, but when he went out the gate he turned around and said to her,

"Don't move. If I don't bring back a divorce agreement when I return, then you can throw all of these plates and dishes at my head!"

She stared at him from beneath those plates and dishes, and nodded.

IV.

Kong Mingliang was hosting an oath ceremony in the town's assembly hall, affirming everyone's determination to have the town be redesignated as a county as quickly as possible. Because this was such a momentous event, the ceremony continued for an entire day and night, and still had not concluded. Eventually, his secretary called him down from the podium. Behind the podium, apart from a curtain, a table, and the auditorium's lamps, chairs, electrical cables, and some drums, there were also some portraits of leaders and some discarded tissues used by couples who had come for secret sex.

When Mingliang retreated behind the curtain, he saw his brother Mingguang standing next to an enormous portrait of a leader. Mingguang's face was sallow, and sweat was running down his cheeks like rain. Before Mingliang had a chance to walk over, Mingguang rushed up to him and exclaimed,

"Mingliang, do you want me to kneel down before you?"

Kong Mingguang proceeded to kneel down in front of his brother. He said, "Don't forget that when you were village chief, this brother of yours wrote your speeches for you. When you transformed the village into a town, this brother of yours wrote the initial drafts of the documents you needed. I wrote hundreds, and even thousands, of pages for you, but now all I want is for you to give me one page in return." Mingguang knelt as he was saying this, and continued kneeling. Mingliang was so startled that he took several steps backward until he bumped into a table. The corner of the table poked him in the back, awakening him from his daze. He glanced over at the town secretary, who had called him down from the stage, and after waiting for the secretary to step aside, he proceeded to pull his brother to his feet.

"If you have something to say, then get up and say it!"

Mingguang leaned forward and said, "I just need one sheet of paper."

"What is it?"

"A divorce certificate."

"Brother, have you gone mad?"

"I've found love." Mingguang became emotional. "I've found love. All I ask is that you give me one sheet of paper. If you don't, then our work to secure this town and its corresponding mayoral seat will have been for nothing. Having a brother as town mayor will have been for nothing. And if tomorrow you were to be appointed county mayor, that will also have been for nothing."

Mingliang stood there staring at his brother.

"If you can't even provide me with this one sheet of paper, then what's the point of having the town be promoted to a county and of you becoming the new county mayor?"

Mingliang stared back at his brother.

"If you can't even provide me with this one sheet of paper, then what's the point of having our Kong family produce a county mayor, a city mayor, or even an emperor?"

Kong Mingliang turned pale. He spat on the ground in front of his brother, then wiped his mouth. After glancing down again at his brother kneeling before him, Mingliang gestured toward the town secretary, who was standing a fair distance behind him, and said a few words to him. Then he led his brother out of the auditorium. The sound of people talking onstage was broadcast over loudspeakers to every corner of the auditorium. The sound echoed off the walls like waves bouncing off a riverbank. The two brothers retreated from this noise, with the mayor walking in front and his brother following behind. They quickly proceeded down the town's main street, then passed through two small alleys. Bathed in sweat, neither of them spoke a single word, as though they were silently going to assassinate someone. When they got home, they didn't see Cai Qinfang but knew that she had gone out to buy some food—since it turned out that after

Little Cui and Mingguang moved out together, Qinfang continued caring for her father-in-law like a maid. Therefore, Mingliang took his brother to the market to look for Qinfang, while at the same time sending someone ahead to find her. As a result, when they ran into Qinfang in front of the town bridge, she was being escorted back.

The bridge was full of people trying to do business. There was shop after shop selling watches and sunglasses. Opera lovers also went to the bridge to sing, expressing their delight through their music. When the mayor and his brother ran into Qinfang on the bridge, the vegetables in her basket were still dripping wet. Vegetables sellers were chasing after her, trying to stuff even more into her basket. They said, "If you take more of our vegetables, it will be as though we are expressing our appreciation to the mayor. . . . So please, take some of our vegetables!" The mayor and his brother reached the bridge, where countless people crowded around and listened quietly as the mayor said,

"Sister-in-law, you should get divorced. For the sake of the Kong family, you should get divorced.

". . . What is so extraordinary about getting divorced? You should approach it as a business transaction. Is forty thousand yuan enough to buy a divorce?

". . . How about eighty thousand?

". . . How about a hundred thousand? Would that be enough for this divorce?"

Qinfang didn't answer. She stared blankly at the mayor, her forehead flushed and covered in sweat. By this point it was already past lunchtime, and the afternoon sun shone down on her face like a fiery red cloth, piercing her eyes. When the people who had crowded around—including those who had just been trying to stuff her basket with more vegetables—realized what the mayor was saying, they began shouting, "A hundred thousand, a hundred thousand! It's really a hundred thousand!" After they recovered from their initial shock, they all began entreating Qinfang on the mayor's behalf, saying, "It would definitely be worth it. Definitely worth it. . . . You would make more from this one transaction than a girl from Otherworldly Delights could make from selling herself for her entire life." They enviously urged her on. Hearing their encouragement, Cai Qinfang gradually calmed down and looked intently at the mayor without saying a word. The mayor became increasingly anxious and took ten blank sheets of paper out of his pocket. Then he squatted down, placed the papers on his knees, and proceeded to sign them, then handed them to his sister-in-law, saying, "This should do it. If in the future you or your family should need anything, just write what you need on one of these sheets of paper. Since the sheets of paper all carry my signature, their instructions will be carried out."

Cai Qinfang accepted the stack of signed pages and looked at them. She carefully rolled them up, then said,

"There is something else."

The mayor said, "Go ahead."

"After the divorce, I want you to continue calling me Sister. Even after you become county mayor, I want you to continue calling me Sister. When I go out, I want to be able to tell people—my brother Mingliang is the town mayor, county mayor, or city mayor."

The mayor agreed.

During this entire discussion, Kong Mingguang was standing to the side behind the crowd that had gathered on the bridge. Not until everyone had dispersed and his wife was walking away did he finally come forward and exchange a final look with Cai Qinfang, then he spat on the ground in front of her as he had just done to his brother. At this point Kong Mingliang said, "You should go get divorced. Even though you are the mayor's brother, you still need to follow the appropriate procedures. Now take your divorce agreement directly to the civil administration board." He then took out another sheet of paper and, while squatting down and leaning it against his knees, wrote two lines and then signed, "Town Mayor: Kong Mingliang." After handing the sheet of paper to his brother, he hurried back to the auditorium to continue hosting the oath ceremony.

By the time Kong Mingguang finally had the divorce certificate in hand, it was already late afternoon. This document—which was printed on stiff red paper that was as large as a man's palm and was stamped with the seal of the town hall office—formally released him and his wife from their matrimonial bonds. He then wanted to marry Little Cui. People were walking into and out of the town hall in a continuous stream, and every office was busy with meetings and telephone calls. People were walking up and down the streets, buying and selling goods, coming and going, friends and strangers, like red and yellow leaves in autumn. Many people nodded or spoke to him, or stopped to chat, but he pretended he didn't see or hear them. Instead, he rushed to his house in back of the town. Little Cui was still lying naked under the tree, and he was afraid that after the shadows moved the sun would shine directly on her body. Perhaps she would get tired of waiting for him, and would remove the dishes from her body and get dressed. Or perhaps she would still be lying naked under the tree, and when he brought the divorce certificate she would let him continue eating the banquet from her naked body, and after eating they could have earthshaking sex right there in the courtyard. After that, he could take her back to the civil administration board to register the marriage, so that they could then spend the rest of their lives together, spending the rest of their days madly in love.

The town was the same as before. But aside from Mingguang himself, no one knew that in that courtyard there was a girl with skin like white jade lying completely naked on a new tatami mat, with eight dishes and two bowls of soup carefully arranged on her chest, abdomen, and thighs. She had prepared those dishes for him while completely naked, and the courtyard was filled with the delicious steam from the food combined with the sweat fragrance from her body. Like an idiot, the rest of the world wasn't aware of a thing. Only the two of them knew about this, and between them they enjoyed many secrets and pleasures.

Only Mingguang knew that the pleasure Little Cui was able to give him was one that most men would never have a chance to hear about, much less experience.

Once Mingguang arrived in the village behind the town, where the streets were almost empty, he practically ran home. He pushed open the gate and, waving his divorce certificate, shouted, "We can now get married!" But then he suddenly froze in the entranceway and stood there motionless for the longest time.

Little Cui was not lying naked beneath the tree, nor was she dressed and waiting for him in the courtyard.

The tree's shadow had retreated to the side of the mat, and the sun was shining down brightly on it. The dishes that had previously been arranged on her body were now scattered all over the ground, and a large number of crows, sparrows, turtledoves, and orioles were busy pecking at the food. There were more than a dozen different kinds of birds, including black, gray, yellow, and red ones, and of each kind there were more than a dozen individual birds. They were all busy eating the vegetables and soup. There were also a couple of wild chickens and peacocks, which no one had seen for many years. It was as if an avian convention were being held right there in the courtyard. The birds that had already eaten their fill were chirping and hopping around, or else were perched on the wall or the tree branches, while the rest were still pecking for food. When the birds heard the gate open, some of them looked at him in surprise, while others ignored him and continued going from one overturned dish to another.

With a sense of foreboding, Mingguang shouted, "Little Cui! Little Cui!" as he made his way through the flock of birds toward the house. When he went inside, he discovered that Little Cui had already left, and her clothing and traveling bag were also missing.

For the next several years, he never succeeded in finding her. It was as if she had never existed, as if they had never been together.

2. TREES

After Little Cui and Mingguang moved out, Kong Dongde rarely spoke. He acted as though he were completely exhausted, and at meal-time he couldn't even extract any flavor from his fish and meat. The only time he managed to have any energy was when he got angry. His wife brought him every meal and entreated him, "Can't you eat just one bite?" When she left, she complained to her eldest daughter-in-law, "Why can't he die? If he died, at least we would be at peace."

When Little Cui had still been living with them, she was most solicitous of Kong Dongde's needs. When he wanted dumplings she would make him ingot-like dumplings, and when he wanted fish balls she would make him jade-like fish balls. Once she stuffed some dough with meat filling, carefully fashioned it into the shape of an official seal, then boiled it and served it to him. Another time, she cut the dough into the shape of hundred-yuan bills, then painted them to make them look like actual money. On another occasion, she labored in the kitchen for the longest time, trying to roll some dough into the shape of an official seal, but the dough was too soft and consequently after she boiled it, it came out looking more like a woman's breast.

When she brought out that bowl of pasta resembling a cross between an official seal and a woman's breast, he kept staring up at her chest. Little Cui stood there and let him look at her, and only after he had finished did she take the bowl and walk away.

Eventually, Little Cui and Mingguang had become intimate.

They then moved out of the house together, and Kong Dongde never saw Little Cui again, spending the rest of his days fuming and refusing to eat. On that particular day, he suddenly said to his daughter-in-law Qinfang, "I want to eat dough in the shape of an official seal, but leave the dough on the soft side. Also, cook me several dishes of tender vegetables, so fresh that they are still dripping water." Qinfang went to the kitchen to knead the dough, and went to the market to buy fresh vegetables. But the moment she left the house, a boy from the village came running in and handed something to Kong Dongde before running back out again. At that point, Kong Dongde was sunning himself in the courtyard and had just dozed off. He took a look at what the boy had handed him and immediately woke up. He became so emotional that he couldn't speak, and his blood surged to his head. He abruptly stood up, then went inside to take off his old clothing and put on a set of neatly pressed new clothes. Then he walked outside.

His wife was there rinsing grain and asked, "Where did you go?"

He snapped back, "I went to die!"

His wife stared in shock and asked, "Where did you go to die?"

Without turning around, he said, "My sickness is cured. No one needs to worry about me."

Holding the object the child had given him, he headed out. His legs felt as strong as they had when he was younger, and when he stepped over the threshold he didn't need to lean on the door frame but rather hopped across like a child. His wife was astounded. She watched him until he disappeared from sight, then said, "It would be good if he just died." Then she returned to rinsing the grain.

Kong Dongde proceeded to a small wooded area to the east of the town. The area was located on a hillside about half a *li* away and was not far from where Hu Dajun—who at the time had been town mayor but by this point was already county mayor—had erected that enormous stele for Zhu Ying, while also erecting a number of other crooked steles along the edge of the woods. Little Cui was standing next to the stele waiting for him. It was early autumn and the trees were still green, while the thick dark leaves were covered with a layer of dirt. On the tree branches there were some plastic bags that had been blown over by the wind, making it look as though they were covered with the white paper blossoms used in the Qingming grave-sweeping festival. There were also some northern birds flying overhead, and when they were tired they would perch on Zhu Ying's stele. Little Cui was wearing her old clothing—straight-leg pants, a tight-fitting top, and a shirt with a small collar—which was quite different from what the Balou Mountain residents typically wore. She was standing there waiting for Kong Dongde and had a large travel bag, which was sitting on the stele's platform. She was like a girl waiting for a man of her grandfather's generation to come over, but at the same time she also resembled a young woman waiting for the lover she hadn't seen for many years. She watched as Kong Dongde approached, then stepped forward and stood in the middle of the road. She looked around and saw that the village was like a magnificent painting spread out on the ground. On the other side of the mountain, Liu Gully and Zhang Peak were connected to the town, and a forest of buildings grew between them. The mountain road, which by now had already been paved, was full of trucks rumbling down from the mines. After waiting for the trucks to pass, Kong Dongde stood in front of her. His face was pale, but beneath his pallor his pulse was racing. His eyes were glazed, but beneath the glaze there was a glittering warmth.

She smiled at him and said, "So you've come?"

He looked at her travel bag, and asked, "Where are you going?"

"Come over here."

After cautiously looking around, Kong Dongde followed her toward the forest. He watched her carry that travel bag while waving her empty hand, like a peacock carrying something in its mouth while spreading its wings to fly. He hesitated for a moment but then continued to follow her into the forest. This had previously been farmland, but after the village developed into a bustling town everyone started earning money to stop farming the land. After a few years, the farmland became covered with weeds and trees. The area had once been planted with pagoda trees, paulownia trees, chinaberry trees, and elms, together with apricot and persimmon trees that grew from the seeds carried over by birds and the wind—they had all grown to the point that each trunk was as wide as a plate. There was a persimmon tree that had been full of oranges and tangerines as fiery red as autumn persimmons. As a result of the combined influence of the wind, insects, and village children, however, the oranges and tangerines had long since disappeared, leaving behind only a single bare branch, as if the tree were holding up an orange-colored red lantern. The ground beneath their feet, once a rich carpet of asparagus, was now covered with wormwood-like weeds and a variety of multicolored flowers reaching for the sky. The old man and the young woman proceeded into the wooded area, while the stele and the road behind them stood like centuries-old artifacts that had been left in place. The sound of cars driving by was ear-piercingly loud, though it also seemed as though it were coming from another world. When they reached the persimmon tree in the middle of the forest, Little Cui placed her bag on top of some underbrush, then turned around and smiled at Kong Dongde.

"Your eldest son tricked me. Ever since I was young, I didn't have a mother or father, or a grandmother or grandfather, so when I met you I regarded you as my elder.

183

". . . You are the one I really care about, but your son Mingguang won't let me be nice to you.

". . . He took advantage of me, and now I'm no longer able to give myself to you. No one would tolerate it if anyone knew I had first given myself to your son, and then had given myself to you."

Then Little Cui began to cry. In the sound of her weeping, there was a pink wildflower that, in the blink of an eye, became a sorrowful grayish black. Tears streamed down her face and fell onto the leaves on the ground. The tree leaves wept as well, as did the tree's branches and trunk. As she wept, she bit her lower lip and struggled to swallow her sobs. Eventually, her shoulders stopped shaking, and she was able to stagger out of that pit of sorrow. She wiped the tears from her face and licked her lips. Then, looking intently at Kong Dongde, who was staring off into space, she quietly made an earth-shattering statement:

"I can't give myself to you, so you should only take a look."

The wind blew in through the trees, blowing toward the west and around toward the north. Upon saying this, she began to unbutton her clothes. She lifted her arms to take off her shirt, then raised them again to remove her undershirt, leaving only her fiery-red bra. Apart from the wind, the forest was deathly quiet, but the sound of thunder and lightning emanating from Little Cui's body continued to rush past him.

Her clothes were strewn over the grass and draped over tree branches, like multicolored flags fluttering in the woods.

Just as she, a little earlier, had stripped in front of Mingguang, she rapidly proceeded to remove her clothes. As she was about to take off her bra, an earthquake shook the mountains. The trees swayed back and forth, and after she calmly removed her underwear, the trees and mountains continued to shake. Throughout the earthquake, tears poured out of her eyes as she smiled at him. With each smile, each bare tree branch became filled with red and yellow flowers. The dead grass came back to life, as a springlike smell of grass and plants rained down on the forest like a thunderstorm. All sorts of birds were singing and flying through the trees. Autumn reverted back to summer, and summer reverted back to spring, until finally time paused in spring. Not until she finally opened her mouth to speak did the season finally return to its proper place.

"I'm returning to my family home. I've let your Kong family down." She let him gaze at her naked body for a moment, then put her underwear back on.

"I know that after I leave Explosion I'll miss you as much as I would miss my own father or grandfather, but I'm afraid that if I remain here your eldest son may strangle me."

She took the red bra that was hanging from a tree branch and put it back on.

"If your son can get along well with his wife and not harass me anymore, then perhaps I'll return to Explosion—and return to your house to work as a maid and wait on you . . . everything will be even better than before!"

After she had gotten dressed and picked up her bag to leave, she told Kong Dongde one final thing: "I really want to spend the rest of my life with you, cooking and washing for you until you pass away. And after you depart, I too would disappear from this world." Then, carrying her travel bag, she slowly made her way out of the forest. After proceeding a few steps she looked back. Although she was still smiling, her face was nevertheless increasingly covered in tears. In this way, she walked toward Zhu Ying's enormous stele. From the stele she headed toward the main road, and on to the world outside Explosion.

Trucks full of mined ore rumbled past her, and following them she, too, disappeared.

3. RIVERS

In the main building of Otherworldly Delights, a white candle produced a black light, and a blue lightbulb produced a purplish red light. The rows of tiny lightbulbs hanging from the electrical cord that stretched from the wall to the ceiling included gray bulbs that glowed white and red bulbs that glowed blue. In the hallway, the reception area, and the living room, there were black, yellow, and green lights all mixed together, and the walls, the floor, and the space in between were lit up in bright colors. After receiving clients throughout the night, the girls slept during the day. In the afternoon, they would sleepily get out of bed and, still half-naked, proceed from the third floor down to the second floor, and from the second floor back up to the third floor. The sound of their ablutions resembled a waterfall. After washing their faces and cleaning their bodies, they stood in the doorway or sat on their beds, smoking, holding all sorts of small mirrors, putting on lipstick, painting their eyebrows, and applying perfume and powder to their bodies. They also compared themselves with each other to see who had the most fat, and who was the thinnest with the largest breasts.

On this particular day around noon, as the girls were preparing to receive their clients, Zhu Ying suddenly appeared. The girls quickly put away their eyebrow pencils, lipstick, and toiletry cases, then in unison they all cried Mother or Sister. They watched as the red light from the green bulbs shone on Zhu Ying's no longer vigorous face, sketching a pattern of happiness, melancholia, and discomfort.

"Have any of you received any clients in their seventies?" Zhu Ying looked around at that group of girls who were all in their twenties. When they merely stared back at her in confusion, she added, "He is my father-in-law, and is seventy years old. He has a thin face, and his hair has gone gray. When I started at Otherworldly Delights, it was precisely so that one day I could bring him here." Hearing one of the girls tittering in amusement, she glared at the girl until she stopped, as all of the other girls fixed their gazes on their madam's face. They saw her complexion alternate between red, yellow, black, and white, making her appear as though she wasn't even real. But her voice was clear and animated, and she announced, "In the next few days, he will definitely come to Otherwordly Delights to pay us a visit. In the next couple of weeks, he will definitely come to see one of you." As she said this, she again looked at those girls with their gleaming skin. She paused, then said more loudly, "Everyone remember what I told you. No matter whom he comes to see, you should receive him with your highest skills. He is my father-in-law, but I view him like my own father. Whatever you do, you should make sure he enjoys himself. You also must not accept a single cent of his money, and let him understand that he won't be charged if he returns, either. I want him to become a frequent guest. The next time he requests a room with one of you, I won't merely give you the amount of money you would have earned with five or ten clients, but rather, as long as he keeps coming, I'll make sure you receive any sum of money you want!"

The girls did not fully understand what Zhu Ying was saying. How could they have this dad-like father-in-law come to Otherworldly Delights, and then become a repeat customer? They watched her with bated breath, as the light continued to change colors, with the red lights shining red and the white lights shining white. Zhu Ying's face returned to its normal color. In her typical rosy complexion there was a trace of pallor, and she had wrinkles on her forehead and around her eyes. What's more, she had prominent bags under her eyes.

As she stood, without painted eyebrows or face powder, among this group of highly made-up girls, her bare face made her look even older and more decrepit. No one had any idea what she was thinking, or how heavy the secrets were that she was bearing in her heart, which pressed down on her so much that her voice was hoarse. The waiting room was full of the scent of perfume, and the trace of light that shone in through the permanently closed window illuminated the girls' backs and Zhu Ying's shoulders. As the girls were quietly listening to Zhu Ying, one of them asked very solemnly,

"What if this seventy-year-old man dies while he is with one of us?"

Everyone laughed brightly.

"If you are able to have him die while he is with you . . ."—Zhu Ying fixed her gaze on the girl—"Isn't your name Ah Xia? Ah Xia, if you are able to have him die while he is with you, then whoever you later wish to marry, I will find him for you, and however much money you want, I'll deposit it for you. In fact, if you want this entire brothel, I will give it to you as well. You'd be the madam, and I would return home and obediently serve as the mayor's wife."

Ah Xia replied solemnly, "What if I don't want this Otherworldly Delights brothel but rather want to marry the mayor myself?"

Zhu Ying's heart skipped a beat, and her legs again felt weak. She realized that Ah Xia must have had relations with the mayor, but she didn't hate her for it. Instead, she examined Ah Xia's appearance, then immediately stood up and, with a smile, she said, "OK." She then wiped the smile from her face and added, "As long as you can have Kong Dongde die while he is with you, and as long as the mayor is willing to marry you, I will divorce him and move out of his home." With this, the meeting concluded. Zhu Ying told all of the girls to return to their rooms and either eat or get made up, and prepare to receive the day's new crop of clients. It was afternoon, and they would soon start arriving. At this point, Zhu Ying and Ah Xia were the only ones in the receiving room. Zhu Ying looked at Ah Xia's tall physique and ample breasts, and saw that her face and body were suffused with tenderness and beauty. Not only was she sure that Ah Xia must have had intimate relations with the mayor, she also had a good idea of what positions they must have used in bed, and what sorts of sweet nothings the mayor must have told her. Zhu Ying took a step toward Ah Xia, stared at the pencil-thin ridge of her nose, and after a pause said softly,

"I'm relying on you. . . .

"As long as he comes over here."

After Zhu Ying said these sentences, the two of them separated. At this point, Zhu Ying was about to hold similar meetings at each of the other establishments, but just as she was about to leave, those lights once again began shining different colors, with the red bulbs emitting black light, the yellow bulbs emitting green light, and the purple bulbs emitting milky white light. On the wall, the floor, and the bureau in the reception hall—everywhere that there were lights, red, white, and yellow peony, chrysanthemum, and poppy blossoms grew out of the walls and the windowsills, between the cracks in the bricks, and from the wooden rafters. A thick floral smell filled the reception hall, the corridor, and all of the rooms.

4. ANIMALS

When Kong Dongde went to visit his son Kong Mingguang, he took some fruit, vegetables, and rice flour. For more than a month and a half, ever since Little Cui departed, Kong Mingguang had not left Second Dog's house. Also, no one saw him go out to buy oil, salt, or pickled vegetables. No one knew how he was getting by, without opening the door during the day or turning on the lights at night. No one in the village or town knew what had occurred in the Kong household. Little Cui had taken her bags and disappeared. Then someone from Cai Qinfang's household came to fetch her clothes and belongings, which were loaded onto a cart and hauled away. Kong Dongde's wife urged him on a daily basis to go visit his son, and after she had urged him more than a hundred times, he finally took some provisions, crossed the street, and headed over.

When Kong Dongde pushed open the courtyard gate, he saw Mingguang sitting on a reed mat in the shade under a tree. The ground around the mat was strewn with overturned bowls and dishes, and dried-up vegetables were still caked onto the sides of the bowls and dishes. A number of sparrows were energetically pecking at the leftovers. Mingguang was sitting there motionless, like a corpse. His hair was disheveled, his face was covered in stubble, and his eyes were sunken. In the middle of his exhausted face, his eyes resembled two dark pits.

"You're still alive?" Kong Dongde stood in the doorway.

With considerable effort, his son turned and looked at his father with a blank stare.

Kong Dongde placed the provisions on the mat, then went into the kitchen. He saw that there were some tree sprouts on the chopping board. He peered into the wok and saw several fishes swimming around in the water that was left inside. When he emerged, he looked at his son's and Little Cui's bedroom, and saw the large red marital *double happiness* characters posted on the wall—though after a month and a half in the dark they had faded so much that they looked as though they had already been there for many years. The breeze that entered through the window and the open door blew the *double happiness* characters so that they flapped sorrowfully. On the table, there was a textbook and box of chalk that his son used when teaching at the school. On the pages of the textbook, however, plants were growing, and there was a bird's nest inside the chalk box, while colorful flowers grew from the ends of the pieces of chalk. As Kong Dongde was standing in the middle of the room, he saw that the ceiling and the walls were covered with pictures of Little Cui's tearfully smiley face. As he was about to walk out, Kong Dongde stumbled upon a hairpin Little Cui had left behind. He leaned over to pick it up and saw that as he was holding it in his hand it slowly turned into a flower. He carefully placed this hairpin-turned-flower in his pocket, then walked out and, standing in the doorway, said to his son,

"Go fetch Qinfang and bring her back. You should continue teaching at the school and get on with your life."

Mingguang acted as if he hadn't heard a word.

Kong Dongde took a couple of steps toward him and said,

"The town will soon become a county, and this county will be ours. Whatever you want to do in the county, I'll tell your brother Mingliang to make it happen—as long as you and Qinfang get on with your lives."

Mingguang acted as if he hadn't heard a word his father said.

"You can't simply hang yourself from a tree." Kong Dongde brought over a stool and sat directly in front of his son, and began offering Mingguang advice on life, particularly with respect to his daughter-in-law, Qinfang. He described how Mingguang's younger brother had exhausted himself trying to bring the town prosperity and to transform Explosion into an independent county. He described how Mingliang had run here and there in order to make this town into a county seat. Finally, he said,

"Our entire family should be more considerate of your brother Mingliang, and we should be careful not to give him any additional trouble."

He said, "You should cook your own food, or else move back in with us."

He said, "You should say something, be it good or bad. You can't just sit here without speaking, as though you were dead."

He asked, "So, are you alive or are you dead—sitting here without speaking?"

He said, "If you are alive, good. But if you really have died, I'll go ask someone to build you a coffin. Then I'll ask someone to go to the cemetery to dig you a grave."

Kong Mingguang still sat there without speaking.

Dusk fell. The sound of the setting sun pierced through the noise of the nearby factories and mines, producing a sound like that of flowing blood. But afterward, this was drowned out by loud thunder, pushed aside by the sound of voices and footsteps moving between the town and the village. The birds in the courtyard were all watching the father and son while they sat on the house, the wall, and the tree. Their feathers fell to the ground and cracked open the cement floor, and even shattered one of the stones supporting the courtyard wall. There was a chill in the early autumn air. The son still refused to speak, and the most he would do was raise his cold, white eyes and stare up at his father, or else he would look at the closed door, and then would lie on that reed mat as though he were dead. His father became increasingly anxious and abruptly stood up, angrily kicked his stool, and spat on the ground. "Let me put it this way," he said firmly. "If you are going to die, you should go ahead and do so. But if you plan to live, then you should return home with me, and tomorrow you should go fetch your wife, Qinfang, from her mother's house." Then he stared at his son, as if he wanted to extract a word from his mouth, but Mingguang continued sitting silently on the reed mat, looking at the bare bowls and dishes that were scattered everywhere, as though Little Cui were still lying naked there. His cold white fish eyes stared blankly ahead, as though he had not seen his father at all, as though he had not heard his father at all.

His father became even more anxious and asked, "Do you want to die? If so, then I'll happily accommodate you."

Kong Dongde went back into the house and walked around. When he reemerged, he was carrying a thin but strong rope. He took the stool on which he had been sitting and placed it under the pear tree with a trunk as large as a plate. He stood on the stool, tied the rope onto the highest and strongest branch of the tree, then tied the other end into a noose that was just the right size for a person's head. Next, he put his own head inside the noose to try it out and discovered that in the sunlight on the other side of the noose, all of the clouds were either square, rectangular, or circular, resembling gold bars, gold pieces, and silver dollars. He also saw some clouds that were as white as a young woman's face. He looked in surprise, then pulled his head out of the noose, whereupon all of the clouds reverted back to their former appearance. He put his head back into the noose, and once again the clouds resembled gold bars and gold ingots, and there were treelike clouds and shoe-shaped ingots and the faces of women and children. He said very solemnly to his son,

"You should go ahead and die. If you do, then you can have anything you want."

He got down off the stool, then proceeded to repeat that phrase. He walked over to Mingguang and said, "I've tied the noose for you and placed the stool beneath the tree. The fragrant smell of the pear tree is strong and fresh as the aroma of the cilantro-flavored fish soup Little Cui used to cook. All you have to do is stand on the stool, place your head inside the noose, then kick the stool away. You will then enjoy an existence of silver and gold, and every day you'll be able to enjoy the company of girls like Little Cui."

When Kong Dongde finished saying this, he headed toward the courtyard gate, as though he had already said what he needed to say and done what he needed to do. When he reached the entranceway, he looked back at the noose, then looked at his son, whose complexion was now the color of the eyes of a dead fish. Finally, he softly made a portentous statement:

"Do you know? Little Cui doesn't even like you. Do you know who she likes? Having been without a mother or father or grandparents since she was young, she has come to view me as her parents and grandparents. Did you know that?"

Mingguang's neck vertebrae produced a sound like stones grinding against each other, as he slowly turned to look at his father, who continued talking as he walked out. There appeared a flicker of light in his dull eyes.

"Before she left, she came to see me," his father continued. "She said you were suffocating her, which is why she had to leave. She said that once you and Qinfang were reconciled, she would return to Explosion."

After having said this, Kong Dongde sighed. His body suddenly felt much lighter, as though he were walking on air, and in this way he proceeded to walk out of the courtyard. After he left, he heard Mingguang crying behind him. When he turned around, he saw that his son was crying so hard that his body trembled like an animal on the verge of death.

5. BEETLES

The next day, as Kong Dongde was eating lunch, he smashed his bowl, as well as the pot he used to cook rice. He took down the clock hanging on the wall and threw it to the ground as well. His wife had told him that their son Mingguang, after a good night's sleep, had figured out what he needed to do. He decided that he would not go find Little Cui, but neither would he bring back Qinfang. Instead, he wanted to move out of Second Dog's house and return home to live by himself—to eat, teach, and be a good teacher. Kong Dongde stared at his wife for a long time, then asked her, "He didn't hang himself?"

His wife laughed and said, "Today, I should cook him a good meal."

Kong Dongde began to throw things, hitting and kicking the walls, and cursing. When he noticed the calendar with a picture of beauties, he ripped it off the wall and began stomping on it until each of the twelve calendar beauties was stomped into a ball of crumpled paper. Finally, exhausted, he sat down, and said,

"You know? I'm going to die soon."

His wife said, "Go see a doctor then."

"Go summon Zhu Ying and have her come see me."

His wife went out to find their daughter-in-law Zhu Ying and summon her back. The one place where Zhu Ying often went was a supermarket a short distance from Otherworldly Delights. She had opened that supermarket based on ones she had seen in the city, and it sold daily necessities, clothes, and food, as well as staples such as oil, salt, and soy sauce. Customers didn't need to go up to the counter to buy things but instead could go directly to the shelves and pick out what they needed. Customers were as numerous as grains of sand or piles of leaves. Kong Dongde's wife made her way through this crowd of people until she found Zhu Ying, who was in her office with the fan on, looking over some ledgers the store's accountant had sent her. When Zhu Ying saw her mother-in-law wiping sweat from her brow as she stood in front of her, she knew that things had come to a head.

This day had finally arrived.

Zhu Ying's mother-in-law said, "Return home quickly. Your father-in-law doesn't have long to live."

Zhu Ying pulled her mother-in-law over to the electric fan and poured her a glass of water.

"If he really does die, that actually wouldn't be a bad thing." Her mother-in-law drank some water, then added slowly, "If he were to die, I could then lead a real life."

Zhu Ying calmly prepared a washbasin for her mother-in-law so that she could wash her face, then the two of them returned home together. As they were crossing the streets of Explosion, Zhu Ying noticed that the clouds in the western portion of the sky suddenly resembled a funeral procession surrounded by onlookers. She noticed that all of the shoppers walking up and down the street were talking and shouting as though they were in an open-air performance. She also saw some people fighting and others crowded around watching, shouting, "Fight! Fight! You're not even bleeding yet!" Then, she led her mother-in-law into a calmer area, as they proceeded from the town streets into the old village alleys. In this way, they quickly returned home. When they arrived, they found that Kong Dongde's room was full of shattered dishes and shredded paper, as well as fruits and vegetables that had been stomped to a pulp.

Zhu Ying stood in the doorway and peered in, and saw her father-in-law sitting in the room like a marble statue. She then fixed her gaze on the back wall. There was a small yellow butterfly the size of a copper coin flying through the doorway, and it landed on the wall to rest. The sunlight streaming in shone down on the butterfly, so that its entire body appeared to be enveloped in a golden glow.

"What was so dire that got you this upset?" Zhu Ying asked with a laugh. She began picking up the shattered porcelain on the ground and sweeping it into a pile at the base of the wall. Then, she picked up the clock that had fallen from the wall and adjusted its batteries, so that it began running again. She said, "A clock is life, and if a clock stops working, a person will stop living." As she said this, she hung the clock back in its original position, then turned and saw that the butterfly had flown over and landed on her father-in-law's face, where it was now sitting motionless.

Zhu Ying said, "Father, look at your face."

Kong Dongde removed the butterfly from his face.

Zhu Ying said, "I hear that someone ran into Little Cui at the market."

Kong Dongde crushed the butterfly in his hand.

Zhu Ying said, "I simply can't see anything good about her. She can't even make dumplings."

Tears began running down Kong Dongde's face, like a small rivulet meandering through a dried-up field. At this point, Zhu Ying turned to her mother-in-law, who was still standing by the door, and said, "Don't worry. Father will improve. You should go to the market. Mingliang is about to become county mayor, and the people at the market will want to give you the best and freshest fish, meat, shrimp, and crabs they have. After you've selected what you want, you can bring it back and I'll cook Father a delicious meal." After her mother-in-law took a basket and left, only Zhu Ying and her father-in-law, Kong Dongde, were still in the house, together with the flowers growing out of the dry bark of the elm tree and the grass growing out of the cracks in the courtyard's cement floor, as well as the flock of sparrows and crows perched in the doorway to watch the commotion. The remains of the butterfly that had just been crushed were also lying on the ground, quietly weeping. At this point, the tears streaming down Kong Dongde's face finally flowed past its ridge-like creases, as his lips and entire body trembled so badly, they seemed about to fall apart. He looked at his daughter-in-law Zhu Ying standing in the doorway and said,

"Ying'er, I've let the Zhu family down!"

Zhu Ying stood there silently.

He suddenly slid off the stool and knelt down in front of her, saying,

"You should bring back Little Cui."

Zhu Ying stood there silently.

". . . I'm not a person, I'm just an animal!"

He knelt there, then hobbled over on his knees. Hugging her with both arms, he said, "I'm old, I'm old! Every night I miss Little Cui so much I can't even sleep. I miss her so much I grip my bed and the walls with both hands, and grip my own body so tightly that I'm soon covered in blood and bruises. I even want to get up in the middle of the night and hang myself." He wiped the tears from his face, rolled up his sleeve, then showed Zhu Ying the bruises from where he had gripped himself at night when unable to sleep. Then he rolled his sleeve down again and proceeded to kowtow to his daughter-in-law seven or eight times, saying in a hoarse voice, "Please return Little Cui to me! Please find Little Cui and return her to me!"

At this point, Zhu Ying, who was still standing there motionless, smiled darkly as tears streamed down her cheeks. She looked disdainfully at Kong Dongde but said very gently,

"Father, don't worry. I'll find Little Cui and bring her back. Otherwise, I'll find you a girl who is even better."

Around noon, as smoke was beginning to emerge from everyone's kitchen chimney, Zhu Ying had her father-in-law lie down on the bed, while she went into the kitchen and cooked him some steamed fish and turtle soup; made a casserole with mule meat, dog meat, and deer meat; and also brought him several glasses of Chinese liquor. She let him eat and drink leisurely, and afterward—when the village streets and alleys were virtually empty, and a flock of magpies had landed on the trees in the courtyard and were chirping noisily—Zhu Ying walked over to her father-in-law's bed, collected his dishes, then said very softly,

"Let's go. Let's go find Little Cui."

Kong Dongde gazed at her gratefully. He got down off the bed and changed his clothes, even standing in front of the mirror for a while looking at his reflection. Then, he followed Zhu Ying out of the room.

Kong Dongde's wife was outside and, when she saw that man with whom she had shared a life and raised four sons, she couldn't believe he was really her husband. He suddenly looked ten or twenty years younger, and his complexion was indistinguishable from that of someone in his prime. His face was flushed, and his cheeks glowed like those of a much younger man. His gaze appeared kind and cordial. His expression didn't seem at all hard or sluggish, and even his hair, which had been old and faded, now appeared jet-black. As he walked into the courtyard, Kong Dongde gazed at his wife, who was standing in the doorway. He then pulled out a bankbook he had been carrying around in his pocket all these years and stuffed it into his wife's hands. The bankbook had an astronomically large sum written on it, but he didn't utter the number out loud and instead said softly to his wife,

"I'm going with Zhu Ying to see the doctor."

In the courtyard, the magpies stopped producing their high-pitched cries like peacocks, and the sparrows on the ground stopped squawking and hopping around. The flowers blooming out of the elm tree bark had also disappeared. Everything had returned to the way it had been, and even the air grew still and no longer had that familiar late summer scent of dirt and sweat. They walked through the main gate, one after the other, and down the silent village street toward the tumultuous town. Kong Dongde's wife followed them out, and watched as her husband and daughter-in-law solemnly walked farther and farther away. She yelled out to them,

"I hope you die! I hope you die! I really do hope both of you die!"

The neighbors who were startled by her shouts all came over and asked cautiously,

"What happened?"

Kong Dongde's wife said, "The heavens are about to collapse. . . .

"He appears so young that no one even recognizes him. . . .

"The heavens are about to collapse," his wife repeated. "You just wait. The heavens are about to collapse."

Later, she watched as everyone drifted down the road and gradually disappeared from view.

Kong Dongde walked the town streets following behind Zhu Ying. As he walked, his face appeared flushed, and he made an effort not to look to either side, and didn't respond even if someone spoke to him. When he reached the entrance to Otherwordly Delights he had an odd layer of sweat on his brow, but otherwise he had managed to completely ignore all of the people, sights, questions, and comments he had passed in the street. The entrance to Otherworldly Delights was similar to that of the various hotels they had encountered, and initially nothing appeared out of the ordinary. The main lobby was also just like that of a hotel, with a crescent-shaped long, red table where young men and women were working as receptionists. When they saw Zhu Ying they immediately stood up and bowed, and addressed her as General Manager. Zhu Ying asked if everyone had come to work, and one of the managers nodded, whereupon Zhu Ying led her father-in-law inside. They walked down those long halls, and smelled the rich and fragrant cosmetics. When they reached the stairs, the fragrance became as strong as the smell of wheat during harvest season. As they were going upstairs, Zhu Ying reached out to caress her father-in-law, and felt his entire body tremble as though he were about to collapse. The beads of sweat on his brow, his cheeks, and his chin were larger than peanuts, and when each drop of sweat fell onto the stairs it made a thumping noise that was louder than a stone falling onto the surface of a drum. "Soon you'll be able to see Little Cui," she said. "Father, while you are here, you can do what you want with her. She will be as filial as if she were your own daughter." Then they reached the second floor, arriving at an open area covering half of the entire floor. There was a red carpet underfoot and a couch against the wall. Across from the couch there was a foot-tall wooden stage, as in a theater, and across the stage there was a curtain, as for an opera. The lights were dim and mysteriously red. Zhu Ying led her father-in-law over to the couch and sat down beside him. A young girl poured him a glass of ginseng water, and when Zhu Ying said, "Begin," the curtain onstage opened. Music poured out like water cascading down a waterfall. Suddenly, a spotlight shot out from midair, as bright as though you were to wake up and find the sun shining down directly on your pillow. There was thunder and lightning everywhere, and an earthquake shook the sofa, the walls, and the entire house, as though some machine were violently shaking the couch back and forth. The windows all rattled. At first, six naked girls emerged from behind the curtain, showed off their bodies, and proceeded to stand at the front of the stage. Kong Dongde watched them very attentively as Zhu Ying turned and asked, "Father, which of them do you like? They are all better than Little Cui." She saw her father-in-law sitting there speechless, his face pale and bathed in sweat. She then asked the girls to come to the very edge of the stage, whereupon another ten naked girls emerged from behind the curtain. They, too, proceeded to parade around slowly, showing off their faces, bodies, skin, and private parts. Zhu Ying again turned to Kong Dongde and asked, "What about these? Do you like any of them?" She sat back and summoned another eighteen girls, until the stage was completely full of naked girls, their white skin glittering like lightning and their fragrance surging forward like a flood. Their smiles were so seductive that they virtually made him pass out.

At this point, the music suddenly stopped, and an even brighter spotlight shone down from above. As a result, even from a distance it was possible to discern the color and complexion of the girls' skin, together with every individual pore. The stage became extremely still. All of the girls were watching Kong Dongde intently, as he blushed deeply and quickly looked away.

Zhu Ying asked, "Father . . . which of them do you like?"

She added, "They are all better than Little Cui."

Then she laughed and said, "Whether you want one or two, or even three or five, you can pick any of them you want. They are all yours, because they all belong to our Kong family." As she said this, she turned to Kong Dongde and saw that he had finally looked back at the stage, and his gaze quickly fell on those jade-like beauties, like a child who is permitted to pick any toy he wants from an enormous pile in front of him. His cheeks glowed with delight. With this, Zhu Ying saw that her plan had succeeded; her play had reached its climax and was rapidly approaching its conclusion.

CHAPTER 10
Structural Transformation

1. A DIFFICULT PATH

I.

As officials in the city were debating whether or not to elevate Explosion to the status of a county, Mingliang received the death notice from his family. The notice stated that his father had had a heart condition and had died while lying atop one of the girls at Otherworldly Delights. It was midsummer at the time, and both the town and the county mayors were staying in a hotel in the city. The hotel's luxuriousness was truly astounding, with silver inlaid tables and chairs plated in gold. The rug under their feet was made entirely from the hair of prepubescent girls, and embroidered in the center was a picture of a naked couple with blond and black hair, such that when you walked on it you could smell the sweet scent of a girl's skin and hair.

The hotel was enormous, but there was only one suite with this particular rug. When guests from lower-level work units, who lacked documentation from the higher-ups, wanted to stay for a night, they needed to reserve a room three years in advance, and had to pay more than half a *jin* of gold a night. At first, County Mayor Hu Dajun was strongly opposed to permitting the exceedingly rich Explosion to separate and establish itself as an independent county, because if it did Mayor Hu's own county would become proportionally smaller and the mayor's stature would consequently be diminished. However, after Mingliang reserved this suite and invited Mayor Hu to come stay for two nights, the mayor's attitude softened. He stayed for an additional two nights, and in the end he basically agreed with Mingliang's proposal. A couple of days later, Mayor Hu formally announced that after Explosion increased its population and the number of its factories, and also raised its profits and taxes, he would send the city the official notice that Explosion had been upgraded from a town to a county. Having now reached that specified target, Mayor Hu and Mingliang used a special car to deliver thirty boxes of documents, recordings, forms, and data to city hall, so that the city's political leaders might examine them. They waited in the hotel suite to hear of the city's response, until they were exceedingly anxious and Mingliang, sitting in one room drinking water, began turning the television on and off until he was tearing his hair out. The clock suddenly fell off the wall and onto the pillow at the head of the bed. Startled, Mingliang reached to pick it up, and his face became completely covered in sweat. He stood there in front of the bed for a while, and suddenly rushed into the room across the way, where Mayor Hu was staying, and blurted out,

"Bad news! My father has died!"

The mayor was sitting cross-legged on the rug, reading the newspaper. He stared, and asked with alarm,

"How do you know?"

"The clock fell off the wall. It didn't break, but now the hour and minute hands no longer move."

Mayor Hu put down his paper, placed his teacup on the table, then turned around. He saw Mingliang standing in the middle of the room, staring in shock, and asked him why he didn't go call his family to see if they were all right. It was only at that point that Mingliang finally snapped out of his stupor. He grabbed the phone in the mayor's room, dialed a number, and asked a few questions. He stood motionless next to the telephone, as his complexion turned first pale and then dark, dark red. As his face was going from red to black, he put the phone down and stood facing the window, watching as the birds in the courtyard continued to fly around and people continued to sweep up the fallen leaves and trash. His own gaze simply could not focus on the scene outside.

"What's wrong?" the mayor asked.

Mingliang smiled darkly. "The workings of heaven are not as important as transforming a town into a county."

"Is he really dead?"

"In transforming a town into a county, it's impossible to avoid losing a few lives."

"How did he die?"

"Mayor Hu," Mingliang said softly, gazing at the mayor's face. He paused, then said hesitantly, "After Explosion succeeds in being elevated from a town to a county, I want to give you ten percent of the county's income."

The mayor considered for a moment, then asked, "Aren't you going home for the funeral?"

"Even the largest private act of heaven is not as significant as the smallest public act, and the same applies to the death of a parent." Mingliang was still looking out the window, then added, "I want to go, but today the city just finished reviewing all of the documents, and what would happen if the city mayor needed to find me but I'm not here?"

Mayor Hu half-filled two teacups, handing one to Kong Ming-liang and taking the other for himself. They clinked cups, and Mayor Hu exclaimed, "If all of the county's town mayors were like you, the county would be in excellent hands! And if all of the nation's cadres were like you, the nation would be in excellent hands." He continued with a smile, "In light of the fact that, on account of your dedication to your work, you are not even returning home for your father's funeral, it would be a crime if you were not appointed county mayor after the town is redesignated as a county."

After clinking their cups again, they each took a sip of water and then looked at each other. Mingliang smiled and said,

"I asked a fortune-teller to tell me your fortune, and he predicted you would quickly be promoted to city mayor."

Mayor Hu laughed and said, "Your father's funeral should include all the trappings. I'd be happy to offer an elegy."

When Mingliang returned from Mayor Hu's room to his own, he was secretly grateful that his father had died at that precise moment. He stood there gazing at the stopped clock, then picked it up and shook it. After confirming that the clock's hands really had stopped, he hung the clock back on the wall. Having nothing else to do, he stood in his bedroom, then went to his living room and paced around. He opened the window and saw in front of him the several-dozen-story municipal government building, like a chopstick stuck in a sand table. He carefully counted how many floors the building had, and when he discovered it had sixty-eight, it occurred to him that after Explosion was promoted from a town to a county, he would first construct an eighty-six-story government building right in the middle of the county seat, such that after the county was redesignated as a city, the building would appear neither small nor out-of-date. As he was standing in front of the window thinking about the eighty-six-story building he was going to erect, he noticed that, off in the distance, a window on the sixty-sixth floor was open. The city mayor's face appeared as small as an apple, and he smiled as he leaned out of that window and waved at Mingliang, urging him and the county mayor to hurry up and come over. Mingliang quickly waved back, closed the window, then went to urge Mayor Hu to go with him to the city mayor's office.

They left the hotel and took a taxi, passing through three small districts. After many twists and turns, they finally arrived at the back of the city government building, where they had to fill out endless paperwork, and only then could Mingliang and Mayor Hu proceed inside, where the city mayor was examining many graphs and tables that had been submitted by Explosion. The city mayor was the former county mayor, back when Mayor Hu was still town mayor and Mingliang was still village chief. The city mayor recognized them immediately—his memory being as fresh as the morning sun and as beautiful as a fresh flower. They reminisced about the past and drank some water. Eventually the city mayor, upon noticing Mingliang's excited expression, said, "I know that you're so dedicated to your work that you didn't immediately return home for your own father's funeral. Based on this, in principle I'm willing to support Explosion's application to be elevated from a town to a county."

Mingliang was on the verge of tears.

The city mayor looked over at Mayor Hu and asked, "Have you decided whom you will appoint to be Explosion's new county mayor?"

Mingliang's heart skipped a beat. He turned toward Mayor Hu, his pleading eyes resembling the morning mist along the mountain ridge.

But just as Mayor Hu was about to respond, the city mayor laughed and said, "I actually don't think you should select anyone. Why don't you just promote comrade Mingliang directly from his current position as town mayor to county mayor?" Mingliang watched

Yan Lianke

in relief as Mayor Hu smiled and nodded, then took another sip of the water the city mayor had offered him. As Mingliang was about to refill the city mayor's glass, he noticed that the red hands of the square clock hanging on the wall behind the city mayor were moving very sluggishly and looked as though they were about to stop altogether. At that point, Mingliang's hand paused in midair. He turned again to Mayor Hu and signaled for him to look at the city mayor's clock. He watched as Mayor Hu looked up at the clock. Mingliang clearly saw how with each revolution it appeared as though the clock's second hand were struggling up a steep flight of steps, and sometimes it would fall back down. Mayor Hu, however, appeared as though he hadn't noticed a thing and, face aglow with pleasure, he continued talking to the city mayor as before.

Mayor Hu said, "During these years of deep-level reform, the county has been doing very well."

The city mayor said, "We should grasp this opportunity and follow the tide of the era."

Mayor Hu said, "Come what may, I will follow your instructions. Whatever objective you specify, I swear I'll do everything in my power to make sure our reform attains it."

The city mayor laughed and said, "We should all follow the central directives. We're here merely to implement these central policy directives."

They both laughed. It was then that the second hand of the clock on the wall behind the city mayor finally stopped altogether. Mingliang stared at that red second hand that was stuck between 7 and 8. His face went pale, as sweat covered his forehead. Eventually, he couldn't resist taking a step forward and, inserting himself into the conversation between Mayor Hu and the city mayor, he quietly told the city mayor,

"Mayor, the battery of the clock on your wall needs to be changed."

208

The mayor turned and looked, then turned back to Mayor Hu and asked nonchalantly, "Which liquor do you want to drink today?"

"The best."

At this point, Mingliang realized that not only was the clock's second hand stopped at 7 but—like someone who has climbed halfway up a tree and then starts to slide back down—it suddenly trembled and retreated toward 6. As the second hand moved backward, Mingliang heard a sound that resembled a meteorite falling to the ground. There was a flash before his eyes, a buzz in his brain, and he immediately ran shouting out of the city mayor's office.

"The mayor's second hand has stopped. Quick, give him a new battery! . . .

". . . The mayor's second hand has stopped. Quick, give him a new battery!"

Shouting, he ran through the hallway of the sixty-sixth floor of the city government's administrative building. He sounded anxious, as though some boulders were about to roll down the mountain and crush someone. When the deputy city mayor and the party secretary, not to mention all of the cadres and workers on that floor, heard him, they rushed out of their offices and stood in the hallway staring at him. After the city mayor finally realized why Mingliang was crazily running around and shouting, he emotionally uttered a single sentence:

"All my life, I've been searching for such a loyal underling!"

II.

Walking side by side, the county and town mayors emerged from the city mayor's office, and when they reached the ground floor, Mayor Hu leaned toward Mingliang's ear and whispered, "Kong Mingliang, you're truly a motherfucker!"

As they exited the courtyard of the city office building and reached the main gate, Mayor Hu turned again to Mingliang and said in a voice that was neither particularly loud nor particularly soft, "Kong Mingliang, your father is already dead. Why doesn't your mother hurry up and die as well?"

When they reached the hotel and were about to return to their respective rooms, Mayor Hu shouted down the hallway, "Kong Mingliang . . . you and the rest of your family should simply die . . . don't assume that just because the city mayor has agreed to permit Explosion to become a county, that means it will automatically become a county. Furthermore, don't assume that just because the city mayor has said that you can become county mayor, that you'll automatically become county mayor. Don't try to accomplish things by going behind my back. I have my eye on you."

Mingliang had no idea why Mayor Hu was so furious, to the point of cursing Mingliang's own parents. In order to get to the bottom of this, Mingliang poured Mayor Hu a cup of hot water, washed his clothes, squeezed his toothpaste, polished his shoes, and even picked up the tissue the mayor had used to wipe his mouth and tossed it into the waste basket. But the county mayor still didn't tell him why he was so angry. It was not until they had returned to the county seat, and their car passed through the development zone, business street, public square, and gymnasium, together with the newly built hospital, funeral home, hotel, and children's amusement park, and as Mingliang was carrying Mayor Hu's luggage and escorting him home—only then did Mayor Hu turn to him and remark rather obliquely, "When you get home to bury your father, think carefully about this."

Mayor Hu lived in a garden in the center of the city. He didn't allow Mingliang to escort him back to his house and instead stopped Mingliang at the entrance to the garden, saying, "Your father has been lying in your home for three days waiting for you to bury him. You should go take care of his funeral arrangements." Mingliang insisted on escorting Mayor Hu to his home and made a point of not giving the mayor his luggage. "If you don't tell me why you're angry, I won't leave. I won't leave even if my life depends on it!" He obstinately followed behind Mayor Hu until they reached the entrance to the courtyard of the mayor's house, where he continued to whisper fiercely, "Mayor Hu, if you don't tell me why you're angry, then I won't leave even if my life depends on it." As they entered the house, he lowered his voice even further and said, "If you want to see me as your underling, your brother, your soldier, then you have to tell me why you're so angry." When they entered Mayor Hu's living room, which was somewhat smaller than an assembly hall, a soldier came to get his luggage and quickly helped Mayor Hu change his shoes, then served him some tea. He also turned on the air-conditioning and brought out a basin for Mayor Hu to wash his face. As the soldier was doing this, Mingliang said in an even softer voice,

"If you don't tell me, I'll kneel down before you.

"Mayor Hu, don't you believe I'm willing to kneel down in front of you?

". . . Not only will I kneel down in front of you, I'll continue kneeling here until I die."

Just as Kong Mingliang was preparing to kneel down, both the hour and the minute hands of the clock on the wall of Mayor Hu's living room reached 12:00, and inside that oval mahogany frame, the clock struck twelve. The sound was bright and brittle, like that of clocks and wooden fish in temples and monasteries. Seeming to realize something, Kong Mingliang looked at the clock, as if searching for the origin of that sound, his expression resembling a ray of sunlight shining through the clouds. Mayor Hu put on some slippers and came over. Staring at Mingliang, he laughed coldly and said,

"Don't worry. The clocks in my house will keep running for at least another hundred years." Mingliang looked at Mayor Hu, then back at that clock, as his rigid expression began to relax. With an expression of regret, he watched as Mayor Hu walked over and sat on the sofa beneath the clock, then lightly slapped his own face.

"I've figured it out," Mingliang told Mayor Hu. He slapped his face again, this time more forcefully. "The batteries of the city mayor's clock are dead, but I actually shouldn't have reminded him that he should change them so that the clock could keep running uninterrupted." As Mingliang was saying this, he plopped himself down in a seat across from Mayor Hu, as though he were about to throw himself out of there. "If the mayor's clock stops running, he will probably get sick and have to go to the hospital. And if he goes to the hospital, that will mean his illness will be difficult to cure—and if he develops an incurable illness, then his position would become available."

Upon saying this, Kong Mingliang looked at Mayor Hu regretfully. "I really do have a pig brain!" He lightly tapped his foot on the ground, then continued. "If the city mayor dies from his illness, won't it be your turn to be mayor? And if you are mayor, won't it be entirely your decision whether or not Explosion is elevated from a county to a city?!" He didn't say anything more and instead just watched Mayor Hu sigh, as though he had succeeded in bringing an enemy's dead horse back to life, only to have that same horse kick him in the leg and kill him. Mingliang sat several meters away from Mayor Hu, as though waiting for the mayor to forgive him.

But Mayor Hu didn't say anything. He was like a character in a film, sipping his freshly steeped tea and using the lid of the cup to push aside the tea leaves that were floating on top. After blowing the hot tea a couple of times, he suddenly put the cup down and said softly,

"You were originally one of the city mayor's people. It is only natural that you would be loyal to him."

Mingliang knelt down and said, "Mayor Hu, even if you beat me, I'd still be your man."

Mayor Hu asked, "Can you offer any proof?"

Mingliang pondered for a long time and finally said, "How about this? Mayor Hu, I know that the entire country is currently undergoing a major reform in funeral practices, and demands that after people die they should be cremated and have their ashes stored in an urn. I also know you recently constructed a new funeral home and crematorium for the whole county, but so far there hasn't been anyone willing to be cremated there. Beginning with me, which is to say beginning with my Kong family, in order to prove that I am yours, and that I will follow you in life and in death, I will bring over my father's body for cremation—making him the first person in the entire county to be voluntarily cremated."

Mayor Hu stared at Mingliang.

"If a town mayor sends his own father to be cremated," Mingliang said, "then surely the crematorium's business will gradually improve."

Mayor Hu continued staring at Mingliang. The clock on the wall chimed again, like the sound of a wooden fish in an old temple or monastery. The sound drifted over from a distance, but as soon as people heard it they would quickly understand everything that was happening in the world.

2. AGONY

I.

When Kong Mingyao rushed back from the military barracks to handle his father's funeral arrangements, he took a car down from the mountain ridge. Standing on the ridge, he was astounded by the change Explosion had undergone. Believing that he must have gotten off at the wrong stop, he turned to the car, which was driving away, and shouted, "Stop, come back!" But the car had already disappeared in a cloud of smoke. He stood there and stared, until he finally noticed the enormous stele that had been erected in the middle of the square in his sister-in-law's honor, and it was only then he realized that the thriving metropolis in front of him was in fact Explosion. Because he had been focusing on his regiment, he almost couldn't remember how many years it had been since he last returned home. The last time had been in order to help elect his brother as village chief, while now not only was his brother town mayor, he was about to become county mayor. Mingyao stood in an open area on the mountain ridge, gazing at the town's houses, bridges, alleys, and factories, and the crowds of people along both sides of the river. Just as he was standing there at a loss as to what to do, his sister-in-law Zhu Ying, with a combination of happiness and sadness, walked onto one of the old roads to meet him. It was dusk, and in the light of the setting sun, the clouds became gold nuggets, gold bars, and shiny gold coins, though the elm and pagoda trees lining the road were all blooming with enormous black flowers that had blossomed after his father's death. In the light of the setting sun, those black blossoms shone with a doleful glow. Zhu Ying approached Mingyao, and when she was in front of him she asked him balefully,

"Third Brother, you've returned?"

Mingyao stared in surprise at the town of Explosion at the base of the mountain and eventually asked in surprise,

"Sister, is this really Explosion?"

"Father died from a heart attack," Zhu Ying said. "He died while in bed with a girl."

Mingyao looked up at black flowers blooming on the elm and Chinese toon trees lining the road, then stared at his sister-in-law and asked, "What about Second Brother?"

"In a few days, each of you will receive an inheritance from your father. I've discussed this with your elder brother, and as long as you don't interfere with your father's cremation, our hundreds of thousands of yuan will go to you."

Mingyao was even more astonished that his sister-in-law would refer so casually to hundreds of thousands of yuan, and that she would offer to give him all of that money. As he was following Zhu Ying back to the village, he asked slowly, "Do each of the four brothers get several hundred thousand yuan?"

Zhu Ying said, "Your elder brother is about to become county mayor. Now that your father has died, all of the county's residents should take the opportunity to bring the Kong family gifts."

Mingyao therefore began to look forward to the funeral arrangements.

During the process, Kong Dongde's corpse sat out for seven days, as the arrangements were conducted in a frenzied manner. There were twenty tons of ice just to keep the corpse fresh. In Explosion's main square, the family erected an enormous mourning shed and an accountant's room. Everyone knew that the mayor's father had died saving a girl working in Explosion. A truck carrying ore had been driving down from the mountain ridge, and it ran over a girl who had just gotten off work. The mayor's father rescued her, but in the excitement he had a heart attack. Before he died, however, his final words were that he wanted to be sent to the newly constructed crematorium and be cremated according to the new custom. Furthermore, after he died, his son, the mayor, was in the city and was so busy helping make the town more prosperous that he completely lost track of time. This incident was written up by Yang Baoqing, who at the time worked in the town's news processing plant but now served as the town cadre in charge of propaganda. The article was published in the newspapers and broadcast on television, and everyone who read or heard it was profoundly moved. People delivering wreaths were as numerous as butterflies and dragonflies around a pond in the summer. All of Explosion's stores, restaurants, and department stores, and all sorts of other shops, closed for three days and hung enormous wreaths on their front doors. The wreaths, in turn, attracted dense clouds of butterflies, which filled the streets and alleys of Explosion for seven days. People traveling from hundreds of *li* away to offer gifts, those people working in the mines and the factories, and those who were doing different jobs in Explosion all donated offerings ranging from hundreds of thousands of yuan to small gifts such as eggs, pillowcases, sheets, and rugs—so that the funeral accountant had to work through the night recording and tabulating everything. In order to give the mayor's father a funerary gift, people lined up over three days from the streets of Explosion all the way to the top of the mountain ridge. Even those Japanese, Koreans, Americans, and Europeans working in Explosion's mines and factories followed its customs and offered the family of the deceased a red envelope stuffed with cash.

In accordance with contemporary practice, after sending the old man's body to the county seat to be cremated, the family placed the urn containing his ashes inside a coffin and then buried it, after which Explosion regained its former order and liveliness. The Kong family also regained a sense of peace that it had not had for years. After the funeral, it was customary to hold a family meeting, but because Mingliang was so busy with work, he made only a brief appearance at the memorial service itself and then disappeared again, having rushed back to the county seat to see the county mayor. Zhu

Ying similarly disappeared after the funeral and didn't even attend the family meeting to discuss how to distribute the hundreds of thousands of yuan they received in funerary gifts.

In this way, the family fell apart.

After everyone left, only Kong Mingguang, Kong Mingyao, and Kong Minghui remained in the Kong household. Kong Mingyao, apart from having a dozen pimples and wearing a crisp military uniform, looked exhausted and depleted. In the army, he was always as busy as a mule pulling a millstone round and round but in the end never managed to produce any flour. He could not serve as a military official or as a hero. Instead, empty-handed, he sat in the family meeting like an ordinary person in a crowd of ordinary people. The mother sat next to her three sons, boiling them water and bringing them peanuts and walnuts. To encourage them to eat, she even shelled the peanuts and placed them in a bowl. She also cracked open the walnuts and placed them in another bowl. After each bowl was full of nuts, she placed them on the table in front of her sons. On the table were also the accounts and receipts for all of the presents that Kong Dongde received after his death. In the account book there were precisely two million yuan, meaning that each of the four sons would receive five hundred thousand. There were also several storerooms full of condolence gifts people had sent, so many that each of the four sons could have one roomful. Kong Dongde's funeral portrait was sitting on a table in the room. The image appeared warm and kind, and smiled as it gazed out at everyone. The room, meanwhile, was warm and quiet, like Kong Dongde's face in the funeral portrait. A fly landed on the portrait and left some droppings, then flew to where the three brothers were sitting. At that point, Mingyao looked at his two brothers and said,

"Let's split up the family."

Mingguang and Minghui looked at Mingyao without saying a word.

"Second Brother and Second Sister-in-Law said that they wanted to give me their portion of the inheritance." As Mingyao said this, he took out a sheet of paper, explaining that Zhu Ying had written that she was afraid he would prevent their father from being cremated, which is why she had decided to give Mingyao her portion. Mingyao took several sips of water, then added, "Also, when Second Brother was about to be elected village chief, I brought a gun back from the army and gave him a military salute. If at that time he hadn't been elected village chief, how would he have been later appointed town mayor? And if he hadn't been appointed town mayor, how would he have later been promoted to county mayor?" The implication was that Mingliang's current position was entirely thanks to Mingyao's initial assistance, and in giving Mingyao everything he owned, Mingliang was also thanking him. Finally, Mingyao fixed his gaze on Mingguang and asked with a smile,

"Brother, do you also want your portion?"

Mingguang replied, "Is this how the family is going to be split up?"

Mingyao then turned to Minghui and asked, "Fourth Brother, do you want yours?"

"Where did Second Sister-in-Law go?" Minghui quietly asked Mingyao, then looked to their mother. He noticed that she was no longer shelling peanuts and walnuts but rather simply sitting there staring into space, as though she didn't even know these sons of hers. Her face was pale and her lips were dry and cracked. "Is the family going to split up?" When she asked her sons, they stared at her in surprise. Mingyao abruptly smiled in recognition, as he shifted his gaze from his mother's body to his elder brother's face. He then looked at his younger brother and announced loudly,

"That's right. Our family is going to split up. After all, there has never been a family that did not ultimately break up."

Upon saying this, he looked at his brothers, then turned back to his mother and saw that she was crying. He then turned to the picture of his father, and in a moment of deathly silence, he heard his father shouting inside the portrait,

"Don't split up the family . . . I'm begging you!

". . . Don't split up the family . . . I'm begging you!"

II.

At the end of the third seven-day mourning period following their father's death, the Kong brothers originally should have gone to his grave to burn paper money and incense. But on this particular day, when the sun was in the western sky, Minghui walked out of the town government building and, not wanting to see or speak to anyone, he looped around beyond the town's streets, the village, and the river. Avoiding the stream of workers leaving the factories along the two mountain ranges, he proceeded to a remote location in the back of the mountain ridge. The sound of explosions from the distant mines reverberated through the evening, and then there was a deathly silence. The setting sun burst into a pool of bloodred water. An enormous ball of red exploded out of the sky. The trees turned red, as though they were full of blood flowers. The songs of the birds also turned red, and the path back to their nests was covered in their feathers. A wild hare looked fearfully at the clouds of dust and exclaimed, "Heavens!" and then began running back to the village. The grass seeds were frightened by the explosions and entered the birds' stomachs, while the flowers and leaves were shaken down by the explosions and hid in the mouths of the cattle and sheep. Minghui stood in that silence following the explosion, then began walking toward the grave. On the way, he encountered red air, filthy spring water, terrified moths, and sick ants foaming at the mouth. There was also a homeless dog that was so parched that it seemed to be on the verge of death. The dog followed after him. He gave it some water, and after he found it some food, he proceeded to the grave, while the dog waited for him on the mountain ridge. By this point it was already mid-autumn, and many plants and flowers had already begun to dry up and turn yellow. The Kong family's hundreds of graves were covered in gray thatch and wormwood. Minghui saw his father's grave from far away—a pile of fresh dirt and a paper wreath lying on the ground. He saw his father sitting inside that wreath waiting for him, his face sallow and sickly. "I'm in pain . . . I'm in pain!" Minghui heard these soft cries coming from his father's grave. In the end, however, he didn't walk over to the grave. He suddenly had a strange sense of terror and anxiety. In principle, on this day of the sacrificial offerings at the end of the third seven-day mourning period, the brothers and their wives should have taken their firecrackers and offerings, laid them out in front of the grave, burned incense, then kowtowed and wept loudly and exclaimed that the dead had left the living in a state of loneliness, longing, and agony. Those who couldn't cry simply knelt there and kowtowed toward the grave, silently opening their hearts to the yellow earth. At this point, the ones who were weeping may have stopped, or perhaps they may have begun weeping even more fervently at the urging of others. Minghui was about to go weep at his father's grave. There was a lot he wanted to tell his father, including how he and his three brothers had decided to split up the family, and how his eldest brother was now using his portion of the money to buy a set of new houses in the town's development zone. Mingyao received both his portion and that of Mingliang, and decided to use it to start a business, so that he would become an influential personage like Mingliang. As for why Mingliang and his wife didn't want their portion of the inheritance, and instead gave it all to Mingyao—for that he had no explanation.

Mingliang was very busy and didn't even have time to return home for his father's burial, and Zhu Ying also left before the burial. Mingguang and Qinfang got divorced, and there was an enormous distance separating the two of them, though Minghui didn't really know why this was. Minghui wanted to kneel down in front of his father's grave on the last day of the third seven-day mourning period and tell his father these things. Neither Mingguang nor Mingliang came to pay his respects, and Mingyao took a large wad of cash back to his military regiment. While Minghui thought that he would have a chance to see Mingguang, Mingliang, and Zhu Ying at his father's grave, none of them came. Minghui realized that after their father's death, the Kong family would topple like a tree or a building. Many years earlier, when the family had been so poor that they couldn't even afford salt to cook their rice, they remained completely upright. Now, Mingliang was about to be become county mayor and Mingguang was apparently about to be promoted to school principal. Originally Mingguang had aspired merely to become a model teacher, but with a single telephone call Mingliang had arranged for Mingguang to be not only a model teacher but also school principal. As for Mingyao, he also had gone crazy in pursuit of money. But as a result, the family collapsed, to the point that no one came to pay respects and burn incense at the end of the third seven-day mourning period. As Minghui sat under the setting sun in an open area several dozen meters from his father's new grave, he suddenly heard the sound of ripping cloth. The summer warmth and heat were circulating and piling up around him. Several ladybugs climbed on a blade of grass in front of him, but the black dots on their bodies had disappeared and been replaced by red dots, as though several drops of blood had fallen on the grass. Minghui looked up from those blood-like dots and shouted into the mountain ridge, "Aren't you coming? Aren't you coming?" When the dog heard

Minghui's voice, it began walking slowly toward the grass in the middle of the grave.

Minghui no longer had any hope that his brothers and sister-in-law would join him at the grave. When he remembered what Eldest Brother and Second Brother had said after their father's death, his heart lurched with pain. Mingguang had said, "Father is a pig. How else could he have died while lying on a woman?" Mingliang, meanwhile, had looked over at their father lying in his coffin, then kicked the coffin and said, "Let's cremate you. That way, we can be counted as supporting the county mayor's directive on cremations." Mingguang had said, "Cremation is good. If we burn the corpse, my heart will also be purified."

The family transported the father's body from Explosion to the county seat's new crematorium. In order to celebrate the arrival of the first corpse to be cremated voluntarily, the crematorium was decorated with fresh flowers and banners, and there was frenetic drumming as though it were a holiday. Afterward, they pushed their father's body into the oven, and then deposited the ashes in an urn, which they placed inside a coffin. Mingliang took the lead in writing an article about his father's cremation and printed it in a prominent location in the county, city, and provincial newspapers. The television stations repeatedly broadcast this news, as excitedly as though they were frying beans in a pot. Newspapers even printed the father's photograph, saying that before his death he managed to rescue someone who had come to Explosion to work, while after his death he became the first person to offer himself on behalf of the new directive encouraging cremations.

Seeing those newspaper articles and photographs, Mingliang laughed and tossed the newspaper aside. Mingguang looked it over as well, then spat on it—but from the spittle on the newspaper a seed formed and grew into a red apricot tree full of mangoes and pomegranates.

An icy breeze blew in from somewhere, and the ladybugs that had been crawling in front of Minghui turned into dragonflies and flew away. It looked as though it were about to rain. Minghui gazed at the setting sun, which was obscured by clouds, and then at his father's portrait in the middle of the funeral wreath. The portrait was being licked by that dog—so that after the father's corpse had been cremated and his face had been reduced to ashes, the portrait was moistened by the dog's licking, as though the pain of being cremated was being washed away from his face and body. Finally, Minghui walked over toward his father's grave, where he kowtowed three times and heard his father say,

"Go home. It is about to rain."

In the rain, Minghui left the grave and slowly made his way home.

CHAPTER 11

Assessment of the New Era

1. ASSESSMENT

I.

When Mingliang found Zhu Ying in her house, he noticed that the former globe-trotter now resembled a peasant who had never left the confines of her own house. Her courtyard and the table in her entranceway were filled with her father's funereal portraits and tributes. In front of every portrait, there were three incense sticks, each as thick as a man's arm; and on either side there were a pair of red couplets. The upper couplet read, "It's not that there isn't karma, it just isn't time yet," while the lower one read, "When the time comes, karma will kick in." Inside, the room was full of smoke, and there was quiet music playing, as if a summer stream and evening breeze were circulating throughout the Zhu household. From the day of Kong Dongde's death, Zhu Ying had closed her outer gates. She would occasionally go to this memorial table to replace the incense sticks in front of her father's portrait, and would pour three glasses of wine and kowtow as she offered the wine to the portrait, saying, "Your daughter has already done everything that needed to be done. You can therefore rest in peace." She would then proceed to the next portrait, replace the incense sticks, pour some wine and sprinkle it in front of the portrait, and say, "Father, that bastard Kong Dongde is dead, and everyone in the village—and even the entire town—knows he died while lying on a woman. They all spat at him behind his back, to the point that his entire body is now soaked in spittle."

For seven days, Zhu Ying almost didn't have a chance to close her eyes. The outer gates to her house remained tightly shut, and no one in the entire town knew where she was, or that she was in fact at home doing these things. It was not until the evening of the seventh day, after Kong Dongde's ashes had been buried, that Zhu Ying—who was dozing off in a chair in her courtyard—suddenly opened her eyes and saw Kong Mingliang standing in front of her. He had a disdainful and mocking expression, as though he were watching a child at play.

She glanced at the front gate, which remained tightly shut, and asked, "How did you get in?"

Kong Mingliang laughed coldly and said, "I hope you're satisfied now."

"Has the town been redesignated as a county?"

"I've come to tell you that in a few days you and I will be divorced." Mingliang sat down in front of her and glanced at the funeral portraits and tributes, then waved away the incense smoke. He laughed and continued, "It was on account of the Kong family that your father drowned in spittle, and it was on account of your

Zhu family that my father was completely covered in spittle after his death. In this way, our fates have now been settled, and there is nothing left for us to discuss."

After he said this, dusk fell. The entire courtyard and house were filled with a sorrowful evening light. There were mosquitoes flying around, but because of the dense smoke they didn't land on anyone, and the sound of their buzzing filled the air. The area next door to where the Explosion Village committee had been located had now been bought up by a vegetable oil company. More specifically, the company extracted oil from sesame and peanuts, then converted it into rubber and water to make leather belts, and into paste to make rubber soles. One *jin* of sesame seeds could yield three *jin* of oil, while one *jin* of peanuts could yield three and a half *jin* of oil. Business was good, and soon the two-story building was expanded to three stories. All four sides of the building were encased in brown glass, and when the setting sun shone on the building it looked like a flaming torch. Beneath that torch, Zhu Ying's house remained brightly illuminated without her even needing to turn on any lamps. Under that light, she saw that Mingliang was holding a set of blueprints for Explosion County. She leaned toward him and said very gently,

"I've done everything I was supposed to do. All that remains is to serve as your wife and help you succeed in becoming county mayor."

Then she asked, "Have you stopped to consider how you'll be promoted to county mayor if you divorce me?"

She laughed and added, "No man can stay away from Otherworldly. Without my Otherwordly Delights, Explosion would never be upgraded to a county, and you could forget about being promoted to county mayor."

Then night fell, and it became so dark that it seemed as though the entire world had disappeared. Kong Mingliang also disappeared like a shadow.

II.

By the evening of the final day of the third seven-day cycle following Kong Dongde's death, Zhu Ying finally emerged from her house. She was pale and gaunt, and suddenly had two streaks of gray in her hair. By this point she was thirtysomething but looked as though she were already in her forties. Her face's former radiance had almost completely disappeared. In town, people who knew her took a few steps back in surprise when they saw her. They stood there by the side of the road, with their mouths wide open but unable to say a word. She looked at one person and smiled, and only then did he nod back at her. She asked, "Have you eaten?" or "Has your business taken off?" But the other person merely muttered, "Yeah, yeah," and immediately dashed off to do something else.

She shouted in surprise, "Don't you recognize me?"

The other person froze and replied with a laugh, "You do look familiar, but I can't quite place you."

She shouted, "I'm the mayor's wife, and the owner of Otherworldly Delights. Don't you know me?"

The other person immediately wiped away his smile and scurried away. With this, Zhu Ying realized that the people of Explosion didn't even recognize her. At first she was confused, but then she rushed along the bustling street. She half-walked and half-ran, and from a distance she could see that Otherworldly Delights was empty and peaceful, and she saw that the light-box sign in front of the entrance had disappeared. On the door, there was an enormous sheet of white paper with a giant "X" written on it. The ground was covered with shattered glass, rusted barbed wire, and discarded glue bottles that had been used when the door was sealed shut. She ran to the sealed door and stood there, her face suddenly covered in sweat. A car drove up behind her, and some people buying and selling goods in the market darted into and out of her line of sight. Water, used by several restaurants to wash their vegetables and rinse their rice, flowed out of a drain at the base of the wall across the street from Otherworldly Delights, as it had in the past. The sun was already well into the western sky and the people who had come into town for the market began packing their things to head home again. After standing before the front door for a while, Zhu Ying proceeded around to the back door, where she saw that the old doorkeeper was in the process of moving all of the courtyard's tables and chairs and placing them in a corner next to the wall.

"What's wrong? What happened to Otherworldly Delights?" she asked. When the doorkeeper heard her, he spun around and the two wooden chairs he was holding fell to the ground.

"Are you Zhu Ying? You've returned!"

Exhausted, the old man took a couple of steps forward and stood in front of her. In a voice as hoarse as tree bark, he told her that three days earlier the mayor had personally brought some people over, who then proceeded to demolish Otherworldly Delights' business. They beat the girls who worked there and drove them away, and then the mayor had stood on the second floor where his father had died and announced,

"Father, I've destroyed Otherwordly Delights. From this point on, Zhu Ying is no longer the wife of the town or county mayor. Instead, I, Kong Mingliang, hereby express my filial devotion to you." The old man reported that after Mingliang finished making this announcement, he proceeded to spit several times in the direction of the selection stage and repeatedly kicked the row of couches. He ordered that those couches, where countless customers had sat, be taken away, to be either dismantled or burned. With this, the mayor angrily stalked away. The old doorman followed behind Zhu Ying as he was recounting all of this. They walked one behind the other, and after the old man finished his report he ran to catch up with Zhu Ying and asked,

"Is it true that the mayor divorced you?

". . . Look at how after you spoke of getting divorced you became so thin that we almost don't recognize you. Are you really the same Zhu Ying?

". . . If you haven't already gotten divorced, then you definitely shouldn't get divorced now," the old man urged her. "He'll be promoted to county mayor in a few days, and as long as you don't get divorced, you will still officially be his wife, meaning that you will be one of the most powerful people in the county." The old man proceeded from the first to the second floor, where sunlight was streaming in through the ripped curtain. He rested for a moment in the hallway, in the stairwell, and in the door that kept opening and closing. In just a few days, countless weeds had sprouted on the floor of this previously bustling building. Cobwebs in the corner of the room happily stretched over an area the size of a tatami mat, while in the washrooms that the girls and their clients had used there were now tiny fish and shrimp in the porcelain sinks and everywhere else where there was standing water. Meanwhile, the places where there had been no standing water were now overgrown with weeds, since everything was so humid and fertile. There were even bonsai plants in some of the toilet bowls, and their leaves and branches had grown so fast that they almost blocked the light coming in through the windows. A cricket crawled onto her foot, chirping loudly, and then started to crawl up her pants leg, whereupon she kicked it away. In one luxurious guest room there was an enormous, round water bed, which had been warm in winter and cool in summer, and girls and their rich clients would lie on the bed, feeling as though they were sleeping on a cloud. Although there was no longer anyone around to sleep on the water bed, it was still plugged in and the water was completely frozen, so that now it was like a huge black ice cube sitting in the middle of the room. When people approached the doorway they would feel a bitterly cold breeze. Because it was so cold, even the water faucets had frozen, and the liquid soap and shampoo in the bathroom had also frozen solid. Zhu Ying stood there trembling from head to toe. The old man went inside and struck the frozen water bed with a brick of frozen soap, as though he were striking one stone with another.

When Zhu Ying reached the stage on the second floor, she saw that the wooden stage had been completely destroyed. The curtains had been ripped down. Behind the stage, the dress racks the girls used when they were changing were strewn around, like a grove of trees that had been chopped down. The wardrobes lined up against the wall like people lined up in a bathhouse were empty, and the girls' clothes, dresses, bras, and underwear were strewn across the floor. Needless to say, as the girls were up onstage performing naked, the town mayor—who was about to be promoted to county mayor—had rushed in with the police, and the girls and their clients must have been as startled as a flock of sheep suddenly encountering a pack of wolves. At first they must have stared in shock, and then they must have run away, leaving their purses scattered across the floor, like pumpkins scattered across the stage. Their makeup kits had fallen out of their purses, and from each of them countless roses were blooming. Unfortunately, because the roses hadn't had any water or sunlight, the petals had fallen off and begun to rot. Zhu Ying smelled the stench of rotting grass and flower petals. She stood in front of the mess onstage and noticed a condom peeking out of one of the purses. Inside the condom several tadpoles had grown, but they had died from lack of water and their shriveled bodies were lying in the opening of the condom, like so many beans. When Zhu Ying saw all that death her eyes filled with tears, but before the tears dropped she quickly wiped her face with her hand. Then she suddenly shouted in the direction of the stage,

"I, Manager Zhu of Otherwordly Delights, am still the mayor's wife!

". . . I want all of you to remember that I, Manager Zhu of Otherwordly Delights, am still the mayor's wife!"

After shouting this a couple of times at the top of her lungs, she turned around on the stage and screamed even more loudly in the direction of where customers used to sit when making their selections. "When Explosion becomes a county and Kong Mingliang is appointed the new county mayor, he mustn't dream of discarding me. Even after he is promoted to city mayor or emperor, he will still be my husband, and no one should even think of trying to take him from me. . . ."

After screaming crazily from the stage, Zhu Ying turned again and began yelling in the direction of the streets of Explosion. She shouted in the direction of Explosion's town hall to the south, and in the direction of the factories and coal mines on the outskirts of town. Eventually, her voice grew hoarser, as her throat and lips were ripped apart by her screams, and blood started coming from her mouth.

Just as the day's final rays of light were fading, Zhu Ying charged into the town hall's meeting room. The room was located on the easternmost side of the eighteenth floor, and if you opened a window you could see a vast provincial-level metropolis like Beijing, Shanghai, and Guangzhou, while inside there were the desks of the county mayor, the city mayor, and the provincial governor. On that day, just as the town mayor was in the meeting room reviewing the county government's directive to transform the town into a county, Zhu Ying suddenly burst in. When this building was first completed, she had come several times to the town mayor's office, and they had even had sex on his desk and his couch. This, however, was the first time she had entered this eighteenth-floor meeting hall. Standing in the doorway, she gazed coldly at this hall that was as big as a family's courtyard. She saw that in the center of the room was a table as large as three houses, on which there was an enormous city map depicting all of the buildings, streets, parks, and squares. She shifted her gaze to her husband, Mayor Kong, and noticed that he appeared to have grown taller and more portly. He was wearing a suit and dress shirt, just like the county mayor and the city mayor. Had it not been for his distinctively taut face and the mole in the corner of his mouth, she almost wouldn't have recognized him. Fortunately, when he turned toward her, the mole at the corner of his mouth moved, allowing Zhu Ying to see that he was indeed her husband—and the town mayor who had not yet been promoted to county mayor. She stared at him for a moment, then grabbed a chair from the other side of the table and took it over to the window. Grasping the window frame with both hands, she looked out, then turned back, and when she saw her husband staring at her in astonishment, she said,

"Kong Mingliang . . . do you still want to be appointed county mayor? If I were to jump from here, then even if Explosion were to be designated a county you still would have no chance of ever being appointed county mayor!"

Zhu Ying looked at the men who were rushing toward her and shouted,

"Just stand right there! If you take another step, I'll jump. . . . Right now, I want you to tell me something: Do you still want to divorce me? If you so much as utter the word *divorce*, I swear to God I'll jump—and if I jump, that will make you a murderer. In that case, not only will you never become county mayor, you won't even be able to hold on to your current position as town mayor!"

Zhu Ying screamed,

"No one come near me! If anyone takes another step toward me, I'll jump. . . . Everyone, stand still . . . don't move. Kong Mingliang, I'm asking you a question: Do you still want to get divorced?

". . . And if you don't get divorced now, will you want to get divorced after you are promoted to county mayor?

". . . And if you don't get divorced when you are county mayor, will you want to get divorced after you are promoted to city mayor?

". . . And if you don't get divorced when you are city mayor, will you want to get divorced after you are promoted to provincial governor?

". . . Everyone, listen closely. All of you cadres from the town government, did you all hear what the mayor just said? Now, I have one question: Why did you shut down Otherwordly Delights but let Peach Blossom Spring continue operating? What is your relationship to Cheng Qing, the owner of Peach Blossom Spring? Is she your mistress, your concubine, or your whore? You must tell me now what she is to you. If you tell me, then I'll get down; but if you don't, I'll jump. Actually, from up here I can see Cheng Qing's whorehouse. Hers has become an exclusive business, and beginning at around dusk all of those officials, rich men, and foreigners with dicks as large as sticks—they all drive to Peach Blossom Spring. . . . Right now, the Peach Blossom Spring courtyard is so crowded that cars can't even park in front. The street in front of the courtyard is full of the cars and bicycles of men inside Peach Blossom Spring. . . . Cheng Qing's business is amazingly good, and many of my own girls end up going to work for her! Kong Mingliang, you're my husband, and I'm the one who helped you become village chief and town mayor. But did you not help destroy and shut down my business, while enabling that whore's business to thrive? Kong Mingliang, you listen carefully! As my husband, you must immediately send someone over to shut down Peach Blossom

Spring, just as someone did to Otherworldly Delights. I want Cheng Qing to weep because she has lost her business!

"... So, are you going to destroy her business?

"... I'll ask you one last time, will you or will you not destroy her whorehouse?"

Zhu Ying gripped the window frame as she shouted, but when her arms and legs began to tire, she shifted her position. As she was doing so, she glanced at the crowded meeting room, and saw that everyone was terrified and covered in sweat. Outside the room waiting to get in, there was an additional crowd of town government cadres and others who had come to watch the excitement. There was a sea of faces in the hallway, as people craned their necks and watched with their mouths open, and because they were standing on tiptoe, their pants were hiked up, revealing their bright red ankles. Zhu Ying peered down at them, then looked back at Kong Mingliang standing in front. She saw that he no longer had the solemnity of a town mayor, and instead appeared terrified and had broken into a cold sweat, a look of embarrassment plastered on his face. He didn't seem to know where to put his hand, as if he half wanted to reach out to the window but at the same time was afraid to. When she hopped down from the ledge, he started to reach out to her but immediately pulled back, leaving his hand suspended in midair. She knew she had succeeded in using her reputation as his wife to bring him down. So she turned and shouted three orders to him and everyone else in the room:

"Send someone to destroy Cheng Qing's Peach Blossom Spring!

"... Not only as county mayor, even when you become provincial governor you'll still need to do what I say!

"... As long as you do what I say, then I'll cook for you and wash your clothes, bear you a son, and raise your family."

The sky turned dark.

With a thunderous roar, darkness fell.

The final rays of sunlight came down like a window curtain, casting the world into darkness. Afterward, lights appeared in the town, in the factory, and in the distant mines. Everything began to glow brightly, including the stones in the riverbed, the electricity poles lining the streets, and the crops and weeds in the fields outside town. It seemed almost as if the dark night was even brighter than daytime. As Zhu Ying was leaving the town hall building with her husband, there was no one in the streets who didn't recognize her. Everyone who saw her nodded and greeted her, and said that she looked even younger than before, her skin was better, and even in her thirties she looked as though she were still in her twenties.

2. VICTORY

I.

Coincidentally, the day Zhu Ying gave birth happened to be the same day Explosion was officially redesignated from a town to a county, and her husband was promoted from town mayor to county mayor. That was the nineteenth day of the third month of the following year, just as the entire world was waking up from its hibernation. The ceremony celebrating Explosion's redesignation as a county was held in the location where the authorities planned to build a sports stadium, and there were so many people in attendance that the shoes they lost in the bustle were enough to fill five trucks. Each night, the trucks hauled the shoes back from the meeting site to a local shoe factory, where they were cleaned, repaired, matched up, then shipped to shoe stores in different cities. In this way, one of Explosion's shoe factories was able to double its profits overnight. That day, everyone drank so much soda and bottled water that the taps of several local beverage companies ran dry, and it took more than a hundred sanitation workers, working continuously for three days and three nights, to collect all of the discarded bottles to send back to the factory for recycling. So many fireworks were used that several fireworks factories were rescued from bankruptcy, and so many slogans were posted on the walls that several paper companies ran out of paper. Explosion held a celebration that ran nonstop for several days, and with this the county's economy, culture, and politics improved.

The day Zhu Ying gave birth happened to be the same day the town hospital was redesignated as a county hospital. On that day, the hospital discharged all of its patients, and the entire hospital was cleaned so that the mayor's wife could come to give birth. There was a six-wheeled float parked in front of the building, every hallway was full of fresh flowers and bouquets, and the maternity room and bathroom were scented with French perfume. The hospital had purchased an expensive piece of equipment for the express purpose of confirming whether or not Zhu Ying's fetus was in the correct position, and later paid an enormous sum for a Japanese-produced ultrasound machine. The birth was personally overseen by the director of the hospital, and the director of the maternity ward—a woman in her fifties—had prepared eight different contingency plans to address potential complications, and had even prepared blood plasma for a potential transfusion. But when Zhu Ying was transferred to the maternity ward, no sooner had she lain down on the sterilized sheets and said a few words to the hospital director than the baby immediately popped out.

The hospital director had asked, "How do you feel?"

Zhu Ying had replied, "The perfume in the hospital is very pungent."

The hospital director then said, "You should prepare for excruciating pain."

Appearing unsettled, Zhu Ying had asked. "What's wrong with my belly? What's wrong with my belly?" She then screamed loudly, "Why has it collapsed like a mountain?"

The hospital director and the director of the obstetrics ward lifted the sheets and Zhu Ying's hospital gown, and saw that her cervix was already as large as a city gate, and after the baby passed through, it silently fell into a pool of blood and amniotic fluid.

News of the successful birth was immediately sent to the office of the county mayor, which had just removed the town government signs and replaced them with county government ones. Kong Mingliang, exhausted from having spent the day attending events celebrating Explosion's redesignation from town to county, had just sat down in his leather office chair and his staff had just brought him some tea and placed it on his desk, when the hospital director excitedly ran in and told the mayor, "Your wife's cervix was fully dilated, and the birth went smoothly. It's a boy, who weighs eight pounds eight ounces." When the hospital director finished saying this, the mayor stared at him intently. "Is it really a boy?" The hospital director said solemnly, "It is indeed a boy, eight pounds eight ounces—which is a very auspicious number." Then, the ballpoint pen on the governor's desk burst into bloom, and a variety of colorful plants and flowers suddenly appeared on his papers. Even the wooden armrest and back of the couch in front of him started budding with new growth. There was a fresh aroma of spring plants, which slowly circulated through the office. Looking at those plants and flowers, Kong Mingliang broke into a broad smile. He looked at the hospital director's joyful expression and quietly asked, "Did you say that my wife's cervix was very dilated?" The hospital director nodded and replied, "She is built to have babies. If the mayor wants to have another child, I'd be happy to pull together the medical documentation permitting her to have a second child and send it over." Then, the county mayor stood up and shook the director's hand, and said, "Go back and tell my wife that our child will be named Victory. The plan to have the town redesignated as a county has achieved victory, and our child will also be called Victory. Tell her that after I've finished with some county business, I'll come to see her and the baby."

The hospital director left.

After the director left, the mayor called in the office manager and told him to immediately draw up a directive to send out. "Fuck, not only did a lowly hospital director see my wife, he even dared say that her cervix was very dilated. . . . I want a directive terminating his position to be drawn up immediately!" The office manager immediately drew up the document, printed it, and attached the county government seal as well as the county mayor's own personal seal, thereby terminating the hospital director's position. He then transferred the director of obstetrics to oversee the hospital's trash collection and grounds maintenance. In the same document, he also announced to all of the residents of the county that the mayor's family had a baby boy, whose name was Victory Kong.

II.

The postpartum month of rest is every woman's vacation. During this period, Zhu Ying needed only to reach out her hand and someone would bring her some clothes, and she needed only to open her mouth and someone would bring her some food. Everyone was so busy that the household was like a city street where no one even has time to sit down and relax.

Zhu Ying was putting her son to sleep when she heard someone knocking at the front door. She went downstairs, and in the courtyard she saw that the trees and the courtyard wall were covered by a dense flock of magpies singing loudly, as though a waterfall had suddenly appeared in that space. Staring at all of those magpies, she asked,

"Aren't you concerned that you'll wake up my son?"

The magpies perched in the trees, on the house, and along the courtyard wall immediately stopped singing.

She then gestured toward the sky and said, "Go on, begone!"

The magpies immediately flew away. So as not to wake up the baby sleeping inside, they muffled the sound of their wings flapping, like tree leaves falling to the ground. Once the birds had disappeared, the courtyard was silent again. Zhu Ying went to the gate and saw five or six nannies waiting with their luggage, each of them holding a letter of introduction. Some of them had been recommended by various county departments, including the county's business bureau and the county's agriculture bureau. The youngest one, who had just given birth herself, had been sent over by Yang Baoqing, the director of the county's propaganda department.

"I need only one nanny," Zhu Ying said, looking them over.

They all replied, "Then keep me!"

They proceeded to argue right there in the entranceway, each of them afraid that if, after having been sent over by her department, she was not allowed to serve as Zhu Ying's nanny and have the privilege of looking after the mayor's son, the department's director would curse her. Therefore, they all boasted about their skills and why they were each uniquely suited to being nannies—each of them claiming that *she* was the most qualified. After they had argued like this for a long time, Zhu Ying finally took their respective letters of introduction and recommendation, looked them over, then said that she wanted her son to drink human milk, not cow or goat milk. She added that she herself didn't have enough milk and asked which of the prospective nannies did.

In the end, Zhu Ying selected the twenty-year-old who had just given birth, as well as an older woman who was very skilled at cooking. One of them would be responsible for looking after Zhu Ying's son, while the other would be responsible for Zhu Ying's meals and clothing, so that Zhu Ying herself would be left entirely idle. On the third day, Zhu Ying realized that Kong Mingliang had not yet come to see their son. On the fifth day, she spent the entire day thinking one thought, which was that no matter how busy the mayor might be, he should still see his son! She called him, but it was Cheng Qing who answered the phone, and as soon as she heard Zhu Ying's voice she immediately hung up. Zhu Ying called again, and at first no one answered, and when eventually someone did answer, it was Cheng Qing again, who asked,

"Don't you have enough nannies working for you?

". . . Mayor Kong belongs to the people of the entire county, and he is not just your husband.

". . . I'm his office manager and handle all of his business. If you should need anything, let me know."

After putting the phone down, Zhu Ying rushed over to the county government building, as though blown there by a tornado. When the sentry in front of the building tried to stop her, she screamed, "Don't you know who I am? I am Zhu Ying, the mayor's wife!" When she reached the elevator, she roared at the elevator monitor, "Don't you know? I am Zhu Ying, the mayor's wife!" When she reached the floor of the mayor's office, all of the workers came to the doorway and bowed to her. Only Cheng Qing was left standing in the hallway, like a tree full of branches and leaves blocking her way. Cheng Qing wasn't as tall as Zhu Ying, but today she was wearing milky-blue high heels and the sort of small-collared jacket that female cadres liked to wear. She was also wearing a snow-white shirt and appeared very dignified, bearing little resemblance to the former owner of Peach Blossom Spring. Standing there like a national cadre Ying, Cheng Qing laughed and said quietly,

"Sister-in-law, how are you?"

Zhu Ying slapped her face.

Cheng Qing stopped smiling but continued in a quiet voice, "Do you dare slap me again?"

Zhu Ying snorted and proceeded to slap her again.

Cheng Qing swayed back and forth, and struggled to remain upright. In a trembling voice, she asked, "Will you dare assure your son that his father is definitely the county mayor? Won't you be concerned that when your son grows up, he may end up resembling someone else?" As Cheng Qing said this, the smile returned to her face, like a flower blooming again in the middle of a field. She took another step closer to Zhu Ying, holding her inflamed cheek as though trying to prevent blood from spurting out, and added in an even lower voice,

"Ms. Zhu, you should leave. If you treat me well, I promise I won't tell the mayor anything.

". . . Ms. Zhu, you mustn't come back here. This is my territory, and you have your own house. If you treat me well, I'll let you keep your title of first lady.

". . . Ms. Zhu, go back and try to come up with a way to make sure your son grows up to resemble Mayor Kong, and not anyone else."

Zhu Ying stood in the hallway in front of Cheng Qing, beads of sweat gradually appearing on her forehead. On that day, the sunlight streaming in through the window twisted and turned in midair. A gorgeous oriole flew over and alighted on the windowsill. It peered in at Zhu Ying and flew away, but as it did so all of its yellow and red feathers fell out, drifted through the air, then disappeared. The featherless oriole, meanwhile, became a bald house sparrow. After chirping a few times, it flew toward the other sparrows. Zhu Ying was so dizzy she felt as though the window, the hallway, and everyone's face were spinning around. Afraid she was about to fall over, she glanced at Cheng Qing. When she noticed that Cheng Qing didn't have even a trace of wrinkles around her eyes, Zhu Ying felt a rush of confusion and quickly leaned against the wall. Just as she was about to collapse, she heard her two-week-old son in her house, wide-eyed and kicking, as he screamed,

"Ma . . . Ma . . ."

This scream was long and robust, and had the effect of supporting Zhu Ying and preventing her from collapsing. As she was saying good-bye to Cheng Qing, Zhu Ying stood in the hallway and screamed, "Kong Mingliang will remain my husband for as long as I live! Explosion will continue to belong to our Kong family for as long as I live!" Then, as Cheng Qing and the others watched, Zhu Ying turned around and headed back in the direction from which she had come.

When she arrived home, she found that the two nannies had already left. From that point on, no one was left in the compound but her and her son, together with an air of bleakness following the loss of prosperity.

CHAPTER 12

National Defense

1. A HERO'S STORY

I.

After returning from Explosion to his barracks, Kong Mingyao asked his commander,

"Are military commendations for sale? Can I purchase one?

". . . Commander, just name a price. I really want to buy a third-class commendation.

". . . Despite having been in the army for so many years, I've never managed to earn a commendation. Therefore, I want to purchase both a third-class and a second-class commendation, to give to someone back home. Money is no object."

At that point, the barracks were shrouded in a post-dinner dusk, as each regiment had been marching in formation in the field, like a city wall moving back and forth. The trees along the edge of the field were all chanting *One, Two, Three, Four* into the wind. The soldiers were holding rifles and handguns that they had a chance to hold only during training exercises, and like an engaged but unmarried couple, they were sweating with anticipation. It was at this moment that Kong Mingyao, carrying his travel bag, returned to the barracks. He was so happy he felt he was about to explode, and delight flowed from his heart like a river, enough to float a ferry. He never imagined that one day he would have this much money, nor that a tall, slender woman would come up to him just as he was about to return to the barracks. She smiled at him, whereupon a green vine began growing from the ground beneath his feet. As he was staring at the vine, the tall, slender woman walked over. Standing there with a calm expression, she said quietly, "You look just like my brother. My brother looks just like you." He had stared at her in confusion and saw that her eyebrows were black and radiant, and as a long as a finger. Shaped like a pair of crescent moons, they hovered over her seductive eyes. Her smile was like a ray of morning sunshine. He had never before stood this close to a girl, nor had he ever smelled a woman's scent while he was stationed in the barracks. Her scent was so fragrant that it seemed to be perfume, though it was clearly emanating from her breasts. She was smiling as she spoke to him; her face was like a summer flower exploding into bloom.

"Can you walk with me through the streets of Explosion?

". . . If you really want to become a soldier, then you should take me out to eat.

". . . You could take me to get a room in the hotel up ahead, so that we can chat for a while."

Up until he returned to the barracks, Mingyao couldn't bring himself to believe what had occurred that day before dusk. He couldn't believe he had really done what he did. Sweat had poured down from his head and face, as the vine at his feet burst into bloom and an array of red, yellow, and purple blossoms appeared on every branch. The flowers' scent was so strong that his entire body went limp and his legs turned to rubber, and he almost fell onto that blooming vine. Then he followed the girl, leaving behind the flower-covered vine, but when they reached the street corner, a millstone that had been there since he entered the army suddenly sprouted camellia blossoms. When they reached a restaurant, the stone lion in the entranceway was suddenly transformed into a pair of welcome bouquets positioned on either side of the door. The bouquets included roses, chrysanthemums, hibiscus, and bright red poincianas, and the effect was as if there were a couple of torches burning on either side of the entranceway. Eventually they arrived at a hotel that initially appeared particularly luxurious, but when he was about to unlock the door he saw that it was painted yellow, and through the cracks in the paint curled-up strips of wood were visible. The instant the key entered the keyhole, however, the door was suddenly covered with fresh red paint, and the smell mingled with the scent of her body. This odor swept over him like a wave, nearly drowning him. He couldn't remember the number of the hotel room where they were staying, nor could he remember how the room was decorated. Instead, all that he could recall was that the moment he opened the door, he was confronted with an enormous, snow-white bed adorned with colorful silk blossoms, and when he lay on the bed he would either sink into the soft mattress or slide off the silk blossoms.

They did it on that flower-covered bed.

She taught him how to do it.

After they finished, the silk blossoms were stuck to his body, which was drenched in sweat. When he covered his body with the sheet while trying to remove the silk blossoms, she was already out of bed and getting dressed. As he was thinking that he wanted to do it again, she took out a wallet-size photograph of herself and placed it in his hand, saying, "You look like my brother, and ever since I was young I've wanted to give myself to him. But since I couldn't do so, I can now give myself to you instead."

Then she added, "Do you want to marry me? If you do, then you'll have to leave the army. Remember that I'm called Fragrance, and to tell the truth, none of the girls in Explosion or even in the entire world—no girl you will ever encounter in this lifetime—has skin or a body as good as mine. If you want to marry me, though, you must leave the army. I've been waiting for you for years—because you look like my brother, and ever since I was a child I've wanted to marry my brother."

After this, she disappeared from that blossom-filled room, explaining that she had an urgent matter to which she needed to attend and couldn't stay to keep him company. She told him that if he missed her, he could look at the photograph, and if he still missed her, he should immediately leave the army. Without waiting for him to get dressed, she disappeared from that hotel room, like a beautiful cloud blown away by the wind. For a moment, he didn't know what had just happened, as the love that had fallen from heaven was like a soap bubble in his palm, and in an instant it burst, leaving behind a layer of water. Only after he watched her walk away and then close the door did he inspect the photograph in his hand. He immediately recoiled, as though the photograph had burned him. He dropped it onto the bed and looked at it again, and saw that the photo was of her naked body. She was sitting on the edge of a bed, with an enormous red rose between her legs.

The next day, he headed back to the army.

He arrived back at the barracks just before dusk, and a surge of excitement swept over him, as though he were surrounded by spirits. When he remembered the feeling she had given him, he found himself bursting with desire. Moreover, when he remembered that he already had a million yuan, he wanted nothing more than to piss all over someone's face so that he could then use his hundred-yuan bills to wipe it clean.

As he was about to enter the barracks, he stood in the entrance-way looking around and couldn't help smiling. In order to confirm that the previous days' events had really happened, he reached into his pocket to stroke that photograph printed on immaculately white paper. Then he picked up his luggage and, his chest thrust out, proceeded inside. The door was flanked by two sentries, who saluted him when he passed through. He not only returned their salute, he even slipped into their pockets a fistful of candy into which he had inserted a hundred-yuan bill. When one of the sentries reached into his pocket to get the candy, he noticed the money and looked at Mingyao in astonishment. Mingyao asked him, "If I told you I'm a millionaire, would you believe me? You can take this hundred yuan to buy a good meal." As Mingyao was saying this, he hurried off, afraid that the sentry would try to give him back the money. Throughout the barracks, he distributed hundred-yuan bills in this manner, but each time he gave the candy and money to a fellow soldier, Mingyao would quickly leave, afraid that the soldier would discover the money inside the candy and try to return it to him. Occasionally, one soldier would in fact find the money and say, "Commander, here is some cash that got mixed up in the candy you gave me." Mingyao would then push the man's hand away and ask, "Are you looking down on me? If I told you I'm a millionaire, would you believe me?" If the soldier stared, then laughed and took the money and walked off, then they would both be happy. If, on the other hand, the soldier insisted on trying to return the money, Mingyao would take it and immediately rip it up, shouting, "Did you think that I was trying to bribe you? Do you really think you're worth that? How many years have you been a soldier, and how many years have *I* been a soldier? Others have been calling me Boss for a long time, yet you dare call me Uncle when you happen to run into me in the street!"

He would continue reprimanding the soldier in this way, while at the same time reaching into his pocket to caress that photograph. It was as if as long as the photograph was there he could speak in this way, but without it he wouldn't have the courage. At dusk, all of the soldiers in the division who did not have evening training—including cooks, janitors, herdsman, and sentries who had just finished their shift—came to his dormitory to pay their respects. They called him Squad Leader, and sat around his cot asking him how his family was doing and whether his father's funeral had proceeded smoothly. They asked what his father had died from, noting that a funeral for a seventy-year-old counts as a celebratory funeral, even though nowadays it is not unusual for people to live to be eighty or ninety.

Then, the sun set and the soldiers doing evening training returned to the barracks. The sound of their military chants mixed with that of the whistle summoning everyone for a squad meeting, like a chorus of guns and bullets. Everyone left Mingyao's room. By this point the entire regiment knew that their former squad leader, who had also served as acting platoon leader, had gone home to see his family and then came back with so much money that it seemed as though the bills were growing on trees. Everyone was shocked by this development, and those who believed it exclaimed, "Fuck!" while those who didn't pondered for a long time as they shook their heads and asked, "How can this be? How in the world can this be?"

After the lights had been turned off in the barracks, the company commander sent someone to summon Kong Mingyao. Previously, Kong Mingyao would voluntarily go to the commander's office whenever the commander needed anything, but this time he waited until the commander had summoned him three times before going to see him. The commander's room was on the eastern side of the regiment's building, and inside there was only a cot, a table, a chair, a face-washing basin, a washbasin stand, a plastic bucket, and a rifle hanging on the wall over the bed, while on the opposite wall there were maps of China and of the world. Before he entered, Kong Mingyao stood in the doorway and shouted, "Reporting for duty!" and then saluted the commander.

The commander said, "Upon returning from leave, you should first report to me."

Mingyao smiled.

The commander said, "Are you not interested in advancing? How do you dare break the rules?"

Mingyao smiled.

The commander said, "Remember, the promotion announcement is still in my hands. I still haven't submitted it to the authorities."

Kong Mingyao continued smiling. He sat in the commander's chair, while the commander sat on his own bed. Then Mingyao said three things:

"Commander, can military commendations be bought? Can I purchase one?

". . . Commander, please name your price. I'd really like to buy a third-class commendation.

". . . After working so hard as a soldier for so many years, I've never received a commendation. No matter what it might cost, I'd like to buy a third-class commendation, as well as a second-class one. I'd like to give them to someone back home."

As he was saying this, Kong Mingyao gripped the photograph in his hand. It was as if he were holding a ball of flame, as sweat poured out of his palm. He was afraid he might get the photo wet, so when the commander wasn't paying attention, Mingyao returned the photograph to his pocket. Then, when he left the company commander's office, he walked very deliberately, like a hammer striking an anvil. As the commander opened the door to see him out, he paused and wondered whether he should have an army physician examine this soldier. After all, how could it be that Mingyao had gone home to take care of his father's funeral arrangements, and upon returning acted as though he had gone mad?

It was then that Kong Mingyao suddenly resolved to withdraw from the army.

It was on a very ordinary night that he decided not to continue in the army. As he was lying in bed with ejaculate between his thighs and unable to sleep, he took that fragrant photograph and looked at it for a while, then abruptly sat up and, without giving the matter a second thought, resolved to withdraw from the army.

II.

After Mingyao decided to withdraw from the army by the end of the year, a series of odd events took place in the regiment. Every week the regiment elected a model soldier, and that week Kong Mingyao was elected unanimously. Every month the regiment elected a model soldier, and that month Kong Mingyao was again elected nearly unanimously. During a marksmanship competition, everyone fired ten bullets, and while the maximum number of points was technically a hundred, Kong Mingyao's target nevertheless ended up with twenty-five bullet holes for two hundred and forty points. Every day, the local post office delivered countless letters praising Kong Mingyao, saying that when he wasn't helping people buy what they needed he was at the hospital helping patients cover their hospital fees—either because they had forgotten to bring the money or because they simply didn't have enough. The families of soldiers from poor mountainous regions received remittances from their sons, although the soldiers themselves claimed they hadn't sent anything—and therefore realized that this must be money Kong Mingyao had sent of his own accord.

To thank him, they bought pig's heads, peanut rice, beer, and *baijiu* liquor, and on weekends the soldiers invited Mingyao and more than a dozen others from the same hometown region to go into the small forest behind the barracks, where they placed some newspapers on the ground and proceeded to eat and drink. The soldiers drank until they were tipsy, then raised their glasses to Kong Mingyao and said,

"Squad Leader, there is no need to say anything . . . Toast!"

Several bottles of wine knocked together in midair, as the wine disappeared.

The soldiers drank again until they were even tipsier, and again several bottles knocked against one another. Holding the bottles in midair as if they were holding grenades to swear an oath, they said, "Commander, what do you need for us to do? Just say the word." Kong Mingyao replied that there wasn't anything he needed, and instead told them all to go back to their rooms and collect their medals of merit and certificates of commendation. He then told them to hang these certificates and medals on his chest, so that he could have some pictures taken. They therefore all went back to collect them. Shortly afterward, Kong Mingyao's chest was adorned with ten third-level gold badges and four second-level ones, while in his hand he had a pile of red certificates as thick as a book. Standing on the military review platform, he took countless photographs. His fellow soldiers asked him what he wanted to do, to which he replied that half of the soldiers would be a red army and the other half would be a blue army, and they would both follow his instructions and undertake a practice battle.

Everyone drank another half bottle of *baijiu*. Then the soldiers deposited their beer and *baijiu* bottles in the forest, and when they reemerged they stood on either side of the sentry post, with Kong Mingyao in the middle holding different colored flags. When Mingyao raised the red flag, the red forces would advance and the blue ones would retreat, and when he raised the blue flag, the blue forces would advance and the red ones would retreat. When he raised the yellow flag, soldiers from both sides would crawl forward on their arms and knees and hide in the grass. When he held the red and blue flags in front of his chest, the two armies would face off and begin fighting—punching and kicking one other. Those who fell gritted their teeth and continued crawling forward, while those who were injured grabbed clumps of earth and placed them on their wounds, and then resumed the fight. They continued fighting until Mingyao finally lifted the yellow flag. At this point, both armies finally called off the fighting and all the soldiers returned to the pile of bottles in the middle of the forest, wiping the blood from their faces and shaking the dirt from their bodies. One said, "Squad Leader, your commands are even more professional than the captain's." Another said, "Squad Leader, if you never become a hero or a general in this lifetime, it will truly be a pity and a waste of your talent." After they praised him and drank the remaining wine, the call to assemble sounded. As they were about to hurry back to base, they saw that Kong Mingliang was still sitting under a tree as though he had not heard the call.

Everyone paused and looked at him.

"Squad Leader, we will do as you say. If you tell us to go back, we will go; but if you tell us to stay here, we will stay."

"And if you are reprimanded because you don't return to the base?" Mingyao asked.

"That is fine," they replied.

"And if they give you demerits?"

"That is fine too," they replied.

"And if they kick you out of the army?"

"That is fine as well!" they replied.

Kong Mingyao broke off some tree branches and used them to cover up that pile of empty bottles. Then he quickly organized more than a dozen soldiers by height, and after they formed a line he shouted, "Attention! . . . At ease! . . . Turn left! . . . Run! . . ." Then, he and the entire squadron ran in the opposite direction from the base.

They headed toward an isolated point on the moat surrounding the local market town, to a bridge from which people would frequently jump to their deaths.

III.

On that particular day, Mingyao and his squadron, all covered in sweat, ran from their barracks to the moat's northern bridge. There, the railing on the old bridge had broken and part of the town wall had collapsed, with the remainder resembling a mouth missing half of its teeth. After a few days of rain, the grass growing from the crevices in the town wall would cover the entire wall. The river was several meters deep and was so full of plants that it resembled the smoke emerging from the town's chimneys. People from the town rarely came here, and consequently this was the best place in the entire province to commit suicide. Also, since no one erected any office buildings or residential buildings here, this became the best place to either commit suicide or rescue someone attempting to do so.

At around two in the afternoon—after Mingyao brought his squadron over, but before his soldiers had time to stop and wipe the sweat from their brows—they saw a young woman with disheveled hair standing on the bridge. She had a distressed expression, as though trying to decide whether to live or to die. Just as Mingyao and the others arrived, the woman jumped into the water. The soldiers shouted, "Squad Leader, come quick! Squad Leader, come quick!" Mingyao immediately began unbuttoning his clothes and taking off his shoes. The soldiers exclaimed, "There isn't enough time. . . . If you get undressed, you'll be too late!" Therefore, Kong Mingyao simply kicked off his shoes as he ran, then leaped in the same direction as the woman had jumped. With a beautiful swan dive, he entered the river cleanly, like a fish.

Several other soldiers quickly followed him into the water.

In short order, the woman was rescued.

It turned out that the woman had tried to kill herself over a broken heart. As the crowd of onlookers grew, the woman's parents and boyfriend rushed over and thanked Kong Mingyao and his squad. The soldiers politely excused themselves and departed without even leaving their names.

When the weather turned colder, the army began the process of helping older soldiers retire. Thousands of people traveled from the provincial seat into the army barracks. They were beating drums and waving flags, and each of them was carrying a letter of recognition or commendation. When they arrived at the entrance to the barracks, they raised their fists and shouted, "Let's learn from Comrade Kong Mingyao! . . . Let's learn from Comrade Kong Mingyao!" It turned out that over a period of several months, Kong Mingyao had anonymously rescued a total of seventeen people—an average of four people every month, though there was one month when he rescued no fewer than seven people from the stone bridge of the old river. Some of the people he rescued were trying to commit suicide on account of a broken heart, while others had gone bankrupt and wanted to use their death to repay their debts. There was even a mother who had taken her child to play on the bridge, but then accidentally pushed the child into the water—but no sooner had she called for help than Kong Mingyao dived into the water to rescue the child. There were also three people who wanted to kill themselves by lying across train tracks, but just as the train was approaching Kong Mingyao happened to be passing by and, heedless of his own safety, proceeded to rescue them. Not only were those young people granted a new life, the train was able to arrive on time at its destination, thereby allowing it to meet its Reform Construction goals.

Although Kong Mingyao would never leave his name after rescuing someone, all those he rescued ended up with him engraved in their memory and searched frantically for this mysterious hero. Eventually, one day, as he was saving a college student who was trying to kill herself because she couldn't afford to pay her tuition, his army ID card fell out of his pocket and onto the riverbank. In this way, everyone finally learned that his name was Kong Mingyao, that he had been in the army for most of his life, and that he was an enlisted soldier in the eastern provincial infantry battalion. One weekend thousands of ordinary citizens and people who had been rescued all marched up to his barracks and demanded that he be issued a commendation for exemplary service.

In the blink of an eye, the news spread through the entire barracks. The company, battalion, and regiment commanders hurried to the entrance of the barracks to receive letters of commendation from the people assembled outside. They used two enormous cardboard boxes to collect those gifts and letters of commendation. That evening, when the people's calls on behalf of the formerly anonymous hero Kong Mingyao finally subsided, the provincial governor called up the barracks to say that he wanted to erect a bronze statue of Kong Mingyao at the same bridge where Mingyao rescued seven people from drowning in a single month—which would serve to encourage everyone to learn from Mingyao's heroic actions, but also to warn others not to take their own lives. The lesson was that those people happened to jump when there was a hero nearby, but what would have occurred if no one had been there to rescue them? Before the governor had even finished his call, the general, from his own phone in front of his war map, had already called the office of Kong Mingyao's division commander.

"A true hero!" the general exclaimed. "If we were still in war-time, then Kong Mingyao would have been promoted to general at an even younger age than I was."

The division commander then called up the regiment com-mander's office and said, "Call upon the entire regiment to learn from Kong Mingyao. Also, please immediately send me a copy of the announcement of his receipt of a first-class commendation."

The regiment commander immediately drove to Kong Ming-yao's former barracks, where he summoned Mingyao's battalion and company commanders, then proceeded to smash a teacup on the floor and exclaimed, "Such an extraordinary individual was sitting under your eyes, and you didn't even realize it. If an enemy spy had infiltrated the barracks, would you have noticed?"

That night, the company commander once again summoned Kong Mingyao to his room. It was after the call for lights out, and the other soldiers, who had spent the day in a state of feverish excitement, had already gone to sleep. Kong Mingyao had responded to so many greetings and congratulations that his lips were numb.

Following the company commander into his dormitory, Kong Mingyao noticed that the dormitory had changed from when he last saw it a few months earlier. For instance, as soon as he walked in, the map on the wall began making a grinding sound of paper being cut, as countless strips of confetti rained down. In the blink of an eye, the map became a paper-cut image celebrating Explo-sion's pursuit of prosperity, while statistical records relating to the military company's training also became celebratory announce-ments that the regiment and the division were about to release. The bedding folded neatly on the cot no longer resembled old bricks from the blockhouse or the town wall but rather now resembled a modestly sized garden where countless plants and flowers were growing. There was a smiling, naked woman standing among the flowers. She waved at Kong Mingyao, then mumbled something he couldn't quite make out.

Mingyao stood there in the middle of the room.

"This has become a big deal," said the company commander, who was standing next to him. "Maybe they'll give you a special commendation and promote you directly from being an enlisted soldier to an officer."

Mingyao smiled.

"My prophecy has come to pass. . . . As long as you are willing, you should be promoted to company commander in a few days' time," the company commander said with some embarrassment.

Mingyao pulled over a chair and sat down. He let the commander make him a cup of tea and drank it as the commander himself remained standing in front of him, until finally he also took a seat. That evening, Mingyao told the commander many things, to which the commander repeatedly nodded in agreement. They talked from ten at night until four the next morning, and when Mingyao was about to leave he showed the commander the photograph he was holding. As the commander looked at the photograph, the room's table legs, chair legs, washbasin stand, and rifle stand all started sprouting flowering vines, and the entire room began to resemble a chaotic greenhouse. The flowers' scent was so strong that for a long time the commander felt he could barely breathe.

2. A HERO'S RETURN

After accepting the special commendation certificate from the higher-ups, Mingyao withdrew from the army and returned home. This was the dead of winter and the barracks were covered in snow, but on that particular day the trees, the walls, and the training field were covered in red, yellow, and purple blossoms. The flags posted on either side of the road cast a gentle light against the cold sky and the snowy ground, so that every soldier who passed by felt as though he were walking through a spring day. The general had wanted to go in person to the barracks to award Mingyao that certificate of commendation adorned with a bright military flag, five stars, and the national emblem. He also wanted to organize a parade, where he would read the directive from Beijing instructing the soldiers to all learn from Mingyao and follow his example, at which point the cold barracks would be thrown into a fit of fiery excitement. In the parade, Mingyao and the general stood side by side on the observation stand, as one squad after another marched in front of them, like so many embers blowing past. From those squads, they heard thunderous chants that were so loud that the snow fell from the roofs and branches, and the birds were so frightened that their feathers fell off. But after the parade, as the general and Mingyao were speaking to each other in private, Mingyao disappointed the general.

The general said, "You have brought glory to our army. What would you like now?"

Mingyao considered for a moment, then said, "I want to withdraw from the army."

The general looked at him in surprise and said, "What are you talking about? It has already been decided that you will be promoted."

Mingyao gazed at the general, as though trying to decide whether or not this was true. Once he decided that the general must be lying, he laughed and said. "I really do want to return home. I want to return and earn some money, because I have discovered that with money, you can accomplish anything." The general was surprised and gazed regretfully at this underling who was obsessed with fame but was nevertheless not very bright. The general paced back and forth, then paused in front of Mingyao and asked,

"Did you think that I was only promoting you to the position of platoon leader?"

The general gazed at Mingyao and asked, "What about if I make you deputy company commander?"

After a while, he added, "Forget it; how about we simply make you company commander?"

Eventually, he asked very earnestly, "Could it be that you want to be promoted directly to battalion commander? If so, then I can indeed make you battalion commander."

But Kong Mingyao kept repeating the same thing. "I want to withdraw from the army and return home. I've discovered that with money, you can accomplish anything."

Even in the face of thousands of entreaties that he stay, Mingyao insisted that he wanted to withdraw from the army. The day he left the barracks, all of the commanders and soldiers, as well as local civilians from the town, came to see him off—forming a line on both sides of the street that stretched for more than ten *li*. They were all holding plastic flowers and colorful flags, which the army had issued them or which they had made themselves. Their shouting and drumming was so loud that it sounded as if a national leader or a foreign head of state had come to visit. After he was jostled onto the train, Mingyao gazed out the window at that cheering crowd and the sea of colorful flowers. Not until the whistle sounded, signaling that the train was about to depart, did he finally sit down and relax, thinking, *Spending a little money has had enormous results. Just think what I'd be able to accomplish if I were willing to spend millions and millions of yuan.*

3. THE GENERAL'S TEARS

The day Mingyao returned to Explosion, after the celebration of his return had subsided, something occurred that made him realize his decision to withdraw from the army had been a huge mistake. Explosion and Mayor Kong gave Mingyao a welcome that was far more magnificent than the army's ceremony had been. Although Explosion's welcome did not feature as many fresh flowers and colorful flags, or as much applause, as the departure ceremony hosted by the army, the county's newspapers, television, and other media nevertheless all trumpeted the news that he had returned. The local television station even made a live broadcast from the moment he got off the train to when his escorts led him home and he embraced his mother. The mayor's underlings knew that his younger brother had returned from the army, and they arranged to invite him to come eat and work in their bureau or department. Every bureau and department chief declared, *You can have your pick of jobs, even being appointed deputy bureau (or department) chief. If you just give the word, then even if you want to be appointed bureau (or department) chief, I'd be happy to step down and give you my position.* On behalf of the county mayor, the mayor's secretary gave Mingyao a dinner invitation from every county unit, with the list of invitations running fifteen pages. Even if Mingyao had eaten all three of his meals out every day, and each meal had fulfilled one of his dinner invitations, he would still have needed a year and five days to work his way through the entire list of invitations.

It was already dusk by the time Mingyao returned home. As soon as he arrived, Mingliang immediately called him to welcome him back but said that he was too busy with county business and couldn't return to see Mingyao until later that night. Mingliang's wife, Zhu Ying, also sent a message to say that she was currently in the middle of her prescribed postpartum month of rest and couldn't leave the house, but invited Mingyao to come visit her at home. On the pretext of going to visit Zhu Ying, Mingyao went out into the street. Carrying a bag full of badges to use as presents, he proceeded to where Fragrance had told him she worked, but when he arrived he discovered that this was not a cultural organization, as Fragrance had claimed, but rather an enormous construction site with a forest of steel scaffolding reaching into the sky. He asked someone where the cultural company had relocated, but the people at the construction site said that there had never been a cultural organization; rather there had just been a handful of hair salons and foot-massage stalls, together with scores of call girls and streetwalkers. Mingyao wanted to show someone the sweat-soaked photograph of Fragrance he was always carrying in his pocket, but since she was naked in the photograph he couldn't simply take it out, and instead continued gripping it tightly as though it were a bubble that was about to float away. He asked some people doing business along the street whether or not they had heard of someone named Fragrance, describing what she looked like and what kinds of clothing she liked to wear. However, they said they had not seen or heard of this person, and asked if perhaps she was a prostitute from the former entertainment district. They noted that the girls there were particularly fond of giving themselves names like Fragrance, Sweetness, and Little Rouge.

Everyone stared at Mingyao in surprise, as though he were a john who had been caught in the act.

Confused, he proceeded from Explosion's main street to one of its back alleys. He simply couldn't accept the possibility that he might not find Fragrance. However, the words *streetwalker* and *call girl* echoed ominously in his ears, and he felt as though a fish bone had gotten caught in his throat. As he walked to where he and Fragrance first met, he brought his hand to his face, and only then did he notice that he had crumbled the photograph into a ball, and his sweat had made it dissolve into a pool of muck. When he extended his hand, the ink-colored water dripped through his fingers, and all that remained were stains on his palm.

At that moment, he vaguely realized he had done something wrong—that he had treated a dream as though it were reality. The girl called Fragrance had made him fall into a reverie, but he had mistaken that reverie for reality. He returned home and, for dinner, his mother prepared him the sort of meal he normally couldn't eat while working away from home—including salted vegetables with meat and chicken stew with mushrooms, as well as winter leeks and scrambled eggs with tossed cucumber. As the entire family sat around the dining table watching television, he was confronted with another completely unexpected event. It was as though a noxious object had flown in from somewhere and struck him in the face. The object's stench immediately entered his mouth, stomach, and lungs. The television, meanwhile, suddenly cut away from its regular programming, and instead there appeared an anchor dressed in black with a white flower on her chest, announcing in a sorrowful voice that early that morning the Chinese embassy in Yugoslavia had been attacked by an American B-2 stealth bomber, and four laser-guided bombs had entered the building through the roof—of which three had detonated while the fourth had not. There were three Chinese fatalities and more than twenty wounded. The announcer reported that the reason US forces did this was that China had been supporting Yugoslavia's resistance to American and NATO forces. The anchor's voice was low and hoarse, full of indignation and sorrow. When Kong Mingyao heard her report that the embassy had been bombed, his chopsticks froze over his rice bowl, and when he heard that there had been three fatalities and over twenty wounded, he spat out the food in his mouth. Finally, when the anchor observed that this was utterly unbearable, Kong Mingyao stood up from the table and announced to his mother and his brothers,

"War has broken out. I have to return to the barracks!"

Mingguang looked at him, then turned back to the television. Pointing to the television screen, he said, "Quick, look! . . . Quick, look! These are students from our school dancing."

Minghui turned toward the television and now saw an ox plowing a field. Because it was so hot, the ox's tongue was hanging out and mucus was dripping from its mouth. Meanwhile, the gray-haired cowherd grasped the plow handle while wiping away his sweat, his sunburned skin flaking off like cicada wings. "He doesn't even let the ox stop to drink some water," Minghui thought indignantly as he looked away. Then he reflected, "I should tell Second Brother that they should issue that peasant a tractor." Then, he and Mingguang saw that Mingyao was hurriedly packing his bags, taking off his civilian clothes, and putting on his military uniform. Mingyao moved very quickly, and in a few seconds he had put on his uniform, shoes, and cap. When his mother entered with the food, she said, "Mingyao, it's dinnertime. Where are you going?"

"I have to go fight," Mingyao replied, "after having been a soldier for so many years. This is the day I've been waiting for."

His family stared at him. They watched as he put on his munitions belt, then kicked aside his gray civilian clothes and his dusty leather shoes. Just as he was about to walk out the door, however, the telephone suddenly started ringing. The rings sounded like gunshots, and he immediately dropped his luggage and ran forward to answer it. He listened for a second, then screamed into the receiver, "What kind of fucking commander do you think you are? The nation has reached this crisis point and must go to battle, yet you're still talking about wanting to go eat and drink?" Then he listened as the person on the other line said something, whereupon Mingyao lowered his voice and said fiercely, "I have no interest in listening to your explanations. As long as I'm not dead, if I don't try to overthrow your hedonistic ass after the war is over, then not only do I not deserve to be called

a Kong, I will even shoot myself in the middle of the public square."
With this, he slammed down the phone, picked up his bags, and
rushed out into the courtyard.

His mother followed him, shouting, "Mingyao, you just got
home. Where are you going now?"

Mingguang ran up to him and grabbed both his arm and his
luggage. He blocked Mingyao's way and shouted, "You've already
changed careers, don't you realize that?"

He then reminded Mingyao, "Don't you realize that your uniform doesn't even have any medals or badges?" As he was saying
this, he grabbed Mingyao's hand and placed it on his empty collar.

Mingyao's hand froze on his collar, as he stood there in the
courtyard. At this point, it finally occurred to him that he might have
made a huge mistake. He bit his lip as though biting the finger of that
girl named Fragrance. Some rays from the setting sun wafted over
from the west, as if long dyed hair were waving in front of him like
a gauze curtain. The old hen was preparing to go back to her nest
with her chicks, and, clucking away, they walked over, half-stumbling
and half-dancing. Just as they were about to pass in front of him, he
leaned down and grabbed one of them, then hurled it to the ground.
He stood there and watched as the chick convulsed a few times, then
died without a sound. Meanwhile, the old hen continued leading her
remaining chicks to the nest, as Mingyao suddenly squatted down
and began wailing,

"The nation is in crisis—how could I possibly have picked this
precise moment to withdraw from the army?

". . . How could I have picked this moment of national crisis
to withdraw from the army?"

As he tried to cover his face, tears poured from between his
fingers like a mountain spring gushing out of a crevice in the rocks.
Soon, it seemed as though his tears had drenched an area of the

ground half as large as a tatami mat and his leather army boots were completely soaked. That night, the entire family was watching television, with everyone watching his or her own program. When Mingyao saw the US military and that asshole president named Bill Clinton claim that the bombing of the Chinese embassy was a result of faulty GPS data and that mistakes are inevitable in wartime, he stopped thinking about that girl called Fragrance. Instead, he got out of bed, got dressed, put on his shoes, and proceeded from the old streets of Explosion to the new square that had been constructed in the county seat. He saw the new skyline to the north, while the streets of Explosion were full of peasants from the mountains. In the middle of the night, these peasants were using oxcarts, horse carts, and even wheelbarrows to haul away bricks, stones, and other construction materials, which they took to countless other construction sites. When an ox or a horse defecated in the middle of the road, however, these same peasants would stop and collect the excrement into a bag they had brought for that purpose, so as to maintain the square's cleanliness and sanctity.

Mingyao stood in a corner of the square watching the peasants with their oxcarts, horse carts, and motorcycles. After a while, he went up to a peasant who was using a horse cart to haul bricks into the city and was in the process of cleaning up horse feces with his bare hands. Mingyao stood in front of the peasant for a while and saw that the peasant was actually a young man about the same age as himself. He was wearing a tattered, filthy black padded jacket and a cotton cap. Mingyao asked him, "Where are you taking these bricks?"

The man looked up at him and gave him a mysterious smile. "I figure that if this county becomes a city, then all of the clay in the entire mountain range won't be enough for the bricks they'll need."

Mingyao said, "If we go to war, will you join the army?"

The man said, "Life is much better now than before, and my family has recently built a tile-roofed house."

Standing under the streetlamp, Mingyao gazed at that mountain of bricks sitting in the horse cart, and at the horse breathing heavily; then he looked down at that man with his oddly pleased expression and said,

"Did you know that the United States just bombed the Chinese embassy in Yugoslavia?"

"Hauling away a cartful of bricks is equivalent to sowing a field for a month," the man said with a smile. "The country has become rich and is not at all like the country it once was."

"If they were to recruit you to join the army, would you do so?"

"I haven't even graduated from elementary school. This sort of menial labor is the only thing I'm able to do."

Mingyao let the man leave with his cart. After the man disappeared into the distance, Mingyao once again went into the middle of the street and stopped a tractor full of lumber. In the middle of the night, the tractor was producing not smoke but rather bright flames. Mingyao stood in the middle of the road with both arms raised, and after he made a military salute the tractor came to a stop right in front of him. The driver stuck his head out of the cab and cursed,

"Are you fucking trying to kill yourself?"

Mingyao proceeded over to the tractor and asked,

"Did you know that the United States just bombed the Chinese embassy in Yugoslavia?"

The driver opened his door a crack.

"The lunatic asylum is on the edge of the city, and if you want to go I'd be happy to take you."

Next, Mingyao stopped a middle-aged man leading an oxcart and saw that he was wearing a military-style cap. Mingyao said gently, "My name is Kong Mingyao, and in the army I received a special commendation. Today, I withdrew from the army. It looks as though you are also a former soldier. Did you see today's news? Do you know that China and the United States are about to go to war?" He then asked, "If I were to give you some money, would you go with me to join the army? When the country is in trouble, the troops have a responsibility. Did you not hear this saying when you were in the military?" Eventually, the middle-aged man walked over, holding the bridles of two yellow oxen. He glanced at Mingyao with a strange expression, walked around him, then headed toward a nearby location where developers were about to build a shopping center.

By this point the sun was about to come up, and the stars were beginning to fade. Under the sky, which was as dark as a sheet of black ice, dew was falling over the enormous cement square. It was so humid that if you reached out your hand, you could feel the streams of dew on your fingertips and palms, and soon your hand would be drenched. Mingyao proceeded into the center of the square, where there was no typical hero memorial, nor a memorial of a national founder or a saint, but rather a newly erected fifteen-meter-tall bronze statue of Kong Mingliang on a pedestal about fifteen steps high. However, Kong Mingliang's name wasn't inscribed on the base, and instead there appeared the word *Trailblazer* written in vigorous characters. Standing below the statue, Mingyao gazed up at his brother's face, which was bathed in light and covered in dew. In a mournful tone, he exclaimed,

"Brother, there is an important battle to be fought, but no one here knows anything about it."

Then he sat under the statue, staring out at the square and at the shopping center, the International Conference Center, and the World Trade Center that were being built all around him. He suddenly burst into tears, and the sound of his crying was as loud as the Yellow River plunging down the Hukou Waterfall.

CHAPTER 13

The Post-Military Era

1. WOMEN AND THE MILITARY

At dawn of the second day, as the moon was still hanging in the sky but the sun had already begun to rise in the east, Mingyao suddenly stood up and looked out into the empty square. His eyes were completely bloodshot, but his pale face had a look of firm resolve. It was as if his realization the preceding evening had helped him understand something. As he was about to leave—just as everyone who tended to wake up early was in the square running around or spitting on the ground—Mingyao saw Zhu Ying walking toward him. When she saw him, her face lit up with delight, as though she had opened a door and found her lost keys.

Zhu Ying reminded him of Fragrance's slender and voluptuous body, and an odd feeling of discomfort began to rise in his breast. He stood in the middle of the square, waiting for Zhu Ying to approach. He stared at her and noticed that although she had already washed her face and applied her makeup, her features nevertheless revealed her age. Her eyes were surrounded by crow's-feet like autumn branches, and even her forehead was no longer as resplendent as before. But when he peered more closely into her eyes, he saw that they were still as fiery as he remembered. The two of them stood next to a flower pond on the east side of the square, silently staring at each other. Eventually he asked, "Sis, where are you going?" She replied, "I've been searching for you for so long that my feet are swollen." Zhu Ying glanced down at her feet, then looked around. Upon seeing that no one else was nearby, she turned back to Mingyao and suddenly exclaimed,

"So, I wasn't mistaken. It was in fact on account of Fragrance that you decided to leave the army and return here."

She added, "Fragrance no longer lives here. Other than myself, no one else here knows where she is. If you want to see her—if you want her—then you must do as I say."

As Zhu Ying said this, she broke into a pleased smile. She raised her head and saw that the red-tinted sunlight had receded from the square, and the moon overhead now illuminated the entire square in white light, as though the sun had suddenly returned in the middle of the night. She could also make out the sound of cocks crowing in the distance.

"If you come back and work with me, I can give you a lot of money, and can arrange for Fragrance to return and wait on you every day.

". . . But right now, I have something I need to ask of you— could you arrange for Cheng Qing to leave your brother? If you can arrange for that whore to leave your brother and return him to me, I will not only return Fragrance to you, I will even give you several hundred thousand yuan.

". . . How about a million yuan? You've served in the military for so many years and have been awarded so many orders of merit, let me give you a million yuan, and all you need to do is find someone to go break Cheng Qing's arms or legs, or throw acid in her face.

". . . If you feel it's not safe for you to do this, I have an even better idea, which is that either you or someone else could invite her out somewhere, and then rape her in an abandoned area behind the hotel. If you or someone else rapes her, I'll give you a hundred thousand yuan, and if you rape her ten times I'll give you a million yuan."

Zhu Ying paused, then looked around again. She saw the moon shining in the sky, and the cars in the streets driving up to the square all had their brights on. Meanwhile, the people who had gotten up early to exercise were also looking up at the sky, appearing as though they were saying something while gazing at that crescent moon. Turning back to Mingyao, Zhu Ying saw that he was still wearing his military clothing, which in the night light appeared to have a thick layer of green. As he looked at the sky along with everyone else, he bit his lower lip until it had snowy white teeth marks.

"Does Explosion really have a girl named Fragrance?" he asked Zhu Ying. "How do you know her? Fragrance is actually a whore, a mere streetwalker. Isn't that right?

". . . I'm telling you, Fragrance tried to seduce me, saying I looked like her brother, but I deliberately ignored her. Of all the fucking women in the world, there isn't a single one who can seduce me, just as there isn't anyone capable of suddenly making this town square collapse into a bottomless pit. Fragrance summoned me to a hotel and wanted to take off her clothes, but I slapped her face and she ran away in tears."

As he was saying this, Mingyao gazed out at the square. He looked around in all directions, then back up at the sky.

"The sky seems different," he said quietly. "Something momentous is about to occur in Explosion, as well as in all of China. This momentous occurrence will dwarf anything concerning Fragrance or Cheng Qing, just as the ocean would dwarf a small creek or a mountain would dwarf a broken tile.

"I didn't return for that girl, Fragrance." He looked once more at Zhu Ying, as his voice became even firmer and more affirmative. "It was on behalf of Explosion that I withdrew from the army and came home. I returned on behalf of the future of Explosion, and of China.

". . . The embassy has just been bombed by the United States, and if I were now to be distracted with romantic concerns involving Fragrance and Cheng Qing, it would mean that all those years I served in the military would have been in vain." As Mingyao said this, he glanced at the moonlit sky and saw that the moon was gradually receding like a piece of silk after getting wet. A golden red light pressed down on the moonlight, covering it like a red cloth covering a white one. That red cloth was thick and bright, and as its eye-piercing light landed on the white moonlight, the dim moonlight appeared dark and suppressed, like a sheet of white paper that has been exposed to fire and bursts into flames. "OK!" Mingyao said very emphatically. "I'll do as you say and break Cheng Qing's arms and legs, or destroy her face. In return, I don't want a single cent of your money, and instead I just want you to find me a gun.

". . . Get me a gun, and I'll break one of her limbs. Find me two guns, and I'll break two of her limbs. Get me three guns, and I'll make sure she disappears from my brother's life altogether, without his even knowing a thing. Brother will obediently return to your side, to be your man and your husband, while the entire county of Explosion will belong to you and my brother.

". . . Can you find me a gun?

". . . The embassy has been bombed, killing three Chinese diplomats and wounding more than twenty others. Can you make the United States apologize for what it did?

". . . Can you help me establish an army in Explosion?"

As Mingyao was asking Zhu Ying these questions, his gaze bore down on her face like a pair of flames. By this point, the moon had receded and the moonlight disappeared completely from the sky. The people and cars approaching from a distance to come in to work were all illuminated by the winter sunlight, which rushed into Explosion like a flood of water pouring into the square. Seeing that Zhu Ying wasn't answering and instead was staring at him as though she had mistaken him for someone else, Mingyao walked out of the square. After he was far away, he heard Zhu Ying shout something that he would regret for the rest of his life:

"Mingyao," she shouted, "if you, your brother, and I could be united, we could accomplish almost anything. We could elevate Explosion from a county into a city, and then from a city into a metropolis. By that point, your Kong family would be regarded as having performed a meritorious service, and its name would go down in history. Can you believe it?!"

Zhu Ying stared at Mingyao from a distance, while Mingyao turned around under the bright sunlight and looked back at her. He gazed at her as though he were looking at a nun standing in the middle of the square. After a while, he turned and walked on.

2. THE POST-MILITARY ERA (1)

Mingliang and Mingyao met up two days after Mingyao saw Zhu Ying in the square. Because Mingliang was so busy, he didn't have enough time to return home and he offered to meet Mingyao in his office. Apart from being fairly large, Mingliang's office was actually no different from that of any other local official. It consisted of several rooms, each of which was several hundred square meters in size. His room had a couch against the wall, and an exquisitely trimmed bonsai plant, a hibiscus plant, and a rubber plant—often called an ingot plant. The walls were covered in maps, the desk was covered in documents, and one wall was filled with floor-to-ceiling bookcases that were full of books ordered from a list provided by a scholar. The books included the twenty-four dynastic histories and classic works such as *Comprehensive Mirror to Aid in Government* and *The Hundred Schools of Thought*, in editions that included both the original literary Chinese and a translation into modern Chinese. Two bookcases contained more than a thousand volumes, including *Dream of the Red Chamber*, *Romance of the Three Kingdoms*, and the other four Ming-Qing master novels in both hardback and thread-bond editions. Foreign books included *On the Origin of Species*, *The Essence of Christianity*, *The Decline of the West*, *The New Science*, *Utopia*, *The Republic*, *The City of God*, and other world classics. When Mingyao entered the office, Mingliang was in his conference room holding a meeting in preparation for elevating Explosion from a county to a city. Mingyao therefore waited alone in his brother's office. He stood in front of the bookcases, and suddenly felt that he had grown apart from his own family during his years of struggle in the military, to the point that now he almost couldn't remember his brother's name or even what he looked like. He stood for a moment in front of the wall of books and then suddenly he pulled down a well-thumbed copy of *The Carnal Prayer Mat* and began rapidly leafing through it as though shuffling a deck of cards. He remembered Fragrance's slender and voluptuous body, while at the same time dimly recalling his own brother's name and appearance.

As Mingyao was leafing through that copy of *The Carnal Prayer Mat*, he saw that his brother had marked many passages in red, and was surprised that all of the marked passages contained descriptions of sexual scenes and techniques. Bewildered, he wanted to throw the book away or rip it up, but at the same time he had an intense urge to read those underlined passages. In the end, he quickly returned the book to its position on the shelf. After he managed to calm himself, he found himself looking down on his brother while remaining optimistic about his own future.

Fortunately, during this moment of calm following his initial excitement, he managed to remember what his brother looked like. As a result, when the door opened and he turned to see his brother enter, Mingyao discovered that his brother did indeed look exactly as he remembered him. The only difference was that while his brother had previously worn a homespun cloth shirt, after being appointed village chief he had begun wearing a uniform. Later he was promoted to town mayor, and then to county mayor . . . and as he led Explosion from a village to a town, and from a town to a county, and after he had helped all of the natural villages in the Balou mountain region become prosperous counties in their own right, Mingliang began wearing brand-name suits. During this period, Mingyao was merely serving in the army, having been promoted from private to private first class. In the end, Mingliang had his success, while Mingyao had his. Therefore, when Mingliang came in and shouted Mingyao's name, Mingyao turned around and suddenly remembered what his brother looked like. He smiled briefly, then became serious and said in a resentful and mysterious tone,

"Brother, yesterday the United States fucking bombed our embassy. Did you know that?"

Mingliang stared at Mingyao and asked, "What kind of tea do you want?"

"Did they issue any statement?" Mingyao continued. "Not only did Clinton not fucking apologize, he even claimed that, in war, it was completely normal to bomb the wrong target."

"Here I have half a *jin* of high-quality Longjing tea," Mingliang said. "It sells for three hundred and fifty yuan a *jin*."

"War is about to break out." Mingyao pulled over a chair and sat down, as his look of disappointment changed to one of dejection. "But I picked just this moment to return home."

Mingliang gestured toward the door. There was clearly no one there, but as soon as he lowered his hand, a girl promptly walked in like a nymph emerging out of a pool of water. She brought two cups of steeped tea, in which each individual tea leaf appeared bright green. Mingyao stared in surprise, but after a moment he noticed that his brother's hair was beginning to turn gray and his forehead had some prominent wrinkles. "You look older than you are," Mingyao said. "Ma says that you've been so busy that you haven't been home in over a year, and when she wants to see you she needs to come to your office herself."

With a wan smile, Mingliang replied,

"Tell me, Brother, why is it that you've come back to Explosion? Explosion County belongs to our Kong family. Do you want to go into government or business?

". . . In the army you were not promoted to cadre, but if you want to enter the government all I need is to say the word, and in less than an hour you'll be designated a national cadre.

". . . Eldest Brother is a fool, and although Fourth Brother is quite smart, if he sees a feather on the ground he will feel a pang of anguish on behalf of the sparrow from which it fell. Our Kong family, therefore, must rely on you.

". . . I thought we could have Eldest Brother go into government and have you go into business. After a few years, when Explosion is redesignated from a county to a city, Eldest Brother could become mayor and you could have several tens of million yuan, or even a billion or a trillion.

". . . In the mountains there are gold, copper, and coal mines. Coal is a huge industry in China, so how about if I were to transfer the country's largest coal mine over to you?

". . . Just think how, in this day and age, if you have money there isn't anything you can't do. In the army, you weren't even promoted to cadre, but if you have enough money it's entirely possible for you to be promoted to regiment commander."

When Mingyao was about to leave his brother's office, his face was as bright as the sun, shining in all directions, to the point that you could even clearly discern the size and shape of the bright specks of dust hidden inside the dark cracks in the wall. In the instant Mingyao passed in front of Mingliang, he turned and, taking advantage of the soft light coming in through the window screen, noticed the astonishment with which his brother was watching him, like a sheet of frozen soil staring up at a sky full of thunder and lightning.

Mingyao drank that cup of three-hundred-yuan-a-*jin* tea but, apart from a faint fragrance and a leafy aftertaste, there didn't seem to be anything particularly extraordinary about it. Mingliang, however, said that if someone drinks this tea, it is like drinking two thousand eight hundred yuan in one gulp. For the people of Balou, two thousand eight hundred yuan is equivalent to two oxen or a manual tractor. When Mingliang mentioned that every tea leaf in the tea was as valuable as an ox leg, two sheep legs, or four pig legs, Mingyao was stunned into silence. Eventually, he smiled proudly and said,

"Brother, we are truly corrupt."

Mingliang also smiled but didn't say a word.

Afterward, the two brothers walked out of the office together. In the hallway, Mingyao saw Mingliang's six secretaries and four attendants. They were all holding cups of steeped tea, and some of them were also holding documents and newspapers. They were waiting for the mayor's summons and permission. Standing in a row in front of the door, when they saw Mingyao they smiled, nodded, and greeted him. When they saw the mayor, they all bowed ninety degrees, until their torsos were perfectly parallel with the ground, even as their heads remained oriented upward, so that the mayor could see their bright, smiling faces. When the two brothers walked past these attendants, Mingyao was reminded of the division commander and regiment commander walking past row after row of soldiers standing at attention. He was reminded of the magnificence and might of a soldier marching next to a general after having received a commendation. A sense of ambition rose up in his chest following his initial disappointment, and his blood began surging to his head. The two brothers passed these secretaries and attendants, then reached the door of the elevator in the middle of the building, whereupon Mingliang softly told Mingyao two things:

"I'm astonished by how ambitious you are.

". . . Even if I were the provincial governor, I'm afraid I wouldn't be able to accomplish what you ask."

The elevator attendant helped Mingyao press the "down" button. When the elevator doors opened, Mingyao looked at his brother's aged but vivid face. "Brother, in a few days you'll know why I'm like this, and you'll realize the significance of what I'm doing." Then, the two brothers waved good-bye, and the elevator door closed.

When Mingyao walked out the door of the county government building, he proceeded to stand in the middle of the road next to a flower garden. He turned to look back at the newly constructed eighty-six-floor government building, standing like an enormous column. The people entering the building hurried past him. He moved away from the middle of the road, where it was most crowded, to the side of the road. He used the knowledge of explosives he had gained in the army and calculated that if he were to blow up this building, he would need at least three and a half tons of TNT and one thousand six hundred twenty detonators. If he started on the first floor and then made a series of blast holes at one-meter intervals, he would probably need eight thousand sixty blast holes in all. But if he used the sort of laser-guided bombs that the Americans had used to bomb the Chinese embassy, he would need only a handful to complete the job. Upon completing his calculations, and with his hands covered in sweat, he rushed out through the outer gate of the government building complex. The two sentries stationed at their post looked at him but didn't salute. He asked, "Why are you not saluting me?" With a confused expression, they stared at him, and just as they were about to speak, Mingyao added, "Very soon, whenever you see me you'll have to salute." Then he proceeded alone into the crowded street.

3. THE POST-MILITARY ERA (2)

I.

Mingyao finally succeeded in erasing Fragrance and the other girls from his mind, and consequently was able to focus his attention on making money. The office building of the Explosion mining corporation was in a development area to the east of the city, and on the sign in front of the sixteen-story building, all of the characters were embossed in pure gold. In order to prevent people from stealing the sign's gold lettering, Mingyao put forth a considerable sum and hired some retired soldiers, and had them take turns standing guard in the entranceway to the building. Each shift would consist of six soldiers standing guard, with three on each side—standing at attention just like the soldiers stationed at the entrance to the capital square or the presidential palace. Every time Mingyao came into or out of the building, all six sentries would immediately stand at attention and salute him, and the sound of them clicking their heels together would be like sticks striking each other in unison. The sentries were perfectly coordinated, like Tiananmen Square's flag bearers saluting and standing at attention. These sentries worked in shifts of two hours, and from the first shift they attracted astonished and delighted stares, as everyone crowded around and applauded. From eight o'clock in the morning until evening, the streets were full of people surging back and forth, and from this everyone came to know that the Explosion Mining Corporation had been established. The people knew that the director of the corporation was the mayor's younger brother, Mingyao. They also knew that Mingyao had previously been recognized as an exemplary hero by the military but was now Explosion's richest tycoon.

Just how rich was he? Mingyao had as much money as there was water in the river flowing through the county, and as much money as there was gold, copper, tin, and coal in the surrounding mountains. But no matter how much money Mingyao had, every morning at 6:10, as the sun was coming up in the east, he would put on his army uniform, get a national flag, and march a procession of soldiers out of the office building's eastern entrance. Then he himself would go to the square in front of the building and slowly raise the flag to the height of a four-story building. He would watch as the soldiers standing guard marched over to the entrance to the company building, where they would stand at attention, would salute, then would have a changing of the guard. Afterward, he would lead the six sentries back to the eastern entrance of the building.

After the sentries returned to their dormitory, Mingyao would take the elevator back to his office and begin a day filled with assorted issues of extraction, excavation, sales, contracts, expenditures, and revenue.

This continued until the first day of the eighth lunar month. The entire city was preparing to go to work as usual when suddenly, at eight o'clock, loudspeakers, trumpets, and bugles began blaring out of the office building's windows. Initially they played cacophonous opera music, but soon this transitioned into an extraordinarily loud and clear rendition of the national anthem. Next, Mingyao, dressed in his military uniform, led the way, marching out of the main entrance of the building. Behind him, at one-meter intervals, were three young men holding military flags. Behind them, there was a phalanx consisting of eighteen soldiers, in which everyone was blowing a trumpet, performing military songs and the national anthem. Another three meters behind them, there was another regiment marching in a square phalanx in which all of the soldiers were carrying red flags, with two-meter-long flagstaffs plated in pure gold. Another three meters behind them there was another bugle-blowing phalanx, followed by another flag-bearing phalanx with gold-plated flagstaffs. In this way, the precession, consisting of one phalanx followed by another, marched westward from the entrance to the mining company headquarters, until it arrived at a building that had been under construction for a number of years but, for unspecified reasons, was never completed. The marchers stopped there, blew their horns, and then proceeded to perform opera songs and the national anthem while facing that dilapidated building surrounded by collapsed scaffolding and steel rebars. Then Mingyao led the twelve-phalanx procession around the dilapidated building, whereupon the scaffolding disappeared, as did the rusting steel rebars. In less than half an hour, not only was this building that had remained incomplete for years suddenly completed, but it was completed using the city's trendiest Italian porcelain tiles.

The procession passed in front of this newly erected building and proceeded west. The rising sun was shining on the marchers' backs, as though every phalanx was covered in an enormous sheet of natural glass. Mingyao's clothing was soaked in sweat, which dripped onto the ground like a thunderstorm. Initially, the tide of people going to work—including those biking, driving, walking, and taking the bus—simply stepped aside to let the procession pass, but later they started following behind, and eventually they started organizing into similar phalanxes of their own. Music poured forth like a river, and the military sounds permeated half the city. There was a recently built overpass, for which the builders had dug a pit twenty meters deep. Laborers worked continuously to drain water out of the pit, but when the procession passed by and performed in front of it and saluted in unison workers on the construction site, the bridge piers suddenly rose up in the middle of the street and the procession had to circle around them, whereupon the underpass itself rose up out of nowhere.

At precisely noon, the procession arrived at the square. By that point the procession had grown so large that it was impossible to say how many people had joined or what form it had taken. Apart from Mingyao's phalanx, which still retained its original organization, the remainder of the procession was like a chaotic assembly. When it passed an old house that had already been slated for demolition, the entire procession shouted in unison and the marchers proceeded to demolish the house themselves. When they passed a residence that was in the process of being built, the procession played music and shouted slogans in front of the construction site, and in no time the building was completed. They passed a road that was being built, and when they walked over those broken bricks and shattered tiles, they left behind a brand-new asphalt road.

The buildings in the square functioned as the symbol and the heart of all of Explosion's architecture. Initially, the three-hundred-*mu* concrete square sat under the open sky, and it took a while for the surrounding Hall of the People, World Trade Center, and International Conference Center to be erected. Meanwhile, Mingyao himself eventually arrived in the square and instructed his troops to rest in front of the memorial stele for the trailblazing oxen. They wiped away their sweat, drank some water, replenished their crackers and milk, and then stood once again in formation. Mingyao took several special recognition medals printed with the national emblem, military flag, and five stars and pinned them to the left side of his chest; below them he pinned row after row of second- and third-class medals, until his uniform was completely full of medals. Then he turned around and looked back at the soldiers in the various phalanxes and saw that on their chests they had all sorts of merit badges and medals of honor. These medals sparkled in the sunlight as though all of the gold in the mine's storehouses had been laid out under the sun. Kong Mingyao gazed at those medals and was half-blinded by their bright reflection. After his eyes had grown accustomed to the gold's brilliance, he lifted his fist and shouted,

"Is there anything the people of Explosion cannot accomplish?"

The troops all raised their fists and shouted in response,

"No matter how vast the earth and sky might be, they are still dwarfed by the resolve of the people of Explosion."

Mingyao waved his fist and shouted,

"Into what kind of city are we going to build Explosion?"

They pounded their chests and shouted back,

"We are going to transform Explosion into the likes of Beijing, Shanghai, Tokyo, and New York!"

Mingyao jumped onto the podium under the memorial to the trailblazing oxen. Opening his mouth until it was as large as a city gate, he shouted at the top of his lungs,

"Comrades, brothers . . . for the sake of Explosion, for the sake of the People, for the sake of the Reform and Opening Up campaign, for the sake of the modern reconstruction of traditional China, and to enable China's construction to overtake that of Japan, America, and Europe, and become a socialist superpower, everyone please put aside your selfish desires and march with us. Forward! . . . Forward! . . . Forward!"

Each time Mingyao shouted *Forward!* he raised his fist higher and shouted louder and louder, to the point that the third time his fist came so close to the sun that it burned the back of his hand and he shouted so loudly that he shredded the back of his throat and blood came gushing out. He smelled the blood and saw that as the troops were shouting with him, they were clenching their hands so tightly into fists that they ripped open their blood vessels, and they were all shouting so loud that their voices became hoarse. At that point Mingyao hopped down from the memorial statue and gave one final shout: "Comrades, follow me! Forward, march!"

Mingyao began marching the same march that he had practiced countless times while in the army, with his fists to his chest and his knees lifted high, and his feet parallel with the ground. He marched forward step by step, so that all of the medals on his chest jangled in unison with his footsteps. The troops continued until they reached the site where the Hall of the People was being built, and then they marched around the scaffolding three times. Instantly, a Hall of the People large enough to hold fifty thousand people sprang up like a tree. They marched three times around the half-finished World Trade Center; then he ordered his troops to stand in silence, staring straight ahead, whereupon Explosion's tallest twin towers were erected. Finally, he led the troops and virtually all of Explosion's other residents who were following behind them, and together they proceeded to the International Conference Center on the other side of the square. He then ordered the crowd behind him to spread out, and once they had completely surrounded the construction site, he stood on the roof of a crane truck that was being used to construct the center. Raising both fists into the air, he shouted into a microphone,

"Great Explosion! Great construction!"

He shouted again,

"Let's set our sights on Beijing and Shanghai! Let's set our sights on Tokyo and New York!"

Everyone then shouted with him,

"Great Explosion! Great construction!

". . . Let's set our sights on Beijing and Shanghai! Let's set our sights on Tokyo and New York!"

In the midst of those shouts, an iconic egg-shaped building was erected.

The gray steel beams and light brown glass produced a tinkling sound under the setting sun, and everyone noticed with surprise and delight that as the sun set in the west, it shrouded this city in the northern mountains with a beautiful red glow. Then, as though the sun became somewhat exhausted, it slowly sank below the horizon. Once a city assumed its modern form, the county mayor agreed to hand over all of Balou's mines to his brother Mingyao and his mining company.

II.

An American CEO, who had previously spent six years in Vietnam, eventually decided to establish the world's largest automobile factory along the border of the Balou Mountains, about sixty kilometers from the Explosion county seat. What ended up eventually influencing his decision was not only Kong Mingliang's wining and dining, but also his amazingly fast construction process, which was a result of Mingliang's having bribed the people of Explosion. At first Mayor Kong had granted the American the most favorable policies and the prettiest girls, and brought in some master chefs from Beijing, who even imported their MSG from kitchens in Southeast Asia, but even after having enjoyed the fine food and having slept with the girls, this group of a dozen or so Americans still wanted to build their car factories on the coast.

The negotiation had taken place in the conference room of the county government building, around a large elliptical conference table that reminded people of the American CEO's enormous belly. In the center of the table were some plants and flowers, like the hair on the body of that sixty-year-old CEO. On one side of the table sat Kong Mingliang, with more than a dozen deputy county mayors, industry bureau directors, and beautiful female interpreters he had hired for the occasion. On the other side of the table sat the American businessmen. Two girls who had gone to bed with the Americans the night before were off to one side preparing coffee and Chinese tea. When the two girls went to pour the American CEO some more water, they tossed him a smile—their eyes bloodshot and their faces still covered in makeup from not having slept the previous night. But the Americans, after spending that previous night exerting themselves on top of the girls, couldn't be rinsed clean by the coffee. They yawned while also smiling at the girls, and the CEO announced, "Oriental girls are as beautiful as flowers, while Western ones are as coarse as grass." But what he said next left the mayor so disappointed that he immediately wanted to kneel down in front of him. The CEO added, "But no matter how good Chinese girls may be, they still can't compare with the girls I saw in Vietnam. I'll never forget them, and will never again experience the feeling I had when sleeping with Vietnamese girls during the war." The American looked at everyone, then concluded sorrowfully, "It's really a pity, but I'm afraid I won't be able to establish my car factory in Explosion."

Mingliang stood across the table two meters in front of the CEO and saw that the American's mottled face was crawling with tropical fire ants, ladybugs, and Vietnamese dung beetles. His cavernous belly, however, was covered with the dollar bills and gold bars that everyone in the world desires. Mingliang said, "Then, how about if tonight, rather than giving you two Chinese girls, I instead give you four Vietnamese ones?" He continued, "In order to grant you Americans a heavenly existence, how about if I build you a Vietnamese-style gambling parlor?

". . . All of your workers at the level of technicians or above will be permitted to sleep with girls free, and Explosion will cover their gambling losses.

". . . What if I issue a directive ordering the people of Explosion to nod and bow whenever they see any of you Americans?"

Finally, Mingliang said, "Let's go! I want to take you back to the Vietnam from forty years ago." As he was saying this, he wrote a note and asked someone to deliver it. Then he took those former US soldiers, most of whom had fought in Vietnam, and led them out of the county government building. After crossing several old streets, they reached a newly constructed street. Following a directive by the county mayor, all of the walls in the county had been covered in green to resemble a forest from the south, and had been painted with images of Vietnam's rivers and palm trees. The men of Balou were wearing the same coarse white gowns and wide-leg pants that Vietnamese peasants had worn forty years earlier, while the women were wearing homespun shirts and dresses, and bamboo-leaf pointed sun hats, and they were carrying bamboo baskets. Peddlers selling vegetables, meat, and French bread had built roadside shacks that featured a combination of Vietnamese and Yunnan elements. In this way, the entire street was designed to be a precise replica of a Vietnam street from forty years earlier. Even the people pedaling three-wheeled carts and pushing wheelbarrows had traditional Vietnamese large-wheeled carts and wooden-wheeled wheelbarrows. To the Americans' astonishment, a group of several dozen women from Balou walked up, chatting and laughing, and appeared to take the Americans' presence in this Vietnam as quite commonplace. While the Americans stared in astonishment, the women glanced at them as though they were ordinary neighbors.

"In this group, do you see the girls you remember from when you were based in Vietnam?" Mingliang asked the American CEO.

Another dozen or so Vietnamese girls walked over, and again the Americans stood on the side of the road staring at them.

Following the seventh group of Vietnamese girls, the eighth group consisted of the same girls who had been in the first group. By this point, the Americans arrived at a small village on the edge of the town. That village featured a tragic scene following the conclusion of America's Vietnam War. There were houses that had been bombed by the Americans and smoldering cowsheds. There were rotting corpses lying along the fields, and an old woman was sitting in the yard of her collapsed house. The woman's clothing was ragged, her hair was gray, and when she saw the Americans walking over she appeared surprised and uneasy, as her teeth started chattering loudly. When the Americans reached this postwar village, they stood there without moving. The potbellied CEO had a nostalgic expression, and when he heard the sound of an American helicopter taking off or landing, he turned away from the old woman and looked east. There, he saw a stone-filled Vietnamese riverbed, and in the man-made tropical rain forest snakes were crawling amid the painted palm trees. Because it was so quiet, the river sounded like a barrage of gunfire in the distance.

The Americans stopped in front of the river.

A solitary eagle soared over from what appeared to be a fire-filled sky.

Standing beneath the burning sky, each of them was parched with thirst. As they were about to lean down and drink directly from the river, a curious Vietnamese boy ran over from a smoldering house. Then there was a loud explosion, as the young boy stepped on a mine. A lifelike rubber arm flew into the air and landed right in front of the American who was bending over to drink some water.

The entire river quickly turned bloodred, and the American who was drinking from the river broke out in a cold sweat and quickly rejoined the rest of the group.

Next, they proceeded up the river, with Kong Mingliang leading the way like a Vietnamese peasant in wartime, crossing back and forth from one side of the river to the other, standing in the middle of that jungle made from plastic foam, wire, and pigment, then returning to a rope bridge over the river and standing there for a while. In front of them there appeared a small Vietnamese town. The town had American military barracks, Vietnamese restaurants, and cafés, as well as dance halls and brothels designed specifically for US soldiers on leave. Next to the brothel there were beer halls and gambling halls with the roulette that Americans at the time were particularly fond of playing. There were Explosion men dressed as US servicemen walking up and down the street, as though they were looking for something. There were several girls from Guangxi, who had been brought over to Explosion because they looked Vietnamese, with light yellow skin, flattened noses, high foreheads, and sunken eyes but an attractive gaze. They were wearing translucent gowns and were sitting in front of the brothel chatting happily. When the girls saw the real Americans approaching, they smiled and waved. A sixteen- or seventeen-year-old Vietnamese girl emerged from that gaggle of prostitutes and stared at the group of Americans with their enormous bellies. She stood coquettishly in front of them and looked at them shyly. At this point a couple of older prostitutes walked over from behind the younger one and said,

"Commander, war is tough. Come in and enjoy yourself."

They caressed the younger woman's head and shoulders and said,

"She is not even seventeen yet. You have come here from America, and we Orientals prize newness . . . and particularly the deflowering of virgins."

The two older prostitutes pushed the teenage Guangxi girl up to the hulking Americans and said,

"War is hell, and you never know if you'll survive from one day to the next. If you enjoy this girl tonight, then even if you were to die on the battlefield tomorrow, you would still be able to die without regrets."

The Americans entered a building labeled Garden of Red Delights. Bashful young girls led the potbellied men into the brothel's innermost rooms. They went inside, closed the door, opened the small Vietnamese-style window, then turned on the Vietnamese-style rotating fan mounted on the wall—and after half an hour, all of the guns in the Vietnamese town discharged at once. After the American soldiers emerged from their respective rooms, Vietnamese guerrilla fighters and soldiers from the American barracks proceeded to do battle in the town's streets, shooting at one another. There were several American corpses, which the Vietnamese guerrillas had hung from the branches of a nearby willow tree. After the guerrillas emerged from the center of town, the American soldiers rushed over from the barracks and proceeded to search the town, executing Vietnamese soldiers as casually as one might slaughter a chicken. By evening, the entire street was lined with piles of dead and wounded Vietnamese, their blood flowing like a river toward the Americans' feet. After emerging from the brothel, the Americans proceeded to a beer hall, but the foamy red Vietnamese blood flowing past the brothel also followed them there. They emerged from the beer hall and proceeded to a French patisserie, but the blood from the beer hall, the brothel, and the patisserie kept following them around, pushing them into a public square in the center of town. It turned out that the entire square was filled with the bodies of the Vietnamese that had been brought here from throughout the town, including dead and wounded, old and young, men and women. A helmet-wearing American was forcing Vietnamese men to bring all of the corpses into the square and pile them up. The ground was soaked as though it had been raining blood. In order to get away from these mountains of corpses and rivers of blood, the Americans circled through a bamboo-filled hill behind the town. But just as they were about to sit down to rest and recall what had just happened, they saw hundreds or even thousands of Vietnamese running out of the bamboo forest and kneeling down in front of them. The Vietnamese started shouting in unison,

"After having killed so many of us, you should come here to invest! You should come here to invest!"

Next, a group of Vietnamese men and women, young and old, emerged from who knows where. They knelt down and began weeping and shouting, "Let bygones be bygones! Why don't you establish your automobile electronics factories here? As long as you invest here, those dead Vietnamese will overlook the fact that you invaded and murdered them."

They shouted, "For the sake of your conscience, you should invest your money here."

They promised, "If you open a factory and start an industry here, we will give you our last baguette and our last cup of Vietnamese coffee."

They kowtowed to the Americans and said, "You should invest here—not just for our sake, but also for America's. Each of our households has lost someone to the Americans, and in every household there is a table with memorial tablets inscribed with the names of our ancestors, brothers, and sisters whom you killed. If you invest here and help us to become prosperous, you will thereby be absolved of your sins. On the other hand, if you invest somewhere else, your conscience will never be clear, and after you die your souls will not go to heaven."

Finally, thousands upon thousands of residents of Explosion gathered under the light of the setting sun. They were all wearing Vietnamese clothing and were carrying the bodies of people who had been shot and killed by the Americans, and embracing the bodies of children killed in war. They were kneeling down together and loudly exhorting the American industrialists, saying,

"For the sake of your conscience, you should invest here!

"For the sake of your God and your sense of justice, you should let your money take root here."

Darkness fell.

After darkness fell, the American industrialists signed an investment agreement with Explosion for tens of billions of yuan. For the sake of their collective conscience, they decided to select Explosion and its outskirts as the site for their car factory, electronics factory, and hundreds of other production companies.

III.

Mingyao's office was more luxuriously furnished than a general's war room. He had completely blocked off most of the entrance to the floor, leaving only a small doorway leading to his immense office. Right next to the doorway was a freestanding two-meter-wide copper globe, and on either side there were a pair of sand tables that were each ten square meters in size and contained maps of the world. The map on the right featured the Eastern Hemisphere, while the one on the left featured the Western Hemisphere. On the Eastern Hemisphere map, China was drawn in red, Japan was drawn in black, and the other countries—including South Korea, North

Korea, Vietnam, Thailand, and Cambodia—each had different colorations and elevation levels based on the nation's status, wealth, prominence, and military power. All socialist countries were drawn in sunny red, while all capitalist countries were in funereal black. But even among the socialist countries, North Korea's red had a hint of yellow, making it appear shallow and a bit childish, while Vietnam was light red, making it appear poor and boring. In the Western Hemisphere, Europe's Russia was drawn in a combination of red and black, while France, England, and Germany were each outlined in funereal black, though for France Mingyao had added another layer of shiny black in recognition of the country's refined and cultured relationship with China, as though it had a layer of fire and magical power. New Germany was formed out of a united East Germany and West Germany, with socialist blood flowing through a capitalist body, and therefore Mingyao made Germany's black different from Russia's reddish-black. Mingyao could still hear England spreading rumors about China in the newspapers and on television, from when it handed Hong Kong back to China, and therefore he added a layer of white to the black that he used for England, so that the entire model of England resembled a funeral procession in which black and white were clearly distinguished.

In Latin America, Cuba and Venezuela appeared in red, while the remaining countries were either winter gray or autumn yellow. In Africa and Central Asia, the anti-American countries appeared in light red or pink, whereas allies of the United States appeared in black and gray. On the sand tables, the entire world was divided into Chinese red and American black. Every day, Mingyao would adjust each country's color and elevation based on corresponding changes in the nation's political status. In his office, no one was permitted to enter the room with the sand table maps—with the exception of the cleaning staff who would periodically come by to lightly dust them with a feather duster. Mingyao had installed a television in this room and had subscribed to a number of magazines and papers dealing with military, national, and political matters, so that he could sit in his office every day reading the newspaper, leafing through his magazines, and watching the news on television in order to catch all of the Chinese news relating to international affairs, and based on this he would continually readjust the color and boundaries of each country on his maps and would plant red, black, and white flags on the countries' territories.

That year, Mingyao rarely thought about ephemeral topics like women. Instead, from the beginning of March he locked himself in his war room and didn't permit anyone to approach—with the exception of mealtimes, when someone would knock and bring food to his door, and his second sister-in-law Zhu Ying, who for two days would repeatedly knock on his door and then slide a couple of envelopes under it.

One day in March, just like the day when the Chinese embassy in Yugoslavia was bombed, the sky was as dark as though there was a total solar eclipse. On that particular day, a US EP-3 spy plane collided with a Chinese J-811 interceptor fighter jet. The Chinese plane broke in half and crashed into the sea. The pilot, whose name was Wang Wei, parachuted out but was lost. The American plane, meanwhile, suffered only minor damage and proceeded to land without permission in the Lingshui military airfield in southern China. When Mingyao heard this news, he was in his war room standing in front of the map of the Western Hemisphere, hesitating over whether or not he should add a white flag to the map of Italy, since in its recent elections the prime minister had invoked China to gain votes, claiming that at the peak of China's socialist construction in the twentieth century, it had used bodies of people who died of starvation as fertilizer, burying them in the fields. Mingyao definitely did not believe that this sort of thing could have happened. He found Italy rather curious and couldn't decide whether to give this country two or three white flags as punishment for viciously attacking China. As he was hesitating, the map of China on the wall behind him suddenly began to shake, as though it were being blown by the wind, though the maps of surrounding nations, including Vietnam, Japan, South Korea, and India, did not move at all.

He knew something momentous had occurred.

When he turned on the television, he saw the news of the collision between the Chinese and US planes above Hainan Island, whereupon he immediately sprang up from the couch, paused for a second, then closed the door to his war room and, apart from the person who came to bring him his food, didn't allow anyone else to enter. No one knew what he was doing in there, much less what he was thinking. Even the dozen or so must-read military newspapers that were delivered every day had to be slipped under his door. On the seventh or eighth day, Zhu Ying came several times to knock on his door, but when he didn't respond she eventually slid two identical envelopes under it. In each there was a letter that said the following:

> *Mingyao, my brother,*
>
> *Ever since you returned to Explosion, I've been thinking day and night that if the three of us—you, your brother, and I—were to unite, we could accomplish great things. But you are the only person who would be capable of uniting us. You are the only one your brother listens to, and the only one who can get rid of those sluts who hang around him. . . .*

No one knew Mingyao's reaction after he read these two letters, or whether he even read them at all. After Zhu Ying stuffed the letters under his door, she stood at the entrance to his war room, shouting in a loud voice,

"Mingyao, please read those two letters and open the door. Let me say a few words.

". . . Open the door so that I can say a few words.

". . . If you don't want to open the door, please at least read the two letters I gave you."

At that point, Mingyao responded from inside the room, saying something that made those standing outside the room stop in their tracks. He said, "Everyone get the fuck out of here. . . . At this moment of national crisis, anyone who bothers me can expect to be treated poorly. . . . Everyone get the fuck out of here!" After this, there were no longer any voices or footsteps in the hallway outside Mingyao's war room. In the surprised silence that followed, his sister-in-law murmured, "I've done everything I can." She quietly turned and walked away, but as she was leaving two crystalline tears appeared in her eyes.

In the days that followed, the entire building was as silent as a grave. But on the tenth day, someone quietly slipped a document from the county seat under Mingyao's door, whereupon this tomblike room once again began to show signs of life. This document was issued by a US car company that had finally decided to build a factory in Explosion, and the day after the first group of elite businessmen moved in with their considerable investment funds from the United States, the county mayor issued a directive that whenever residents of Explosion ran into foreigners in the street—regardless of whether the foreigners were there as investors or merely as tourists—the locals always had to nod and say, "Hello!" and then bow down to them and step out of the way so that the foreigners could proceed down the middle of the street. This was intended to fully demonstrate the high level of civilization of a country known for its rituals and order. Less than three minutes after this document was slipped into his room, Mingyao roared and threw open his door. Everyone standing outside saw Mingyao—who had just spent ten days locked up in his war room—suddenly appear in the doorway with sunken eyes. The two letters that Zhu Ying had slid under the door had been tossed aside like empty cigarette boxes. The directive from the county government, meanwhile, had been ripped up and scattered like snowflakes all over the sand table model of the Western Hemisphere. Even the US territory and the Pacific Ocean were covered in paper and spittle from his cursing.

With his clothes under his arm, Mingyao strode out of the war room. After he left, a few people entered and began to clean the shattered plates, bowls, and cups that were scattered over the floor. When they saw the sand table model of the United States, they noticed that Mingyao had repainted in snowy white everything that had previously been painted black. America's vast mountains, deserts, plains, and cities—including New York, Washington, San Francisco, and Seattle, together with Cleveland and Miami—were painted in Chinese-style funereal white. In this whiteness, every US city, every piece of territory, and every stretch of forest was inscribed with the characters for *Offering* and *Libation*, which one normally finds only on Chinese coffins.

Those former soldiers—with some of them having served as civil servants for a major general, and others having served as sentries for lieutenant generals and full generals—cleaned up the plates, chopsticks, and discarded food and scraps of paper that were scattered all over the war room, and realized that something momentous was about to unfold. When they returned home, they took out their military uniforms, caps, shoes, and munitions belts, which they had previously locked away, and proceeded to clean them and place them on the table and the bed.

Mingyao rushed into the county government building and immediately stepped inside the elevator. He hit his head against a half-open window in the hallway and shattered the windowpane. Then he proceeded into the county mayor's office, where he saw his brother Mingliang discussing with several advisers how to help American investors profit and thrive in Explosion—and how to have them serve as bait to lure large businesses from rich European and Asian countries. Mingyao rushed in and overturned the conference table, throwing teacups to the floor. The water and tea leaves poured across the floor, with porcelain shards sitting in the water like islands in the ocean. "How can you, at a time like this, issue a directive instructing the people of Explosion to bow and give way to foreigners when they meet them in the street?" Mingyao howled, "You are a turncoat, a traitor, a slave! Don't you know?"

Mingyao kicked a teacup that had somehow remained intact and sent it flying into the wall. "A Chinese plane has been struck by an invading US plane, and the pilot drowned in the ocean, yet the authorities are doing little more than voicing feeble resistance. At a time like this, how can you be sitting here discussing how to help former US soldiers enjoy themselves and make money while in Explosion? . . . Kong Mingliang, if you were not my brother, I would push you out the window to fall to your death on the concrete ground below!"

Mingyao rushed up to his brother's desk, grabbed him by the collar, and attempted to lift him. He said, "I want you to send someone right now to go rescind that directive. If you don't, I'll immediately arrange for both the county government building and your office to be burned to the ground!"

Mingliang pushed Mingyao away, then slapped his face. "The economy is the nation's top priority, you know?" He howled, "I'm telling you, all I need to do is give the word, and your mining company will immediately collapse, your assets will be seized, and your accounts will be frozen!"

Mingliang furiously sat back down. "Do you really want to go against your elder brother? Do want to see whether he is able to ruin you, or whether you can succeed in removing him from his position as county mayor?

"Don't forget!" Mingliang roared as he pounded the table. "If it weren't for your brother, you would currently have no standing at all in Explosion!"

After everyone had retreated from this confrontation between the mayor and his brother, and all that was left in the room was this fraternal fury, Mingliang laughed coldly and said, "You focus your attention on earning money, but what can you do with that measly amount of money? Can you buy an aircraft carrier? Can you buy an atomic bomb that you could fire at the United States whenever you want? From my position as county mayor, I'm telling you that Explosion is now extraordinarily poor, but if it really becomes rich then I will be promoted to city mayor. China is now extraordinarily poor, but if it becomes rich then it would be able to purchase the US presidency.

"Go home." Mingliang brushed away the tea leaves and drops of water that had splattered over his clothing. "You should go home and find someone to marry. If you don't even think about women, then who will you ever be able to love, and what will you ever be able to accomplish?"

Before Kong Mingyao emerged from his brother's office, he snorted and said, "Are you not going to retract your directive instructing the residents of Explosion to bow down to every American or other foreigner they encounter?" He then declared, "If you don't, then I'll retract it for you. I can get those Americans to leave Explosion without even having to utter a single word!" After saying this, Mingyao walked out of the county government building. The afternoon sun shone into the hallway, illuminating his body as he walked away, like a string of shells shot out of a gun. Mingyao's face was the color of bronze and glowed brightly in the sunlight. It turned out that he had originally rushed into the office building because he didn't know how to respond to the news of the collision between the US and Chinese planes. Now, however, as he was arguing with his brother, he realized what he had to do in order to resist American imperialism. He virtually ran out of the county government courtyard, and when he reached the main road he ignored everything else as he proceeded toward the company building. He completely forgot that he had arrived at the county government building in a sedan, and that the driver and the car were still waiting for him in the garage.

Forty minutes later, Mingyao approached the empty plot where his mining company's central administrative building was being constructed. As he had expected, his troops, soldiers, and militia, together with those soldiers who had withdrawn from the army but had been lured back by the high salaries he offered, were all waiting there anxiously for him. In the army they had been soldiers, squad leaders and platoon leaders, and company and battalion commanders, but after arriving in Explosion's richest mining company they entered a peculiar half-military, half-civilian lifestyle, where Mingyao might summon them at any moment. After the US and Chinese planes collided over Hainan Island and the US plane landed on Chinese soil without permission, these former soldiers knew exactly what they had to do. They waited a total of ten days, until finally Mingyao emerged from his war room and then ran out of the county government building.

The main street in the county seat was still as crowded as before, full of people buying and selling vegetables. The people in the factories and office buildings were still going to and from work, but behind the mining company building, in a courtyard surrounded by a tall brick wall, there were three reinforced militia battalions with uniformed soldiers clustered together. The soldiers' military company was their new administrative work unit, and they stood in formation across three basketball courts. Those who had been designated as battalion commanders and company commanders included some who had served as company commanders while in the army, while there were also others whom Mingyao had appointed himself. On this day, they had all been hurriedly summoned by a deputy regiment commander in charge of training, who issued a report that made their blood boil. It turned out that the deputy regiment commander (who had been a battalion commander in the army) saw Mingyao soaked in sweat and facing the training field. He stood at attention, marched up to him and saluted, then announced that the entire regiment had reported for duty and were awaiting their orders. Then Mingyao wiped the sweat from his forehead and flung it to the ground. He collected himself, took a deep breath, and looked out at his forces. He was silent for a moment, and after his breathing had stabilized he began walking slowly toward a wooden stage in front of the regiment. That stage was as large as a house and a meter high. When it was not in use, it was pushed over into the field and covered in a tarp, and when it was needed it was covered in a red carpet.

Now, the wooden stage had been carried to the center of the three basketball courts, and under the midday sun the rug sparkled as if it were on fire. When Mingyao walked up onto the stage, warm blood seemed to surge from the stage into his veins and then rush to his head. As soon as he got onstage, the thousand-odd soldiers in the audience all stood at attention and saluted him—and as they were doing so, you could hear the swooshing sound as their hands moved through the air, as though a series of lightning bolts were whizzing by. This scene made Mingyao's blood boil with excitement. He gazed down at the crowd, then gathered his energy to shout to them,

"Comrades!"

The thousand-odd soldiers shouted back, "Commander!"

Mingyao shouted, "Comrades, you have worked hard!"

The soldiers shouted back, "Serve the People!"

Mingyao asked, "Do you all know what happened recently?"

The soldiers shouted back, "Overturn American imperialism! Drive the Americans out of Explosion!"

Mingyao shouted to the troops, telling them that they had spent a thousand days training for this one moment. But this moment of combat ultimately consisted not of fighting the Americans directly but rather of using their own poverty to attack their opponents' wealth, using their own weakness to attack their opponents' strength, and using their wisdom to attack their opponents' stupidity. In short, they proposed to use Explosion's prestige to attack America's arrogance and insanity. After everyone had quieted down, Mingyao proceeded to speak for half an hour, as though giving his soldiers a lecture on military strategy. Eventually, he ordered the soldiers to disband and wait for further orders while he summoned all of the cadres at the level of the company or higher to his war room and proceeded to hold another military strategy meeting. In the end, they came up with three basic strategies in response to recent developments:

1) Wait for one's opportunity, and maintain absolute secrecy.
2) Overcome firmness with gentleness, and use the element of surprise.
3) Swear that they will never rest until they reach their goal.

Two days later, when the county mayor went into the city for a meeting, something happened that left America and the Americans astounded. Those former US soldiers who had come to Explosion to invest in the automobile factory were all living in a European-style villa complex on the outskirts of the city. A two-hundred-meter-wide, man-made river flowed through the villa complex, and the air there was much more humid than in the city. The northern elms were blooming with southern ceiba blossoms. The pagoda tree blossoms were large and red, just like the phoenix tree blossoms that you normally find only in Hong Kong and Shenzhen. It turned out that now, in early spring, the wormwood, thatch, and dogtail plants, all of which were indigenous to the area, were blooming like a Vietnamese garden in the middle of summer. In the villa complex there were persimmon and apple trees, which had already begun to sprout mangoes and coconuts. In the center of this fruit orchard was a flower garden, and on the tenth day of the fourth lunar month, the flowers were blooming and the fruit was fragrant. But by the eleventh day of the month, that first group of Americans arrived and enjoyed the local nightlife, and when they woke up after ten o'clock the following morning, they opened their windows and saw that a two-story white canvas tent had been erected in the flower garden. In the center of the tent a rusty chimney rose into the air, and on the side facing the Americans' villa complex there was the word *CREMATORIUM* in English, together with the correspond-ing Chinese characters, 火葬场, and below this there were a dozen corpses. The corpses were each covered in a white sheet, and on the sheets were written, in English, the names of President Bill Clinton, his wife Hillary, their daughter Chelsea, Secretary of Defense Colin Powell, the Speaker of the House, and the Senate majority leader, together with the names of the commander of the EP-3 spy plane and the other American pilots. Standing at attention behind this group of corpses were all of Mingyao's troops, dressed in full military uni-form. They had solemn expressions and were standing in formation in the garden, trampling on the flowers underfoot. The Americans didn't know when these Chinese soldiers had arrived in the garden, and neither did they know when exactly the Chinese had built that impromptu funeral parlor with a crematorium inside. When the first American noticed this unusual scene outside his window, a young soldier from Explosion had just pulled down the US flag in front of the funeral parlor. When a second American opened his window with surprise, another of Mingyao's soldiers lit the US flag on fire. When all of the remaining Americans rushed outside to stand in front of the mortuary, Mingyao—wearing a commander's uniform, shiny black shoes, and a bright red leather munitions belt—came to the front of the soldiers. Facing an American who had just come running outside, he saluted them and then made a gesture, whereupon two soldiers approached carrying a corpse on a stretcher.

Several Americans stood directly in front of the crematorium with shocked expressions. As they watched, Mingyao slowly pulled back the white sheet and revealed a real corpse, in full makeup, underneath. The corpse was large and tall, and was dressed in a suit, with short hair and thick eyebrows. Its face looked exactly like Bill Clinton's, and even its tie was the same one that Clinton liked to wear. The Americans stared in surprise. When the American standing in front of the group first saw the corpse, his arms froze and he fell back a step. He swayed from side to side and looked as though he were about to collapse, but was supported by a couple of his companions. With a hard, eerie smile, Mingyao pushed the Bill Clinton corpse aside and pulled over the Hillary corpse, followed by the Chelsea corpse. Finally, he brought over the corpse of the pilot of the US spy plane. He slowly lifted the white sheets covering each of them, as though removing an article of clothing, so that the Americans could see the made-up face of each corpse. Each of them looked exactly like an American. At this point, the cremation began. The mortuary workers turned on the electricity and opened the gas pipe leading to the furnace, then transferred the first corpse—which was the Bill Clinton one—from the stretcher to the crematorium cart. Mingyao told the Americans to take a final look, before he slowly pushed the cart into the crematorium. The door to the crematorium was as wide as that of a warehouse door and was directly facing the Americans standing outside. Two mortuary workers dressed in white uniforms—including one who was outside Mingyao's line of sight—pushed a button, and the door clanged open and a flame shot into the oven and immediately filled the furnace with fire. A wave of heat surged out of the crematorium, pushing back the people standing outside. After this, another mortuary worker slowly pushed the Clinton corpse into the oven, then closed the inch-thick iron door.

Above the crematorium there was a series of sunlit clouds moving across the clear sky, such that the soldiers, the Americans, and other onlookers standing there alternated between being covered by clouds and enjoying a cool breeze, on one hand, and being baked under the blazing sun and engulfed by hot air from the crematorium, on the other.

The news that twelve corpses had been cremated, including those of the US president, Bill Clinton, and the First Lady, Hillary Clinton, permeated every corner of Explosion. Immediately, the residents of the city and the surrounding rural regions all crowded around the villa complex. To prevent a disruption of the ceremony, Mingyao and the troops held hands and surrounded the crematorium. The people who had come to watch began shouting noisily, and those who couldn't see proceeded to climb atop a rockery, fruit trees, and the roofs of the foreigners' villas.

Someone was leading chants that included "Overturn American imperialism!" and "Kick the Americans Out of Explosion!" Initially the chants were rather chaotic, but they quickly became quite rhythmic, as though the thousands of citizens had suddenly become soldiers.

But just as these chants were reaching their peak, everyone suddenly became quiet, and the only thing that could be heard was the sound of muffled breathing. After thirty minutes, the crematorium button was pressed again. The gas nozzle closed and the flame died down. The Bill Clinton corpse had already been reduced to ashes and was ready to be removed. A soldier wearing a white gown brought over an urn made from white marble, and the lid was printed with Bill Clinton's name in both Chinese and English, together with his official portrait. The soldier opened the urn and let the American businessmen look inside, inviting them to verify the quality of the materials and their workmanship. Then he went to the opening in the back of the furnace, where one mortuary worker was holding a wooden box while another was using a small shovel and a metal broom, designed expressly for crematoriums, to sweep up the ashes. After they finished, they brought the wooden box to the front of the crematorium and proceeded—right there in front of the Americans—to dump the ashes into the urn labeled with Bill Clinton's name.

There was a thighbone and a vertebra that had not been completely reduced to ashes and were too large to fit into the urn. The mortuary workers looked to Mingyao, who was standing beside them, and asked, "What should we do?"

"Smash them!"

The mortuary workers therefore took the small hammers they had brought with them and began striking the two bones. Shards flew everywhere, covering the Americans' faces and bodies. As the mortuary workers smashed the bones, they cursed, "Serves you right for bombing our embassy! Serves you right for having your plane collide with ours." After they had finally succeeded in smashing the bones into dust, they scooped up the bone dust and deposited it in the urn.

Next, they began to burn the Hillary corpse, followed by the Chelsea corpse, and then the pilot corpse. In each case, the sequence

was the same—they would allow the Americans to view the corpse
and bid farewell; then would place it in the furnace, close the door,
and turn on the gas; and finally they would collect the ashes and
crushed bones and place them in an urn. However, when they
were burning the pilot corpse, as soon as they ignited the flame,
the mortuary workers came out and told Mingyao, "We don't have
enough gas." Mingyao replied, "Then use an electrical flame." In this
crematorium, if the gas nozzle was not working they would have
no alternative but to incinerate the corpse with an electrical flame
and use a crucible to reduce the bones into ashes. But for some
reason, when they burned the pilot corpse, the flesh was reduced
to ashes but the bones remained intact. Those bones—including
hip, leg, arm, and toe bones—were removed from the oven like
a pile of leftover kindling and dumped in front of the American
businessmen. All of Mingyao's troops lined up in a row and the
soldiers, wearing gloves, took turns going up to the pile of bones
and smashing them with a hammer, whereupon they would each
say a word and then step aside so that the soldier behind could do
the same. They collected skull or vertebra fragments, placed them
on a brick, and then began smashing them with a hammer. As they
did so they cursed angrily, saying,

"Let's see if you dare collide with another Chinese plane!"
Another hammer strike.
"Do you want peace or a good fight? It's your choice!"
Another hammer strike.
"The world belongs not only to America, but also to China."
Another hammer strike.
"When it comes to war and peace, we in China love peace!"
They finally succeeded in reducing all of the pilot's bones to
ashes, which they then placed in an urn. The sun hung overhead for
a long time, and as the spectators from Explosion watched this final

scene, they shouted, "Let's smash the United States! . . . Let's smash the United States!" But as the mortuary workers were placing those twelve urns to the side, the residents of Explosion suddenly grew silent, as everyone waited for the next step. In this moment of silence, the sound of China's national anthem suddenly could be heard coming from inside the crematorium, as solemn as the morning sun rising in the east. Then, twelve soldiers, all of whom were over 1.8 meters tall, marched out of the crematorium. They stopped in front of the row of urns and stood at attention, then each took one urn and marched over to the group of Americans. At this point, the broadcast of the Chinese national anthem ended and was replaced by the US national anthem. The latter was as commonplace as the sun setting in the west, but when the Americans heard their own anthem, their expressions became very serious, as they adopted a look of curious anticipation. At this moment, the first Chinese soldier solemnly handed them the urn containing the ashes of the Clinton corpse, as though it were a bar of gold. The second soldier then handed them the urn containing the ashes of the Hillary corpse, and the other soldiers handed them the remaining urns. The Americans received the urns, with pale, expressionless looks, as though they had no idea what was happening. They stood there in shock, holding urns containing the ashes of the entire First Family, Secretary of State Colin Powell, and the other US political leaders. They heard Mingyao read out a statement titled "Arrogance Will Lead to Extinction," then inform the Americans that China wanted peace but would not tolerate being bullied, and that the people of Explosion sought greater prosperity but would not tolerate fraud and deception. He stated that the outsiders who had come to Explosion to conduct business must be fair, just, and polite to the people of Explosion, and if they weren't, then all they would receive would be these cremated corpses and urns full of ashes.

At this point, Mingyao led his troops away.

He expected that the first thing the Americans would do, after returning to their villas with the urns containing the ashes of the First Family, would be to purchase plane tickets back to the United States. After leaving the Americans, who looked as though they had just watched a performance, Mingyao gestured, and his troops proceeded to dismantle the crematorium. He gestured again, and the troops returned to their original formation, and then left this Explosion economic development zone.

As the soldiers, urbanites, and peasants were saying good-bye to the Americans under the setting sun, they raised their fists and shouted, "We've achieved victory; we've kicked the Americans out! . . . We've destroyed your president; you should go back to where you came from!" Afterward, the villa complex fell silent. Apart from the plants and flowers that had been trampled underfoot, the assorted scarves and shoes that the residents of Explosion had left behind hanging from trees, and the tissues that were scattered over the villa roofs, together with the leftover bones from the First Family, the secretary of state, and the Speaker of the House, which were scattered on the ground where the crematorium had previously been—everything else was calm and clean. The stream coming from the villa complex and the pond they had built there both contained water that was clean and blue, and the air was full of mist. Meanwhile, overhead there were flocks of wild geese flying home, together with a flock of pigeons that stopped flying north and instead settled down in Explosion. The grasshoppers and wasps in the grass all became naptis and eye butterflies, and the world began to improve. Holding their urns, the Americans stood in the middle of the garden. They didn't know whether to send the urns back to the United States or deposit them somewhere else. At the end of the day, the urns merely contained bone ash. As the Americans were discussing how to proceed, Kong Mingliang returned from the city, and before his car had even come to a stop, he jumped out and went up to the American investors.

"If I don't use the law to restrain these disruptive people, then I'll have to resign as county mayor!

". . . You can believe that Explosion has hooligans, but you can't doubt the fact that Explosion would offer you the very best investment environment.

". . . Give me these urns full of bone ash. I need to deal with these disruptive hooligans, as well as also investigate those residents of Explosion who are selling people's corpses to the hooligans.

". . . Can you believe what I'm telling you? If you don't, I can arrange for all of the residents of Explosion to kneel down before you to apologize and offer self-criticism."

From the garden on the former site of the crematorium to the American investors' villa complex, and from the villa complex to the conference room in the villa's guildhall, every time Kong Mingliang said something, a different flower would wilt. As he apologized to the Americans, the leaves of the bamboo plants on the side of the road dried up. There were a pair of potted pines in the entranceway to the guildhall, but under the sound of his cursing the pots cracked and the soil and plants spilled onto the ground. This continued until he and the Americans were all seated on couches in the guildhall, and attendants brought them coffee, beer, and red wine. The Americans accepted and drank the coffee, beer, and wine, and with a sigh of relief they told him that their investments spanned the entire globe. They had personally investigated more than a quarter of the world's countries, but there was not a single country or a single people capable of doing something as amusing as what the people of Explosion had just done. They said that they had gone to Beijing, Shanghai, Guangzhou, Shenzhen, and Hainan, but none of these places was able to rival Explosion's democracy and freedom, permitting people to assemble and demonstrate in this way, and permitting them to burn the entire First Family in effigy. The Americans added that the fact they had come to Explosion to invest was not only a result of their wisdom and good fortune, but also a gift from God. They claimed that not only had they come to Explosion to invest and do business, they also wanted to mobilize their fellow countries in Europe and around the world to come to Explosion as well.

When the Americans finished saying this, the twelve funeral urns that had been placed on the table in the conference room began broadcasting, as though they were loudspeakers, a deafening sound of applause.

CHAPTER 14

Geographic Transformation (2)

When US and Japanese automobile manufacturers decided to relocate to Explosion in the Balou Mountains, they were joined by Singaporean construction companies and South Korean electronics and handicrafts factories, together with Australian mining companies; French clothing and service sector companies; German road, rail, and bridge transportation companies; Italian clothing and briefcase factories; Spanish sports equipment factories; and companies specializing in carved black wooden statues from Kenya and grilled meat, coffee, and olive oil from Brazil. The city was divided into an east side, a west side, an old city district, and a new development zone. A highway linking this city to others was built overnight. Whereas previously a train would pass by every half hour, now one would come rumbling through every three minutes. The train station located more the twenty *li* outside the city was expanded so that it could accommodate up to eighteen trains at once, making it a hub station capable of receiving the tens of thousands of passengers surging into Explosion. In a valley about fifty kilometers to the south, the railroad company constructed a station for freight trains traveling north to south. Meanwhile, following official orders, sewage and toxic materials from the factories and manufacturing plants were dumped into wells up to a thousand meters deep, from which they would flow into underground rivers leading who knows where.

Explosion continued to expand day by day, and it was as if there were countless zippers on the ground that could be repeatedly opened and closed, lifted up and buried, permitting the city to undergo an unprecedented open heart surgery. In the city's central zone, there was a street reserved for foreign businessmen engaging in sightseeing, negotiating, flirting, and bullshitting. In imitation of small European towns, the citizens built coffeehouses, beer halls, food stalls, and souvenir shops. There were also foot-washing stalls, massage halls, hair salons, and back-massage booths reserved for foreigners. Exotic enterprises ranged from Thai transsexuals to Arab teahouses and China's very first Indian roti shop—no one even knew when they all arrived and set up shop in Explosion. Every day, all sorts of foreign music could be heard in the streets, which were also filled with the sound of English, German, French, and all sorts of strange languages, not to mention Chinese and the local Balou dialect.

The foreigners always had more money than they could spend. It was as if they lived in order to drink coffee and beer, listen to music, and flirt with women. They would sign contracts, transfer funds into bank accounts around the world, and then return to their riverside villas outside Explosion for the night, and the next day they would return to this same street. The people of Explosion didn't know what exactly had happened, but they felt that all of a sudden the city had been dramatically transformed. Buildings that had been constructed only a few years earlier were demolished to make room for even newer ones, and the public square where people had just been singing and dancing was now roped off, since the brick-and-cement pavement had to be removed and replaced with granite imported from Australia. The city's orderly chaos resembled a spinning flywheel, as the people gradually came to feel that the Explosion they had known no longer existed and that it now belonged to others—to foreigners. It reached the point where the government specified that the county's development should serve as a model for the entire country, and when high-level officials came from Beijing to observe Explosion they each personally toasted the county mayor three times in a row, saying that they wanted to have Explosion quickly promoted from a county to a city, and to have Kong Mingliang promoted from county mayor to city mayor. The Kong family and the people of Explosion were no longer amazed by this news, and instead treated it as an eventuality they had long expected.

Meanwhile, on the street that had been dubbed Kong Street, which had been set aside for foreigners to drink coffee and beer, listen to music, flirt, and conduct business negotiations—when they heard that Explosion was going to be promoted to a city, all the foreigners and foreign-owned businesses hung red lanterns in their doorways and when the foreigners went outside they each carried a little red flag. The walls on both sides of the street, the sidewalks, the street itself, and even the sewers were decorated with roses, camellias, and all sorts of red, yellow, and purple flowers from China and abroad. The result was that the entire world was filled with the sound of laughter and toasts extolling these extraordinary blossoms.

In this way, the city of Explosion was established, as though in a dream. The day it was announced that Explosion was being redesignated from a county to a city, the city hosted an extravagant celebration, and Zhu Ying locked herself in her room to drink and smoke away her sorrows. She was first surprised and then infuriated by the fact that her husband, Kong Mingliang—in the space of three years and without her assistance or knowledge—had transformed the county into a city and managed to be promoted from county mayor to city mayor. As a result, she locked herself away at home and, after night fell and everyone grew quiet, she cried up to the heavens,

"Kong Mingliang, you'll regret this!

". . . Kong Mingliang, I'll make you regret this!"

She had never expected that Explosion would be promoted so quickly from a county to a city. It was as easy as a car rolling downhill, which needed only a tap on the gas pedal to take off.

That night, she drank alone until she was half drunk. Then she went to look at her son, who was sound asleep in his bed. She lightly slapped his cheek, and cursed, "It's all your fault, you little beast. It's because of you that your father never returned to this household and stopped talking to me!" She waited until her son woke up, stretched, and started bawling, then took him out to the courtyard. She sat there with him until the moon set and the stars faded, and after he fell back asleep she finally was able to calm down. It was at that point that she began muttering to herself, "I'll make you regret this! I'll make you regret this!" She took her son inside, and after putting him to bed, she headed to the women's vocational school she had established a year earlier. She wanted to convene an urgent meeting to recruit and train some specialized girls, in preparation for another battle with the men.

CHAPTER 15

Culture, Cultural Relics, and History

1. REALISTIC CULTURE HISTORY

Mingyao didn't know how he ended up as the director of the town's civil administration bureau, nor how he ended up as the leader of the county's civil affairs section, or even how he ended up as the director of the city's development bureau. The day he was appointed bureau director, thousands of Balou residents all wanted to have their peasant household registrations reassigned as urban ones, resulting in a line that stretched from the development bureau downtown all the way to the outskirts of the city. They brought their original household registration booklets, which identified them as peasants, and they also brought a variety of local specialties to serve as gifts, including peanuts, walnuts, and mushrooms and other edible fungi. They were smiling appreciatively as they waited for the office workers to collect their peasant household registration booklets and issue

315

them new urban ones as well as ID cards with their photographs printed on them.

"With this, do we now become urbanites?" They walked out of the civil administration bureau carrying their new household registration booklets. They looked at the new booklets with their dark red covers and said to each other, "From now on, we're no longer fucking peasants." They laughed and lifted these booklets into the air to show those who were still waiting in line to receive theirs, then they stepped into a restaurant to eat and drink.

To celebrate, they all got drunk.

There was even someone who, upon becoming reassigned as an urbanite, suddenly had a heart attack and died before even making it to the hospital. After the county was redesignated as a city, the civil affairs bureau spent half a month replacing thousands of peasant household registration booklets with urban ones. An ambulance from the hospital was even parked in the bureau's courtyard to treat people suffering heart attacks and strokes as a result of the excitement, and even though seventeen people still ended up dying, the medical workers were nevertheless able to save a hundred and twenty-eight others. After changing their household registration they thereby became urbanites. They placed the gifts they had brought next to the desk of the department official responsible for reassigning their residence permits, or else handed them directly to the workers responsible for filling out, approving, and stamping the forms.

"How can you not accept our gifts?" the peasants asked. "We have now become urbanites, and this is an enormous accomplishment.

"Will you accept them?" they asked. "If you don't accept our presents, we'll simply smash them on the ground."

So the bureau workers had no choice but to accept the gifts.

These presents piled up everywhere—on tables, behind doors, inside rooms, and out in the courtyard. Several professional moving companies worked continuously to transfer all of the cigarettes and wine from the civil affairs bureau's main office to its warehouse. Some people had even added cash to those packages of cigarettes and wine, wanting to take advantage of this opportunity to register the children they had over the official one-child limit. Others, who wanted to help their relatives in the distant mountains transfer their residency permits to the city, stuffed rings, necklaces, and pendants directly into the pockets of the people in charge of residency permits, while saying things like *Here's a peanut!* or *Here are some sunflower seeds you can shell after you return home.*

Minghui's office was located in the middle of the development bureau's courtyard, since applicants needed his signature before they could begin the process of requesting forms, completing them, getting approval, and paying the requisite fees, and then they would need his signature again in order to receive their new residency permit and ID. As a result, Minghui's room was filled from floor to ceiling with gifts, to the point that the gifts forced him and everyone else out of the room and into the courtyard. In the end even the office wasn't big enough to hold them all, and the gifts were deposited in the development bureau's courtyard, where the cigarette cartons were piled so high that they reached the branches of an elm tree in the courtyard and the cigarette smoke stained the tree leaves yellow, so that the old elm became addicted to nicotine. For years afterward, someone would need to periodically open a packet of cigarettes and place it under the tree. Without cigarette smoke, the tree leaves would curl up and die. Across from the elm tree, there was a persimmon tree, under which there were boxes and boxes of wine and alcohol. Because that happened to be the season when the persimmons bloomed, all of the persimmons that year reeked of alcohol and anyone who consumed three or more of them would fall over drunk. When there was no more room under the elm tree for cigarettes, and no more room under the persimmon tree for red wine or *baijiu* liquor, Minghui simply stood in the middle of the courtyard of the development bureau and personally tried to prevent those gift-bearing visitors from entering. He stood on a stool and saw that the line of people who had come to change their residency permits was several kilometers long. The line wove through the square and ended beyond the city limits.

In order to stop these people from bringing gifts, Minghui went to his brother Mingyao's place and recruited eight young soldiers to stand guard in the entranceway, instructing them to stop anyone bearing gifts from entering the development bureau's courtyard. The problem eventually began to subside, until finally there was no longer anyone attempting to bring gifts into the courtyard. As the city revised the residency permit of one household after another, the population of Explosion City began to snowball. Within a month, virtually all those whom the directive had indicated should have their residency permits reassigned to the city had done so. At this point, a rumor began circulating that the mayor's younger brother, Kong Minghui, had developed a psychosis such that if anyone gave him a present he would immediately throw it out the door, and if people stuffed money into his hand he would throw it back at them.

Everyone was dumbfounded.

Everyone knew that Minghui had developed this mental illness.

One person, though, tried to determine whether Minghui was really sick or merely faking it, and one morning he waited at the entrance to the development bureau office, and when he saw Minghui approaching he shouted, "Bureau Director Kong!"

Kong Minghui was bureau director, but he didn't allow anyone to address him using the honorific title Bureau Director Kong and instead asked everyone to call him by his actual name: Kong Minghui. With this, everyone knew that he really was ill, and furthermore that the illness was quite serious. However, people had no choice but to nod to him and smile, then quickly walk away. When it was time to finish work, the associate directors of the development bureau all watched as Minghui slowly left for the day, and it was only then that they dared come out of their offices and get into their company cars to return home. If they happened to catch up to Minghui on the road, they would have the cars turn around to avoid him. They would also try to avoid those people who would wait on the side of the road every day for Minghui to walk by—as the sight of the mayor's younger brother walking to work had become a local spectacle. Every morning at seven thirty and every afternoon at five thirty—half an hour before work started at eight and before it ended at six—the city's residents would crowd around the bureau entrance, standing on both sides of the road, to watch the bureau director who refused to ride in his own car and instead insisted on walking to and from work.

One day, when the crowd of people watching Minghui was unusually large and there was a traffic jam in the square, the mayor happened to drive by. "What's going on?" Mingliang asked. His driver stuck his head out the window to look around, then reported, "Everyone is here to watch Director Minghui, who has a car but insists on walking to work." The driver then laughed and added, "Mayor, more people come here every day to watch the bureau director walk to work than go to the square to watch the flag being raised." Mingliang remembered the time when the four brothers had gotten up in the middle of the night, and how that night he had found an official seal that foretold his current political position. That night, Mingyao had encountered a military truck hauling a cannon, which similarly foretold his current power. His youngest brother Minghui, meanwhile, had encountered a gentle cat, which anticipated his current weakness. Looking though the car window into the distance, Mingliang didn't say anything else. He watched as Minghui walked over from the other side of the intersection. Minghui appeared thin and frail, and was carrying one of the black briefcases that had been issued to all of the city's cadres. As everyone watched, he proceeded forward, like a sick cat scurrying out from under people's feet. He took short steps and didn't say a word, as he walked away from that crowd of people watching him from a distance. The observers, meanwhile, said regretfully,

"He really is ill."

". . . He really is mentally ill."

As the car passed the crowd standing by the roadside, the mayor gazed at his brother and sighed.

That evening, when it was time to get off work, the sun shone down feebly on Explosion. Because the elm and persimmon trees and the grapevines in the development bureau courtyard were addicted to nicotine, alcohol, and sugar, if they were not supplied with cigarettes, wine, and candy their leaves would promptly shrivel up and fall off. After the cadres and workers at the development bureau got off work and Minghui was left alone, he opened a pack of cigarettes under the elm tree and tossed some wine and candy onto the ground beneath the persimmon tree and the grapevines. The director of the city's mental asylum walked over, wearing a white coat, and he looked around and then stood in front of Minghui for a long time without speaking. His hands were clasped in front of his chest, and he seemed as if he wanted to ask Minghui if he could borrow something, but didn't say a word.

"Do you want something?" Minghui buried several pieces of candy under the grapevines and then patted down the earth with his foot.

"The mayor asked me to take you to stay in the hospital for a few days, so that we could give you a complete exam."

Minghui stood there speechless, still holding a fistful of candy wrappers. He scrunched the wrappers into a ball, then permitted the director to lead him back to the hospital for an exam.

2. A HISTORY OF CULTURAL DISLOCATIONS

I.

After Minghui's mother fell ill, Minghui stayed home from work for three days to take care of her. Initially, this did not even appear to be a terribly serious illness, as she was simply running a high fever and talking in her sleep, saying, "I'm going over there, I'm going over there. . . . Over there is better than over here, over there is better than over here!" After the fever began to subside, she emerged from her room and looked markedly thinner. The house was still the same as before, as was the courtyard. In the courtyard there were the same elm and paulownia trees as before, which would bud in the spring, flourish in the summer, and turn yellow in autumn. Even the ants and other bugs crawling up and down the trees were the same as before. They would pant as they crawled up and would skip happily on their way back down. The spider in the web behind the door was still the same old spider that had been there when the family suffered a setback many years earlier.

"You definitely must not move," Mingliang had said coldly. "Even if I am appointed emperor, you definitely must not move, so that people from around the country can come here and observe my family's holiness."

So his mother didn't move.

She continued living there.

After Explosion was redesignated as a city, their house was preserved as a cultural relic. The trees that originally lined the streets of Explosion had all been labeled with plaques noting their species and their identification number. A millstone that had previously lain abandoned and forgotten in one of the village alleys had now been rediscovered and excavated, and was written into the city's cultural chronicles, and a glass enclosure was built around it for protection.

321

The graves originally located in the village square were all relocated to an empty field in the mountain ridge behind Explosion, and it was there that you could find the tombs of the martyrs who gave their lives so that the city could be established. The grave of the mayor's father, Kong Dongde, was transferred to the center of that new cemetery, and in front of the grave there was a tombstone that read: A PIONEER IN ESTABLISHING THIS CITY. Zhu Ying's father, Zhu Qingfang, who had that bitter rivalry with Kong Dongde, was now lying—together with his immediate relatives—in this martyrs' cemetery, and the tombstone at his feet was inscribed with the phrase TOMB OF A PIONEER.

It is said that the mayors of the town and county to which Explosion had belonged when it was still merely a village have now been appointed as city mayor and deputy provincial governor of another province, but they nevertheless each specified that after their death they wanted to be buried in the Explosion cemetery. On their tombstones, they wanted the phrase "This city's pioneers!" Mayor Kong, however, asked Yang Baoqing—who at the time was the director of Explosion Village's news production factory, but who by this point was the director of the city's propaganda bureau—to personally write the former county mayor a letter, saying that when the mayor eventually passes away Yang would erect a statue in this city's public square, on which he would inscribe the phrase *Father of the City*. He also wrote the former town mayor—and current city mayor—Hu Dajun, the following brief message:

> *We look forward to your death, which will be a great honor for us. If you could enter the Explosion cemetery as soon as possible, it would make the people of Explosion very proud!*

By this point, Explosion was definitely one of the nation's great cities.

The entirety of Explosion's past consisted of reality, history, and people's memories.

On account of this tension between reality and history, Explosion's old streets and the new city became divided into two distinct worlds.

The city's east side, west side, and development zone extended along the river, where new buildings stretched out like a multicolored forest. The glass surface of the buildings made the temperature in the city center always several degrees warmer than in the suburbs. Meanwhile, in the old city area, where there was a street named Explosion Street, there was barely anyone at all apart from a handful of people who came for sightseeing. Even Mayor Kong Mingliang and the city's richest resident, his brother Mingyao, rarely returned home to this street. It was as if they had already forgotten that they were originally from Explosion Street, and apart from New Year's or their mother's birthday, they almost never visited their former residence. They were all very busy as business took off. After Mingguang and his wife got divorced, Mingguang didn't end up marrying Little Cui, and instead bought an apartment at his school and stayed there. He, too, forgot to return home. As a result, it was left to their mother to look after the household. She would cook for Minghui and wash his clothes, and have him walk to work every morning and then walk home every evening. Minghui continued this practice of walking to and from work until one day his elder brother asked the director of the city's mental hospital to take Minghui in for an examination, whereupon their mother began running a fever that lasted for three days. To express his filial devotion, Minghui looked after his mother until she was able to emerge from her room. She stood in front of the table like a living corpse and stared for a long time at her husband's photograph, then turned to Minghui and said,

"How old am I now? I should go find your father and keep him company.

". . . I don't want to live any longer. I should go find your father and keep him company."

One morning three days later, the early summer sunlight was shining down on the courtyard, and the city's buildings at the base of the mountain were shimmering like ripples in a pond. Their mother slept for a while; then she dressed herself in the sort of clothing one would give a corpse and wandered out of her room. The nanny was in the kitchen heating some milk for her. At this point, Minghui was about to go into work, but as he was washing up he discovered that after his mother recovered from her illness, she was no longer the same person she had been three days earlier, but rather now there was a thick death veil over her face. He didn't know what she had endured during her illness, but she suddenly looked like someone who had died and come back to life. Her skin was dried up, her face was sallow and wrinkled, and she stood there like an old ghost cut out of gray and yellow paper. She stood in front of her husband's ghostly photograph, then used her sleeve to wipe away the dust on the photograph's glass frame. She mumbled to herself, "I'm going to go find you! . . . I'm going to go find you!" It was as if her husband were inside the glass stamping his feet as he waited anxiously for her.

When Minghui heard this, he froze.

"I just want to die." His mother then heard a sound behind her and turned around. Looking at Minghui, she said, "Your father is over there stamping his feet and waiting for me."

"Then I'll stay home every day to keep you company." Minghui added, "After all, I don't want to go to work anymore."

His mother stared at him without saying a word, as her eyes lit up.

"I'll stay with you for the rest of our lives." Minghui added, "I don't want to work one more day at the bureau."

When his mother heard this, her sallow complexion became a little rosier, and she began to look more like a living person. Then, the sunlight streaming into the room became as bright as a mirror. The sunlight shone in all directions, and even illuminated the corner behind the door, which had been shrouded in darkness for thousands of years. At first, the old spider behind the door could not adjust to the sudden brightness and stood motionless in the sunlight. But eventually, after it adjusted, the spider danced happily across its web, which bounced up and down like a trampoline. The old hen that walked in lay down beneath the spiderweb for a while, and left behind a nest with five blood-veined peacock eggs.

Just like that, Minghui decided not to go to work anymore, and not to serve any longer as bureau chief. When he went to discuss his decision to step down with his eldest brother, the latter simply said, "You should discuss this with your second brother." When Minghui went to discuss his decision to step down with his second brother, Mingliang, he first had to make three appointments with his brother's office manager, Cheng Qing, and only then could he meet with his own brother. When Mingliang heard Minghui's decision, he was furious, saying, "You piece of shit. You're the youngest bureau director in the entire city. Don't you realize that?"

Mingliang added, "How many more days does our mother have to live? She has money and a nurse, so if we designate her a Mother of the Nation, we will have fulfilled our filial obligations."

When Minghui went to discuss his decision to step down with Mingyao, he was able to meet with him very promptly. At the time, Mingyao was in a hidden gully several dozen *li* outside the city limits, where he had erected quite a few basic military buildings and had recruited countless retired soldiers and militiamen. He was training them and paying them a monthly salary. They were wearing military uniforms, and every month they would perform a military parade on a specially constructed concrete training field. On the eastern side of the training field there was a reviewing platform, which had been constructed to conform to the contours of the mountain ridge. The parade ground was located in the gourd-shaped gully on the other side of which there were military barracks. This was the training field, and under the scorching sun of the eighth lunar month they had lit a fire inside the gully, and the rivulets of soldiers' sweat gushing out of the gully converged in a ditch and then continued to flow out of the gully. Mingyao was wearing a military uniform and was standing on the review platform under a parasol, watching the troops march back and forth in front of him. The magnificent military music coursed through the troops' feet and chests, like steam in a steam engine. After Minghui arrived, Mingyao brought those military exercises to an end. Minghui stood on the edge of the platform and watched as one squad after another passed by on the way to the barracks, as the troops' chants caused the platform to tremble under his feet. The rhythmic sound of their footsteps resembled the excavation machines that could be heard throughout the city every night. After waiting for all of the troops to pass, Mingyao walked over and smiled at Minghui.

Minghui said, "I don't want to be bureau chief anymore."

Mingyao looked over at the final military company that had passed by him and shouted, "Hey, Third Company Commander, let's post some sentries at the entrance to the gully. No one should be allowed to enter this training area without my express permission!"

Minghui said, "I want to stay home with our mother, but Second Brother won't let me."

Mingyao gazed intently at Minghui, then snorted. "Sooner or later, Second Brother will need to listen to me."

"But you're so busy." Minghui looked at Mingyao and added, "I'm leaving, and won't be eating here with you."

Mingyao patted Minghui's shoulder and said, "After I succeed, you'll be able to become a general or even a commander if you want to."

When Minghui emerged from his brother's training gully, he stood on the empty mountain ridge and saw the mountains behind him, shimmering in the sunlight. A loud rumbling sound could be heard coming from his brother's barracks, which were hidden in the gully, while in front of him, in the hazy city of Explosion, skyscrapers jutted into the sky, like a glimmering sheet of fog covering the earth. Standing between that sound and the bright buildings, Minghui suddenly realized that something was going to happen between his second and third brothers, and that it would be as monumental as an earthquake or a volcano. When he realized how huge this event would be, Minghui's legs grew limp. He squatted on the mountain ridge, like an ant trapped under an elephant's foot, as tears began to appear in the corners of his eyes.

II.

Minghui went to tell his sister-in-law Zhu Ying that he didn't want to serve as bureau director anymore. Many people would be willing to sell their own wife and daughter for the chance to serve as a bureau director in a new city, but Minghui was emphatic that he definitely didn't want to serve. After finding that he couldn't discuss this momentous decision with his own brothers, he decided to go see his sister-in-law Zhu Ying. It occurred to him that he hadn't seen her for a long time, given that the last occasion must have been his nephew's birthday party. He had bought his nephew a tree that could be made into a house and plants that could be used for food, together with colorful plastic eggs that could hatch into real birds that would fly off into the sky. As Zhu Ying prepared a tableful of food, Minghui played with his nephew while calculating how many years it had been since Mingliang—after being appointed county mayor and city mayor—had last returned home. Upon calculating that it would take only forty minutes to walk back to the old Explosion streets from the city government building, and a mere ten minutes by car, Minghui was astonished that Mingliang, despite living in the same city, had gone for so many years without returning to see his own wife and son.

"Do you want me to go find him and bring him home?" Minghui asked Zhu Ying.

"He'll be back," Zhu Ying laughed. "And when he does return, not only will he kneel down to me, but if I choose to ignore him he will die at my feet." Upon saying this, Zhu Ying looked outside, then turned back to Minghui. "That day is not far off. I promise you'll live to see it."

Minghui couldn't really understand what Zhu Ying was saying, but he didn't hear much anger or resentment in her voice. Instead, he heard a principled shrewdness, which convinced him that she was truly extraordinary. He felt that Zhu Ying's smile was mysterious and inscrutable, so that it was impossible to glean anything useful from it. Originally Zhu Ying and Mingliang had been working side by side, equally determined to make Explosion prosperous. They had been determined to have Explosion—originally a small village that resembled a fallen fruit—become a village committee in charge of overseeing other natural villages. They had been determined to have Explosion be promoted to a town, and even a county. And now, it had in fact become a bustling metropolis. But after Zhu Ying got pregnant and gave Mingliang a son, she rarely went outside anymore and instead spent all of her time at home raising her son. In the end, she had been through a lot. She had given birth to this city, and what she had seen and experienced was in no way inferior to her husband's experiences. When Minghui went to discuss with her his decision to step down as bureau director, he also went to see his nephew, who was getting bigger by the day. Minghui first went to a department store to buy his nephew a gift, and got him a pear from an apple tree and a date from a persimmon tree, together with a cocoa tree imported from abroad. As long as the cocoa tree was exposed to sunlight, small cocoa beans would grow, and later you would be able to pick chocolate fruit directly from the tree and eat it. He bought a plastic horse, stable, and pasture, and if you took the white horse out to the pasture, its belly would expand and some green grass would disappear. After the horse had eaten its fill, it would return to the stable to sleep, and after a while it would give birth to a tiny foal. The foal would then grow up, eat grass, and give birth to yet another foal. After several days, your home would become a veritable farmyard, and you would become the farm owner.

When Minghui arrived at the front door of the building that was originally the village committee building—and which subsequently became an industry building and was now a nursery school—he saw that there were many parents dropping off their children. He stood in the doorway for a while, but when he didn't see his sister-in-law and nephew, he proceeded on to his sister-in-law's house. Mingliang had paid to have the industry building demolished and then hired a Danish architect to design the nursery. All of the nursery's walls and ceilings were decorated with lively colors and pictures, to look like a Danish town. When Minghui walked past that town, he saw that the pigeons sitting there were also colorfully decorated in red and yellow. The real pigeons were just like fake ones, and the fake ones were just like real ones, but he found this mixing of reality and imitation to be completely unremarkable. He therefore continued to his sister-in-law's house. Zhu Ying had built what at the time was Explosion's most extravagant three-story house, though now, compared with all of the modern buildings and imitation European villas, it appeared old and dilapidated. In the entranceway to the two-decade-old house, however, there was a bronze plaque that said CITY HISTORICAL SITE, as a result of which the house and courtyard appeared dignified and distinctive. Explosion's original main street was now Explosion City's old city street, and all of the bricks and trees were cultural relics. But among these cultural relics, the old Kong family house and Zhu Ying's house were particularly prized, and years later they would be designated as museums and the former residences of local notables. Therefore, Zhu Ying continued living on this street—and just as her mother-in-law continued living in the old Kong family mansion, Zhu Ying similarly kept watch over the Zhu family home, which she had built with her own money.

Minghui rang the doorbell.

He rang the doorbell again.

Finally, someone arrived to open the door. When it swung open, he saw that a seventeen- or eighteen-year-old girl was standing there. She was wearing a translucent silk shirt and shorts that were so short that they reached only the top of her thighs. Minghui was startled by her white jade-like thighs, flirtatious features, and carefully painted eyebrows and lipstick. He stepped backward, thinking that he had come to the wrong house. But when the girl saw Minghui step back, she smiled at him and asked,

"Who are you looking for?

"Come inside," she added.

After he entered, she closed the door behind him. Then, like a host, she led Minghui to Zhu Ying's living room. It was there that he saw Zhu Ying standing in the middle of the room, and in front of her was a row of girls all wearing the same outfit and with the same makeup as the teenage girl who had opened the door for him. They looked at Minghui in surprise. They all had flirtatious expressions and were red hot, as though they had suddenly met the man of their dreams, as though they wanted to devour him with their gaze. Minghui stood in the doorway, his forehead covered in sweat. He immediately dropped the gifts he was holding, and as he was reaching down to pick them up, he looked around for his nephew.

"He's gone to the nursery." Zhu Ying accepted the packages Minghui was holding, then said to the girls, "This is my brother—you can go upstairs now."

The girls reluctantly tore their gazes away from Minghui. Laughing and chattering, they all ran upstairs. Their footsteps on the stairs sounded like drumbeats. One girl's red high-heeled shoe fell off, and several hundred-yuan bills flew out. As she was gathering the money, the other girls burst out into peals of laughter. Eventually, Zhu Ying glared at the girls, and only then did they quiet down. After the girls left, Zhu Ying turned back to Minghui and said, "Come in. They're all students from my women's vocational school."

Minghui woke up from his daze and entered Zhu Ying's living room. On the couch, there was the thick smell of girls' perfume and body odor. Between the couch cushions, there was a red hair clip with crystal and diamond pendants, which one of them had dropped. Zhu Ying pointed to the couch and said, "Please sit." Minghui, however, did not sit on the couch, and instead he pulled over a chair. Then he looked away from the couch and saw that on the wall there were several pictures of his second brother, Mingliang. Beneath the portraits, Zhu Ying had written in red pen: MINE TO THE DEATH!!! The three exclamation marks that appeared at the end of the phrase resembled the string of grenades that Minghui had seen at his third brother's place. Then he noticed that on the wall next to him there were several more portraits of his second brother, below which was written a similar phrase: YOU AND EXPLOSION COULD ALL BE MINE, followed by a similar string of three exclamation marks. Then he looked into the living room, the dining room, the kitchen, the bathroom, the wine cabinet, and the pantry. The walls in each of these rooms were just like the walls of the staircase he had just walked up. Everywhere Zhu Ying would usually go around the house, the walls and the furniture were all plastered with photographs—both in color and in black-and-white—of Second Brother as a boy, as an adult, getting married, and working, and also speaking at various meetings, cutting ceremonial ribbons, and shaking hands after being appointed city mayor. All of the photographs had similar phrases scrawled over them, followed by the same three exclamation marks. The old photographs had been reprinted, while photographs of him as city mayor had been cut out of magazines and newspapers. The result resembled a photography exhibit of the mayor's life. After Minghui saw all of these photographs, he didn't know why his sister-in-law had posted them everywhere. He finally turned back to Zhu Ying, who smiled and said,

"I was afraid that if I didn't post these pictures, I might forget what your brother looks like."

Her eyes grew red and bitter.

"He's so busy that often he doesn't return home for years at a time."

Finally, Zhu Ying wiped away her tears, then smiled confidently and said,

"He will return soon. He will soon return to see me. He wants to transform this midsize city into one of China's largest metropolises—a megalopolis as big as an entire province. He wants Explosion to become a top-level metropolis directly under central government rule, like Beijing, Shanghai, Tianjin, and Guangzhou. He wants the officials in Beijing to agree with his plan. After all, hasn't he been giving them gifts all this time? What has he not given them? Eventually, he will realize that giving material gifts is not as effective as distributing students from our women's vocational school." As Zhu Ying was saying this, she glanced upstairs, then wiped the smile from her face. She said, "I've already selected two hundred students for your brother, and eventually plan to have several hundred. When your brother needs them, he will have to come back and ask me—he will need to ask me to give him these several hundred beautiful female students, so that he can send them up to Beijing. At that time, your brother will come back to ask for my help, and if I decline he won't be able to elevate Explosion into a provincial-level metropolis. He will have no choice but to kneel down and bang his head against the wall, begging for my assistance."

Zhu Ying smiled and drank some water, then passed Minghui a pear she had picked from the persimmon tree. Minghui didn't eat the pear, but when he accepted it he noticed that his sister-in-law had deep wrinkles around her eyes. In the blink of an eye, her previously tender skin had aged dramatically, and she looked as though she had aged several decades in the course of just a few years. She now appeared middle-aged and resembled not his sister-in-law but rather Explosion's city mayor or the provincial governor—looking as though she had already undergone countless trials and tribulations and could handle anything thanks to her age and experience. Minghui once again looked around the room at the portraits of his brother, then looked upstairs at all of the girls Zhu Ying had prepared for him.

"Does he want to have Explosion promoted again?" Minghui asked. "When will it become a provincial-level metropolis?" Finally, he placed the pear he was holding on the table.

Has my brother truly gone mad? Minghui asked himself.

"I don't want to serve as bureau director any longer," Minghui said out loud, as he stood up and looked as if he were about to leave. He had originally come to discuss with Zhu Ying his decision to step down as bureau director, but now, upon hearing that his brother intended to transform Explosion into one of China's provincial-level metropolises, Minghui suddenly made up his mind and therefore no longer had any need to discuss the matter with Zhu Ying. It was as if his brother's decision to transform Explosion into a provincial-level metropolis had reinforced Minghui's own decision to step down from his current position as the city's youngest bureau director. Sunlight was streaming in and shining on Zhu Ying's face and shoulders. Her face came to resemble a dust-covered mirror. Minghui took one of the gifts he had brought with him—a plastic pasture and stable set—and created a green pasture in front of him. This endless expanse of pasture stretched all the way to the base of the mountains. It was as if he and his sister-in-law were the only two people left in the entire world. They stood there in that endless expanse of pasture, and Zhu Ying gazed at him as though she were looking at her own brother and son.

"Do you really want to step down as bureau director?" she asked him in surprise.

". . . Have you discussed this decision with your elder brother?

". . . You should remember that night when you were still young, that night everyone in Explosion Village emerged from their homes to see who or what they would encounter. The first person I ran into was your second brother, which is why I was fated to spend the rest of my life married to him. After your brother found an official seal, he was fated to serve as village chief, town mayor, county mayor, city mayor, and provincial governor. Did you really encounter a cat that night? If you didn't, then you shouldn't be so indecisive now, treating major events as though they were completely inconsequential.

". . . Did you really first encounter a cat that night?

". . . Think carefully. Perhaps it wasn't a cat but rather something else?"

When Minghui emerged from Zhu Ying's house, the girls upstairs crowded up to the windows to wave good-bye. Minghui looked upstairs, then quickly turned away. Zhu Ying came out to see him off and stood in the courtyard under a chinaberry tree watching him. Because some crows had deposited melon seeds under the tree, there were melon vines crawling around it, and there were loofah melons, yellow melons, bitter melons, and summer squash. There was also a watermelon as big as a man's head. Minghui stood under the tree next to a melon, as Zhu Ying urged him to think carefully about what he had encountered that night, saying that once he was sure, he would know what he should or shouldn't do in this life, and specifically whether or not he should step down as bureau chief. The courtyard was filled with a strong smell of melon and wildflowers. There was also the sound and smell of cars driving up and down the streets of Explosion. Zhu Ying finally told Minghui, "When you have time, you should take me to the cemetery to weep. It has been several years since we last went."

III.

When Minghui left Zhu Ying's house, the sun was directly above the eastern entrance to the old village street. When he had arrived there the shadow from that tree in the middle of the street filled the crevices in the wall surrounding the house, and now that he was leaving, the tree's shadow was once again in the same crevices. He had said a lot in his sister-in-law's house and had sat there for what seemed like ages, but the sun didn't appear to have moved at all. Time was frozen. As he gazed down from the hillside at the old streets during that period of frozen time, he saw a tide of people in Explosion bottled up like water behind a dam as they attempted to go to work. Here in the old street, however, everything was extremely peaceful, as the young people had all gone into the city. The people who had rented houses along the old street had also gone to work, leaving behind only the houses, various cultural relics, and the sunlight and tree shadows. Minghui stopped under this tree and looked at the cracks in the wall and the stationary shadows. At this point another cat emerged from behind the tree.

The cat ran along the courtyard wall, then disappeared.

Minghui's heart skipped a beat, as he recalled that night many years earlier. The moonlight had flowed like water, as all of the village's mothers and fathers dreamed the same dream, and they all let their children leave home to see what would be the first thing they would encounter or pick up. That night, he had left home with his three brothers, and they had parted ways in the square. Minghui's eldest brother had gone east, his second brother had gone west, his third brother had gone south, while he himself had proceeded north. Along the road he had seen many walls and trees, together with moonlight and a cat. The cat meowed, then ran under a willow tree, heading south—climbing over a wall and then running off toward the houses. At that point, Minghui had sat under the tree, just as he was doing now, and turned his gaze away from the direction in which the cat had scurried away. He knew he should go back and meet up with his brothers, and wanted to tell them that the first thing he had encountered had been this cat. But just as he was about to leave, he saw that under the same willow tree there was a dusty and tattered book. He picked it up and leafed through it. It was a well-thumbed, wire-bound almanac, the pages full of saliva stains from someone wetting a finger to turn them. There was also a musty smell coming from the volume. In that era, every household would have had one of these almanacs, which would have contained a sixty-year table correlating traditional lunar dates with modern solar ones. The almanacs would have been printed with the twenty-four solar terms and the weather, and after every several dozen pages there would have been a page with an explanation of how to calculate the reader's trigram fortune.

Minghui had leafed through that book, then tossed it into a hole in the old willow tree. In the end, given that the first thing he saw that night was the cat, and not the old almanac, therefore all this time he had thought that his subsequent gentleness and weakness were because the first thing he encountered that night was that cat. If he had encountered a dog, he could have followed his second brother's footsteps and become a loyal official or a good general; if he had encountered a tiger, he could have followed his third brother's footsteps and become a public official; and if he had encountered an ox, he could have claimed a plot of land in Explosion to cultivate. But what he encountered was instead a weak cat, and therefore he had no choice but to stay home and look after his mother while his three elder brothers pursued their careers. Now, however, Minghui stared after the cat that had just run away, and began marching forward. The intersection in front of him now had a traffic light, and the area where several dozen local martyrs had been buried had been made into a circular lawn with a stone statue of a trailblazing ox. Walking lightly, he headed north and then turned. The entire way, he kept looking at the old houses and other buildings lining both sides of the street, until finally, near an old millstone that had been gated off as a cultural relic, he found that old willow tree that had been designated Cultural Relic #99. The willow had transformed into a cypress, though the tree itself remained the same—its trunk so wide that it would take two people to reach around it, and at the height of two meters it abruptly bent to one side. The tree's branches were curved and jet-black, and at waist height there was a basketlike black hole. When Minghui saw that cypress that had previously been a willow tree, he sprinted over to the hole in the tree trunk and stuck his arm in. He felt inside, then pulled out that almanac he had tossed there so many years before. The book was damp and mildewed, and tree sap had seeped into its pages, turning them red. Minghui gently shook the book, and several pages fell out, whereupon he picked up these loose pages and carefully returned them to their original places. Then he opened the book to a random page, which happened to be precisely that same year, month, and day. He looked at a blank space on the chart matching the lunar dates to the solar ones, and found that someone had written with a brush:

Lost but found again.

Those four words, *Lost but found again*, warmed his heart like a fire on a winter day. He looked around, but apart from a car that drove past him there was no trace of movement. He tried to find the day he left school and returned home, and found two words written in small script: "Failed exam." He found the day he went to town to work, and there was the single word: "Mistake." He then turned to the day that he was appointed branch head, and there were two word: "Major mistake." Finally, he turned to the day when his brother appointed him as the youngest bureau director in the entire city, and once again there was only a single word: "Resigned."

Minghui stared in shock.

The almanac trembled slightly in his hand. It turned out that the first thing he encountered that night when he went out was actually not the cat but rather this almanac. It turned out that the cat had scurried across his path simply to alert him to the fact that there was a book beneath this tree on the side of the road. All these years, he had thought the first thing he encountered that night was the cat, and therefore he had tossed the book into the hole in the tree. The autumn sun was warm, but the old cypress that was originally a willow shaded him like a giant parasol. Now this book was back in his hands and upon quickly leafing through the volume he found that all of his previous events were carefully recorded inside. A mixture of wonder and regret surged inside him, developing into a sense of unadulterated joy. He stood under the water-like shade of the tree for a while, warming up like a child, then hugged the book close to his chest, looked around, and rushed back home.

His footsteps flowed down the street, like a boat floating down a river.

3. CHRONICLE OF THE HISTORY OF THE HEART

I.

Minghui wanted to bring Cai Qinfang back from her mother's house, so that she and Mingguang could be reunited. This was something that was clearly specified in the almanac. With that almanac, Minghui no longer needed to worry about what the future might bring. It turned out that someone had used a script as tiny as a fly's legs to write all of the details of his past and future into this almanac. Unfortunately, after having sat in this hole in a tree for so many years, the almanac was now completely damp and its pages were stuck together, so that everyone's fate was similarly stuck together. Every few pages, some of the tiny script had gotten wet and formed a blob. During that period, Minghui abandoned his job as bureau director, and instead remained at home locked in his room, where he attempted to peel apart each page from the almanac's most recent sixty-year cycle and return all the pages to their original condition. In attempting to understand the almanac, he became fascinated by Chinese astrology, solar terms, and divination. He bought many books and used the explanations they provided to supplement the almanac's incomplete entries and illegible characters. First, he tried putting the almanac in the sun to dry out, then he tried putting it under a light breeze. When neither of these approaches helped separate the stuck-together pages, he placed a table in the courtyard in the middle of the night, put the almanac in the middle of the table, then sat down next to it to keep watch. As the night fog dampened the pages, he was able to carefully pull them apart. The pages that he separated each night he would then read the following day. He slowly separated one page after another, and by early winter he had succeeded in separating a third of the book's pages. In a dense block of writing from the beginning of the fourth lunar month, he discovered two words that he recognized: "Go fetch . . . Sister-in-Law . . ."

Minghui therefore decided to go fetch Mingguang's wife, Cai Qinfang, and bring her back.

First, he went to see Mingguang himself. Mingguang didn't know why he had been appointed the deputy dean of the newly established Explosion City Normal College. He didn't want to serve any longer, and instead simply wanted to be a good teacher who met with his students every day. But the higher-ups said that his wanting to be a good teacher was a noble aspiration and therefore insisted that he serve as deputy dean. The construction team and the trucks that hauled cement and bricks to the construction site ultimately left the site completely covered in dust and dirt. Mingguang was the school's dean and was responsible for overseeing all of this. He pulled aside a driver at the construction site and began cursing him, saying that he was driving too fast and had run over a small pine tree and smashed the car's windshield. "Although the windshield doesn't feel any pain, the tree definitely does. You know?" Mingguang screamed at the driver, whose head was covered in blood, "Don't you see that the tree is also bleeding, and that the white marrow is the tree's bones?" The driver wiped the blood from his head, then squatted down like a child. At this point, Minghui appeared, and from a distance called out, "Brother! . . . Brother!" When Mingguang turned in Minghui's direction, Minghui saw that his brother's temples had turned gray.

He looked middle-aged, and his blue uniform was stained with dirt from the construction site and chalk dust from the classroom. The moment Mingguang looked at Minghui, the winter sun shone directly in his eyes. Standing next to the construction site, Minghui and Mingguang spoke for a while, as close to each other as the wind and the clouds. Minghui asked how it was that Mingguang's hair had already turned gray, and Mingguang laughed and replied, "I'm a professor now, haven't you heard?" Minghui observed that over the past several years Mingguang had spent all his time at the school and suggested that he should return home for a visit. Mingguang said, "You always wanted me to be the school principal, but all I wanted was just to be a teacher." As Mingguang was saying this, he caressed the pine tree that had been run over, as the driver—holding his bloody head with one hand and the steering wheel with the other—dragged the car's shattered windshield behind him, toward the construction site's warehouse.

When the two brothers were the only ones left in the road next to the construction site, a winter wind blew in from the northwest and the yellow sun disappeared from the sky. In that cold wind, Minghui told his brother about finding the almanac, and how the almanac had told him to go to Cai Qinfang's house and bring her home. As Mingguang was listening, he leaned over to pick up a fistful of soil from the ground and caked it onto the pine tree's broken trunk. He also pulled up some plants and placed them around the tree like a tent, until the tree was completely protected from the cold wind. In this way, the tree began to sprout new growth from where the trunk had been broken. When he was done with the tree, Mingguang turned back to Minghui and continued listening. Minghui said,

"Brother, you can't live alone for the rest of your life.

". . . If Sister-in-Law returns, she could cook for you and help wash your clothes. She could take care of the housework, and might even be able to give you a son or daughter. Your family would be the envy of everyone in Explosion.

". . . I know Mother misses you," Minghui continued. "You should definitely find time to return home and see her."

He added, "The almanac says I need to fetch Sister-in-Law, so I will."

Mingguang listened and gazed at Minghui's face. He didn't say a word and seemed to be deep in thought. But now, when he looked away from his brother, he noticed that the sun was coming out from behind the clouds. With this, all of Explosion, including the city's east side, its high-rises, and its smokestacks, as well as its newly constructed cloverleaf intersection, all shone brightly. The new growth sprouting from the run-over tree was like a glass window in the warm winter sunlight, and the sunlight sparkled on the branches.

"You said you needed to bring Sister-in-Law home, but can't I just focus on my research?" Mingguang asked his brother.

"I want to write a book," Mingguang added with a laugh. "As soon as it is published, I'll be the most accomplished professor on campus."

As Minghui was preparing to leave Mingguang, he suddenly began to tear up. He had thought that the reason why Mingguang didn't return home had to do with the divorce and Little Cui's disappearance. He had assumed it was because of this that Mingguang had decided to remain at the school, living in solitude with his chalk, his blackboard, and his students. But now Mingguang was not in the classroom but rather on the construction site in his capacity as school principal, and Minghui was distraught not only at the sight of the truck's broken windshield but even more so at the sight of the pine tree that had gotten run over. Even though it was winter as Minghui and his brother were separating, the new growth emerging from the pine tree's broken trunk was already as tall as a chopstick, and one by one the pine needles were turning from light to dark green, and black resin, which helped the tree resist the winter chill, had appeared on the pine needles. As the two brothers were bidding each other good-bye in front of those black-green branches, Mingguang happily told Minghui, "As construction site manager, I theoretically could embezzle a lot of money, but I actually don't want any of it. All I want is to become a first-class teacher."

Mingguang asked, "Aren't you going to stay for lunch?"

He added, "Perhaps your sister-in-law has already established a new family."

Then he exhorted Minghui, "You should go visit your sister-in-law on my behalf."

With that, Minghui left Mingguang, leaving behind the construction site, the city's east side, and all of Explosion. When he glanced back, it was as if he were looking at a dissipating cloud of smoke.

II.

Cai Qinfang's family lived in the depths of the Balou Mountains, and in order to ship out the copper, iron, tin, and platinum ore from the mines, the mountain road had been widened to the point that it could accommodate four large trucks driving side by side. The road was made from a combination of crushed stone, cement, and steel rebars, and the day the new road was completed Mayor Kong cut the ceremonial ribbon. He took a large pair of scissors from a tray, and as he was cutting the red silk ribbon that had been extended across the road, countless gold bars and crystal beads, jade pendants and agate clasps all spilled out onto the road. Hundreds of earrings and bracelets rolled into the grass. From the site of the ribbon-cutting ceremony, there was torrential applause from the officials and city residents assembled there. Amid this applause, people scurried to collect the gold, jade, and necklaces scattered along the road, but in the chaos some people were trampled to death. When Minghui saw this scene on television, he called Cheng Qing in the city government and, with her permission, was able to speak to his brother.

"People were trampled to death," he told Mingliang.

Mingliang reflected for a moment, then replied, "The first phase of construction has yielded two hundred and thirty-two kilometers of road."

Minghui exclaimed, "My god!"

"The second phase has now begun," Mingliang added. "And in three years' time we plan to transform all of the surrounding rural areas over which Explosion has jurisdiction into roadways, so that our people will be able to lead even better lives than the Americans and Europeans."

Minghui discussed some family matters with his brother, then hung up the phone. By this point he was on the same stretch of mountain road where Mingliang had cut the ceremonial ribbon and all of the gems and jewelry had fallen to the ground. The cold, dry winter air covered the entire mountain range. The trees lining both sides of the road were crying out from the cold as wind tore through them. Minghui could easily have taken a car to the house of his sister-in-law's mother. All he would have needed to do was pick up the phone and call someone up, and say that he was Mayor Kong's younger brother, Kong Minghui, and immediately several sedans would come to meet him. But the almanac had said he must walk ten thousand *li* before everything would become clear, and therefore he decided to walk. Countless empty trucks drove past him, heading into the mountains. There were also many trucks full of coal driving down from the mountains, heading toward the smelting plants on the outskirts of Explosion. He walked along the side of the road and saw that the dust from the trucks had completely buried a tree. He saw birds struggling to fly but falling to the ground because they were coughing so badly. On the side of the road he also saw a plot of wheat belonging to some village, but because the dust was so thick, the wheat seedlings had peeked out and then ducked back underground. He watched as the seedlings tried to dodge the cars, coal, and dust—as though they were playing hide-and-seek. Minghui stood for a long time next to that field, until the sun in the west looked like a fiery ball about to dip into a lake, and only then did he leave and proceed to quickly follow the road into the mountains.

He walked to the end of the paved road, like someone reaching the end of a stretched-out strip of cloth.

He walked to the end of the dirt road, like someone reaching the end of a piece of hand-woven cloth.

He reached the end of the path, like someone following a rope until it suddenly breaks off. Under the light of the setting sun, the fields, villages, and gullies were all peacefully arrayed along the mountain ridge. Because it was so quiet in the mountains, Minghui could hear the blood rushing in his ears. Along the road he asked several people for directions but still took a couple of wrong turns. Eventually, however, he reached Cai Qinfang's home before nightfall. It was then that he saw the village, known as Zhang-Wang Village, sprawled out over the hillside. This was an old village with a combination of thatched-roof and tile-roof houses, and it looked much the way Explosion Village had looked years earlier. Qinfang's house was the second one at the entrance to the village, and when Minghui arrived at her front door, he found her feeding her semi-paralyzed father. The setting sun cast a light yellow glow on her face, and each strand of white hair on her head resembled dried-up grass. Minghui had asked for directions at the first house in the village, but when he arrived at Qinfang's house he was suddenly reminded of his elder brother. As he remembered his brother, Minghui suddenly slowed down. When he was standing in front of Qinfang, he asked quietly,

"Are you my elder sister-in-law?"

Then he added, "Sis, how have you become like this?!"

Qinfang sat up and turned around. When she saw Minghui, she immediately dropped the bowl she was holding, splattering egg noodle soup all over her pants. Staring at Minghui's face, she opened her mouth as though to say something, but nothing came out. Tears poured down her cheeks, and her hands trembled as she held them in midair. Standing in the doorway to this thatched-roof house, Minghui and Qinfang stared at each other, until finally she opened her mouth and exclaimed, "Minghui!" She took two quick steps toward him, then stopped and asked how he had managed to find her. She said, "How did you find this place? How many years has it been since we last saw each other? Brother, how are you? You've barely changed and still have that boyish look." At that point, it occurred to her to invite Minghui to come inside and sit for a while. She asked a relative to straighten up the house, wipe down the table and chairs, start cooking some rice, and pour Minghui some water to wash his face.

She asked him,

"What would you like to eat?

". . . Would you like to start with a bowl of egg-drop soup?

". . . It takes more than half a day to get from Explosion to Zhang-Wang Village, even if you're driving. How long did it take you to walk here?"

Qinfang's entire household sprang into motion, while her neighbors also helped. Soon, the entire village was hard at work, with everyone bringing Qinfang eggs, walnuts, and peanuts, all hoping that Minghui would try their own family's delicacies. Someone even brought over an old hen and asked Minghui whether he liked to eat chicken—adding that if he did, she would immediately make him some chicken stew. Someone else brought over some black wood ear fungus and asked Qinfang to cook Minghui a bowl of black wood ear and white sugar soup.

Everyone crowded around Minghui and asked,

"Are you really the mayor's younger brother?

". . . If you are the mayor's brother, then why did you walk all the way to our village?"

Qinfang was the wealthiest person in the village, and even though she was divorced, it was nevertheless still true that she had been married to the brother of the former town, county, and now city mayor. This brother who had arrived, meanwhile, was now a university president, and furthermore had come to Zhang-Wang Village to fetch Qinfang and take her to her former husband's house, where she could live in harmony with Mingguang. After Minghui said that he wanted to take Qinfang back and have her remarry Mingguang, the entire courtyard fell silent. Everyone stared at Minghui and asked, "Really? Really?" Then someone tugged at Qinfang's arm, saying, "Your hard work has finally yielded results." They said that from now on, the mayor would call her Sister, and all the section chiefs, bureau chiefs, and department heads would address her as Sister. They tugged at Sister-in-Law's sleeve while crowding around Minghui, saying that it was no wonder that two days earlier thousands of magpies had flown over to the village and spent the entire day singing, while a day earlier two peacocks and two phoenixes had flown over Qinfang's courtyard wall and opened their wings to her, like the sun coming up over the horizon.

The sun, which was shining down on the villagers' happy faces, slowly set behind the mountains.

As the sun was setting, Qinfang squatted down and began to cry. Then she suddenly rushed out into the courtyard, grabbed her father, who was lying down in his chair, and exclaimed, "It's over, it's over! Your illness will be healed!" It was then that Minghui learned that when Qinfang agreed to get divorced, Mingliang, who was town mayor at the time, had signed ten sheets of white paper. He told Qinfang that if she wanted to build a house, she just needed to write down what she needed on a sheet of that paper, and it would be delivered to her. He told her that if she wanted to sow a field of crops, she just needed to fill out one of the sheets and some cadres would issue her a ready-made contract to sublease the land. If she had any legal troubles with a family in the village, she simply needed to fill out one of those sheets explaining the situation, and she would win the lawsuit and keep her reputation. Those ten sheets of paper could help Qinfang accomplish ten critical tasks. But after she returned home and her father heard that she had divorced Mingguang, he immediately fell silent, and the next morning they discovered that he had had a stroke and had been left partially paralyzed. She therefore began filling out those blank sheets of paper—using them to have the hospital send its very best doctors to visit her father, and to obtain ingredients with which to brew Chinese medicine for her father to drink. She begged him to hang on to life, even if it meant that he would be partially paralyzed.

Once, when her father collapsed in the mountains and looked as though he were dead, Qinfang asked someone to quickly write several lines on one of those sheets of white paper, requesting that doctors from the hospital in the mountains come over as quickly as possible. Those doctors rushed over, out of breath and bathed in sweat, and they managed to pull her father from the brink of death. Another time, when her father was at home and fell down in the courtyard, he began foaming at the mouth, and not even a trace of breath could be detected from his nostrils. Qinfang knew that her father's time had finally arrived and that, even if the doctors came rushing over, they still wouldn't be able to save him. She therefore took all of the blank sheets of paper that Mingliang had signed, rolled them into a ball, and stuffed them into her father's mouth, while crying, "Father, Father . . . My brother-in-law is no longer the town mayor, but is now the county mayor!" With this, she was able to bring her father back to life. To this day, she still kept one of those blank pages signed by Mingliang, and no matter what happened, she refused to part with it. At most, she would, at a crucial junction, take it out and wave it in people's faces, telling them that her brother was Kong Mingliang, the city mayor, and if they didn't believe it they could see his signature right there! When her father suffered an aneurysm on the coldest day of the year and fell into a coma, she knelt by his bedside and held up that signed sheet of paper, crying out, "He is the mayor! He is the mayor!" Then the room gradually warmed up, the blood flow to her father's head returned to normal, and he became so clearheaded that it was as though he were not ill.

The moment the sun touched the western mountains, the mountain ridge became as peaceful as a silk cloth fluttering to the ground. In the fields of Zhang-Wang Village, all of the wheat sprouts were green, as they turned their leaves in the direction of Qinfang's house. The bare tree branches also beckoned in the direction of her house, while the grass and flowers around the entrance to her house also had a hint of green. When her father heard that his middle-aged daughter wanted to marry back into the Kong family and return to her former husband's house, he didn't say a word and instead he merely raised his hand—the same hand he had not raised for many years owing to his paralysis. He caressed his daughter's head and face as the tears falling on his hand, wrist, and arm bloomed like flowers and emitted an early spring fragrance.

Shortly afterward, the villagers surged toward Qinfang's house, asking Minghui if it was true that he had come to fetch her and take her back to Explosion to remarry his elder brother.

Minghui nodded.

"Has your brother agreed?"

"My brother asked me to look after the family," Minghui responded solemnly. "It goes without saying that he would agree."

Next, someone began lighting fireworks outside Qinfang's house, and someone else went to fetch some musical instruments. The sound of drumming and fireworks filled the courtyard and the entire village, radiating in all directions, making everything as festive as New Year's. Everyone surrounded her and lifted Minghui up, grateful that he had come to fetch her and take her home. The villagers congratulated her on once again becoming a member of the Kong family and asked, "Now that you'll be married back into the Kong family, and will once again be the mayor's sister-in-law, could you not take that final unused sheet of blank paper that the mayor—back when he was still only a town mayor—signed for you, and write something on it? We are enduring an unusually cold and dry winter, and are about to enter a period of drought. Could you not write on that sheet of paper, 'Let it snow! Let it snow!' That way, the heavens might dump a heavy snowfall onto our fields."

When Qinfang heard this request, she returned to her room and opened the chest at the head of her bed, and from the bottom drawer she took out an envelope. From the envelope, she removed the final signed letter, which had begun to yellow, and wrote, "Let it snow! Let it snow!" Then the villagers crowded around her and Minghui, and under the moonlight the two of them proceeded to the front of the village, where they knelt down and waved that sheet of paper in the air, chanting, "Let it snow! Let it snow! It is the mayor who is calling for snow! It is the mayor who is calling for snow!" They chanted, "A snowstorm is an omen for a prosperous year. It is the mayor who is calling for snow!" Sure enough, the air was soon filled with moist, dirty snowflakes, and under the moonlight the moonlike blossoms fell onto the uncultivated fields at the head of the village. As soon as the ground was covered in a dusting of snow, everyone knelt down, whereupon Qinfang lit a match and set the sheet with the mayor's signature on fire. Then she lifted the burning sheet into the air, and the snowfall turned into a blizzard. The snow continued to fall heavily all night, blanketing the village and the surrounding fields, as well as the entire mountain ridge. The snow ended up being a foot deep, and all the wheat sprouts, trees, and grasses were warm and moist, as though they were hibernating, and there was no need to worry about the future because prosperity was in sight.

The next day, Minghui and Qinfang extracted themselves from this snowfall and returned to Explosion, where Qinfang and Mingguang were reunited and resumed a peaceful life.

4. CULTURE AND CULTURAL RELICS

There was also a snowfall in Explosion.

After the snow stopped, the entire city was put on display. The buildings and overpasses in the distance looked as though they had been constructed out of bricks of snow. Meanwhile, the trees and street signs were all wrapped in snow. After fetching Qinfang from her mother's house and taking her to Mingguang's house and helping her straighten it up, Minghui returned home.

On that snowy night, the moonlight shone through as dimly as a sheet of gauze. When Minghui reached the former village square, he picked up a shard of moonlight from the ground. This shard was about the same weight as a window shade but was as cool and slippery as a piece of wet silk. After returning the shard to where he found it, Minghui walked home through the snow. By the time he arrived his mother was already sound asleep, like an old cat curled up next to a stove. Minghui opened the courtyard gate and heard his mother ask in her sleep, "Have you returned? Are your eldest brother and sister-in-law OK?"

Through the window to her room, Minghui nodded to his mother, who then turned over and fell back asleep. Seeing that everything was all right, Minghui went to his own room, but as he was about to fall asleep he remembered the almanac under his pillow. One page had partially peeled away from the others, but apart from the words *Second Brother*, the rest of the text remained buried in a blob of ink. The ink resembled dried mud from a pond, and the tiny fly-like writing resembled wisps of water plants. Minghui had already looked at this dried pond and its plants thousands of times, but he was unable to discern any trace of the plants' former greenery, nor was he able to make out anything regarding Second Brother's life. He also had no way of knowing what this almanac wanted him to do on his brother's behalf.

Lying in bed, Minghui thought about that half page dealing with his brother, and then abruptly sat up and grabbed the almanac. He turned to the half-moistened page concerning his brother and looked at the date—"third month, third day"—which turned out to be Second Brother's birthday. On this page, there appeared an ink splotch half as big as a fist. Minghui remembered that shard of moonlight he had found in the old city street, as well as this old almanac printed on coarse paper that had been used for who knows how many years. Because of the dampness of the hole in the tree, all of the pages had stuck together. He had taken the old volume out into the sun, whereupon the pages dried up and became even more tightly stuck together, and it was not until he took the book out into the night mist that several of the pages had begun to dampen and peel away from one another. Minghui had to mist the page on Eldest Brother and Sister-in-Law for three nights in a row before he could separate it. As for this page on Second Brother, he had to mist it for fifteen straight nights before he was able to peel away even a single corner, but because he had misted it for too long, the ink on the page had run together. But now, it suddenly occurred to Minghui how he could decipher the page on Second Brother. While in the sun the pages would dry and stick together, and in the night mist they would moisten and peel apart though the ink would then run together, in this mist of snowy night the stuck-together pages could be peeled apart. The light of the cold winter moon could suck out moisture better than the sun could, thereby allowing him to dry out those pages so that the indistinct writing could once again resemble a muddy pond streaked with water plants.

When this approach occurred to Minghui, he jumped out of bed and ran over to the window to look at the snowy-night moon, which at that point was shining down on the old street. He quickly grabbed a table, which he placed in the middle of the courtyard. Then he opened the almanac and put it in the middle of the table. He walked to the area between the two courtyard walls where the moonlight was falling and carefully picked up the brightest shard of moonlight from the ground. Slowly, he carried the shard to the table and placed it upright next to the almanac. When he went back to the courtyard wall to get another shard, he noticed that the spot where the first shard had been was now jet-black, and this blackness had dimmed all of the remaining shards at the corner of the wall. Minghui stood there for a while; then he turned around, opened the courtyard gate, went out into the street, and brought in a second shard of moonlight. He went to the former square and brought back a third shard. Finally, he went to the area on the outskirts of the old street and brought back a fourth and a fifth shard.

Upon returning home, Minghui first leaned the shards of moonlight against the table legs. Then, after locking the outer gate, he took one shard after another, each of which was a different size and shape, and placed them all erect on the table, arranging them into a square.

He brought over the largest square-shaped shard and placed it on top of the others. In this way, on this snowy night, he was able to cover his almanac with a tiny house made of moonlight. Minghui stood quietly next to this moon house, looking at the opened almanac lying peacefully in its home. The humidity of the snowy night gradually moistened the page discussing Second Brother together with the following page describing the events of the fourth day of the third month. The walls and ceiling of the cool, dry moon house absorbed the moisture and steam emitted by the pages as they dried. The moon gradually moved from directly overhead toward the western part of the sky, and while during the first half of the night the moon was in its waxing phase, in the second half of the night it entered its waning phase. When it transitioned from a round full moon into its waning phase, Minghui saw that a corner of the page describing Second Brother had begun to separate from the page beneath it. He carefully moved aside the shard of moonlight directly in front of him, then reached into the moon house with both hands and carefully lifted the page for the third day of the third month until he was able to separate the entire page from the one beneath it.

He saw that what had previously been merely a dark smudge of ink was slowly clearing up, and eventually he was able to discern the two characters for *Zhu* and *Ying*. The *Zhu* character appeared very clearly, while the *Ying* one was somewhat indistinct, though the right-hand portion of the latter character appeared as clear as though an autumn leaf had fallen on the page. When Minghui discovered that he could discern the characters for *Zhu* and *Ying* within that smudge of ink, his hands froze as he realized that the almanac wanted him to do something involving Second Brother and Second Sister-in-Law. Minghui was elated, as though he had finally succeeded in solving a riddle. His hands started trembling, to the point that he almost knocked down the moon house he had just built.

CHAPTER 16
New Members of the Clan

1. ZHU YING

The day after the snowfall, before Minghui went to see Mingliang, he first went to see his sister-in-law Zhu Ying. She was in her courtyard in front of a large pile of snow she had swept up. In the snow she had drawn a picture of Second Brother with her finger, and over his belly she had written the word *Die!* However, her entire house—inside and outside, on the walls and ceilings, upstairs and downstairs—was still covered with photographs and newspaper clippings about Mingliang, and beneath them there still appeared countless phrases like *Mine till death do us part!* But over these phrases, Zhu Ying had used a thick red marker to draw the sort of red *X* that one normally would see on a poster announcing someone had been sentenced to death. Every inch of wall in the house was covered with postings and writing, and in addition to the earlier photographs of Mingliang that had already been there, now there were new ones from the national and provincial papers of him giving speeches and shaking people's hands. The phrases such as *He is mine!* and the red *X*'s were like fireworks on a holiday. Minghui stared at these red *X*'s and realized that Zhu Ying's hatred of Mingliang had already driven her insane. This made Minghui even more convinced that he needed to go see Mingliang.

Minghui stood in front of Zhu Ying's house and looked around, but on this occasion, unlike his previous visit, he did not see the girls Zhu Ying was training in preparation for Explosion's transformation into a city or even a provincial-level metropolis or even a province. Instead, he stood directly in front of Zhu Ying in her living room and gently said,

"I'm going to see Second Brother.

". . . Second Brother hasn't been home in years, has he?"

Zhu Ying bit her lower lip as she thought for a moment, then said very deliberately, "There is no need to see him. His business is about to collapse, and once it does he will be begging to come home—to come back to me. But when the time comes, even if he is literally dying at my feet, I won't necessarily rescue him, as I did before."

As Zhu Ying said this she smiled coldly, but behind that smile she was secretly beginning to cry. Without waiting for the tears to appear, she quickly wiped her eyes with her hand, then invited Minghui to sit on the couch beside her as she pulled out an exquisitely decorated small wooden box. She opened the box and took out a leather pouch. Clenching her jaws, Zhu Ying removed from the pouch a collection of photographs of her son Victory, beginning with the day of his birth and continuing through his first month celebration to his first birthday to his enrollment in nursery school. The photographs were wrapped in paper consisting of a series of documents and directives specifying that Zhu Ying was not permitted to visit Mingliang in the city government without Mingliang's express permission, so as not to interfere with the work he was doing on behalf of Explosion's development. The earliest of those documents was dated three days after Mingliang was appointed city mayor, while the most recent one was from the preceding month. Upon looking at these photographs of his nephew, Minghui proceeded to examine each of the documents and noticed that their language became progressively sharper, to the point that the final document concluded with the line, "If you return again to city hall to disrupt the mayor and the government's work, you will receive either a certificate of divorce or a letter assigning you to reside in a mental asylum in perpetuity."

With a look of shock and horror, Minghui read though all of those documents line by line. The winter sunlight shone in through the window, shining down on his body like a sheet of ice and chilling him to the bone. To warm himself, he wanted to embrace Zhu Ying or drape his body over the stove.

"Sister-in-Law, did you try to see Second Brother again last month?

". . . Did you go see him several times, only to have him refuse you?

". . . Is he in fact a person, or rather a cold-blooded beast?"

Biting her lower lip, Zhu Ying took those documents back from Minghui, carefully folding them as before. Then, with a bitter laugh, she handed him the most recent photograph of his nephew and said,

"Perhaps you could go see him. After all, the two of you are brothers.

". . . If you see him, please do one thing on my behalf: Have him look at this photograph and ask him whether or not his son resembles him.

". . . Does his son resemble him or not? That's all I need to know."

After Minghui left Zhu Ying's house, the sky over Explosion was finally sunny and warm. The thick clouds and fog had been washed away by a heavy snowfall that blanketed the earth, so that now the sky was left thoroughly cleansed and appeared brand-new. As Zhu Ying was walking Minghui out, she choked a bit on that new freshness. They walked out one after the other, then came to a stop under the apple tree that, several years earlier, had been transformed into a pear tree. They both stared silently at that apple-pear tree, though now it appeared that it was no longer a pear tree. The tree's bark had been maroon-colored and was covered in wrinkles, but now the bark glowed brightly and was completely green, as though it were about to become a walnut tree. Perhaps, in spring, it would indeed become a walnut tree. Seeing that the tree branches were no longer curled like chicken fingers but were rather long and straight, Minghui said to Zhu Ying,

"Pears symbolize departure, while walnuts symbolize union. After I visit Second Brother this time, you'll definitely be successfully reunited with him."

Zhu Ying laughed softly as the flush faded from her cheek. "He won't look back. I've already decided to ruin your second brother, and even if his life were threatened, I still wouldn't help him." Then she caressed Minghui's head, hesitated a moment, and added, "In the Kong family, you are the only good and upright one. I trust you. Do you want to know where your second brother will fail?"

Minghui stood there staring at his sister-in-law, with no idea of what she was talking about. After looking at him for a moment, Zhu Ying took his hand, turned around, and walked away. She quickly passed through the courtyard and the living room, and went upstairs. From her pocket she produced a key and unlocked the door to a room. She then went inside, opened the window, and let in a ray of sunlight. Finally, she pulled in Minghui, who had followed behind and was in the doorway, and gaping in astonishment.

The room was oriented toward the south, was about twenty square meters in size, and didn't have a single piece of furniture. Instead, it consisted of just four snowy-white walls, each of which was full of countless photographs of naked girls. Some of the girls had shoulder-length hair, while others wore their hair longer. All of the photographs were in color, and they were all full-frontal images. Each of them had been enlarged to one foot and two inches, and each of them had a name and number written in the lower right-hand corner. Several of the girls were wearing bras and lacy panties, but most of them were completely naked except for a peony or rose placed strategically between their legs. The photographs were arranged in a row, so that all of those girls' eyebrows, smiles, breasts, and genitals were neatly aligned. The wall was filled with flirtatious faces, each of them smiling happily like a flower on a snowy day. This series of pert breasts and strategically placed peonies and roses made Minghui break out in a cold sweat.

"Can you hate and curse me?" Zhu Ying asked him with an odd smile. "These are all top students from the women's vocational school, and they can make your brother return and kneel down before me. They can reduce all of the men in the world to the status of mere animals, and make them belong to me—to women.

". : . All of this was prepared so that Explosion could become a provincial-level metropolis." Zhu Ying paused for a moment, then quickly resumed. "In no time, Explosion will become as large as Beijing and Shanghai, and I had thought that when the city was redesignated as a provincial-level metropolis your brother would definitely return and ask me for these girls to send to Beijing as gifts. But now that he has your third brother to help him, he won't come back to see me. He won't use them and also won't ask for my help, and as a result he'll fail at their hands.

". . . You are the person I trust the most, so I'm begging you not to tell your brother about any of this." Zhu Ying paused to grind her teeth, as a sallow smile appeared on her face. "You've been good to me, but I have nothing with which to repay you. Why don't you see which of these girls you like, and I'll summon her for you." She gestured toward a beautiful girl with the number 1949, and asked, "How about her? She's one I prepared for a certain bureau director in Beijing." Seeing that Minghui was not looking at that girl, Zhu Ying finally smiled and said solemnly, "If you don't want one, that's fine. If you don't want one, that merely reassures me that in this world there is still one good person and that I still have a reason to continue living."

As Minghui retreated from the room, the cold winter air brought him to his senses. It occurred to him that perhaps his sister-in-law had gone mad, and he should follow the almanac's instructions and quickly summon Mingliang to her side. Only by having Mingliang return to her side could Zhu Ying's illness be cured, and if he did not return, both the Kong family and Mingliang's own family would be destroyed, like snow under the hot sun.

2. KONG MINGLIANG

When Explosion had been redesignated as a city, there had been only two sentries stationed at the front of the government building, but now there were six policemen stationed on the sentry stand. Their uniforms were neatly pressed, and the rifles they were holding sparkled bloodred. Originally, the government building gate had been thirty to fifty feet wide, with a pair of stone pillars on either side, but now the entrance was three hundred feet wide, and in the middle there was a new sliding gate. The gate was completely closed, and it would slide open only when a car drove up, while pedestrians used a separate entrance on the side. The officials going inside were all carrying municipal entry permits, and anyone who lacked this permit would have to go to the police office next door to register.

As Minghui was about to enter the building to visit his brother, he stared in surprise at the new entranceway, and the six sentries all turned to look at him. After he took a step forward, four of the sentries promptly surrounded him and sternly asked him,

"What do you think you're doing?

". . . You say you're looking for your second brother? Who is your second brother?

". . . You want the mayor to be your brother? Don't you know that *everyone* in Explosion wants the mayor to be his godfather!"

As the sentries said this, they grabbed Minghui's arm and pushed him into the police office. Inside, there was a burly thirtysomething policeman. He pushed Minghui down into a chair with his gaze, then repeated what the sentries had just said. At this point, Minghui took out a photograph of himself with Mingliang and showed it to the policeman. Then he took out a picture of all four brothers and showed it to him as well. Finally, he took out a family portrait from several years earlier and showed it to him. Upon seeing the third photograph, the policeman, who was a strong fellow, became gentle and compliant, as his oversize uniform hung on his thin frame like a set of barrels on a wooden stand.

When Minghui left this entry room, he was personally escorted by the policeman, who went to open the door for him. As they were leaving, the policeman even walked Minghui down the stairs and remained with him until they were inside the city government's main building. Holding the photograph of him and his brother, Minghui walked through one doorway and then another, until finally they reached the building's innermost doorway, where there were two sentries. Not only did these sentries not attempt to stop him, they even rushed forward to salute him. The sudden sound of their approaching footsteps startled Minghui to the point that he simply stood frozen in the doorway. In shock, he saw the city government's administrative secretary, Cheng Qing, walk toward him, smiling, as though a firepot in the middle of winter were facing him.

Cheng Qing had gained weight, and her face, which had previously been egg-shaped, was now quite round. When she laughed, that firepot resembled an enormous egg yolk swaying back and forth in midair. She asked, "How many years has it been since we last saw each other? Do you still remember that the mayor is your brother?" She then wiped the smile from her face and asked coldly, "All these years, no one from your family has come to visit the mayor."

Minghui took the elevator up with her, then proceeded down a hallway. The entire way, Cheng Qing kept going on and on about how the mayor worked day and night on behalf of the citizens of Explosion, working his heart out on behalf of the people. She recounted how one day someone came from Beijing to inspect the city's infrastructure from the perspective of its potential redesignation as a provincial-level metropolis, and to prepare for the inspection the mayor didn't sleep for three full months. Exhausted, he became as limp as a scarecrow, and as soon as the inspectors from Beijing departed, the mayor was so drained that a gust of wind could have blown him away. Cheng Qing told Minghui, "It would have been nice if either you or your family had come to see the mayor. If you had, he wouldn't have become so estranged from your family." As she was saying this, Cheng Qing arrived at the office of the city government's administrative secretary. She pushed the door open and sidled in.

Cheng Qing's office was far more spacious and luxurious than he had imagined. It was as large as five houses, and the desk alone took up half of the entire floor. The folders on the desk were sorted by color into red, yellow, green, and so forth and arranged in piles. On the other side of the table there were red, black, and blue telephones. In addition, as in all other offices, there was a couch, a television set, a newspaper rack, and a water fountain, together with an array of bonsai plants and flowers in colors ranging from light green to jet-black. Minghui stood in the doorway staring at the office, a look of astonishment on his face. "If you hadn't given up your position as director of the bureau of development, perhaps you would have such a large office?" Cheng Qing smiled and said, "Do you regret it? Do you still want to return to work?"

The tea on the tea table had grown cold, but Minghui still didn't take a sip. When they had poured the water in, the green tea leaves had swirled in the boiling water, but now, even though the water had long since cooled and stopped steaming, the tea leaves were still swirling in the cup as fast as before. "I don't need anything; I just want to see my brother." The first time Minghui said this, the sun outside the window was bright yellow like a firefly; the second time he said it, the sun was fiery red; and by the third time he said it, the sun had entered a twilight color somewhere between red and yellow. Twilight had arrived without his noticing it, and within the room's warmth there was a layer of coolness. Cheng Qing's face had lost its former fiery brightness, and her yolk-like smile had also turned the color of twilight. Sitting in front of Minghui, from dawn to dusk she said the same thing:

"If you need anything, all you have to do is tell me. The mayor represents the citizens of Explosion, not only your Kong family. He is so busy that he doesn't even have time to stop and breathe."

Regardless of whether it was spring, summer, fall, or winter, Minghui kept saying the same thing:

"I don't need anything; I just want to see my brother to say a few words to him."

In the end, as the sky was turning dark, Cheng Qing went into another room in the office and made a telephone call, then returned. With a relieved smile, she said, "The mayor has gone to the city's east side to host a leadership restructuring meeting. He'll be back by nightfall, and if you want to wait for him, he said that you may wait in his office."

Minghui therefore proceeded to his brother's office. It was not very far and was on the same floor as Cheng Qing's—with the two offices separated only by three conference rooms. The only difference between the two spaces was that outside the mayor's office, there were two bodyguards, while next door there was the office of his administrative secretary, whom he could call whenever he wished. The bodyguards and secretaries all reported to Cheng Qing, and when they saw her they smiled and said, "Good day, Chief Secretary!" Cheng Qing nodded lazily, then gestured for Minghui to enter the mayor's office. Inside, she exchanged a few more words with him, then slipped out, as though trying to avoid a leper.

"Just wait here patiently.

". . . If you want some water, you can serve yourself.

". . . Don't touch your brother's things. He never permits anyone to wait in his office alone."

When Cheng Qing left, she shut the door behind her. The setting sun hung behind the enormous window like a piece of red fabric. This was the first time Minghui had entered his brother's city mayor's office. He didn't see anything extraordinary about the office's decorations or contents. There was a large red desk, but his brother Mingyao also had one of those; there were two evergreen trees, but Mingyao's office had these as well. As for the rest, there was a couch, some newspapers, a telephone, documents, a water fountain, and a bookcase full of thick scholarly books. What else was there? Across from the red bookcase, there was also a display cabinet containing a variety of exquisite artifacts that foreign guests had brought as gifts when they had visited. But apart from this, the only thing that was somewhat unusual was the curtain hanging over the window. The curtain's fabric was extremely thick and heavy, and was covered on both sides in high-quality cloth with embroidered borders. Also, next to the display cabinet containing the foreign gifts there was another room with the key still in the keyhole.

Minghui walked around the main room for a while, then opened the door to the other room.

The room was the office's relaxation space. When Cheng Qing had told Minghui not to touch anything in the mayor's office, she had probably meant that he should not enter this particular room. Minghui hesitated a moment but in the end still proceeded inside. He was the mayor's younger brother, and when he entered the inner room he felt as though he had just entered the home of a close friend. There was a bed, wallpaper, a lamp, a white ceiling, and a desk piled high with newspapers and documents, while on the floor there was a dark-colored wool carpet. Minghui didn't know that the carpet was made from the hair of sixteen-year-old girls, but when the light was turned on the carpet radiated a soft skin-like glow. The floor felt a bit slick, and it occurred to him that rather than the carpet, it would have been better to put down a bath towel. He opened the door to the washroom to take a look, and apart from the pristine white bathtub, a gold-rimmed urinal, a gold-plated faucet, and a solid gold soap dish, there was nothing else that struck him as particularly extraordinary. The light in the bathroom was pure white, and various bathing utensils were also made of pure gold, each of them so heavy that he almost couldn't lift them. This made him feel a bit faint, as if he had accidentally entered the wrong room. He again remembered Cheng Qing's instructions that he not touch anything in the mayor's office, but as he was tearing his eyes away from those gold artifacts, he noticed that in the waste basket next to the sink there were some remains from a sexual encounter. When he saw this, his stomach began to rumble and he felt as though he were about to vomit. As he was rushing out of the bathroom, he noticed that next to the towel rack there was another door, on which there was a wooden sign that read, ENTRY PROHIBITED. Moreover, just like the "Mine until death do us part" that Sister-in-Law had inscribed below all of those pictures of Second Brother, the *Entry Prohibited* inscription was followed by a string of three exclamation marks. He now realized what Cheng Qing had meant when she said that he shouldn't touch anything. He stood in front of the bathroom staring at that door. He wanted to walk away, but without realizing it he instead grasped that solid gold or gold-plated door handle. To his surprise, on one side of the door his brother had posted a plaque saying NO ADMITTANCE!!! while the secret door itself was unlocked—like a secret room in a bank when, because no one ever goes in, the staff doesn't bother to lock it anymore.

After hesitating for a moment, Mingling pushed open the secret door.

As he had expected, there was a light switch on the wall next to the door.

He flipped the switch, and the light came on.

Under the white light, Minghui initially looked around in confusion, but he became increasingly alarmed as he gradually understood what he was seeing. There were several rooms with the windows all tightly sealed, as in a storeroom. Against the white walls there were shelves made from the most expensive yellow pear wood. Each shelf must have cost several hundred thousand or several million yuan, but they were full of the least expensive objects imaginable. Minghui entered that storeroom and stood in the middle, staring at those shelves that looked like something one would find in a palace treasure room. He inspected each shelf and saw that they had an array of different-sized boxes, and in each box there were exceedingly ordinary items collected from different hotels, including toothpaste, toothbrushes, slippers, hand towels, bathrobes, and disposable razors or hair dryers. Furthermore, under each item there was a date and the name of a hotel. In another display area, there were pen cases, pen racks, staplers, pencil sharpeners, and all sorts of fountain pens and ballpoint pens that he had collected from all sorts of different conference halls. Beneath these items from around the country, there was also a date and the name of the organization to which the hall belonged. In the display area beneath it, there were artifacts collected from countless foreign banquet halls, including forks and knives, Korean tin chopsticks and Japanese copper ones, together with an occasional ordinary dish or bowl. In the fourth display area, there were some slightly more valuable artifacts, such as an oddly shaped telephone and several cigarette lighters in the form of a handgun. There were also drinking glasses with PEOPLE'S MEETING HALL or ZHONGNANHAI printed on them. It was when Minghui's gaze alighted on the final display area, however, that he felt he had finally found his brother—and specifically his brother's fraternal warmth. In the darkest inner corner of the display case, there were several pieces of coal and coke, cheap cigarettes and wine, and the sorts of cheap suits, clothing, hats, and shoes that only peasants from rural areas would wear.

Minghui felt as though a bucket of cold water had been poured over him and gradually realized that Second Brother was still the same brother he had known—the same Kong Mingliang who had led the residents of Explosion on those secret expeditions. After he was appointed town mayor, Mingliang once took some people to beat those residents of Explosion who were unable to stop stealing, though he himself never completely abandoned the habit either. After he was appointed county mayor and city mayor, he definitely wouldn't openly steal anymore, though he never did cure himself of the habit of casually taking things. All of the carefully dated slippers taken from hotel rooms and towels taken from airplanes, together with a matchbox filled with three-inch-long matches taken from the home or reception room of some official in Beijing—these demonstrated that Mingliang not only stole when he was village chief, but also continued stealing whenever he had a chance even as town mayor, county mayor, and city mayor. The only catch was that he never stole anything of value but rather merely pocketed an assortment of random items, the same way that many people, after they finish eating, will take the toothpicks and napkins sitting on the table. Mingliang brought these stolen items home, then he carefully placed them on display in this secret room. Here, Minghui rediscovered the Mingliang he had once known, and as he was reminiscing he heard the sound of Mingliang's footsteps approaching.

Minghui looked in the direction of the footsteps and, without turning off the light, he walked out of the secret room, passed through the bathroom, and returned to the display case of foreign gifts on the eastern side of Second Brother's office. He saw that in the office doorway, a young man even taller than Second Brother was standing, handsomely dressed in a suit, with a crew cut, and a face so white that there wasn't even a hint of color. Meanwhile, the briefcase he was holding was so black it looked fake. However, his bright smile was utterly genuine.

"I'm Mayor Kong's secretary, Secretary Liu. In order to have Explosion City redesignated as a metropolis, Mayor Kong has had to return to Beijing to make a report. Before he boarded the plane, the mayor told me to ask you what happened at home that has made you so anxious."

Minghui stood flabbergasted and, after a moment, responded, "Nothing has happened at home. I just need to see him."

With a soft smile like an autumn leaf falling on that square face in the doorway, it felt as though an extreme chill had suddenly fallen, as if all the warmth in the room suddenly disappeared. Minghui saw Mingliang suddenly disappear from in front of his eyes, like a breeze blowing through a crack in a door.

3. KONG MINGHUI

Because his heart was icy cold, the ground outside was frozen, the marble stones in the city square were covered in frost, and even the oil left behind by a car had become lumps of ice. The car had stopped by the side of the road, and the driver was hunched over, blowing on his hands while stomping his feet and cursing nonstop: "Fuck, Fuck!" But he couldn't get the car started again.

Unable to endure the bitter cold, Minghui decided to go see his third brother, Kong Mingyao.

Minghui's visit with Third Brother was exactly the opposite of his visit with Second Brother and was as straightforward as opening and closing a door. He went to the base of the mining company building, where he told the sentry that he was Kong Minghui, the fourth brother of Kong Mingyao, whereupon the sentry quickly called up the office building. As soon as Minghui entered the building, Mingyao was there waiting for him in the first-floor hall. All of Explosion—including the old city district, the city's east side, its west side, and the development zone—was frozen solid and covered in snow. Minghui trudged in from outside, trying to get warm, and saw Mingyao wearing a munitions belt and standing in front of a Lohan bamboo. Because of the cold, the bamboo plant's leaves had fallen off, but at that moment, as Mingyao looked at the bare plant, he removed his arms belt and placed it next to the bamboo, and the plant began emitting warm sounds as it produced streaks of green.

Mingyao then touched the plant, and countless green buds appeared on the bare branches.

Minghui walked over, looked at the new buds, then looked at his brother's face. Just as Minghui was about to say something, his brother asked,

"Is it very cold outside?

"It's somewhat warmer upstairs," Mingyao added, as he took Minghui to his sand table room on the eighth floor. Apart from the maps of the world, the United States, England, France, and Germany hanging on the wall, next to the map of the United States, which was half as large as the room itself, there was an equally large map of Afghanistan and Iraq. On the eastern side of the office, in addition to the sand table maps of the United States, Japan, and Taiwan, there was an unfinished sand table map of Afghanistan and Iraq—some craftsmen were in the process of using Bakelite and clay to create a sand table model of Iraq, but when they saw Minghui and Mingyao approach, their clay-covered hands were suspended in midair. Mingyao gestured for the craftsmen to continue their work, while he sat down with his brother and had someone pour them some water. Seeing that Minghui was warming up and was no longer shivering, Mingyao asked him why he had come.

After recounting how the previous day he had failed to see Second Brother, Minghui sighed and said,

"It's as if we weren't even brothers anymore."

Mingyao saw Minghui's expression and then reflected for a while before saying,

"The United States might attack Iraq."

Minghui said, "It's as if Mother were sick, because she keeps talking about you every minute of every day."

Mingyao said, "I never expected that the world could become so chaotic, and it's entirely the fault of the United States."

Minghui said, "If only Eldest Brother and Sister-in-Law were here. . . ."

Mingyao was silent for a moment, then asked, "Do you want me to remove Second Brother from his position as mayor? Do you want me to have him return home to live with Second Sister-in-Law?"

Minghui didn't know what to say and instead just stared at Mingyao.

Eventually, Mingyao realized that Minghui wasn't going to say anything, so he continued softly, "Brother, you should leave. It's too soon to bring Second Brother down. You should look after things at home, until the situation in the Middle East has been sorted out and I have restored peace to the world—if Second Brother still hasn't returned home by that point, I can force him to return, and can organize a dinner for all four brothers, where we can discuss our family responsibilities." Then Mingyao stood up, looking as though he were about to see Minghui out. Minghui stood up as well, placed his unfinished cup of tea on the table, and watched in astonishment as Mingyao went over to the sand table to tell the craftsmen to make the city of Baghdad twice as big, so that every street and alley could be clearly visible. Then Mingyao escorted Minghui out.

4. MOTHER

Mother died.

With a warm smile, she departed this cold world.

Not even heaven could have anticipated that that year's winter would be so bitterly cold. After Minghui left Mingyao's office, he ran home. He rushed inside and closed the courtyard gate, and the first thing he saw was that the trunk of the courtyard's old elm tree had frozen solid and developed several finger-size cracks, revealing the pristine white wood inside. He saw that a rice bowl that had been forgotten on a windowsill had frozen and shattered, with shards scattered all over the ground. When he walked inside, he saw that the hour and minute hands of the clock on the wall over the bed were frozen in place, while the red second hand had fallen off completely and was stuck in the bedding like a needle.

Minghui froze.

He stood in the doorway for a long time and then eventually ran toward the inner room. "Mother . . . Mother . . ." he shouted, his voice like a piece of bamboo that has been split open. Before he had even run out of his own room, his voice had caused the door to the main room to open. He proceeded to the doorway and shouted, "Ma, are you OK? . . . Ma, are you OK?" His cries caused the curtain to his mother's room to open, and he rushed inside and saw that his mother was still lying in bed. Her complexion, however, was no longer bright and rosy, as it had been when he left her, and instead it was pale and mottled. She was facing the interior of the room, her eyes were half open, and she looked as though she had just seen something on the wall. It was as if a gust of bitterly cold air had blown through that wall and onto her face.

"Mother is going to leave tonight, so you should tell her the truth. Have your eldest brother and his wife gotten back together? Has your second brother reconciled with his wife?

". . . Has your third brother married and started a family? Did he marry a woman from our old Explosion Street?

". . . You yourself are already one of the elders of our street. If you don't hurry up and get married, this is the one thing I won't be able to get over.

"Minghui," his mother added in a very weak voice, "you must answer these questions. After you do, Mother must go find your father."

Minghui did not know how he had suddenly become so composed, as though he had known all along that his mother would die. When he heard his mother's questions, he slowly took several steps forward and then stood in the middle of the room, as though he were an incense stick stuck in front of her bed.

"Eldest Sister-in-Law is pregnant with twins—a boy and a girl.

". . . Second Brother has taken Second Sister-in-Law into his home in the city hall complex, and every day when Second Brother goes in to work, Second Sister-in-Law stays home to cook and take their children to and from school.

". . . Third Brother is married. His wife is an instructor from Explosion and teaches my nephew, Little Victory.

"I'm also engaged, to that girl you saw while sitting in your doorway before winter fell. She is pretty and virtuous, and works in the hospital. We plan to get married later this year."

When he finished saying all of this, his mother turned over and faced him. On her lips she had a trace of a smile, which lasted several seconds, after which she closed her eyes for good.

Before burying his mother, Mingliang signed a directive from Beijing ordering that the weather of Explosion City must improve, and therefore the weather warmed up and the sun overhead became so hot that people wanted to take off their padded clothes. When Minghui finally received a phone call from Mingliang, he told Mingliang that their mother had died, whereupon Mingliang said that Explosion's redesignation as a provincial-level metropolis was about to be approved. Minghui asked Mingliang if he was going to return home for the funeral, and Mingliang suggested that they leave things as they were for the moment, because the most important announcements were about to begin. When Minghui tried to find Mingyao to tell him about their mother's death, he discovered that Mingyao was not at the mining company headquarters but rather had installed himself in some military barracks deep in the Balou Mountains. On that particular day, Mingyao was wearing his military uniform and was leading a spring training mobilization meeting for his troops, saying that the Japanese prime minister had again gone to visit the Yasu-kuni war shrine, while some Rightists had landed on China's Diaoyu Islands. Taiwan's Democratic Progressive Party had already secretly drafted a new constitution in anticipation of Taiwan's independence. Meanwhile, in an attempt to overturn the Iraqi and Afghan govern-ments, the United States was using the most advanced and most brutal equipment available, for which it was borrowing an enormous amount of money from China—as a result the value of the RMB had skyrocketed, making Chinese people want to hurl themselves from the tops of Beijing's skyscrapers. Germany had originally agreed to sell China weapons but now went back on its promise. Even neigh-boring Vietnam, which was as tiny as a grass seed, was drilling for oil in China's Spratly Islands. A Philippine printing company had even included China's island on its own map, which was about to go to press. The messenger Minghui had sent to inform Mingyao of his mother's death returned and told the rest of the Kong family,

"Throughout history, there has never been a hero who has mastered the ideals of both loyalty and filial piety."

Together with Mingguang and his wife, Minghui dressed their smiling mother's body and placed it in the coffin. Without troubling any of their neighbors, they buried their mother. That unusual winter snowfall had already melted on the sunny side of the hill, but the opposite side was still covered in pristine white snow, and a cold breeze was blowing over. From there, you could make out only the tops of Explosion's distant high-rise buildings, just as you could see only the crowns of the trees in that forest in the ravine. From behind the buildings, however, a continuous rumbling sound could be heard coming from mining and quarry sites.

After burying their mother in the same grave site where they had previously buried their father, Minghui and Mingguang were both exhausted, so they sat down in front of the grave to rest. They gazed out at the tops of the city's buildings, the smoke from the mines, and the snow on the mountains in front of them. They could hear the sound of a train approaching from the other side of the mountains, as well as planes landing at the airport. Mingguang said to Minghui, "Let's go back. It's time to eat. For lunch, we can have dumplings."

They stood up, grabbed their shovels, and prepared to leave. At that point, however, Mingguang went up to Minghui and, with a smile, said quietly, "Your eldest sister-in-law is pregnant, with a son."

CHAPTER 17
Great Geographic Transformation (1)

1. MEGALOPOLIS (1)

Mayor Kong Mingliang did not wake up on his own that morning but rather awoke in a shock. He initially didn't want to open his eyes, so with his eyes still tightly closed he tapped on his bed's yellow pear-wood headboard with his fingers. When the assistant standing outside his room heard the mayor tap three times on his headboard, he immediately went outside and used a bamboo pole to shoo away all of the sparrows that had gathered on the windowsills overnight. The assistant also summoned several young people and told them that if any sparrows or crows flew to the windows or to the trees in front, they should use the bamboo poles to shoo them away. But later, after everything had quieted down, the mayor could still hear something flying around, so he tapped even louder on his headboard.

The assistant became anxious and instructed the three sentries standing guard in the courtyard of the city government building complex that they should stand a dozen meters from each other and that each of them should hold a long bamboo pole—and in this way they could prevent all sparrows from flying over. The courtyard's garden was in the process of awakening from its winter slumber and, regardless of whether it was the flowers planted on either side of the stone path or the trees and flowers planted around the mayor's house, everything had turned so green that it appeared as though the sap was about to gush out. The peonies in the greenhouse were the first to burst into bloom, looking as beautiful as a young girl's face. When the sun came out, it shone down on the road that the mayor, after he woke up and got out of bed, would follow to go to work. That morning, when the gardeners were tending the flowers, the young men with the bamboo poles gestured toward their feet, indicating that they had taken off their shoes, whereupon the gardeners quickly removed their own shoes. Afraid of making a racket as they were arranging the flowers, they covered the edges of the flowerpots with their fingers and didn't remove them until they had put the pots down.

The enormous courtyard was like an ancient garden and was located several li to the east of the city government building. There was no one of consequence—only a vast wall and a set of empty villas and other buildings, together with cooks, gardeners, electricians, and other service workers. These people all gathered in the courtyard, like grass seeds in an empty field. They walked very quietly and whispered when they spoke. When they saw one another they would quickly nod. Particularly when Mayor Kong was about to go to sleep, the workers would remove their shoes. When his personal attendants entered his room, they would change into soft-soled slippers imported from Japan. They kept quiet not in order to avoid waking the mayor but rather because he had grown accustomed to silence. In the tile-roofed house Mingliang had built in the center of the city government courtyard, there was a corridor with many twists and turns, and the rooms were all linked to one another. Among those rooms there was a large meeting hall, a small meeting hall, a large and a small dining hall, a teahouse, and a coffeehouse, together with a workers' dormitory that was located where the sun didn't even shine. When the mayor was in his bedroom, if he needed anything he wouldn't pick up the telephone or ring a bell but rather would simply tap the table or headboard, and this would notify his assistants. If he wanted to have a certain girl come sleep with him, he would tap his headboard with a slightly different intonation and his assistants would understand. Given that Mingliang worked very hard all day, he was even more appreciative of peace and quiet. In the morning, apart from the sound of the sun rising, there was no other sound to be heard. His assistants would even hold their breath as they were removing their shoes and shooing away the birds. But in this silence, Mingliang still felt that there was some sound coming from somewhere, and just as he was about to tap on his headboard out of annoyance, it occurred to him that the sound was not coming from the courtyard but instead was coming from the preternatural silence in his brain and the extreme isolation of the courtyard. When he realized this, his finger—which was about to tap on the headboard—suddenly froze.

After dinner the previous evening, the ninth observational delegation from Beijing—which was there to examine Explosion's qualifications for being redesignated as a provincial-level metropolis—had told Mingliang that within a month Beijing would host its final discussion of whether or not to redesignate Explosion as a provincial-level metropolis on the same level as Shanghai, Guangzhou, Tianjin, and even Beijing itself. The delegates said that the key consideration was not the city's population or the speed and dimensions of its economic growth, but rather whether Mayor Kong could capture the attention of the experts and the government officials charged with making the decision, because these questions of redesignation necessarily came after discussions of national personnel. They added that by that point it would already be time to eat and, in order to retain the delegates' attention, he would need to ensure that any further discussion would be at least as appealing as the expected food. He would therefore need to prepare the rhetorical equivalent of delicious dishes and pair them with rare wines—and only then would the officials be willing to put off their meal and continue their discussions in the meeting hall. As the delegates were saying this, everyone was in the meeting hall next to the city government's dining hall enjoying dinner, and after the delicious meal had ended the investigation team and several people from the city government stayed behind in the conference room. In front of each of them there was a wooden basin, on which seven or eight bottles of Maotai *baijiu* wine had been poured for them to soak their feet. The room was full of the smell of *baijiu*. Several one-of-a-kind beauties were also on hand to give the men massages. When the head of the investigation team had been fully massaged, he faced the mayor. Then, with his sixty-year-old feet rubbing together in the *baijiu*, he said that he had never before used *baijiu* to soak his feet and that it was making his toes a bit numb.

At that point the mayor gazed at the investigation team, whose gray heads and wrinkled faces were all glowing radiantly. He pondered for a while, then said three things—each of which seemed to be part question and part observation:

"In Beijing, does no one care about women and money?"

He added, "Does no one care how quickly the city is developing?"

He added again, "If I can build a one-hundred-kilometer subway line and the largest airport in Asia in less than a week, is it possible that no one would take an interest?"

When he made this third statement, the eyes of everyone in the investigation team widened, like a row of red lanterns lined up in front of him. "Can you really build a hundred-kilometer subway line in only a week? Can you really build the largest airport in Asia in only a week?" The head of the investigation team rubbed his feet together in the *baijiu*, repeating these two questions over and over again. Finally, when they were about to leave to board the airplane, he asked these questions again while staring at Mingliang. After Kong Mingliang had escorted the investigation team onto the airplane, he went home to sleep. During the entire eighteen days that he had spent with the investigation team, he had been responsible for every-thing—even the chopsticks they had used were ones Mingliang had picked out himself and had personally distributed to each member of the team. He was bone tired after escorting this ninth investigation team around for eighteen days, and felt as he had back when he was village chief and was taking the villagers out to the railroad tracks to unload goods. But he was no longer as young as he once was, and rest, recuperation, and quiet were now as important to him as air and water. He slept so soundly that he would have no memory whatsoever of what he had said and what he had done, but as he was falling asleep something kept buzzing in his brain. He could hear people asking him the same question over and over again: "Can you really construct a subway line in only a week?" He nodded several times, while the people kept asking him, "Can you really build the largest airport in Asia in less than a week?" In the end, it was as if everything was decided at that juncture, and as long as Kong Ming-liang could build a hundred-kilometer subway line and the largest airport in Asia in less than a week, Explosion's redesignation as one of China's provincial-level metropolises would be all but guaranteed. Kong Mingliang lay in his enormous bed, opened his eyes, and saw that the ruby-encrusted hair clip of one of the women from the night before was still lying next to his pillow. He took the hair clip and placed it on his bedside table and reminisced about the woman. Then he sat up, grabbed his clothes, and got out of bed.

He suddenly grasped the thing that was ringing in his head—which was that he had to go see his third brother, Mingyao. In order to construct a subway line and an airport within a week, he would need Mingyao's help, and specifically he needed Mingyao to offer the services of his soldiers. As Mingliang was about to put on his shoes, he coughed lightly and someone immediately brought over a pair of slippers that had been custom-made by a specialty store in Japan. When he went to the bathroom door, he knocked and someone immediately squeezed out his toothpaste and also placed a disposable towel—printed with a future image of Explosion—next to the faucet. When the faucet was turned on and started producing the sound of running water, the staff in the dining hall began placing all sorts of breakfast food and drinks at Mingliang's seat at the table.

After taking several gulps of milk and eating several bites of his favorite pickled vegetables and fried egg, Mingliang did not knock on the table or say a single word to anyone. The workers knew that after eating, the mayor liked to stroll through the garden alone, and therefore they retired to their respective places, to allow him to stroll around in peace. The assistants who didn't have a chance to retreat in time stood by the side of the road, and as he walked by they would smile and bow, and softly say, "Greetings, Mayor." By this point the sun was already high in the sky and shining down on the eastern half of the courtyard. It looked as though molten gold had just solidified into an orb with a golden halo around it. As Mingliang was following the corridor under the courtyard's grape trellis, he found that even though winter was over there were nevertheless several grapevines with branches that were still white and bare. Most of these branches were full of spring greenery, but there was one that seemed about to break off and did not yet have any green buds. Mingliang walked down the middle of the grapevine corridor and looked out. He knew that there were workers standing at his side and behind him, and all he needed to do was cough lightly or stop and turn, and they would immediately appear before him and ask, "Mayor Kong, what do you need?" It was as if they had been standing and waiting for millennia for him to say those words, and now that the opportunity had finally arisen the excitement was clearly visible on their faces. All of this had been arranged by Cheng Qing, who had been by his side ever since they were children in Explosion Village. Cheng Qing was the administrative secretary of the city government and was responsible for looking after Mingliang' life, work, and talks, and when he felt lustful and wanted a woman, his old passion for Cheng Qing would be awakened. He knew that Cheng Qing was in one of the villas in this courtyard, and that all he had to do was give the word, and in a few minutes she would be in front of him. But at this moment he didn't want to see her, nor did he want to see anyone else. He simply wanted to walk alone for a while, to consider how to discuss with Mingyao the question of building a subway line and an airport in a single week.

He therefore went for a walk alone.

The sun shone down through the half-green grape trellises, so that one large round golden orb after another appeared over the corridor, like the Olympic rings. A squirrel ran over from the pine trees in the field to one side, stood beneath one of the grapevines, and saw that the mayor had an amused gleam in his eye. This squirrel was one of many that Mingliang had told his worker to bring down from the mountains. In all there were several hundred of them, and they frequently appeared in trees and on the roadside. The previous year Mingliang had been strolling through the courtyard when he happened to remark that it would be nice if this garden had some squirrels, and soon enough there were squirrels everywhere. Similarly, one night the previous summer he had been walking through the courtyard and it occurred to him that he didn't hear any crickets, and he asked why there were no crickets. Upon hearing his question, the government promptly sent all of the city's residents into the mountains to catch hundreds of thousands of crickets and bring them back to the garden. Now, this squirrel ran up to him as though it had some business to attend to. It had a pleading look in its eyes, and when Mingliang walked over to it, it didn't run away and instead faced him and sat down on the side of the corridor. The benches along the way were made of pine and their red paint smelled like a palace garden, like Beijing's Palace Garden. However, Beijing's Palace Garden was as crowded as an anthill, while this city government garden, which was not much smaller, had only Mingliang and this squirrel. Mingliang stood in front of the squirrel. The squirrel quietly chirped at him a few times, whereupon Mingliang squatted down and the squirrel eagerly ran up to him.

Mingliang knew exactly what the squirrel wanted. He glanced over at the field and the forest, and saw that apart from the sunlight and the wind, there was no movement. He thought to himself, "Are there any more squirrels over there? If so, they should come out, because this one is rather lonely." Then he saw several squirrels in the forest turn around, and their uneasy eyes were like stars in a winter sky. Annoyed by those squirrels that had turned in his direction, he shouted, "I am Mayor Kong and order you to come here. Do you hear me?" Upon hearing his shouts, several dozen gray squirrels ran out of the forest together. The squirrel sitting near the bench saw the group of squirrels approaching and, after wagging its tail at Mingliang, quickly ran to join the others.

Seeing the group of squirrels run away, Mingliang felt a surge of joy. The city government garden was now as quiet as a reflection on the surface of a pool of water, except that there was the sound of the footsteps of the squirrels running through the field and the forest, together with the faint sound of cars in the city and of clouds floating overhead. Standing in that quietness, Mingliang suddenly had an urge to pee on the ground, like a boy. He chuckled, looked around, then stood on one of the benches, as though suspended in midair, and proceeded to unzip his pants and pee onto the ground.

He peed out a city mayor's piss.

He regretted that earlier that morning someone had already escorted him to the restroom. He wanted his pee to be golden-colored, the way it had been when he was village chief and town mayor, but ever since he became city mayor his doctor made sure that he didn't have a hint of illness, and even his pee was perfectly clear. He gazed down at this clear pee as it arced through the air and landed in the grass. His pee disturbed only a cricket, which came out and sat in the sun on leaves of grass, shaking the water off its wings.

Mingliang looked at that old cricket. He suddenly pouted and, like an overgrown child, said, "Tell the others to come out." The cricket hopped down from the blade of grass. "Tell all of the bugs and all of the sparrows to come out . . ." Mingliang shouted again. "Spring has arrived, so all of you should show yourselves!

". . . I am Mayor Kong, and all of you should show yourselves!

". . . I am Mayor Kong, and all of you should show yourselves!"

Quickly, from behind a rockery in a corner of the corridor, in the middle of a cluster of bamboo plants, he entered the main room of his five-suite courtyard, where several dozen secretaries, gardeners, electricians, plumbers, security guards, and other workers suddenly stood up. Everyone stared in alarm at Mingliang, who was simply standing, and no one could understand what was happening. The workers weren't sure whether they should rush toward him or wait until they had figured out what he was doing before deciding whether they should go or not. Therefore, they remained frozen in their original positions, with a look of terror on their faces. By this point the sun had almost reached its apex and was radiating bright yellow light. The warmth of the fifth lunar month was like the beginning of summer, and the walls of the surrounding buildings were lazily lounging about, as though they were a group of men squatting in the sun. Only after they heard the mayor shouting angrily did they express any surprise or excitement. Some magpies flew over, alighting on the tree branches and chirping excitedly. In no time, the garden's sparrows had also returned and landed on the grass and the tree branches, chirping up a storm. The squirrels also came running back from where they had been hiding in the depths of the forest and were scurrying up and down the trees in front of Mingliang, their fluffy tails even wider than their bodies. The crickets were also summoned back by the mayor's fury and the warmth of the sun, and thousands upon thousands of them were standing or lying down on individual blades of grass. Some of them extended their wings and began to chirp, whereupon hundreds or even thousands of crickets began to chirp in unison. The entire city government building courtyard was full of the happy chirping of crickets and singing of sparrows. Mingliang couldn't see the grasshoppers, but their singing was interwoven with the chirping of the crickets, as though they were sopranos leading a chorus.

Butterflies also playfully flew around on that noisy spring day.

Those secretaries and other workers all retreated. Kong Mingliang now stood on a stone in the middle of the garden and was moved by what he saw around him. He had a smile on his face, but tears kept running down his cheeks. Explosion was his. The entire world was his. Even the insects and sparrows listened to him. With a smile, he swallowed his tears, then repeatedly gestured for the secretaries, security guards, and workers to retreat even farther to where he wouldn't be able to see them, and regardless of what he might say, they shouldn't come back out again. Next, he hopped down from that stone, looked at the sparrows and insects that were flying around him, then sat in the grass like a child and watched the large black crickets crawling over his feet and legs. He then watched a pair of green grasshoppers singing together as they sat on the chrysanthemum blossoms in front of him, together with a pair of orioles that sang as they flew around. The scent of grass and flowers flowed into his nostrils and through his body like a warm stream, making him feel more relaxed and at ease than he had ever felt before. He knew that not only was this two-thousand-*mu* municipal garden all his, the city government building and all of Explosion also belonged to him. "I'm the mayor, don't you know?" he quietly asked the black cricket sitting on the end of his shoe. "Explosion will soon be redesignated as a provincial-level metropolis, don't you know?" As he asked this, he saw that the crickets and grasshoppers sitting on the blades of grass, together with the magpies perched in the trees and along the roof of the corridor, all suddenly grew quiet and stared at him with a contented expression. He then very gently and very slowly shook his foot, until the crickets and grasshoppers perched on his shoes and legs got off. Then he stood up, straightened his clothes, cleared his throat, and said to all of the insects assembled before him,

"You should retire. I want some peace and quiet."

He then shouted to the sparrows, magpies, and gray orioles,

"You should leave. I want some peace and quiet."

He then shouted at the squirrel in front of him, as well as at the hedgehog and the badger that had run into the garden from somewhere, and said, "Get out of my way. I want to try to establish a construction headquarters here for building the subway and the airport. I want to personally oversee the process of constructing the subway and airport in less than a week. Within ten days, the largest airplanes in the world will be taking off from and landing in the new Explosion airport. I will arrange for national cadres to take the first flight into Explosion, and then take the subway from the airport directly to the hotels that I will construct for them." The mayor shouted to the sky and the earth, "All animals, birds, and insects should leave now. This entire courtyard is going to be demolished!" As he was shouting, the rest of the garden fell silent, reverting back to its original state. A large flock of sparrows and magpies flew away, leaving behind only a handful standing around. It was unclear where the squirrels, crickets, and grasshoppers had gone, as they left behind only a soft humming noise. A silence covered the land. An emptiness also covered the land. There was no one else in the garden other than Mingliang. The sun, which was now directly overhead, had gone from yellow to fiery red. Mingliang's forehead and back were covered in sweat, which made him feel even warmer and cozier, as though his chilled body was gradually being immersed in warm water.

From this empty garden, Mingliang glanced at the quiet buildings around him, then began walking toward the pond in the distance. About three hundred meters from the red corridor, beyond the man-made garden, there was a pond and an uncultivated field. The pond was several dozen *mu* in size and was about three feet deep. The reeds were almost half as tall as a person, and there were also waterbirds, fish, and snakes. Even though he lived there, this was the first time Mingliang had come out here. At that point the workers were in the process of planting some grass around the pond, but when Mingliang said to leave, they left the pond the way it was. There was also a wilderness area, but Mingliang wanted to build a headquarters for his airport and subway construction projects, so that a building could arise from the embankment like a flock of birds or locusts suddenly taking flight. The building would be like one he had seen in Beijing, which looked like an oversize goose egg. He had already decided how the building would be furnished, so that it would resemble the ministry office building he had seen in Beijing. Inside, the walls would be covered in milky white wallpaper, which would emit a jade-like glow. Having already planned this out in his imagination, Mingliang picked an empty area next to the pond and then stood there. Facing the sun, he looked through the pond reeds, and after he had decided on the proposed location for his building, he slowly closed his eyes, took a deep breath, and said to himself,

"I am Mayor Kong of Explosion. I am going to build a structure here."

He added, "I want to start building now, and since I am the mayor, what I say goes!"

Then he asked, "Is it necessary for me to send a directive? Isn't it enough for me to stand here myself? Do all of you not recognize that I'm the mayor?"

As he was saying this, he closed his eyes even tighter, waiting for the ground beneath his feet to start trembling. There would be an explosion like a burst of wind or a volcano exploding, and the water plants and mud would go flying in every direction. He would open his eyes, and in front of him there would be an enormous egg-shaped building.

The mayor was waiting for this moment.

He had already prepared himself so that after the earthshaking burst of wind arrived, he would be thrown to the ground, where his head would be smashed open, his clothes would be in tatters, and when he stood up his face and entire body would be covered in mud. But as long as a building could appear out of nowhere, he wouldn't need to discuss his plans for the airport and the subways with Ming-yao. Instead, he would be able to build Explosion's new airport and subway all by himself. "Explosion is mine. I am Mayor Kong, who single-handedly made Explosion what it is today. If I can't build an airport and a subway in a week, then who can?" As Mingliang asked himself this and waited for the earthshaking movement to arrive, in front of his tightly closed eyes there appeared a cluster of dancing gold stars, even as the ground began to tremble beneath his feet.

He thought that the earthshaking tornado was about to arrive, that he would surely be blown away, and he instinctively clenched his teeth and gripped the ground tightly with his toes. He leaned into the wind, but as he waited and waited, he noticed that the ground under his feet stopped trembling and the stars in front of his eyes began to disappear.

An ominous sense of foreboding rose in Mingliang's chest.

Somewhat anxiously, he opened his eyes. As he had feared, he found that everything was exactly as it had been. The city government garden was the same, as was the reed pond in front of him. The waist-high reed plants were still standing in the water, and there were some dragonflies flying around above while mayflies were skimming over the surface of the reddish-black water. Even the grass under his feet was still as it had been, full of tiny yellow flowers. Mingliang felt faint, as though someone had punched him in the stomach and all of his organs were jostling about inside. Staring at a reed in the pond in front of him, he said,

"I am Mayor Kong. Did you hear me when I said I wanted to immediately construct a building here?"

Then, raising his voice, he said, "I am Mayor Kong. Did you hear what I just said?"

Finally, Mingliang watched as his shout skimmed over the surface of the pond, and several waterfowl flew out from behind the reeds. He silently bit his lip and turned pale, and tears started to appear in the corners of his eyes, and then, like a child or an old person, he asked in a tearful voice, "Don't you want Explosion to become a provincial-level metropolis like Beijing and Shanghai?

". . . Don't you want Explosion to be ruled directly by the central government?"

At this point the secretaries and security guards who had been hiding behind trees, behind walls, and in the corners of the corridor all emerged. From a distance, they had watched the mayor standing there but were unsure whether to approach him or not. They each had a look of deep frustration.

2. GRAND PROSPECTS

Mingliang went to find his brother Mingyao.

When he left the city government complex, Mingliang felt sorrow creep over his heart. He had not taken his personal secretary, and instead he took only the luxury SUV that Cheng Qing had arranged for him. When Cheng Qing had seen Mingliang, she said, "Mayor Kong, you didn't sleep well last night." Mingliang replied, "Why don't you go with me?" So they got into the car, with him sitting in the back and Cheng Qing sitting in the front. Before the car entered the urban district, they received an urgent phone call saying that if the mayor was going to use Remin Road, it would be closed off by the police, and if he was going to use Gongde Road, then the latter would be cleared of all cars and pedestrians. With his eyes half-closed, Mingliang leaned back in his seat as the car moved forward like a ship through the sea. After they had left the city with its ten million inhabitants, Mingliang and Cheng Qing exchanged a few remarks.

Cheng Qing asked, "Where are we going?"

Mingliang replied, "Explosion's promotion to a provincial-level metropolis has reached a critical juncture."

Cheng Qing laughed and said, "Your face is as sallow as a sheet of paper." She then added, "You're not so young anymore; you shouldn't keep such late hours."

Mingliang looked at the wrinkles that had suddenly appeared on the back of her neck. He reached out to massage her shoulders, and when she turned to him, her face bright, he asked,

"Do you think that, without Mingyao, I can build Asia's largest airport and a subway line running at least a hundred kilometers in less than a week?"

"Yes." Then a shadow of disappointment flashed across Cheng Qing's face, and she said coldly, "We'll have to see what you arrange for me to do after Explosion becomes a provincial-level metropolis. Can you arrange for me to be the deputy mayor?" The car then left Explosion and headed into the mountain range to the west. This was the mountain ridge where Mingliang had originally planned to build the new airport, and the area had become incredibly vast, as the city of Explosion—which began at the base of the mountains and expanded into the distance—was reduced to a mess of gray and white resembling a realistic painting. The railroad tracks from which the villagers had previously unloaded goods had disappeared, and the old Explosion city that you could still see from there even just two years earlier had also disappeared. Now, there was only a cluster of brand-new buildings in the distance. Mingliang asked the driver to stop in front of a cement path leading to the mountaintop. Then he got out of the car, went into a field next to the path, and stood there—as though trying to get out of Cheng Qing's sight to relieve himself. When he reached a barren slope, he glanced behind him and continued walking away, until he reached a flat area on the hillside. He stood in the middle of that field full of wormwood, white grass, and wild jujube. After looking around, he faced a mountain rising up in the distance, then took out a folded document full of all sorts of red stamps, and after showing it to the wilderness, he closed his eyes and said,

"Can we first build a runway? I am Mayor Kong, and I've brought the documents relating to the airport's construction and its funding."

He pleaded, "Let there be a runway. I am Mayor Kong, and I really don't want to beg Kong Mingyao for assistance."

He closed his eyes, waited, and listened to the wind blowing the pile of documents he was holding in his hand. But apart from this soft sound, he was surrounded by silence. Everything was as still as a grave. When he finally opened his eyes again, he saw the field, stones, and the mountain ridge stretching out into the distance. He felt so helpless he wanted to weep, and felt unbearably depressed. Deeply chagrined, he returned the documents to his leather briefcase, but as he was turning to walk away, he saw Cheng Qing, who was standing behind him and appeared to have seen and heard everything. A dark flame rose up, and he felt his failure had been due to the fact that she had been standing there, but just as he was about to erupt in anger, Cheng Qing brushed the hair from her eyes, and softly said,

"You haven't seen me in three months.

". . . Not having seen me, you owe me.

". . . You owe me for my body, so you should give me something else in return.

". . . I don't have anyone else I can ask. After Explosion becomes a provincial-level metropolis, you should appoint me deputy city mayor, or at the very least should transfer me to an outer province and appoint me deputy provincial mayor."

When they returned to the SUV, they once again sat with one in front and the other in back. Like a married couple in the middle of a fight, neither of them said a word to the other. Mingliang had the car proceed directly toward the mountains to the west, as though they were about to drive into the setting sun. As the forests and fields, the villages and towns—together with the businesses and industrial parks that, for reasons known only to Mingliang, had been built deep in the mountains—receded into the distance, all that was left in front of the car was a vast desolate landscape. By this point they were about a hundred kilometers from Explosion, and the trees on either side of the road left it covered in shade. The road was like an endless ribbon circling around the wooded mountain. The warm fifth-month sun was replaced by a bright chill. Cheng Qing rolled down the window, looked outside, and asked, "Where are we?" Mingliang instructed the driver, "Continue following this road, over that mountain up ahead." Then a sense of surprise and mystery grew inside the car, becoming so heavy that as the SUV attempted to climb up the mountain, it had to proceed as slowly as an old man panting as he tries to walk down the street. Eventually, however, it managed to reach the top of the mountain. The SUV managed to free itself from the forest and parked in a grass lot at the top of the mountain.

A different world appeared.

It turned out that at the base of the mountain, and in the middle of the mountain range, there was an enormous field. The setting sun bathed everything in a bluish green and dark red glow, and Mingyao's navy was in the process of conducting naval exercises on that sea-like field. Mingyao stood on the mountain peak gazing down at the sea-like field below, where several fleets of ships were clustered together in the field, attacking each other and defending themselves. There was the sound of cannons and clouds of smoke, and the field resembled a scene from a painting. Because the ships were so far away, it was like seeing a school of fish swimming along the surface of the ocean. The sound of the soldiers shouting swept toward Mingliang like a wave. There were tens of thousand of men from two or three divisions, all wearing naval uniforms with white ribbons fluttering behind their flat-topped caps, like white birds soaring above the grassy sea.

Cheng Qing got out of the car and stared in amazement.

"Mingyao is going to do something great," Mingliang murmured to himself without removing his eyes from the seascape in front of him, though at the same time appearing to respond to the question Cheng Qing had asked him in the car. He stood on the mountainside in the light of the setting sun, staring down at the grassy sea at the base of the mountain. His face was pale with surprise, but there was also a hint of an excited smile. Leaving the driver next to the car, he accompanied Cheng Qing down the mountain, where they found both sides of the street lined with troops welcoming them. One or two battalions were lined up along the side of the road, and all of the soldiers were wearing crisp new naval uniforms, and in the sunlight they were shimmering like the ocean. At first, the drumming sound was rather erratic, but it gradually cohered into a steady beat, until eventually it became as precise as though it had been cut by a knife. Mingliang walked in front and Cheng Qing followed behind. There was a large sign waving back and forth, which read, WE WARMLY WELCOME THE MAYOR TO INSPECT OUR TROOPS! When Mingliang saw the message on the sign, a naval officer in his fifties—who happened to be Mingliang's former commanding officer back when Mingliang was in the military—rushed out from under it with his clenched fists held up to his chest. He suddenly stopped when he was a few meters away from Mingliang, and proceeded to salute and announce in a shrill voice,

"Reporting to Mayor Kong, sir! Explosion's entire naval base is performing a large-scale sea-crossing and shore-landing military exercise. Participating in the exercise are two naval divisions and one sea missile regiment. Division Commander Gao Qiyi from the second naval division reporting, sir!"

Mingliang stared in surprise. After listening carefully to Commander Gao's report, he initially wanted to return the salute and say something in a similarly measured cadence, but in the end he merely lifted his hand to his waist and said feebly,

"Take me to see Mingyao."

The division commander responded in a forceful voice,

"The commanding officer is waiting aboard the ship."

Upon hearing the words *commanding officer*, Mingliang felt a pang in his chest. He again looked down at the seascape at the base of the mountain, and the seemingly endless array of ships and troops. Then, without a word, he followed the division commander toward the rows of welcoming naval troops. When he arrived in front of them, a chant of "Senior Officer, Senior Officer" could be heard amid the applause. By this point, the sun was already approaching the western horizon, and a red glow filled the sky. The warmth in the air was like mountain camellias blooming in the winter. Mingliang knew that when he heard the troops chanting, "Senior Officer!" he should respond by shouting, "Comrades, you are working hard!" At this point, the welcoming troops would shout in unison, "Serve the People! The Senior Officer is working hard!" In this formulaic exchange, the greeting ritual would reach its climax. But when Mingliang heard Mingyao addressed as "commanding officer," he found himself unable to utter the requisite response "Comrades, you are working hard!" Instead of that enthusiastic response, he merely took Cheng Qing to look around and nod, then quickly withdrew from the welcoming procession.

Upon leaving the procession, Mingliang turned back and saw Cheng Qing behind him. Her excited face was covered in a sheen of sweat, and was so red it appeared as though the excess color might peel off. The division commander, however, was standing right next to her. He gestured at the troops and ships and spat out a string of commands, from which Mingliang could make out phrases like *United States*, *Great Britain*, *President Obama*, and *Japanese Prime Minister*. But in front of him, along a dirt road leading down the mountain, he could see the silhouettes of one truck after another hauling goods. He stood on the side of the road and could see that, at the border of the sea of grass, an enormous naval vessel had appeared. Mingyao and his staff officers were on the ship's deck and were gathered around a sand table examining something. Mingyao kept looking up and gesturing at the assorted vessels and the thousands of troops in the sea of grass before him, together with a fleet of ships in the distance that were arranged in the shape of the character for "person": 人. On this hillside on the edge of the grassy sea, the sun in the western sky shone across to the east. When the wind blew, an endless series of waves moved across the surface of the grass. There was a conifer with leaves similar to both a poplar and a willow, which could be found only on the mountains behind Explosion. In the wind, the leaves kept turning upside down, and their white underside looked just like ocean spume.

Mingliang was astonished by this sight of a navy on a frothing sea, and anticipated that Mingyao was doing something momentous on behalf of Explosion. His sense of unease grew, and a look of confusion passed over his face like a layer of fog. Standing at a turn in the road, he saw the row of sentries. He waited for Cheng Qing and the division commander to catch up to him, then told the commander that he had previously visited this outer county for inspections but had never heard of there being this sort of field in the middle of the mountains. The commander smiled and replied that three years earlier he had discovered that there was this one-hundred-kilometer plain right here in the middle of the mountains. So he planted some additional grass and converted the field into a vast grassy ocean, so that every year the navy could conduct exercises here.

"Does this work?" Mingliang asked.

"We are confident that we could defeat the Japanese fleet in open ocean." The division commander shook his fist and added, "Our objective is to defeat the US aircraft carrier fleet, so that we can land on the US west coast whenever we wish." Then, he pointed to the most distant row of several dozen ships and said, "Mayor Kong, look off into the distance. That farthest ship, which resembles an enormous club floating on the water's surface or a bowling ball floating in the water—that is a newly developed nuclear-powered submarine, which can remain submerged for up to eight months at a time. If it strikes a US aircraft carrier, the carrier would be completely destroyed." While he was saying this, he proceeded forward, and the sentries along the side of the road kept saluting the mayor, the division commander, and Cheng Qing. When the sentries saluted, Mingliang would merely nod to them, while the division commander would stop in front of each sentry and return the salute. In this way, they headed down the mountain, approaching the ocean, until eventually they were assailed by thick steam arising from the fields and a sweet smell of fresh grass warmed under the hot sun.

"Do you smell the ocean?" the division commander asked Cheng Qing with a smile.

Cheng Qing nodded and asked coldly,

"Are there no female soldiers?"

The division commander smiled back and said, "We've already made plans to recruit some."

When they reached the shore at the base of the mountain, they saw that the vast field was budding with green growth and was full of red, white, and yellow blossoms. Amid the military exercises there were also some homeless birds such as petrels flying through the sky. The steel body of the ship Mingyao was using as a headquarters was completely covered in sea paint and was anchored in the grass-sea about three thousand meters from the base of the mountain. No one could walk across these three thousand meters of grassland, because anyone who tried would fall into the water and drown. When they reached the shore, Mingliang used a walkie-talkie to call Mingyao, who was up on the control vessel. Then, after a while, a motorcycle left the ship as though it were a speedboat, and took them to the ship.

It was only as Mingliang was crossing the gangway onto the main deck of that five-story-high ship that he realized just how enormous the ship actually was. He fell into a stupor, as he saw that on the ship's two decks, each as large as a basketball court, a white tarp was covering a shaded area as large as ten rooms. Beneath the tarp, there was an enormous sand table containing models of both the Eastern and the Western Hemispheres, on which there were an array of two-inch red and white flags, together with numerous pictures of the sea covered in red and white arrows and ship icons. When Mingliang and Cheng Qing arrived, the middle-aged and young naval officers stationed next to the sand table all saluted the mayor in unison. Then they looked over at their commander Kong Mingyao, who was standing between the sand tables, and after Mingyao nodded to them they all took their compasses and their binoculars, and retreated to the command deck.

Aboard the ship, there was just Mingliang, Mingyao, and Cheng Qing. It was only then that Mingyao removed his snow-white naval jacket and tossed it onto the US coast on the sand table. He then poured his brother and Cheng Qing a glass of water, which he placed on a white plastic table next to the sand table. Then he pulled over three white chairs and placed them around the table and told his brother apologetically,

"If you had come this morning, you would have been able to see us defeat the Japanese fleet and force it to surrender."

He announced solemnly to Cheng Qing, "The day after tomorrow a fleet of submarines will surround the US mother ship, and it is there that our fate will be decided." Then, turning toward the large ship and small warships under the setting sun, Mingyao looked anxious, because the fate of any future battles remained uncertain. Owing particularly to the light of the setting sun, his anxious expression appeared to carry a trace of sickness or even death—as though someone, following a major illness, had left the sickbed before fully recovering. It appeared as though his resolution and his confidence had completely disappeared, and instead now he simply looked exhausted.

"You've lost weight," Cheng Qing said, looking him over.

"The final battle is upon us, and I can never sleep." Mingyao smiled, then handed the two glasses of water to Cheng Qing and Mingliang. "I hear that Explosion's designation as a provincial-level metropolis will soon be approved?"

Mingliang nodded.

"After it is approved, you will become a ministry-level cadre," Mingyao said. "This will place you higher than provincial governors and party committee secretaries."

An expression of delight flashed over Mingliang's face as he looked at his brother, then gazed silently out at the sea and the naval fleet. In the distance they could hear the sound of fighting and explosions. Several dozen kilometers away, on the far side of an island, fire and smoke were visible.

At this point, Mingyao turned toward Mingliang.

"Do you plan to have Explosion become a nation?"

With a look of surprise, Mingliang stared silently at Mingyao.

"Do you think that one day you'll go to Beijing and assert control over this entire nation?"

As Mingyao asked this, he gazed intently at his brother.

Mingliang continued to stare in shock. He opened his mouth, but no words came out.

Mingyao laughed. He then looked away, and back at the sea and his fleet. "Have you really not considered it?"

When he asked this, his voice seemed to drift over from a far distance, as if in a dream.

Mingliang bit his lip, and in his eyes there was a gleam that demanded silence. The two brothers stared at each other for a moment, then they both smiled and the tension between them faded. Mingyao looked over at Cheng Qing and saw that she had turned pale. There was a sheen of terror-induced sweat on her face, so he smiled at her and said,

"You'll also be promoted. Do you want to be deputy city mayor or deputy provincial governor?"

"Ask your brother." Cheng Qing shifted her gaze from Mingyao back to Mingliang. "Only he can remember all of those who have toiled without recognition."

At this point, a pre-dusk silence descended over the field ocean, like the setting sun slipping beneath the ocean horizon. Under the trembling light of the setting sun, that green of the sea mixed with the red of the evening sky. The ocean generated a feeling of agoraphobia, as though that fear were trying to climb onto the ship, onto the deck, and onto their three faces. They therefore stood on deck on the ship's prow gazing at one another, then gazed out into the distance, where they could see an array of large and small ships, like birds soaring overhead. There were also all of those seamen aboard the ships, waiting for the order to attack. No one said a word; they all let the silence—together with the sound of explosions and fires that intermittently broke that silence—waft over from afar. Finally, as the setting sun was about to sink below the horizon and was lighting up the distant grass in a brilliant flame, Mingliang coughed, then turned to his brother.

"Mingyao, I need your help.

". . . There is no one else who can help with this.

". . . In less than a week, I need to build an airport that not only would be the largest in Asia, but must be one of the two largest in the world. In addition, I have to build a hundred-kilometer subway line. If I don't, then Explosion can abandon all hope of becoming redesignated as a megapolis, like Beijing, Shanghai, New York, and Tokyo."

As Mingliang was saying this, his gaze remained fixed on his brother's face. He was watching to see if Mingyao would refuse him, or would come up with an excuse to pass him on to someone else. Mingliang had already prepared a number of explanations for why he needed to complete these projects in under a week. All Mingyao needed to do was ask, and Mingliang would immediately recite them until Mingyao was left with no possible reason to refuse or to shirk this request.

But Mingliang had predicted incorrectly. Mingyao did not appear to have the slightest intention of shirking the request. He listened intently to what Mingliang had to say and gazed at his brother's pleading expression, and when Mingliang was finished Mingyao glanced out at the naval exercises that were just concluding, then in a soft and skeptical voice said,

"You are my brother, so tell me the truth. Is it really possible that you have not considered that, after Explosion has been redesignated as a provincial-level metropolis it might then be redesignated as a sovereign nation?"

Mingyao laughed softly and added,

"Not only can I, in a week, build Explosion the world's largest airport and a one-hundred- or two-hundred-kilometer subway line, I can even construct several hundred buildings, each of which would be fifty to eighty stories tall."

As the sun was setting, Mingyao looked out to sea, at the fleet of ships that were systematically coming to shore. Finally, he presented his conditions:

"If you want me to build all of this, then you need to find me five thousand severed legs and ten thousand severed fingers.

". . . Without severing that many legs and without cutting off that many fingers, and without thousands of people dying, do you think these construction projects can be completed?

". . . If we are going to build these projects, my forces will be utterly exhausted and I will lose much of my fighting power. Mayor Kong, I don't ask for anything else—I just ask that you celebrate Explosion's redesignation as a provincial-level metropolis by declaring a three-day holiday—during which time you will give all of the city's residents three days off. During those three days, you should lend me your city's residents. I need them for only three days, and afterward I will return every single one of them to you."

There was a long silence, as the sky began to darken. As the sun was slipping under the horizon, Mingliang and Mingyao, standing on the deck of the ship, made a toast using glasses of water in place of wine. The sun disappeared under the horizon, as though as a direct result of their toast.

3. MEGALOPOLIS (2)

The super airport that was constructed on the outskirts of Explosion was virtually complete after only three days and two nights. Without anyone realizing it, in the mountains several dozen kilometers outside the city there appeared a runway long enough to accommodate the world's largest airplanes. People saw that there were reed and bamboo mats in a large clearing, and tall walls made of canvas completely surrounded several mountains. There were also trucks full of soldiers driving into and out of that enclosed section. Everyone assumed that this was a mining operation or a military exercise, and no one surmised that Mingyao was taking his troops to build an airport.

The airport was completed in just a few days.

The mountainside was full of grass and thorns, and all the soldiers needed to do was toss in several dozen bloody fingers and then stomp on them, trampling the grass and thorns until the fingers completely disappeared. First, they followed the construction plans and used white lime to draw the outlines of the projected runway along the mountainside, then they used soldiers to surround a hill rising up out of the plain. The soldiers each had a rifle loaded with bullets, and after they fired at the hill, the hundreds of bloody fingers, toes, and severed legs buried under that hill made it collapse, as though it were a balloon that had been filled with air. Meanwhile, the runway itself remained perfectly flat. They appointed the most experienced soldiers to go up to the trees on the mountainside and along the edge of the cliff, and bury some more bloody fingers—the precise number being dependent on the size of the tree. Then they would lift their bayonets, aim them at the trees, and shout, "Kill, Kill!" Upon hearing this command, they would thrust forward with their bayonets, and the trees' leaves would fall to the ground. When the sand and earth began to assume the form of a runway, Mingyao took the army's battalions and regiments, and combined them to form an enormous phalanx. The soldiers were all wearing leather shoes and, while singing a bright military song, they proceeded to trample the bloody ribs and leg bones that littered the ground. They marched with forceful steps, the sound of their feet resonating between the mountain and the sky. Along the runway there was a one-foot-five-inch-thick strip of concrete reinforced with steel mesh, and the soldiers ended up covered from head to toe in blood.

The division's military strength lay in loading, aiming, and firing at a mountain blanketed in blood-covered finger and toe bones, after which several new runways promptly appeared on the hillside. Then the soldiers surrounded the biggest hill and placed some antiaircraft guns, machine guns, and heavy-duty cannons around it, then piled up the bones from another twenty-five hundred bloody arms and legs, and just as the troops were about to open fire, the hillside transformed into a gully creating an enormous plain in the middle of the mountain ridge. Mingyao then summoned all of the troops and had them hold hands and surround the several-hundred-*mu* plain, and once the earth stopped shaking, they added three to five thousand bloody bones, so that blood was flowing in every direction, making it look like a lake at sunset. Then the soldiers lifted and aimed their rifles and pulled the triggers, whereupon the foundation for the airport's terminal gradually appeared in that plain, amid the sound of the earth splitting open. The troops then shifted to a different formation to surround the foundation that was rising out of the earth, then they brought over some highly sophisticated and never-before-seen weapon, then they proceeded to remove the layers upon layers covering the weapon, and each time they revealed part of the weapon they would make the weapon bleed a bit, and as they did this the walls around the airport waiting area increased by the height of an entire floor. By the time the weapon was uncovered, blood was flowing, covering the entire earth. The dark muzzle of the gun repeatedly shot at the airport construction site and all of the accompanying facilities, and within an hour the airport's infrastructure was completed.

Because it is not feasible to build tall structures at an airport, the tallest buildings were only five or six stories. The only exception was the control tower, which was completed in an hour and a half after being shot at by rifles—but even that was only eight stories. The airport's basic structure was built between noon, when the troops moved in, and the following evening. What was slower and required more attention, meanwhile, was the airport's furnishings, and the installation and testing of its equipment. For this, the troops needed to use their utmost care and diligence. Throughout the entire construction of the airport's foundation, Mingyao did not make a single appearance at the site. Instead, he stayed with his staff in a tent on the top of a mountain, consulting blueprints and directing the first and second regiments on what to do, and the third regiment on how to slowly uncover the precision weaponry. He directed them where they should leave bloody bones, and how many they should use, and instructed them not to immediately take the weapons to the construction site and station themselves there like fools.

But after the basic construction was completed, Mingyao walked around the construction site, then immediately directed the members of this army unit to polish their weapons directly in front of the control tower, then run to the middle of the runway. He ordered them to sit there studying and reading that day's issues of *National Daily* and *National Modern Technology News*. He also told a few military engineers to meet in the airport's instrumentation building to discuss some technical details and review some reports from the United States, Japan, Germany, and England. After the army had completely demilitarized from its former status of war-readiness, as the men were reassembling the various weapons that they had dismantled and cleaned, they simultaneously assembled the airport's instruments and machinery. After all of the weapons were put away and covered up with clothing, by the time they finished using the first five thousand bloody fingers and ten thousand severed toes, the airport's furnishings were already completed and ready for use. As the sound of reading, studying, and singing resonated from the terminal to the tarmac, and on to the fields and mountains beyond, all of the airport's electronic equipment was assembled and installed.

When they needed to paint the inside of the airport, Mingyao told his troops to take the multicolored—but predominantly red—flags that they normally used for celebrations and wave them in the air, whereupon all of the different-colored paints that they needed would suddenly appear.

When they needed to build an expressway linking the airport to the city center and to its environs, Mingyao ordered several tanks to proceed side by side from the airport to the city, sprinkling blood on the ground behind them, and an expressway materialized like a ribbon fluttering in the wind.

In five days' time, both the airport and the subway were completed. Once Explosion had the world's largest airport and a subway line extending in all directions, and once it had more than a hundred buildings, each of which was several stories tall, there would be no reason why Explosion should not be considered one of China's major metropolises. Overnight, Explosion would become one of China's megalopolises.

CHAPTER 18

Great Geographic Transformation (2)

1. PRELUDE TO TRANSFORMATION

Zhu Ying had never been so busy. It was as if she had spent her entire life preparing for this moment. She had not returned home for three days in a row, being unable to leave her work at the women's vocational school. The school was located in the urban fringes to the west of the city, hidden in a willow and poplar grove and removed from both the countryside and the hustle and bustle of the city proper. But in the courtyard hidden in the willow and poplar grove, the masson pines and spire cypresses in front of every building were full of fiery red roses and phoenix flowers all year round, as though they were covered in rosy clouds. But if you looked from the distant road or fields, in addition to willow branches, poplar leaves, and a surrounding wall that was only inter-mittently visible, there were also security guards whom Mingyao had sent there to guard the entranceway, together with a sign that read EXPLOSION VOCATIONAL SCHOOL. But no one knew what the students were actually studying there, who was teaching them, or even what courses they were taking. They were all girls between the ages of sixteen and twenty, with pure and blank minds and bodies, like sheets of blank paper. But after they stayed at the school for three to five months—or, in some cases, for six to twelve months—their minds and bodies were no longer blank, and in their pockets they had deposit books and gold or silver bank cards, and their heads were full of countless things, as they became the most desirable nannies in the entire city.

The school had already graduated thirty classes of nannies, or a total of 1,568 students. They were taken individually by a couple of older girls named Little Qin and Ah Xia to Beijing, Shanghai, Guang-zhou, and countless seaside resort cities. As in planting beans or gourds, the girls were assigned to various business and were selected by different households. Meanwhile, Ah Xia and Little Qin, working as manager and general manager of their company, made countless phone calls every day, kept a registry of the girls' clients, and cursed the girls who had not succeeded in finding men to corrupt. Noting the occupation, position, income, and social connection of the girls' clients, they compiled a detailed inventory, and when it was complete they would send it back to Zhu Ying.

The following month, thousands of economists, urban recon-struction experts, and important members of the national develop-ment committee arrived in Beijing to discuss and vote on whether Explosion should be redesignated as a provincial-level megalopolis. Kong Mingliang and all his cadres from throughout the city were staying in Beijing hotels, as if his entire city government had relocated to the capital. They worked day and night to try to build roads and bridges to facilitate Explosion's transformation.

For three days and three nights, Zhu Ying had not eaten a bite of food or gotten a wink of sleep. Instead, she locked herself in her three-room office in the women's vocational school, plotting how to entrap those men having relationships with their nannies—calculating which of them were in Beijing and which of them were elsewhere, which of the men were important figures in government agencies or public companies, and which of them were the secretaries or drivers of political leaders. She researched the ancestry, background, position, and experience of the men, parents, and children who were being waited on by these young nannies—basically trying to find anything that could be potentially usable. Zhu Ying reorganized all of their names, telephone numbers, and photographs, placing the useful ones on the table and pushing the less useful ones to the side. From the useful pile in the center of the table, Zhu Ying drew one or two flowers below the name of each of the girls, depending on the occupation and status of the men that girl had slept with. If one of the men was either a department or a subministry director, or was the parent or in-law of the director of a government ministry, Zhu Ying would draw four or five flowers beneath the maid's name. Finally, she reorganized the nannies' names based on how many flowers she had assigned them, then copied them into a separate registration form.

The girl named Fragrance worked at Zhu Ying's side like a secretary, grouping all of the girls' names together based on the number of blossoms they had been assigned. As Fragrance was copying down these names, her wrist began to ache, and she could smell a faint plum and osmanthus scent coming from the registry. Later, her wrist became red and swollen, as that faint plum and osmanthus scent became increasingly pungent, and the entire room came to be covered in flower blossoms and petals. She paused for a moment to look at the petals on the floor and noticed that Zhu Ying, who

Yan Lianke

had not rested for three days and three nights, had fallen asleep at the table amid all of those forms and photographs, as her breath wafted over like flowing water. Fragrance looked in the direction that breath was coming from, and saw that a lock of black hair on Zhu Ying's forehead and face was gradually turning gray. First it was just a few strands, but then it was an entire clump, and furthermore it appeared as though the hair was simultaneously drying out—as though a clump of white hemp was on her forehead, below which her face quickly aged.

Fragrance immediately stood up from the table. The pen she was holding fell, striking the flower petals on the ground.

"Miss Zhu," she cried out. "Quick, wake up!

". . . If you really get old and ugly, will Mayor Kong ever come back to you? And if he doesn't come back to you, will you be able to make good on everything you have promised us?" Fragrance initially said this in a gentle voice, but she became increasingly alarmed, until finally, just as she about to shake Zhu Ying awake, Zhu Ying slowly opened her eyes, lifted her head, and looked at Fragrance and around at the registration books that filled the room. She rubbed her eyes, smiled, then tucked the clump of gray hair behind her ear. Looking at Fragrance under the light, she asked,

"How many days have you not slept?

". . . Do you know how many five-blossom nannies we have in Beijing alone?

". . . Fragrance, Kong Mingliang is about to fall from power and will soon beg me to take him back."

As Zhu Ying was saying this, she stood up from the table. She wanted to get a drink of water and say something else to Fragrance, who was standing right in front of her, but as soon as she saw Fragrance's body and face her mouth immediately tightened and her smile disappeared. She saw that Fragrance—who had been working with her all these years, tending to the vocational school's admissions, finances, records, expenditures, and training—must be in her thirties, and yet her face didn't have a trace of wrinkles or even a single mole. Instead, she was still a tender girl, with a thin waist and firm breasts. People could see at a glance that under her clothes her breasts were so firm that she didn't need to wear a bra.

Zhu Ying asked, "My God, how is it that you are so well preserved?"

Fragrance said, "Can you really arrange for the mayor to fall from power?"

". . . Little Sis, can you tell me how I can stay young like you? If you do, I'm willing to give you half of everything I own.

". . . I can even give you two-thirds of everything I own.

". . . Either this month or next month, our meritorious service will be completed and Kong Mingliang can die at my feet. Afterward, what had previously belonged to the Kong clan will instead belong to the Zhu clan—which is to say, it will belong to me. When that day comes, what will you want?

". . . I'll give you whatever you want. As long as you tell me how you keep your face so wrinkle-free and your breasts so firm, I'll give you anything you want. But you must tell me, how can a woman stay forever young? How can she keep her breasts firm when she is in her fifties, sixties, seventies, or even eighties? How can she keep her face wrinkle-free and prevent her hair from going gray?"

Then Zhu Ying poured Fragrance a glass of water, and as she was taking it to her she kicked those useless maid records and flower petals lying all over the floor. After she put the glass in front of Fragrance, she asked her again, and as she was waiting for an answer Fragrance stared back at her with a frightened and skeptical expression.

"Can you really prevent Explosion from being promoted to a provincial-level metropolis?

"... If Mayor Kong returns to your side and becomes your husband again, will you give me a bigger and better reward than Little Qin and Ah Xia?

"... If I don't want anything else, can you really arrange for me to see the mayor's younger brother, Mingyao, again? Can you arrange for us to get married and live happily ever after?"

At this point, as everything fell quiet, the window lit up. The red silk window curtains of this fifth-floor office were covered in the fresh scent of spring flowers and of spring. Drifting in through the curtain, some willow catkins and poplar blossoms were floating through the air and fell to the ground with a swishing sound, with the force of raindrops. The ultralight catkins landed on the registration book listing the nannies by number of flowers they were assigned and the names of the men they had snared, but since the writing in the registration book was smudged and illegible, the room was therefore filled with the smell of salty tears. Furthermore, a catkin happened to fall on the name of a department director from Beijing—and the name and phone number, which were both a mixture of ink and tears, disappeared altogether. As all of this was unfolding, Zhu Ying stood there stiffly, watching the ink from the names and telephone numbers disappear, as her hair turned completely gray.

"What's happening? What's happening?" Fragrance asked repeatedly as she stared at Zhu Ying's gray hair, then noticed that several dozen new wrinkles had appeared on Zhu Ying's face. It was as if Zhu Ying had aged precipitately, and even her back had gotten hunched over. "With respect to the question of whether or not Explosion will be promoted to the status of a metropolis directly under the jurisdiction of the central government, Kong Mingliang already knows who will be voting and he is confident that he can guarantee that at least half of the experts will vote in Explosion's favor." As she mumbled to herself, Zhu Ying's complexion turned sallow and pale, and sweat poured down her face until the entire room was filled with her sweat and her look of desolation. She stood motionless, looking down at the registration book with the names of those nannies and those men that had not yet gotten completely blurred away. After a while, once her tears had begun to subside, Zhu Ying licked her dry, cracked lips and then went over to open the curtains that had not been opened for several days, letting sunlight shine in on that room full of tears and desolation.

"What day is today?

". . . Is it morning or afternoon?

". . . Does the train for Beijing leave this evening at eight ten or at nine thirty?"

As she asked these questions, Zhu Ying looked out the window. In the courtyard of the vocational school, the sun was shining down on the lawn and on the surrounding buildings like a form-fitting gold veneer. The lawn was as large as a ball field, and the green grass imported from Europe was growing rapidly, creating a thick carpet. There were many pigeons and peacocks wandering across the lawn, and the girls who had not yet been sent to Beijing all came out of their rooms. Some of them were sunning themselves on bamboo mats, others were lounging on bedsheets that they had placed on the ground, while others were sitting there putting on their makeup. Makeup cases, a set of eyebrow pencils, and hand mirrors were sparkling in the sunlight. There were also a couple of beauticians who specialized in placing tattoos on girls' breasts, backs, wrists, and ankles, and even their private regions. The beauticians were in their forties and were wearing white lab coats, and because there was ample sunlight, they took their table out into the courtyard. They covered the table with a white surgical sheet and told the girls who wanted tattoos to lie down naked on top of it. Then they placed the box of tattooing equipment next to the girls, and, to help the girls cope with the pain—though in reality it wasn't actually that painful—a towel was rolled up so that the girls could bite on it as they lay there and looked at all of the photographs of tattoos hanging in front of them.

It was not just one or two girls who wanted tattoos, but rather one or two dozen. They loitered in front of the tattoo table, sunning themselves as they waited their turn, like naked beauties on the beach. Zhu Ying opened the window and looked out at the beautiful girls on the lawn. She saw those half-naked and fully naked nannies waiting for their tattoos. She saw that one girl walking under the window had taken off her shirt and was wearing a pair of athletic shorts and sneakers, and resembled a tornado as she walked past. However, on her back where her bra straps would have been, she did not have a butterfly or flower blossom tattoo, like the other girls, but rather had a tattoo of a book. Zhu Ying could see the book's title as clearly as if it were a flower tattooed on her own fingernails.

The book's title consisted of four words: *New Unabridged Chinese Dictionary*.

Zhu Ying had no idea why this girl would want to have a dictionary tattooed on her back. Watching the girl pass beneath the window, Zhu Ying noticed that several Chinese characters were falling out of that dictionary, like tiny black beans. She could smell the girl's perfume as well as the sharp odor of beans. After the girl passed by, the pigeons, peacocks, orioles, swans, geese, and sparrows on the lawn all flew over and began pecking at those beans and at those Chinese characters that had fallen out of the dictionary tattooed on the girl's back. Only then did Zhu Ying turn around, after standing there biting her lip, and say in a soft voice,

"Fragrance, we don't have any other alternative. You should take these eight hundred students from our women's vocational school and escort them to the capital. You should book all available seats on this evening's eight-thirty train.

". . . You should use every one of these eight hundred girls on the academicians, professors, and experts listed in the second flower registration book. Tell the girls that whoever manages to snare an expert or a professor will be awarded five or eight hundred thousand yuan, and if they manage to bed an academician they will be awarded at least one million or one-point-two million yuan. If this academician turns out to be one of the organizers of the voters, the girl who snares him will be awarded at least two million yuan.

". . . I, however, can't leave Explosion," Zhu Ying explained. "If anyone were to see me leave and go into the capital, Kong Mingliang would immediately know what I was up to.

". . . You may think of this as my act of saving you. But at the same time, it's actually true that I'm saving you. You should take eight hundred girls to the capital tonight, and if you don't have enough you can also take the girls who are currently working here as cooks and grounds sweepers. As long as they're under thirty and are reasonably attractive, then you should have them all work the streets and alleys of Beijing.

". . . You have to trust me when I tell you that the hardest men in the world to deal with are those officials. On the other hand, the easiest to deal with are those students who will go on to become professors and experts. Even if you give them a woman in her forties whose beauty is already fading, they will still hug her tight. You have to trust me, because I'm confident that within a few days after you reach Beijing you'll surely be able to snare at least half of the men on that list.

". . . I'm begging you, and if you need to lose your virginity then do so, but as long as you can snare at least half of the men on that list, then Kong Mingliang will be mine. At that point, Explosion will belong to me, and to all of us women. When the time comes, not only will I give you everything that I currently own, I also promise to arrange for you to see my elder brother-in-law, Kong Mingyao. I promise to secretly arrange for him to like you, and even fall in love with you. That way, the two of you can get married and spend the rest of your lives together.

". . . Fragrance, I'm begging you to trust me this one time, or at least trust me when I say that I promise I can arrange for you to see Kong Mingyao, and that I can arrange for Mingyao to like you, love you, marry you, and spend the rest of his life with you."

2. SECOND ACT OF TRANSFORMATION

I.

Half a month after Fragrance went to the capital with eight hundred girls and the list of the names of men they were supposed to snare, the group of 1,110 experts began to cast their votes. The choice was between Explosion and that other city on the southern coast, to decide which of them would be elevated to the status of a metropolis under the direct rule of the central government. The final decision was in the hands of those experts. Originally, all of the delegations from Explosion to the capital projected that 80 percent of the experts would vote for Explosion, but in the end Explosion received only 30 percent of the votes, the other city on the southern coast received 40 percent, and the remaining 30 percent of the votes were abstentions.

Thirty percent of the experts had thrown away their right to vote as though it were a dirty tissue.

The day before the vote, Mingliang returned to Explosion from Beijing. He had already met with all of the officials and experts he needed to see, and had given away his secret extravagant gifts. The experts representing the public out of a sense of public duty should have voted for Explosion for the sake of the future of the nation's development. After all, over the preceding decade the entire nation's reform policy had had the distorting effect of exacerbating the wealth gap between the rich south and the poor north, and if northern China was going to achieve prosperity, then Beijing would have to elevate Explosion to the status of a provincial-level metropolis. Mingliang knew, therefore, that Explosion's promotion was already virtually guaranteed and that the experts' votes were merely a legal formality.

The last time he went to visit and thank one of the officials who would decide which city would be promoted, the old man was sitting quietly in his courtyard. The old man asked,

"Why have you come to Beijing, rather than staying in Explosion?

". . . Don't you realize that it is taboo for you, as city mayor, to be here in Beijing?

". . . The one place where you should be right now is in Explosion. You are Explosion's grass roots, its countryside, and its mountain region. If the city were to have a disaster, such as a devastating flood or earthquake, you should be in the headquarters at the front lines of the disaster zone."

On the logic that once the necessary preparations have been completed one can wait for things to take their course, Mingliang left several deputy mayors and other delegates behind in Beijing, while he himself took several secretaries back to Explosion. He did this not in order to be able to send commands from a disaster zone in the event of a flood or an earthquake, but instead merely because he was concerned that the possibility of a natural disaster like an earthquake, a flood, or a tornado would lead these experts to conclude that Explosion, on account of its geographic location and its natural conditions, was not suitable for promotion. Mingliang decided that it would be fine if he simply waited in his city government building for the experts to cast their votes. Accordingly, on June 1, Children's Day, he told some workers to bring out a tea table from the city government's tearoom and place it beneath the tallest grape trellis in the government building courtyard. He told them to bring out his favorite wicker chair and place on the table a red telephone connecting directly to the heart of the central government. In a tea box beneath the table, he placed two cell phones, the numbers of which very few people knew. Then he dismissed all of the secretaries and workers, steeped himself a cup of Longjing tea that he didn't intend to drink, and proceeded to sit there with his eyes half closed, waiting for either the red telephone or one of the cell phones in the tea box to ring.

Eventually, one of the cells phones rang.

It was ten in the morning when Mingliang sat down there to wait, and at eleven one of the cell phones rang—half an hour earlier than he had expected. As he was reaching to answer it, he didn't stand up and instead scooted his chair forward. But from when he picked up the phone to when he put it down, his expression quickly changed from excitement to a look of icy calm. The call was from a deputy mayor speaking from Beijing's Shangri-La Hotel, and the first thing he said was, "Mayor, you mustn't get angry . . ." The last thing he said before hanging up was, "I'll definitely figure out why things changed course. Don't worry, I'll definitely figure out how things went wrong." After hanging up, Mingliang wanted to throw the cell phone to the ground, but instead he very slowly placed it on the table. Then it occurred to him that the other cell phone should be ringing as well, and in fact it did. He assumed that it must be his administrative secretary, Cheng Qing, calling, and in fact it was. Her voice was muffled and mysterious, as though there were someone next to her listening in. She not only pressed the phone tightly to her ear but also used her other hand to cover her mouth, making her voice sound even more mysteriously soft.

"You know, there were only four hundred and ten votes in favor of Explosion, while there were eight hundred and twenty fucking votes against.

". . . This breakdown of votes in favor and against is identical to that of the vote when you and Zhu Ying were running for village chief. Do you belief in karma? Do you know where the problem lies? At that time, you should have failed but didn't, but now that same evil woman has been responsible for your downfall!

". . . Can you believe it? Today, when those male experts came to vote, half of them had nannies who were in fact whores from Explosion—they were whores trained in that special vocational school in Explosion, of which neither you nor I has any knowledge.

". . . Mayor Kong, you are the mayor of the twenty million residents of Explosion. Do you know who is the principal of that special vocational school? She is none other than your family's old whore—that yellow-faced bitch! All of the whore nannies from Explosion, if they were not able to contact the high-level cadres whom they were targeting, settled for the cadres' drivers, secretaries, and cooks. In this way, they managed to take down those experts, professors, and academicians!"

Cheng Qing concluded with a tearful plea. "Mayor Kong, listen to me. You must divorce your wife either today or tomorrow. You don't necessarily need to marry me—I'm no longer thinking about that. But for the sake of Explosion, and for the sake of the people of Explosion, I beg you to immediately have someone deliver the divorce papers to her. You must cut off her dreams, so that she will no longer think about your and Explosion's future."

When he hung up the phone, Kong Mingliang thought he was calm, but he actually threw the phone. He hurled it into a rosebush in front of him. The rosebush was in full bloom and was flaming red, like a women having sex in the middle of her period. He stared at that flowerpot and suddenly had an evil thought. He wanted to stamp on that rosebush, but it had a single blossom, and the rest was only green leaves. When he went over and lifted his foot to stomp on that single rose, the flowerpot suddenly didn't have any green leaves left and instead, in the blink of an eye, dozens of red roses had bloomed, resembling layers upon layers of flames.

When he looked away, he saw that none of the rosebushes that were located every few meters along the path and beneath the grape trellis had any green leaves left, and instead they had all burst into fiery bloom. Even the cell phone he had just thrown down burst into bloom inside the tile flowerpot.

The mayor didn't know how his evil thought could have made all of those rosebushes simultaneously burst into bloom, to the point that there were no green leaves left in any of the flowerpots. He stared at those rosebushes, until the red phone with a direct connection to the heart of the Beijing government finally began to ring. It rang like an epileptic having a seizure. As he lunged forward to grab that trembling receiver, Mingliang first cupped his hand over the receiver and then, after he caught his breath, said politely and warmly, "Hello!" He waited for the response from some important personage or Beijing official, but instead the voice he heard coming from the receiver was the steely voice of his brother Mingyao.

"Brother, I know everything. From the perspective of our family, we should destroy Second Sister-in-Law. But from the perspective of Explosion and of the nation, not only must you leave her alone, but furthermore you must treat her well."

Mingyao said, "My brother, your entire life you have been foiled by women."

He added, "As long as Explosion can receive at least half the votes in the next round of voting, you can kneel down before Sister-in-Law. You should agree to anything she asks, even if it involves killing someone!

". . . You should have all of the city's cadres kneel down before her. If Sister-in-Law wants someone dead, you should have that person locked away until they die—as long as Sister-in-Law doesn't interfere any further with the voting process.

". . . Your next directive should instruct Explosion's residents to go kneel down in front of Sister-in-Law—for the sake of Explosion and its twenty million residents!"

After putting down the phone, Mingliang overturned the tea table in front of him, broke the red phone's cord, then smashed the telephone to the ground next to the overturned table. Then, bizarrely, he repeatedly slapped the face of the secretary who had run over to help him, and kicked a squirrel that was sitting at his feet watching him. The squirrel spat up blood all over the ground and all over Mingliang's shoes, and after waiting for the squirrel to stop breathing he—with his toes still pointed—screamed like a barbarian at the sky,

"Zhu Ying, you beast, you whore, you slut who has been tormenting me my entire life—if I, Kong Mingliang, don't send you to prison, then I don't deserve to be mayor or even Kong Mingliang!"

He shouted, "All of the people, trees, and plants of the city government, please listen—if I don't succeed in killing Zhu Ying after Explosion has been promoted to a provincial-level metropolis, then I want you to kill me right here instead. That way, this city government compound will become my cemetery and my graveyard."

He added, "Did you hear me? After one of us is dead, you should open your eyes and see that all of my goodwill toward this whore has been for the sake of you and Explosion, and if I manage to kill her you will all kowtow to me and to the city government, expressing your gratitude!"

After making this announcement, Kong Mingliang stood there for a while, his lips bleeding where he had bitten them. There were tears in his eyes, though it was unclear whether they were tears of love or tears of hatred.

II.

By afternoon, Mayor Kong decided to go implore his wife.

He knew that if there were in fact three thousand maid-whores who had been scattered throughout the capital's streets and alleys, penetrating into the homes of experts who were about to vote, then Zhu Ying would be able to prevent Explosion from being promoted to a provincial-level metropolis. He waited under the grape trellises behind city hall until he was able to calm himself down and then, in addition to placing several telephone calls to Beijing instructing his people to undertake a variety of lobbying efforts on his behalf, he decided to go back and see his wife, Zhu Ying, in person. He sent three secretaries to go to Zhu Ying's home and drive her to the city hall, but they reported back that when they arrived at her home, she was not even willing to open the door to them. Eventually, Mingliang realized that he had no choice but to go to her home, the same way that when he was trying to be elected village chief thirty years earlier, he also had to go see her in person. At the time of that earlier visit, the village board was located not very far from Zhu Ying's house, and Mingliang could cover the distance in a dozen steps or so. But now the city government compound was located several dozen kilometers from the old main road, and he needed to take a forty-minute ride to cover the distance. Moreover, he had not anticipated that, even though Explosion's promotion to the status of a provincial-level metropolis had not yet been approved, the streets would still be filled with people marching up and down while waving national flags and hibiscus flowers. Countless youngsters had gathered in the square, in the streets, and in the garden in the city center, and they were taking turns standing on tables and stones while making speeches celebrating the nation's development and advocating that Explosion be promoted. The sound of their chants echoed through the city streets like claps of thunder, as the red flags and banners that were hanging everywhere made Explosion resemble a pot of boiling water. Some cars had stopped by the side of the road and were honking their horns, as though it were a national holiday.

In order to avoid those noisy crowds, Mingliang got out of the car and took some back streets to the old city, proceeding in the opposite direction from the crowds. The sun on this first day of June covered in a gold veneer the buildings, bridges, and twin towers that Mingyao had helped erect. Ever since he was promoted to county mayor ten years earlier, he had never walked alone through his city like this. This was his city, and these were his people. The city's skyscrapers and overpasses, its gardens and its intersections, and every flower and plant lining its streets—all of these fell under his oversight. If he were but to give the word in his next directive, all of the city's willow trees would bloom with scholar-tree blossoms; if it were known that he was on his way somewhere, all of the cars and bicycles in the streets would pull over to let him pass. To prevent people from recognizing him, he grabbed a white flag from somewhere and held it up, as though he were just an ordinary citizen out celebrating in the streets. His face was covered in sweat, and he used the flag to wipe it. After he turned from the main road into a small alley called Deren, he threw down the white flag. Deren Alley led directly from Explosion's main street to the old city road. At the time this alley was being reconstructed, and he had personally assigned it its current name. Because the alley led directly to the old city road, and all of the tumult and excitement was in the new city district, once he reached this alley he was able to sigh with relief. He drank a sip of water from a faucet in the alley, then hurried on toward the old city road.

When he finally reached the opening to the road, the sun in the west reappeared and shone down, scattering red light over the old city streets and covering the houses, walls, and ground in red, yellow, and blue slogans and banners. The slogans and banners all bore the phrase "Welcome back Mayor Kong!" He didn't know, however, whether all these banners on the trees, on the walls, and hanging in midair like late-autumn fruit had appeared on their own or whether someone had arranged for them in advance. The opening stretch of road was as quiet as the wilderness, and it was as if the residents of every house and every building had all gone out to celebrate in the streets and public squares, and even to city hall itself, leaving the smaller alleys completely empty. But when he emerged from the alley, he found himself in the old city streets, where everything was in a great tumult. A red carpet had been laid out leading right up to Zhu Ying's house, and when Mingliang looked out at the red mountains and red ocean, he saw that all of the tree leaves were red, the houses' old blue bricks were now red, and even the sparrows, turtledoves, and crows flying through the sky had turned red. Many of the residents of these old city streets were no longer people who had been born in Explosion, but rather outsiders who had flooded into Explosion after it began to develop. Because Mayor Kong had lived on this street when he was growing up, these newcomers had paid a high price to buy houses there. Standing on both sides of the red carpet, people applauded wildly when they saw Mingliang, and shouts of "Welcome Mayor Kong back to the old city!" echoed rhythmically through their applause. There were also boys and girls wearing matching red scarves, standing on both sides of the road and holding wreaths of flowers as they sang one welcoming song after another. Next, two elementary school students ran up to Mingliang and presented him with flowers and a red scarf. When Mingliang did not express any excitement, a passerby quickly went up to him and whispered in his ear, telling him to stop since Aunt Zhu's home was ahead. Mingliang nodded and grunted in response. Then a worker pointed his right index finger at his left palm, gesturing for everyone to quiet down. Everyone who had gathered to welcome the mayor instantly grew quiet. The people stood along the sides of the road, looking as though they had done something wrong. Some of the leaves and petals from the flowers and wreaths they were holding fell to the ground, others fell into their outstretched hands, and still others hovered in midair, uncertain what to do. In this silence, Mingliang walked along the red carpet toward Zhu Ying's house. He quickly remembered what her door looked like, what the wall around her house looked like, and even what sorts of grass had been growing in the cracks in the wall so many years earlier. He saw that where there used to be a pair of large red iron gates, now the red paint had disappeared, revealing a grayish maroon layer of rust. There were also many rust splotches on the gates themselves, making them look as though they were not thirty years old but rather had been left behind by some dynasty more than a century earlier.

When Mingliang reached those gates, he stopped and looked at the building, the courtyard wall, and the crowds around him, who had all retreated to a reasonable distance. He confirmed that the gates were not locked but rather merely latched. With this, he realized that Zhu Ying was definitely not in the house but rather standing in the courtyard behind the gate, listening and watching the commotion outside. Then he placed one hand on the head of the stone lion to the right of the door.

A chill emanated up from the lion's head into his hand, and he used that chill to help calm himself down. He coughed to clear his throat, then quietly said to the gate, "Zhu Ying, please open this gate. I am the mayor of Explosion, Mayor Kong." Then, after listening carefully for a moment and seeing that there was no response, he proceeded to walk up the steps to the gate and lightly knocked.

The residents who were gathered around collectively held their breath, afraid that if they made a sound they might startle and annoy the mayor, and Zhu Ying standing inside. A sparrow flew over and dropped a feather, which fell loudly to the street like a wooden club. All of the people who had gathered there held their hands to their mouths. They looked in the direction of the feather, until the feather finally came to a rest after bouncing twice, and only then did they turn back to the finger with which Mingliang was gently knocking on the gate.

Mingliang knocked several times, and as he did he said more loudly,

"I am Mayor Kong, the mayor of Explosion!"

Then, he repeated even more loudly,

"I am your husband, Mayor Kong."

And again, as loudly as he could,

"Is it possible that you can't even hear the voice of your husband, the mayor?"

Someone brought Mingliang a stool, and he stood on it in front of the gate and proceeded to scream,

"Zhu Ying—I said, Zhu Ying!—it's all right if you don't want to open the door for me, but there is something I need to tell you in my capacity as mayor. In this morning's vote in Beijing over whether or not Explosion should be promoted to the status of a megalopolis under the direct jurisdiction of the central government, there were four hundred and ten ayes to eight hundred and twenty nays and abstentions. Why weren't there eight hundred and twenty ayes and four hundred and ten nays? Why was this vote identical to that of the elections for village chief thirty years ago? I now understand that you're trying to tell me that the two of us have rendered a meritorious service of creating this city and creating history. You're this city's mother and the bearer of its children, while I am the city's father and the creator of its infrastructure. This city's buildings, roads, airports, train stations, shopping areas, development districts, and foreign residential areas and even its handful of foreign consulates and business offices, as well as all of the city's plants and trees, people and zoos—all of this will be inherited by your children, which is to say our descendants. Explosion now needs to be promoted to the status of a provincial-level metropolis. However, you sent three thousand girls, nannies, and students from your women's vocational school to specific households and official posts in Beijing—so that they could use their status to snare the vote-wielding experts, professors, and academicians. But Zhu Ying, has it occurred to you that if you alter the outcome of this vote, you will be impeding Explosion's future growth and development, while also undermining the hopes and dreams of Explosion's twenty million residents? In this way, you will become Explosion's criminal, don't you know?

". . . Zhu Ying, I'm begging you in my capacity as city mayor—please quickly notify your girls and ask them to tell the men they snared that, in the second round of voting that begins tomorrow morning at nine, they should vote in favor of Explosion. If you don't notify them now, it will be too late and you'll become Explosion's greatest criminal. If this fails, the people of Explosion will tear you to shreds, don't you know?

". . . Zhu Ying, open this door. Open this door so that we can talk things over. For the sake of Explosion, for the sake of the people, for the sake of the past and the future—tell me what you want, and I'll agree to it.

"... Open this door. As the city's mayor, I'm begging you.

"... Open this door. Although I am your husband, I am also the mayor of this city!

"... Open this door. For the sake of Explosion, for the people, and for history, open the door and I'll kneel down to you!

"... I can kneel down before you and let you beat me, curse me, and even spit in my face!

"... For the sake of history, for the people, I won't hesitate to take action!

"... Zhu Ying, what do you want me to do? Not only am I willing to kneel down before you, I can even have thousands of residents of Explosion kneel down before you. As long as you support Explosion's promotion to the status of a provincial-level metropolis, I'm willing to remove any individuals you want from their current positions, and even send them to prison. ..."

As dusk approached, Mingliang stood on that stool and shouted until his throat bled, to the point that all of the city's streets were full of the smell of the blood from his throat. Moreover, because he was shouting for so long, his voice became increasingly hoarse. When it finally reached the point that he could barely produce any sound, he climbed down from the stool, knelt in front of the door to the Zhu family home, and in a deep voice said,

"Zhu Ying, I am your husband, and I have returned to you.

"... Open the door. If you open the door, you will see that not only am I kneeling here, but so are all of the residents of Explosion's old street, together with many of the city's other residents."

At this point, as the old people, children, men, and women standing outside the door were kneeling with Mingliang in front of the Zhu home, and as they were shouting, "For the sake of Explosion, for the sake of the people, please open the door so that the mayor can talk to you" until they became hoarse, and as their cries were flying through the city streets like autumn leaves, and covering Zhu Ying's house and courtyard walls—the Zhu family gate *still* didn't open. There was, however, a mysterious sound that emerged from inside, and everyone thought that the gate was about to open and Zhu Ying would appear in the entranceway. But, in the end, the sound disappeared, and the sound of footsteps approaching the gate once again receded into the interior of the courtyard. After this happened two or three more times, everyone began to believe that Zhu Ying would never open those gates and that she was willing to face off against Mingliang and the people of Explosion until the death. They assumed that she preferred to become Explosion's greatest criminal rather than allow Explosion to become promoted to the status of a provincial-level metropolis, which would thereby allow Kong Mingliang to become the mayor of this new megalopolis. At this point, the sun was setting in the west and its final rays were shining down on the city and on the heads of the thousands of city residents kneeling there. Just as darkness was about to fall, a sharp burst of frustration and anger emerged from the crowd. They kept passing notes up to Mingliang and whispering in his ear, as the words "Break down the gate! Drag her out!" came gushing from the crowd like a river. Some people had begun to quietly stand up, had found some sticks and stones, and were about to break one of Zhu Ying's windows. However, a child who was not yet ten appeared amid that crowd of kneeling people. He was thin, with a long face and a crew cut. On his book bag there was a picture of a cacao tree and an olive tree, and as he walked a trail of chocolate and olive candies fell out. He didn't know what was happening, so he went up to Mingliang and first looked at him as though he were a stranger, then as if he were someone he had once known, and finally he took two steps forward and said in a soft, halting voice,

"Are you my father?"

Mingliang looked at the child. Initially he was astonished, then an excited pallor came over his face, and, finally, he flushed bright red when he heard the boy trying to call him "Father!" He grabbed the child's hand and hugged him tight. Then he put the boy on his shoulders and, under the final rays of the setting sun, he walked over toward those locked gates.

Standing in front of them, he shouted in an excited and trembling voice,

"Zhu Ying, I have returned with our son.

". . . I never expected that our son would look just like me—thin, with a square face, and small dimples that appear when he talks."

At this point, the double gates suddenly swung open.

Light from the setting sun poured through the door, illuminated Zhu Ying—who was neatly dressed and made up. She faced Kong Mingliang, who was holding their son, and stared out at the vast crowd of people who were bowing down on both sides of the street, entreating her to open the gates. First, with trembling hands she leaned against the door frame and looked at her son, who was sitting on his father's shoulders and—like countless other children from Explosion—was wearing a backpack. Then her eyes filled with tears, as the tears drenched her face and dripped to the ground.

At this point, the people and citizens kneeling in front of the gate all stood up and began to applaud, shouting, "Explosion can now become a provincial-level metropolis! Explosion can now become a provincial-level metropolis!"

When the boy reached down from his father's shoulders to hug his mother, the sun had not yet fully set, while the moon had already risen. The entire city and indeed the entire world were jointly illuminated by both the sun and the moon.

3. MEGALOPOLIS (3)

I.

From dusk until dawn, Zhu Ying spent the entire night calling all of the girls who managed to snare someone in the capital, telling them that they must find a way to make sure that the experts and professors would vote in Explosion's favor in the morning. She placed so many calls that she broke two landline phones and three cell phones, and used up several telephone cables.

The next afternoon at one, the results of the second round of voting were announced, and the result was the same as it had been that time when Kong Mingliang and Zhu Ying were both running for village chief. There were 820 votes in favor of Explosion becoming a new provincial-level metropolis like Beijing and Shanghai, and only 410 votes in favor of that famous city on China's southern coast. After the news reached Explosion, the entire city erupted with joy. Every resident went on and on about this glory. In order to celebrate Explosion's promotion, the city's streets and alleys were filled with parades and people chanting. Schools, factories, and companies all declared a holiday, and even all of the city's foreigners were out in the streets with Chinese flags, drinking beer, and discussing how China was one of the world's miracles and how Explosion was one of China's miracles. The small minority of residents and youngsters who either did not want Explosion to be promoted or did not think it would be, were spat upon by the others, and those who tried to keep offering reasons why Explosion should not be promoted were beaten by the others. Accordingly, for those who ended up losing a tooth or breaking an arm, those few days were not terribly fresh and exciting.

In the city's east side, a teacher was even killed over this.

In the southern part of the city, there was a young scholar who asked, "If the city is promoted to a provincial-level metropolis, will ordinary citizens like ourselves no longer be able to lead regular lives?" This question incited an animated debate, during which someone struck him over the head with a club, and he closed his mouth forever, never again expressing a skeptical opinion.

All of the trees along the streets and alleys—including willows and French toon trees—would normally have just started to turn green at the beginning of the sixth lunar month, but at that time they were blooming as though it were midsummer. In the past, pagoda trees would bloom for about a week in the fourth month, after which they would start bearing fruit, but this year the pagoda trees, apricot trees, walnut trees, and elms started flowering again in the sixth month, blanketing the city's streets and alleys in an ocean of blooms. Moreover, during this season, white pagoda blossoms were blooming large and red, while each petal of the red peach blossoms was golden yellow. The largest of these flowers could reach the size of a large bowl or a basket, and if placed on the side of the road or out in the countryside, they could go for an entire month without dropping a single petal. Elm leaves piled up on the tree branches like coins, so heavy that the branches bent over under their weight. The apricots and walnuts, which normally would not ripen until the eighth or ninth month, were already being sold in the streets. All of the flowers began blooming significantly earlier, larger, and longer than usual. All of the seasonal fruits began to mature at lightning speed as soon as they heard that Explosion had received two-thirds of the available votes for promotion and would therefore become a provincial-level metropolis. The apple trees almost didn't have a chance to bloom before they immediately began bearing fruit, and a few days later stores started selling apricots as large as apples—and cherries, mangoes, and pears soon followed.

Grapes were as large as walnuts, and were as bright and translucent as dragon fruit.

Every day the streets of Explosion were full of spring freshness and the scent of summer and autumn fruit. There were more magpies and orioles than in the past. It was if all of the orioles in the world had descended on Explosion. Sometimes flocks of pigeons would fly over Explosion, casting a dark shadow over the earth as though a rain cloud were overhead.

After finishing her telephone calls, Zhu Ying took a quick nap, and upon waking up she learned the result of the vote. At that point, her husband had already left her side, having gone to the city government to begin preparing for the additional work and glory that Explosion's promotion would yield. Zhu Ying felt a surge of post-excitement loneliness, and in order to break out of it and join in the festivities, she got out of bed and washed her face, then left the house and began wandering aimlessly through the streets. When she passed the entrance to a school, she saw that the pushcart in front of the school that used to sell pencils and notebooks was now selling only the flowers and flags that everyone was waving. Furthermore, next to the flags, the stand was covered with dripping wet roses, which normally didn't bloom until late summer or fall, and each blossom and flag could sell for the price of a student's entire semester's tuition. When she turned around to look at the flower pond in front of the school, she saw that in the middle of the pond the evergreen tree (which normally didn't need to be trimmed or pruned) had suddenly grown as tall as a house, and its branches were full of delicate lilac blossoms that were emitting a pungent smell of osmanthus. Many people who walked under the tree would break into fits of sneezing on account of the fragrance, and it was at this point that she truly believed Explosion was going to become a major city—all thanks to her husband's efforts. Then she hurriedly left the school, occasionally breaking into a run. She herself was not sure why she was rushing. She quickly proceeded forward until she reached the Explosion memorial, but when she turned at the intersection, she picked the wrong road, and it was not until she saw the Kong family mansion, which had been designated a first-class cultural relic, that she finally realized what she had been hurrying to see. She wanted to find someone in the Kong family to talk to.

When she reached the door to the mansion, the sun was already hovering over the buildings in the eastern side of the city, and in the sunlight, the shadows cast by trees, people, and buildings all looked twice as large as the originals. An old man out walking his dog came over. Zhu Ying looked at him and realized that he was the same Second Dog who, years earlier, had spat the most at her father. She was astonished to see that he was already so old. She stood there in surprise, then asked him,

"Don't you recognize me?"

The old man slowed down.

"I am Zhu Ying."

The old man stood there thinking for a while, then without a word he turned and hobbled down a different alley. After he left, there was only the yellow dog, whose name Zhu Ying couldn't remember, still standing there looking at her. The dog barked a few times to express its enthusiasm and curiosity, then followed him. Zhu Ying watched as the old man and the dog walked away; then she pushed open the gates to the Kong family mansion, which she had rarely entered. She immediately saw Minghui sitting in a sunny area of the courtyard, leaning against a small table. On that table, there was an oil stove with a small aluminum pot. Over the pot, there was a large slab of glass, on which sat the old almanac with the stuck-together pages, and on top of the almanac there was another glass slab. The steam came up from the stove below and the sun shone down from above, though the steam could not pass through the glass to reach the book. This way, the humidity could finally separate the stuck-together pages of the old almanac. Minghui sat there attentively, staring at the oil stove and at the humidity accumulating between the two glass slabs. After he heard Zhu Ying push open the gate, he looked up and turned to the doorway, then turned back to those final pages of the almanac that were still in the process of being separated—as though he had not heard the gate open and had not seen Zhu Ying.

"Your brother has succeeded. With my help, he has succeeded in making Explosion a provincial-level metropolis." Zhu Ying stood in front of the table, her excited voice sounding like firecrackers. "Everyone is out celebrating. Don't you want to go see?"

Minghui looked up again.

"Along the street, all of the trees are blooming with different-colored flowers. Don't you want to go see?"

Minghui looked down again at the stove and reduced the heat a bit.

"I hear that in the next few days Beijing will issue a directive stating that Explosion is being promoted to the status of a provincial-level metropolis. Your Kong family should definitely celebrate your brother's achievement."

Minghui removed the slab of glass from the almanac, used a paper napkin to wipe away the condensation from the glass, and then began to carefully peel back a moistened page. Throughout this entire process, the only thing he said to Zhu Ying was a mumbled "Wait a moment," after which he didn't even look at her. While holding down the almanac with his left hand, he used the thumb and index finger of his right hand to lift a corner of that top page, as slowly as though he had not only all night, but even an entire season or entire year to complete this task. In the process, he forgot all about Zhu Ying and forgot that there was someone standing in front of him.

After standing there for a little while, Zhu Ying finally left. Before she left, however, she said,

"Minghui, in the entire Kong family, you are the only good one, but you are also the only slow-witted one. You know?"

As Zhu Ying walked out of the Kong family mansion, she discovered that the old city was now as still as a pool of stagnant water, while the sky above the new city's development zone, together with that of the east side and west side, was full of fireworks like falling stars. Staring at that bustling sky and those buildings, Zhu Ying suddenly understood what she had to do. Some of the girls who had gone into the city to snare their targets would be returning later that day, so what she needed to do was to go to the city government and find Mingliang, and have him accompany her to the train station to meet them. They should travel out to the maid-training school in the suburbs to see them. She quickly set off, telling her driver to head toward the city center, to the city government complex that she was now permitted to enter.

II.

On July 1, Beijing officially designated Explosion as one of China's provincial-level metropolises, and Kong Mingliang was appointed a state-level mayor. As of that day, all of the residents of Explosion, together with the residents of the counties and regions falling under Explosion's jurisdiction, would be given a week's vacation to celebrate Explosion's promotion and transformation. From the city to the rural villages, and from the bricks of the high-rise buildings to the grass of the Balou Mountains, the sound of fireworks could be heard throughout the region. On the trees and walls, there

436

were red banners and slogans celebrating Explosion's promotion to the status of a provincial-level metropolis. All of the cinemas and theaters were showing films and performances around the clock, like a row of sugared gourds on a stick. A folk percussion group was performing in the streets day and night, and throughout the celebrations tens of thousands of residents of Explosion didn't eat or sleep for days. Kong Mingliang, in his new capacity as a state-level mayor, signed a directive ordering that all of the metropolis's streets and alleys, plants and flowers, bushes and trees be dyed imperial red and imperial yellow. All of the trees and plants were blooming with dark red, light yellow, maroon, and pink flowers. All of the walls were bearing red apples, yellow oranges, orange pomegranates, and purple grapes. Mingliang wrote and signed another directive, whereupon the weather forecast for overcast skies changed to one for clear skies. The rains that ordinarily would have come in July were instead pushed back to August or September. Several of the city's newspapers printed special issues and special sections, and furthermore every day they printed two editions—thereby covering the development and transformation Explosion had undergone over the preceding few decades. The monthly and bimonthly journals that became weeklies all recorded the miraculous story of how Kong Mingliang had led the people as Explosion was transformed from a small village of only a few hundred into a city with a population of over twenty million. All of the television channels were broadcasting nonstop speeches by the mayor and deputy mayor, together with congratulatory letters from Beijing, Shanghai, Guangzhou, Tianjin, and all of China's provinces. Scores of foreign nations had also either sent congratulatory messages or sent people to deliver congratulatory gifts. But just as the celebrations were reaching their zenith, and even the street-side toilets and trash cans were blooming with flowers and surrounded by people singing and dancing, Mingyao, who had not been seen for several days, suddenly appeared on the television broadcast that was being streamed around the clock to every household in the city. He was wearing a military uniform. His face was pallid and covered in sweat, but he had an outward appearance of calm. He was standing in front of a microphone and telling the people of Explosion that a month earlier he had rowed a boat, alone, departing from Yantai in Shandong province and heading out to sea. He has passed through China's Yellow Sea and several archipelagoes, into the Pacific Ocean, and eventually reached the Atlantic. Along the way, he visited Taiwan, Japan, South Korea, North Korea, and India, as well as Vietnam, the Philippines, and Cambodia. Afterward, he went ashore on America's west coast, and proceeded to New York, Washington, San Francisco, and Salt Lake City. Then, from Miami he rowed a boat to the Port of London. After staying in England for a few days, he proceeded to visit all of the other countries in Europe. He said that he had met with the US president Barack Obama and the UK prime minister David Cameron, Germany's chancellor Angela Merkel, and France's new president François Hollande. While meeting with thirty-eight Latin American heads of state, he confirmed that the root of Taiwan's desire for independence, Japan's arrogance and presumptuousness, and the fact that even small countries like Vietnam and the Philippines had the audacity to shit on China's head—all of this was a result of the arrogance and prejudice with which the United States and Europe viewed China. It was that the fucking United States was supporting and encouraging them, while Europe was quietly cheering them on. Mingyao stood solemnly in front of the camera and recited this entire speech without using any notes. After a few minutes his yellow pallor had completely disappeared, and instead he appeared energized. In a fervor, he proceeded to speak nonstop for two hours and twenty minutes, until finally he announced in a hoarse voice,

"The time has arrived for us to correct the arrogance of Europe and the United States. Citizens of this new provincial-level metropolis, all I need is three days of your time. All I want is that during these three days, you follow me and do as I say. If you do, then China will no longer be the way it is now, and neither will the world be the way it is now. None of those in Explosion will be the way they are now!"

At this point, Mingyao paused and undid the top button of his uniform, as his middle-aged face had a flash of a youthful glow. Then, with a throat that was almost bleeding, he shouted, "Compatriots, brothers and sisters, my beloved people—the world will not grant us very much time or opportunity. But now that the United States has once again been plunged into a severe financial recession and the EU is on the verge of falling apart, please everyone come with me. We can spend three days lending the United States and Europe a hand, after which they will no longer be as arrogant and biased, or as rude and unreasonable.

"In three days, we will first fix all of America's problems, and then we'll fix Europe's. After this, we will proceed to fix China's problems, and even all of the world's. This is an opportunity that has been granted us by heaven, and a responsibility that has been granted us by world history. Accordingly, the people of Explosion and I should shoulder this responsibility. Let us set off proudly from the new provincial-level metropolis of Explosion!!"

After this, an image of Mingyao and his army practicing a march appeared on the television screen. Meanwhile, the entire city of Explosion became quiet, and remained so until dusk, whereupon the whole city began surging toward the airport, toward the train stations, and out to the suburbs. No one in the city had any way of knowing that the mayor, at that precise moment, was in fact dying in his office in the city government compound. His wife, Zhu Ying, had rushed over and parked in front of the entranceway, just as the sun was slipping behind the mountains, and as that entranceway, which was built in imitation of the Arc de Triomphe, was bathed in silence and bloodred light. At that point, soldiers from two companies or an entire battalion were running out of the government compound holding their weapons, their footsteps echoing on the pavement. Zhu Ying had a premonition that something momentous was about to unfold. She followed the wooden corridor with the grape trellis that her husband took every day, and when she burst into Kong Mingliang's office in the city government compound, her husband had already died at that immense mahogany desk. The army had taken away the directive he had been forced to sign just before his death: "Agreement to permit General Kong Mingyao to borrow the city's residents for three days." After the mayor signed this directive, the army had been worried that he would sign another one ordering the recall of those residents who were still en route. When he returned to take care of some business for Explosion or for the nation, a rather ordinary dagger had stabbed him in the back, in such a way that the tip could be seen poking out of his chest. There was a clot of blood on the tip of the dagger, and he lay there at his desk as though he were merely asleep. The blood flowing out of his chest was as black as ink. Not a drop fell onto the desk, however, and instead all of it poured onto his right pants leg and into his shoe, finally pooling on the floor under the desk.

Before he died, the mayor used his right index finger to write a line of characters on his desk using his own blood. The line read,

"My people, I've let you down!"

When Zhu Ying burst into his office, she stood motionless in front of her husband, sweat pouring down her forehead like rain. She stared at the line written in blood on the desk, then lifted her husband's shoulders to see his anguished expression. She paused for a moment in that deathly silence, then walked out of the office. As she did so, she glanced up at the thousands of squirrels and birds that emerged from the fields and forests. They all stood on the lawn, in the orchards, and in the flower gardens of the city government compound, watching Zhu Ying without making a sound. They all had a look of anxiety and foreboding, as though they knew a disaster was about to unfold.

Zhu Ying walked out silently under the gaze of those birds and squirrels.

She did not return to her own home and instead proceeded back to the Kong family mansion. At that point, Minghui happened to have just emerged from his home and was standing in the middle of the street. He was holding the almanac, with the stuck-together pages he had finally succeeded in separating. He was looking out in alarm at Explosion, as though he, too, knew that something momentous had occurred. It was then that he saw Zhu Ying rushing over from the other end of the alley. She stopped in front of him, and said,

"Your second brother has died. He was assassinated by someone sent by your third brother.

". . . Your third brother is now leading the military and all of the city's residents to the airport, the rail station, and the pier. Meanwhile, I will take a thousand girls to go with them.

". . . His army needs these girls. For the sake of your second brother, I'll see to it that your third brother will die either at my hand or at the hand of one of those girls.

". . . I'll entrust your nephew Victory to you. He is the only blood link between your second brother and myself, and is also one of your Kong family's roots."

Upon saying this, Zhu Ying quickly turned and walked away. But before she had proceeded more than a few steps, she walked back and hugged Minghui, who was still standing there in shock, then kissed his cheek with her icy lips. "In this life I have dealt with countless men, but I have never before voluntarily kissed one—including even your second brother." She added, "Today, you're the first man whom I have voluntarily kissed. I'm begging you not to tell your nephew, after he grows up, all of the things that his father and mother have done. Just tell him that his parents were killed in a car accident, and the accident was so bad that their corpses could not even be recovered afterward."

Then she left.

That night, she recruited a thousand girls and had them join Mingyao's army under the name Women's Support Troops. That night, Mingyao left with his army and all of the people of Explosion that he could take. They departed in a chaotically disordered sound of feet marching and truck tires screeching, as Minghui's hoarse voice could be heard everywhere, shouting and beseeching,

"Third Brother, where are you? Please leave behind the elderly and the children!

"Third Brother, where are you? Please leave behind the elderly, the children, and the women!

"Third Brother, as your brother I'm begging you, please leave behind the elderly, the children, the women, and the disabled!"

Following these cries, none of those soldiers, residents, and people heading toward the train station and airport made any effort to stop, though some old people, children, and women were pushed out of the group. Furthermore, when the soldiers passed the city government compound, they followed Mingyao's instructions— they goose-stepped and, while facing the government compound, observed three minutes of silence in memory of the father of the city, Kong Mingliang.

That night, Zhu Ying took all of the girls and left with the army. As for another several hundred girls who had just returned from the capital, they didn't need to leave the train station. For the next several days, all of Explosion's stores and companies closed, and the city was reduced to a virtual ghost town. When someone occasionally came out into the streets, it would invariably be one of the old people, children, weak, or disabled who had stayed behind, who all had a look of fear and confusion in their eyes.

In this way, the city's prosperity abruptly came to an end.

A brilliant historical period reached its conclusion.

One morning a month later, the first to appear in the city's streets and squares was not a person from Explosion but rather a broken clock that someone had thrown out. With this, the city's trash bins, its gardens, and the ground were littered with all sorts of discarded clocks and cheap watches that had suddenly stopped working and couldn't be fixed. Throughout Explosion, the hands of all the clocks and the watches stopped in the middle of the night, and in most cases their hour, minute, and second hands had completely fallen off. In this way, the city came to resemble a junk pile of broken clocks and watches, to the point that the old people and children couldn't even walk through the streets because of all the broken clocks and watches. In this way, the city was buried under a mountain of broken clocks and watches.

After the people who had been left behind in Explosion spent several days cleaning up all of the broken clocks and watches, Minghui dragged his nephew Victory to Mingguang's house. Mingguang was looking after his wife, who had just given birth. Their first child was a son, and this time she had given birth to boy and girl twins. Minghui and his nephew arrived just after Mingguang's wife successfully gave birth, and as Mingguang was carrying a basin with the umbilical cords and amniotic fluid, preparing to throw them out and bury them. The two brothers stood in the front of the house. Facing each other, they had the following exchange:

Mingguang said loudly, "We now have both son and daughter. Our Kong family has its own descendants."

Minghui said, "Second Brother, Second Sister-in-Law, and Third Brother all died in a car accident. Now, you and I are the only ones left."

Mingguang asked, "What day is today? I need to remember my son's birthday."

Minghui replied, "We should go weep at their graves. As Explosion has been transformed from a village to a town, from a town to a county, from a county to a city, and from a city to a provincial-level metropolis, the people of Explosion have lost the habit of weeping at the graves of their relatives."

It was that evening that it also occurred to the people who were left behind in Explosion that it had been several decades since they last visited the cemetery to express their joys and sorrows. Accordingly, several of them headed to their family's grave sites during the period between sunset and moonrise, and by the time the moon had appeared there was the sound of someone weeping as he returned from his family's grave site. Afterward, the entire city—including its old city and new city, its east side and west side—was filled with the sound of weeping. The remaining people of Explosion all came out of their houses and, weeping, knelt down facing the graves of their ancestors, tearfully recounting their miserable fate, calling out the formal and diminutive names of their deceased relatives. In this river of tears and under the light of the moon, some people saw the Kong family emerge, weeping, from their old mansion in the old city section of Explosion. This included Eldest Brother Kong Mingguang; Fourth Brother Kong Minghui; Mingguang's wife, Cai Qinfang, who had just given birth; and Zhu Ying's son Victory Kong. They emerged together, supporting one another. After kneeling down in front of the museum on Explosion's former main street, they proceeded toward the cemetery on the outskirts of the city on their knees, leaving behind a trail of blood.

The next day, the sun should have come up in the east, as usual, but it never appeared. Instead, the sky was filled with a black haze that the people of Explosion had never seen before. Even in the middle of the day, they couldn't see anything more than a few meters away. In this haze, all of the birds, including phoenixes, peacocks, pigeons, orioles, and so forth, were poisoned to death, while the people started coughing up blood. When the haze finally receded thirty years later, Explosion no longer had any birds or insects left. But the people who were still alive thirty years later saw that, along the trail of blood and dried-up tears that they had left behind as they were dragging themselves to the cemetery on their knees, there had sprouted some gorgeous roses and peonies. Meanwhile, along the bloody path that the Kong family had left behind on their way to the cemetery, there were not only flowers but also all different kinds of trees.

CHAPTER 19

Postface

Dear readers, *Explosion* is finally finished, as I, like an old ox, finally managed to drag this train car to the top of the mountain.

The very next day, I had this work printed and bound. Carrying several bound volumes, I excitedly departed from the Beijing airport, sitting in first class (the Explosion city government helped pay for my ticket), and flew directly to the Explosion airport. Upon walking out of the plane, I saw that officials from the Explosion city government were waiting on the tarmac. They shook my hand and chatted with me, offering me flowers. They took me to a company car and, escorted by three police cars, they drove me to a hotel directly in front of the Explosion city government building. There, they put me in the presidential suite, where countless world leaders and dignitaries had previously stayed. For dinner, Explosion's city mayor, Mayor Kong, personally hosted a banquet in my honor. Of course, in real life he and I are just as the manuscript describes us—we are both in our fifties and of average height, and we both have a square face. Although we didn't say much, every sentence was meaningful and resonant. The dishes at that night's banquet were so good that they can only be described as exquisite. If I were to describe the food in more detail, I would have to wait until I'm on my deathbed and these would be the last words I'd ever utter.

While we were eating, I handed my manuscript to Mayor Kong, who was sitting at the head of the table. He excitedly leafed through it, then handed it to his secretary and said,

"If Author Yan runs into any problems, please resolve them. If he needs any money, no matter how much, please give it to him."

The mayor offered me a toast, then we proceeded into another room to take pictures with some important guests representing national institutions, who had arrived from Beijing before me.

After dinner, there was nothing.

The entire night, there was no word.

The following morning at eleven, Mayor Kong's secretary came to the hotel to escort me to Mayor Kong's office. The mayor's office was exactly as I described it in the preceding chronicle, and was located in a "city government complex" behind the main city government building. In the city government complex there were a series of newly constructed courtyards along the grape trellis corridor. The courtyards came in different sizes, ranging from two to five suites, and under the eaves of every courtyard there was an old painting in black, yellow, and red, together with a Buddhist story or legend. I followed the mayor's secretary down the corridor and past all of the Buddhist pictures, and after several turns we arrived at a five-suite courtyard. The mayor's office was in the third suite's meeting room. Because the function of that courtyard's meeting room was different from that of the others, its furnishings and decorations were also different. In the main room of that third suite, because it was the mayor's office, when you entered you would see the sun's rays illuminating every corner of the room, even though the windows did not appear particularly large when seen from the outside. The secretary took me into the mayor's office, then disappeared. I, meanwhile, stood in front of the mayor's mahogany desk, which was about six square meters in size. I glanced at the office's bookshelves, couches, and bonsai plants, and was about to say a few complimentary words about how enormous and luxurious the mayor's office was, when I suddenly noticed that the mayor had been staring at me coldly ever since I entered the room and had not said a single word. His face was livid, and his mouth was clenched so tightly that his lips were turning purple. The inch-thick bound copy of *The Explosion Chronicles* was placed neatly on the desk in front of him.

"Have you finished it?" I stammered. "It's a first draft and still needs to be revised."

"No need!" With this, the mayor took out a lighter and held it up to the manuscript, then set it on fire. As the fire was about to singe his hand, he threw the manuscript down, then kicked it until the pages were reduced to ashes and all that remained was the spine and some burning embers. Then he looked up and said three things:

"As long as Explosion and I are here, you shouldn't even think about publishing this book in China.

". . . If you try to publish this book anywhere outside China, you'll never be permitted to return to your hometown in the Balou Mountains as long as you live.

". . . I want you to leave Explosion today. If you don't leave today, there's no telling what I'll do to you!"

By that point, it was noon and the midday sun was streaming in through the mahogany-rimmed window. In that bright sunlight, I gazed at the mayor's livid face, then smiled and said, "Thank you, Mayor Kong. You are this book's first reader, and your response reassures me that I have written a pretty good work." Then, I retreated from the mayor's office.

I retreated from the city government complex.

That afternoon, I left the Explosion airport to return to Beijing, and shortly after I landed in the Beijing airport, an evening thunderstorm rained down. It rained continuously for four and a half hours, flooding the entire city and tying traffic into knots. As a result, I and countless other travelers were stuck in the airport for more than ten hours. The next morning, I finally returned home from the airport, and when I turned on the television I learned that this was the largest thunderstorm Beijing had experienced in the past six hundred years. Thirty-seven people drowned, and countless houses and lives were inundated. With this, the capital's prosperity became blunted.

Author's Note

1.

For readers, literature often provides an inspiration for life, but for authors, it is life that inevitably drives literature.

Contemporary China is currently hurtling past a series of economic and developmental milestones that took Europe over two centuries to achieve, but in the process all the usual rules and regulations have been displaced by their corresponding objectives. Shortcuts and unscrupulous methods have become a path to success and prosperity, while power and money have colluded to steal people's souls. The result has been a string of terrifying incidents, wherein beauty and ugliness, good and evil, substance and emptiness, value and meaninglessness, all become inextricably jumbled together.

Incidents that at first glance appear utterly illogical and unreal have become increasingly common. For instance, someone did indeed drown in a prison guard's half-filled face-washing basin; on New

Year's day, more than a thousand dead pigs did indeed float down Shanghai's Huangpu River; and just before a certain region in China switched over from burials to cremations, countless elderly people did indeed take their own lives so that they would be buried rather than cremated.

Our nation is new, but at the same time very ancient; it is modern and prosperous, but at the same time feudal and autocratic; it is Westernized, but also intrinsically Asian. The world is transforming the nation, even as the nation is simultaneously transforming the world, and through this process the nation's innovation lies in its use of an unfathomable reality to challenge the limits of human imagination. As a result, the nation has come to acquire a sort of unrealistic reality, a non-existent existence, an impossible possibility—in short, it has come to possess an invisible and intangible set of rules and regulations.

The nation has come to acquire a new logic and a new rationality, as it becomes characterized by the ubiquitous presence of something that could be called the mythoreal. At one time, the Chinese people may have been suspicious of this mythoreal, but they have gradually grown accustomed to it, and have even come to identify with it. As the entire world stares incredulously at contemporary China's miraculous transformation, the nation's authors feel they have reached a point where literature can no longer directly reflect reality. Even the ideologies and techniques associated with world literature would emit a collective sigh of despair if confronted with China's extraordinary events.

China's reality is currently driving the creation of what could be called a mythorealist literary practice—which is to say, a literature that uses an innovative set of techniques to reveal an otherwise invisible region beneath perceivable reality. By having literature follow a spectral path of ghosts and spirits, mythorealism seeks out these invisible regions in order to explode reality's façade.

2.

Just as it is inconceivable for conventional novels to lack a story, plot, or basic character development, they must similarly be grounded on a scientific and logical causality consisting of interlocking elements, such that sunlight makes objects visible, sex results in pregnancy, and the invention of the engine yields new modes of transportation. Here, causal logic's rationality is perfectly obvious.

In works by realist authors, the development of characters and objects is based on a strictly reciprocal, logical relationship. The causal relation may be hidden or implicit, but in these sorts of texts it is definitely not possible for it to be missing altogether. The correspondence between cause and effect is narrative's preeminent logical element. Realism relies on this sort of reciprocal logic, which it then elaborates and develops—and if a work deviates, it can no longer be considered pure realism.

In the opening of Franz Kafka's *The Metamorphosis,* the narrator famously describes how, "One morning Gregor Samsa awoke in his bed from uneasy dreams and found he had turned into a large verminous insect."* Nowhere in the remainder of the work, however, does Kafka ever tell us *how* or *why* Samsa was transformed from a human into a "verminous insect." In this way, the result remains, though the original cause has completely disappeared. This is Kafka's most powerful betrayal of realism, whereby he was able to discover (or even create) within literature an extra-realistic "acausality," in which there is effect without cause, and result without reason. In this way, in works like *The Trial* and *The Castle,* Kafka created a new kind of writing out of which an entire new literature was born.

* Franz Kafka, *The Essential Kafka,* John R. Williams, ed. and trans. (Herts: Wordsworth Editions, 2014).

Similarly, the first paragraph of Gabriel García Márquez's *One Hundred Years of Solitude* describes how:

> He *[the gypsy Melquíades] went from house to house dragging two metal ingots and everybody was amazed to see pots, pans, tongs and braziers tumble down from their places and beams creak from the desperation of nails and screws trying to emerge, and even objects that had been lost for a long time appeared from where they had been searched for most and went dragging along in turbulent confusion behind Melquíades's magical irons.***

Summoned by these magnetic ingots, the nails and screws in the floor struggle to respond. Here, we find a playful return of the sort of causal factors Kafka had previously discarded. However, these causal factors do not have the same relationship with their effect that we would expect to find within realism, but rather they are linked by more of a "semi-causal" relationship. After *One Hundred Years of Solitude* adopted this sort of semi-causal narrative, the rest of the world began to demand a similar narrative structure, thereby bestowing glory on Latin America and its authors like someone handing out steamed *mantou* buns in the middle of a famine.

3.

If it was indeed contemporary China's reality that spurred mythorealism into existence, then under what causal logic does this mythorealism now exist?

** Gabriel García Márquez, *One Hundred Years of Solitude*, Gregory Rabassa, trans. (New York: Harper Perennial Modern Classics, 2006).

It is only recently that the Chinese people have finally begun to understand the absurdity of China's Great Leap Forward. After all, if the only thing you have is a bundle of kindling and a handful of sand, how could you possibly smelt steel? And if all you have is a *mu* of land, how could you possibly produce ten or twenty thousand *jin* of grain? It turns out, however, that even the most absurd aspects of China's history and contemporary reality contain an invisible internal truth, and this truth is grounded on one or more "internal causalities."

These internal causalities dictate the most absurd reality, history, and humanity. Although God, in the Bible, said, "Let there be light," and there was light; then said, "Let there be water," and there was water; and finally separated the light from the darkness, and there was day and night—in China's reality and history, absurdity, disorder, chaos, and incomprehensibility (together with the emotional confusion and spiritual pain they may generate) all remain hidden within an internal causality. When an author finally succeeds in grasping this internal causality, mythorealism's "myth" becomes a reality that cannot be apprehended directly but which may be perceived through literature. Rather than confirming that 1 plus 1 equals 2, mythorealism instead helps people appreciate why 1 plus 1 *doesn't* equal 2—which is to say, it confirms that the occurrence of B is completely *unrelated* to A. In other words, mythorealism not only demonstrates why people in China came to believe that one *mu* of land could produce more than ten thousand *jin* of wheat or rice, it also reveals the origins, process, and underlying "reality" by which this phenomenon became possible in the first place.

In my novel *The Four Books*, the protagonist is an author who has been sentenced to compulsory re-education, and in order to plant a crop of wheat that would yield ten thousand *jin* of grain per *mu* of land, he selected an unusual plot of land. It turns out that the plot was located over the tomb of a former emperor who, when he was alive, enjoyed virtually unrivaled power, and it was in the soil over this tomb that the Author planted his wheat. When the wheat began to sprout, the Author irrigated the sprouts by repeatedly cutting his fingers and mixing his blood with water, and even slicing open his veins and allowing the blood to spurt out and mix with the rain. As a result, by harvest time the plot's ears of wheat were as large as ears of corn, and a single *mu* of land did indeed yield ten thousand *jin* of wheat. In this way, the inner causality of the *mu* of land that yielded ten thousand *jin* of grain was able to reveal humanity's innermost pain and hardship.

While realism rigorously accords with a set of logical causal correlations, absurdity discards this causality, and magical realism rediscovers reality's underlying causality— though this is not precisely the same causality that we find in real life. Mythorealism, meanwhile, captures a hidden internal logic contained within China's reality. It explodes reality, such that contemporary China's absurdity, chaos, and disorder—together with non-realism and illogicality—all become easily comprehensible. In the chaos of today's China, once novels succeed in grasping the wild roots growing under the soil of reality, the significance of reality itself pales in comparison.

Fumbling around in the darkness, *The Explosion Chronicles* attempts to grasp the "most Chinese" cause, like a painter who attempts to paint the uneven contours of an invisible riverbed. Under these circumstances, what is the point of discussing whether or not the river's water is tumultuous or peaceful? What mythorealism seeks is this invisible riverbed; it wants to reveal the nine-tenths of an iceberg that lies hidden beneath the ocean waves, and demonstrate why the minute portion of the iceberg that people *can* see is the way that it is.

Mythorealism was not created for the sake of an ideology or out of an author's imagination, but rather it is a product of contemporary

China's incomprehensible absurdity. Mythorealism is not merely a methodology or worldview, but rather it articulates the most basic spirit of contemporary Chinese history. In fact, mythorealism is not even strictly speaking a literary perspective at all, and instead it marks the very nature, origin, and identity of Chinese reality itself.

—Yan Lianke